CW01650973

'The romantic city of Venice and the glamorous and illusory world of film-making are the subjects of best-selling author Charlotte Lamb's latest novel, *Deep and Silent Waters*. When Laura is invited to the Venice Film Festival with a nomination for Best Supporting Actress, she meets up with her former lover, Sebastian Ferrese, a film director with charisma to die for. And it's death that concerns her – because Sebastian seems to be involved in the lives of so many people who die in mysterious circumstances. But exactly how is he involved, and how can she discover the truth without yet again being drawn into his dark world of passion, desire and fear? To discover the answers, lose yourself in this irresistible mystery . . .'

Woman's Realm

'. . . impossible to put down. The dark and erotic tale of Venice past and present, and lovers past and present, is tailor-made to suck the reader in as sure as every soap opera on day-time television hooks viewers.'

Isle of Man Examiner

Also by Charlotte Lamb

Walking in Darkness
In the Still of the Night

Deep and Silent Waters

Charlotte Lamb

CORONET BOOKS
Hodder & Stoughton

Copyright © 1998 Charlotte Lamb

First published in 1998 by Hodder & Stoughton
A division of Hodder Headline PLC
First published in paperback in 1999 by Hodder & Stoughton
A Coronet paperback

The right of Charlotte Lamb to be identified as the Author of the Work has been asserted by her in accordance with the Copyright, Designs and Patents Act 1988.

10 9 8 7

All rights reserved. No part of this publication may be reproduced, stored in a retrieval system, or transmitted, in any form or by any means without the prior written permission of the publisher, nor be otherwise circulated in any form of binding or cover other than that in which it is published and without a similar condition being imposed on the subsequent purchaser.

All characters in this publication are fictitious and any resemblance to real persons, living or dead, is purely coincidental.

A CIP catalogue record for this title is available from the British Library.

Printed and bound in Great Britain by
Clays Ltd, St Ives plc

Hodder and Stoughton
A division of Hodder Headline PLC
338 Euston Road
London NW1 3BH

Prologue

Venice 1968

He walked out on to the little wooden jetty, shivering in spite of the woollen jacket and trousers he wore. A few flakes of snow blew against his chilled face. The wind was raw, and laden grey clouds sagged like a damp tent roof low above Venice. Mist veiled the horizon so that he could not even see the baroque dome of the church of Santa Maria della Salute, his usual landmark, only a short distance away down the Grand Canal.

Venice in February could be a cold, depressing city; dangerous, too, for a six-year-old boy who had not yet learnt to swim. Sebastian was forbidden to go out alone: it was easy, Mamma warned him, to get lost in the maze of alleys leading off the Grand Canal, or fall into the sluggish, oily waters and drown, not that he had needed to be told. He often saw dead things in the water: cats, dogs and birds floating past, pathetic and frightening because they were not alive – you felt it as much as saw it, the absence of life in them. Once he had seen a dead man bob up with a horrifying gurgle, as if the breath had just come out of him. The face lived in his dreams: bloated and shiny with nothing human about it, the eyes opening suddenly staring at him, then the hands reaching, grabbing.

'Sebastian!'

Her voice made him start: for a second, he had half believed that the dead man had called his name. But it was his mother.

He looked round, face brightening, as she came towards him, snow flying around her, clinging to her hair and clothes.

Behind her, inside the palazzo, a movement caught his eye. A cold, stone face showed at an upper window, between the ranks of tall marble archangels massing along the façade, as though one of them had got inside and could not get out again.

Sebastian stood frozen, staring, but realising he had seen her, the woman inside smiled and waved to him. Uncertainly he waved back: the Contessa was kind whenever he saw her. Sebastian, though, was a shy, sensitive, intuitive child, who found it hard to respond to others. He lived inside his own head, where he had invented for himself a world and space he would never have been able to articulate and which he preferred to the everyday world others inhabited.

Seeing him gaze upwards his mother turned her head and looked up, too. He could not see her expression, only that her face was pale and grave. Something had troubled her lately: he had no idea what it was but it disturbed him to see that look in her eyes. 'Mamma, what's wrong?' he whispered, tugging at her hand.

She glanced back down at him, brushed a lock of his dark hair from his face with a tender gloved hand. 'You should be indoors. It's much too cold for you out here. I don't want you catching a chill.'

'I wanted to watch you leave.' She was going to a party in one of the palazzi along the Grand Canal; the American who rented the house was giving a carnival party, and Mamma was wearing a costume that made her look like a boy in a Renaissance painting, one of those she had so often taken him to see in the city art galleries.

Mamma was passionate about art. Before she had married his father she had spent three years at art school and still painted every morning, once she had finished her domestic routine. First she checked that the servants were doing their jobs, went to the local market to buy vegetables, fish and meat, then discussed with the cook what they should have for lunch and dinner. Painting took second place, which Sebastian thought was stupid. She shouldn't have to do boring chores like shopping: it was like asking one of the angels on the front of the palazzo to sweep the rooms or lay the table.

His mother was a brilliant painter, and he loved to study the colours in her canvases. Gay and bright as sunlight, wild and strong as a gale at sea, they told him so much about her. It was like looking through a window into her head.

He wished she wasn't going out without him – he hated it when she was somewhere else and he wasn't with her, he always felt afraid for her, although he couldn't put his fear into words. He only knew that each time she left he felt panic welling up inside him. He was afraid she might never come back, but he didn't want to put the fear into words – that might make it happen.

'Do you have to go?' he pleaded, eyes brimming with anxiety.

She ruffled his hair gently. 'Yes. Be a good boy for me, go to bed and don't quarrel with Niccolo.'

His mouth turned down at the edges. 'He quarrels with me.'

'Well, try not to quarrel back.'

That was stupid. Once Niccolo was in one of his rages you could only run away. He was crazy, a lunatic, and dangerous, Sebastian's dark eyes said, and she laughed. 'Well, try to keep out of his way, then.'

Mamma always understood: you didn't have to use words to explain, she heard what you weren't saying.

She gestured at herself now. 'How do I look?'

Sebastian had gone with her to the most exclusive costumier in the city, a small shop crowded from ceiling to floor with elaborate, expensive creations, which the assistants reached down from the racks with long wooden poles ending in black iron hooks. Mamma had looked at dozens; it had been Sebastian who had made the final choice.

When he saw the page-boy's outfit, fifteenth-century in style, he had said, 'Oh, Mamma, that one, that one!' He would have loved to wear it himself; he ached to have one just like it.

Mamma had tried it on in the tiny fitting room and come out to show him and the assistants, who all exclaimed, '*Si, si, bellissima!*'

It was perfect on her: the black quilted-velvet jacket that clipped her tiny waist, its fat sleeves and their tight cuffs, the white ruff around her throat, the dark red silk tunic, which ended well above her knees, the tight black wool stockings. Oddly, it did not even look out of place in 1966: girls were wearing very short skirts and often dressed as boys did, in jeans and knee-high patent-leather boots.

'You look wonderful,' he said now, as he had said the first time he saw her in it. She smiled. 'Thank you, my angel.' She often called him that. Was it because they lived in the house of angels? Or because, as she had told him many times, he had lived with the angels before he was born, and was still, Mamma said, very close to them? Sebastian sometimes thought he could hear their wings, catch a glimpse of them, shimmering white creatures of feathers and shining skin.

Gina Ferrese was thirty that year, a slender, beautiful woman with red-gold hair pinned up at the back of her head, her long white neck swanlike as she bent to kiss her son.

'I'll be back late so don't try to stay awake. Sleep well. I'll see you tomorrow morning to walk to church.'

An engine started up in the boathouse adjoining the palazzo; mother and son watched the launch emerge and move towards them through the blowing snow, until it was bobbing beside the jetty. The man steering held out a hand and Gina Ferrese, in her boy's costume, took it and stepped in.

'*Ciao,* Sebastian,' she called, her words echoed by the man standing beside her, his black hair wind-ruffled. '*Ci rivedremo presto.*'

Neither of them looked up at the palazzo, but the face still showed at the window, an oval as blank as a cameo, and when Sebastian glanced round he saw the Contessa smiling down at them.

The boat moved away, slowly at first, with Gina waving at her son, until the engine note picked up and they vanished rapidly into the curtain of white flakes now veiling the canal. It could still be heard when all sight of the boat was lost: sounds travel a long way over water.

That was why Sebastian could hear the other boat zooming along in the white mist of snow. He could see nothing but he heard the terrible crash, screams, the sound of people being flung into the water, struggling, crying out, and an engine revving away past him, heading out towards the mouth of the canal and the invisible lagoon.

He stood there, mouth open on a soundless cry of anguish, trembling like a terrified animal.

He knew before they told him, an hour later, after the police had been out to search through the blizzard, that his mother was dead, had drowned out there in the deep and silent waters while he stood listening.

Chapter One

London, 1997

Laura would never have gone to Venice if she had known she would see Sebastian Ferrese there.

Although it was three years since she'd last seen him she still dreamt about him from time to time. But that didn't mean she wanted to see him again. Whatever her dreams betrayed, Sebastian frightened her: his aura was of darkness and death.

When her agent told her that she had been nominated for an award at the Venice Film Festival Laura's immediate response was, 'You're kidding? Me? I can't believe it.' Then she asked huskily, 'Was Sebastian nominated too?'

'Who knows? He's not my client,' Melanie said, irritated. 'Forget him, for God's sake, will you? You got a nomination for best supporting actress, that's all that matters. It was the poster – that was what did it.'

'It made me look like a hooker.'

'It pulled the audiences in, dummy! Put bums on seats.'

Melanie's expression said, What else matters? She had a strictly cash mind, and would never have allowed Laura to accept the role in *Goodnight, World, and Goodbye*, a low-budget film for which she'd earned just enough to keep body and soul together, if there had been any alternative. But Laura wasn't being offered many parts. Her name had no pulling power, so Melanie shrugged and told her to take it just for the sake of the experience. Better to be in work than out of it.

'Bread on the waters, darling,' she said. 'And it could be fun.'

It was the best fun Laura had ever had. She had learnt a lot from working in an ensemble cast of unknown names, a cheerful, friendly group with not a single star among them. None of them, cast or crew, had believed the film would make any money, let alone attract any awards, but they had all loved working on it and become great friends. Laura still saw them whenever she was in London.

When she first saw the posters she had been amazed to find that she dominated the foreground: sexily posed in black lace bra and panties, her legs looking even longer than they were in real life, her breasts like melons, her green eyes slanting and cat-like, hair a blaze of flame around a face they had made somehow sultry and sensual. Laura had been deeply embarrassed. She had had no training as an actress, and was always afraid of being exposed as a know-nothing fraud. Her professional insecurity was mirrored by her lack of self-confidence in every other direction, all of which sprang from being too tall; since she was a schoolgirl she had felt like a giraffe in a world of pygmies.

Melanie had been her agent since she was offered her first film; but they were friends, too. Laura needed someone to talk to, someone she could trust. She couldn't confide in her showbiz crowd: they loved to gossip and would pass on anything she told them. She certainly couldn't talk to anyone back home, her parents, her sister or her old friends. Not about Sebastian. They would have been so shocked. She couldn't tell them about her pain and grief, the longing she could not suppress although she had tried to forget him, the shameful jealousy of his wife. Rachel Lear was a legendary star, a cinema icon, an ice-blonde with a body men dreamt about, while Laura was just a skinny little red-headed nobody.

Melanie, though, was a tough, sophisticated city dweller,

used to the muddle and confusion of people's lives. Nothing Laura had told her came as any surprise, nor had she been shocked. She had simply said, 'Use your head, lovey, forget him and get on with your career,' and Laura had been trying ever since to take that advice.

'I won't win this award, so I won't bother to go,' she said now.

Melanie knew what was on her mind. 'Look, he's out in the jungles of South America, shooting some weirdo film about a lost tribe. He'll be so late finishing it he can't possibly make it to Venice by August.'

'He *was* nominated, though, wasn't he? For *Instant Death*?'

Pulling a face, Melanie admitted, 'Yeah, he got a best director nomination for that. Thought it was a pretty crappy film, myself, too arty-farty for me. And it didn't do well at the box office – the public obviously agreed with me – but it has a cult following. So I'm told.'

'I thought it was brilliant.' Laura had seen it three times. She saw all his films, had got them all on video and had watched them so often she knew them frame by frame, every word, every look, every gesture. She always hoped they would help her to understand him. There was a darkness in them that reflected the dark centre of Sebastian's mind, a sexual energy, a deeply sensual force.

'Yeah, but you're one of his fans, aren't you, darling?' Melanie said cynically. Melanie detested anything that smacked of élitism. She called herself a socialist, but the truth was that she was one of life's awkward squad, always out of step and spoiling for a fight. Luckily her prejudices happened to coincide with public taste, which made her a wonderful litmus paper for anyone trying to guess which way an audience might jump.

Laura reacted hotly. 'Sebastian is one of the best directors in the world, Mel! He's a genius.'

'You mean he's crazy, always goes over budget, is completely unreliable, spends money like water, won't take advice. Is that what you call being a genius? He needs to do huge business at the box office to make up for all that.'

'And he does!'

'Huh!' snorted Melanie.

'With a lot of films he makes big money, Mel. He can always find somebody to bankroll him for his next film.'

When he chose, Sebastian had the charm of the devil. He could hypnotise hard-headed businessmen into believing every word he said, and he had the same effect on women, especially actresses, Laura thought bleakly. He got good performances out of them by focusing those dark eyes on them and making them his creatures. She had been mesmerised while she worked with him – they had been cocooned together in an intimacy so strong that she had thought she knew Sebastian better than anyone else in the world ever had. Only later did she begin to question that belief.

'God knows how he does it.' Melanie grimaced. 'Whatever you say, I don't believe *Instant Death* has a prayer. It's up against films that have broken box-office records worldwide – and, anyway, he's running so late on this South American film that the word is the backers might pull out before he shoots the last reel.'

'That's crazy! Why can't they let him finish it first?'

'Apparently they haven't even seen any rushes yet. They keep demanding that Sebastian send over some of the stuff he's shot but he ignores them. A couple of the stars have been taken ill – the food is terrible in those places – and they're plagued by mosquitoes. Some of the crew have gone down with malaria.' Melanie shuddered. 'I hate places like that. Insects and dirt and bad food. Give me a city any time.'

Laura laughed. 'Sebastian would agree with you, he hates working in remote places. Most of his films have been shot in cities – London, New York, San Francisco.'

A shiver ran down her spine as she remembered a recurring dream she had whenever she was strained. She could never recall how it began, but it always ended the same way. She was in a shadowy hotel room, impersonal, comfortable, characterless, and she and Sebastian were quarrelling, although she could never remember what about. Suddenly, his hands would shoot out towards her throat which made her back away, aware of an open window behind her, the familiar noises of a city street far below. Then he would give her a violent shove, and she would fall backwards, out of the window, down, down, through empty air, screaming. She always woke up before she hit the ground. For hours afterwards she would sit up in bed, shivering and icy cold.

It had never happened, of course, not to Laura. It had been his wife who had fallen out of a window. Why did she always dream it had happened to her?

Guilt, Laura thought bleakly, because she had been jealous of his wife. She had bought every newspaper that covered the inquest and read every word over and over again. Witnesses had talked of his wife under pressure on her most recent film, arriving late on set, losing her temper, turning nasty when she forgot her lines, or stumbling around so drunk that she kept banging into scenery. A post-mortem had shown that she had been drunk the day she died. She could easily have lost her balance and fallen out of the open window which had a waist-high sill – a dangerous window, the coroner said, and added that her husband should have kept her away from it. His criticisms were mild, though, because another witness had been present, Sebastian's assistant, Valerie Hyde, who claimed that he had been nowhere near his wife when she fell. Rachel Lear had opened the window and leaned out too far.

A thin, brisk, down-to-earth woman, with a direct way of looking at anyone she spoke to, Valerie made a convincing witness. But Laura knew something that the coroner could not have known: Valerie Hyde would go to the stake for Sebastian; would cheat or steal for him. She might have been telling the truth, of course, but she would not have hesitated to lie.

Melanie said abruptly, 'You *must* go to Venice, Laura – this is your first nomination, you *have* to be there.'

Laura shook her head. 'Who am I up against?'

Reluctantly Melanie told her the names, and Laura threw up her hands. 'Well, there you are! They're all better actresses than me, and better known, too. I don't have a chance.'

Furious, Melanie said, 'Well, if you don't go, I can't. I've never been to the Venice Film Festival and I'm dying to. It's a great excuse to buy a really stunning new frock on expenses. It's not often I can do that. And you can't wear just anything to Venice – it's supposed to be even more glamorous than Cannes.'

Melanie loved clothes, far more even than films or plays. Her whole face lit up when she talked about them. She should have become a dress designer, but she had missed her chance, early on, by getting a job as a secretary to a theatrical agent instead of going to college to study art and textiles. Her Russian-Jewish father had been in the rag trade in the East End, and as a child, Melanie had been dressed like a little princess. It had left her with a passion for style and cut, and a taste for the exotic, which perfectly suited her long, straight black hair and huge leonine gold eyes.

Her skin was either olive or golden, depending on her health and mood, and Melanie needed colour to bring to life the beauty buried in her generously endowed flesh. She was larger than life, in every sense of the word, lion-hearted, a fighter, voluble and open-handed. She fell in and out of love with the same fierce concentration.

Over the last three years, she had built up Laura's career with that same intense commitment, but it had been Sebastian who had made Laura an actress. Indeed, it had been Sebastian who had told her she needed an agent, when he first offered her a contract, and who has suggested Melanie, saying he had heard she was good. She didn't have many clients yet, but would work harder for Laura than someone whose books were already full of stars. Some actors might have suspected a secret deal between Sebastian and Melanie, but they would have been wrong. Far from conspiring with him, Melanie couldn't wait to get Laura more money from someone else. She had never had much time for Sebastian, and he knew it. That, to Laura, was testament to his integrity: he had picked Melanie as the best agent for her, in spite of knowing Melanie didn't think highly of him.

Sighing, Laura said, 'Mel, I really don't want to go. It'll be a nightmare – those occasions always are, noisy, overcrowded, flashbulbs going off all the time, hordes of people grabbing at you, . . . like going for a swim in a tank full of piranhas.'

'You're an actress, for heaven's sake. How can you be afraid of an audience?' Mel had never been shy or nervous in her life.

'I've never been on a stage – you know that! Or had any training,' Laura protested. 'I'm not scared of cameras or film crews. They're always too busy with their own job to have time to stare at me, and if I mess up or fluff a line I can always do it again. But on a stage it's live. It can go wrong in front of hundreds of people. You can make a fool of yourself.'

She had learnt her trade by working at it, had picked it up as she went along, by making friends with the camera men, sound men, lighting men. She listened to everything they said and related it to what she already knew, watched them work with such open fascination that they were happy to suggest how she should pitch her voice, how she should move, and to show her how little she needed to do to make an effect. A sideways flick of the eyes could show fear, suspicion, jealousy without a word being spoken.

Melanie changed tack. 'You won't have to act, lovely, just stand there and smile, and say thank you if you win – and winning is a long shot, remember. But you'll see Venice – and it'll blow your mind. Sebastian was born there, wasn't he? I read that somewhere. Born in Venice, but brought up in California, wasn't it? They said he was born in a palazzo on the Grand

Canal.' She gave her cynical little grin. 'I always said he was a fantasist, didn't I?'

Had it been fantasy? When Sebastian talked about his childhood Laura had believed him. It had seemed the perfect place for him to have been born: a Renaissance palazzo in the most beautiful city in the world. Only later, when death had entered the equation, did she begin to doubt him.

During the months they were working together she would have refused point blank to believe Sebastian capable of murder – but after Rachel's death she no longer knew what she believed. How much truth had he ever told her? she wondered and she kept thinking that once you have admitted one doubt you find more hidden inside you, which multiply like flies on summer evenings, becoming a buzzing, stinging multitude in your brain, driving you mad.

'Venice is one of those experiences that change your life,' Melanie said. 'Once you see it, you'll never be the same again.'

That was what Laura was afraid of. She was uneasy about going to a place that had been so important in Sebastian's life. She remembered everything he had said about his childhood in the golden palace on the Grand Canal, with its marble floors and walls, hung with ancient, fading tapestries that made the rooms whisper and echo as they stirred in the chill breeze. Sebastian had talked of long, dark corridors through which you had to find your way, like Theseus in the maze, from room to room, and out at last into the garden full of orange and lemon trees five foot high, in great terracotta pots padded with straw to keep the chill of winter at bay.

It was based on a geometric pattern, he had said, narrow gravel paths between low box hedges within which stood paired statues of Roman gods: Jupiter and Juno, Mars and Venus. In the centre, standing on one winged foot, the other pointing backwards, stood Mercury, his staff angled at the window of one room from which over the centuries, family legend said, several members of the Angeli family had fallen to their deaths.

'Murdered?' she had whispered, ready to believe him if he said yes. Everyone knew about Renaissance princes who bumped off their enemies – the Borgias, the Visconti, even the Doge of Venice himself.

'Perhaps, or perhaps they jumped of their own accord.'

She remembered shivering at the cool, dispassionate voice but she had had no glimpse into the future. Rachel Lear had not fallen from that hotel window for another year.

'Why would they kill themselves?' she had asked.

He had shrugged. 'Why do people ever kill themselves? They had their reasons, no doubt.'

At the time, she had listened like a child being told fairy stories. Now she had dozens of questions she wished she had asked. If he had been born in such a house why had he and his father ever left? Who else had lived there with them? He had never mentioned anyone. Why had they never been back to Venice? Why had he said that the family in the palazzo had the surname Angeli when his was Ferrese? Why had Sebastian so little to say about his family? Especially his mother. It was clear that he had loved his father, Giovanni Ferrese, but he had told her nothing about his mother, except that she had died when he was six. When she had asked what Giovanni had done for a living he had said curtly, 'He had his own business.' And when Sebastian's dark eyes chilled, as they had then, you were wise to stop asking questions.

'You owe it to yourself to go, you know. It's a great honour,' Melanie said.

And she might find the answers to some of those questions, Laura thought. She would look for the palazzo where Sebastian had been born: if it existed, it might tell her a lot about him.

That night she dreamt about him, not the nightmare but the wild sexual dream she had also had so many times. She was back again in the caravan she had used on that first film. Sebastian was with her, talking about the scene they would shoot next day, watching her take off her makeup in front of the scrappy mirror on the dressing table. Laura avoided his eyes, kept her attention on her face, her skin shiny with cream.

She looked like an awkward schoolgirl, like the girl her friends had once called Lanky and made fun of whenever she tripped over her own feet or had to stand up in class, looming over them all. She hated Sebastian watching her: compared to his beautiful wife she was ugly and clumsy. Hurriedly she wiped off the cream and picked up her normal makeup bag, but Sebastian took it from her and tossed it back on the dressing table.

'Don't put anything on your lovely face. Nothing ruins the skin faster than plastering it with makeup day and night. Clea has destroyed her skin with that stuff. It's like orange peel now. Only wear it when you have to, in front of the cameras.'

He called Rachel by a nickname her brother had given her when he was beginning to talk, lazily running her two names together. She preferred Clea to Rachel and even the press often used it now.

'I'll feel naked!'

'There's a thought,' he said, his dark eyes teasing, and she felt her mouth go dry. His face changed; he leaned forward and kissed her softly. She shut her eyes, breathless, her whole body shaking.

In her dreams that was the moment she relived: the hunger and need that flared up between them then. Her arms round his neck, they had clung together as if they were drowning.

'I want you so badly,' he had groaned, his hands moving down her body, caressing her breasts, stroking her buttocks, pressing her even closer.

They had never been to bed together, but the intense attraction between them would have led to that before long if Clea had not caught them.

The caravan door had opened and a cold wind had blown over them.

'So it's true! You are screwing the little bitch,' a hoarse voice screamed. Sebastian stiffened, his head lifting. He let go of Laura, moved away from her, his face dark red.

Laura wanted to die. She did not dare look at the woman in the doorway.

'How long has it been going on?' the famous whisky voice sneered. 'Did you audition on the couch, darling? How many times did you have to satisfy him before you got the part?'

'If you're going to make a scene, make it at home, not here, with fifty people listening outside,' snapped Sebastian.

'Do you think they don't all know what's been going on?'

'Get out of here,' Sebastian muttered to Laura, who ran, hearing Clea yelling, swearing violently, and Sebastian shouting back at her. Crew and cast pretended to be busy doing something else but Laura felt their curious, amused, knowing eyes on her.

A few days later the film had wrapped and she had left for home, to stay with her family. She hadn't been alone with Sebastian in those last days; nor had she heard from him since. When she first heard about Clea's death she had been so shocked she hadn't eaten or slept for several days. Haunted by guilt, she had been desperately afraid that Sebastian had killed his wife. She still was.

Venice, 1997

Melanie got her way. They flew to Venice on one of those August days during a heatwave when the temperature had climbed so high that people wore less and less each day and became more and more irritable. At the airport, everyone was flushed and perspiring. It was so overcrowded that people had to fight their way through, using their elbows, losing their tempers. Most men were in shirtsleeves, girls wore tiny shorts and even tinier cropped cotton tops.

Laura had put on a wickedly simple but expensive black linen tunic from one of London's hottest young designers. Although it left her arms and most of her long, slender legs bare, it hadn't kept her cool during the flight.

So many of the most famous faces in the film world were arriving at the airport that the *paparazzi* had the satiated expressions of sharks that had fed for days on the bodies from a great shipwreck. A few recognised her and snatched some rapid snaps before they hurried off to find more bankable faces coming along behind her. None of the reporters bothered to ask her any questions.

'Nobody expects me to win,' she told Melanie, as they climbed into a hotel launch waiting at the airport jetty to take arriving guests across the lagoon from the mainland to the city.

'You had to be here, to get your face on TV, get talked about. How many times do I have to tell you? A career in films isn't just about acting, you have to sell yourself.'

The launch set off, bouncing over the waves in a way that made Laura feel slightly sick. Outside she saw blue sky, blue water, so bright she was half blinded by the glittering light. Where was the city? She had imagined the airport would be quite close to Venice itself.

When, at last, the launch began to slow down, she could see a long, sandy outline, white buildings rising against the hot blue sky. That wasn't Venice! Where were the spires, the domes, the canals, the coloured façades of the old buildings?

Melanie had been to Venice before, several times. 'That's the Lido, darling. I had a honeymoon here once, years ago, with Lewis.' Melanie had been married several times over the past twenty years although she lived alone now.

'Lewis? You never mentioned a Lewis.'

'You never knew him, he was a bastard, but a rich bastard. I must say we had a terrific honeymoon, at the Hôtel des Bains. I've never been able to afford to stay there again, but it's a dream of a place – the hotel Visconti used when he made *Death in Venice*, remember? Thomas Mann mentioned it in the book.'

Laura's face lit up. 'Of course I remember. Why aren't we staying there?'

'The Excelsior is where the final ceremony is held, so I booked us in there. As I said, we have to see and be seen.'

The boatman was calling out to a man on the landing-stage, his voice fluid and mellifluous. Laura picked out a word or two – she had learnt some Italian during the months she had spent working with Sebastian, so much in love with him that she was obsessed with everything about him. She had longed to be able to talk to him in the language he had first spoken; it would be a way of excluding everyone else. That was why she had learnt so much so quickly about making films; it had been another way of getting closer to Sebastian. Cinema was his obsession so it had become hers.

As they got off the boat, Laura screwed up her eyes against the glare of light outside, and asked Melanie, 'Is this part of Venice?'

'The Lido is a sandbank between Venice and the sea. The city is over there somewhere.' She waved a casual arm to the right, but Laura couldn't see anything through the heat haze.

Along the beach road, Laura could see yellow sand covered with a mass of tanned, scantily clad bodies, some of which were leaping around in the sea, swimming or manipulating sailboards with vivid sails.

'Look at all those people! It looks like Blackpool on a bank holiday. I didn't realise Venice had a seaside resort so close to it.'

Melanie shrugged her plump shoulders. 'Most of the crowds will be day-trippers – they'll leave this afternoon.'

As they walked into the reception lobby of their hotel Laura paused. She felt as if she was back on a film set, not simply because she was confronted by a sea of famous Hollywood faces but because the décor was Hollywood to match – marble and gilt and silk brocade.

'Give me your passport and I'll register. Wait for me by the lift then I'll be able to find you easily,' Melanie said, and began to push her way through the starry crowd.

Laura did as she was told, then stood gaping like a tourist at the famous faces.

She had made only four films and knew few people in the business so it left her dazed to see so many Hollywood stars at close quarters. Beautiful women with instantly familiar faces embraced, posing as if for a photo-opportunity, cooing like turtle doves in American, French, Italian, while their eyes darted down to assess the style, the cut and guess the designer's name or how much the jewellery had cost, and see if the other woman had lost or gained weight, was looking any older or showing signs of wear and tear.

'Darling ... wonderful to see you.'

'*Ciao, come stai? Si, tante grazie* ...'

'*Cherie, ça va? Et ta famille? Bien, oui, moi aussi!*'

Laura felt like a newcomer to the Tower of Babel, and a very underdressed newcomer at that. She was wearing no jewellery and her little black dress was far from eye-catching. She was totally out of place, she shouldn't have come.

All her buried anxiety rose up inside her and she wished she was back in her childhood home, the old farmhouse on Hadrian's Wall with a long, rolling view in front and behind it, the green hillsides of northern England, backboned in rock, scattered with thorn trees that sang in the wind. Whenever she was unhappy or frightened that landscape comforted her. It had outlasted the Roman Empire, the British Empire, seen suns rise and set for thousands of years, it dwarfed all her fears and griefs and put them into perspective.

Melanie came bustling back. 'The porter's taking our bags up to our rooms. Ready?'

Laura pressed the button for the lift. 'Which floor are we on?'

Melanie didn't answer. She was staring across the foyer. Her scarlet mouth hung open. 'Oh, my God, no!'

Idly Laura followed her stare until she saw the face that had caught Melanie's attention. The hair on the back of her neck prickled; her skin turned icy with shock. Sebastian. Walking towards them, in his usual working gear of well-washed but shabby jeans, a white shirt under an olive green sweater, army-style, with patches on shoulders and elbows. Some in that glittering crowd turned to stare at him, stepping back to let him pass.

'Where the hell is that lift?' muttered Melanie. She put her thumb on the button and kept it there. 'Come on, damn you, come on.'

He looked so much older. Laura couldn't believe how much he had changed. When they first met he had been only thirty-one, his skin a smooth golden olive, his black hair thick and sleek, his features so hard and clear they might have been chiselled from stone, high cheekbones and temples, an aquiline nose, and above it those bright, dark eyes.

He looked forty now, but could only be thirty-five. Deep lines had been etched into his brow, around his eyes and mouth; his facial bones showed through his skin, giving him the austere, spare look of a monk.

There were silvery hairs among the black at his temples, his mouth was tighter, reined in, tension in the set of it and in the angle of jaw and throat. Everyone who ever worked with him would agree that Sebastian Ferrese was an arrogant, brilliant, dangerous son-of-a-bitch, and it showed now in that face, as if the rock of his nature, which had once been masked by the beauty of his youth, had risen up into view with the passage of time.

On the other side of the room Laura noted a little cluster of people whose faces she knew – Sebastian's favourite camera man, Sidney McKenna, a quiet, introverted man with a bald head and the blank, sea-gazing eyes of a sailor, Valerie Hyde, and several others from the crew with whom she had worked on her first film. Sebastian surrounded himself with people he respected and trusted. They would all have been with him in

South America. Maybe some of them had been nominated for awards, too.

'Come on,' Melanie urged, tugging at her arm. 'The lift's here.'

Laura turned blindly, but as she did so Sebastian grabbed her other arm with long, tense fingers that bit into her and would not be easily dislodged.

'We're in a hurry.' Melanie would not let go; she was determined to pull Laura into the lift.

Sebastian wouldn't let go either. 'Laura, I have to talk to you.'

She quivered at the sound of his voice – deep, faintly hoarse. How familiar, how oddly American, when she had begun to expect him to sound Italian here in Venice – but, then, he had lived in the States for so long.

Somewhere a flash-bulb exploded, then Laura felt the heat of television arc-lamps on her cheek and realised that a TV crew had spotted them and swung their camera round to start filming.

Melanie saw them, too, and ground her teeth audibly. 'That's all we need!' she muttered. 'Look, will you let go of her and bugger off, Sebastian? Haven't you done enough harm? If her name gets linked with yours again, it could ruin her. At this stage of her career the wrong gossip could be fatal.'

Sebastian's eyes flashed at her, black with rage, but he let go, Melanie tugged, and Laura almost fell into the lift. The doors closed and a second later they were gone.

As the lift rushed upward Laura leant against the wall, trembling. She had seen him. He had touched her. Nothing had changed.

Melanie watched her worriedly. 'That was bloody bad luck. Don't worry, I'll be around while we're here. Just don't let anyone into your room until you've checked through the spy-hole, don't answer the phone, and don't go anywhere without me, okay?'

Laura didn't answer. Her face was white, her green eyes jagged with fear, shards of broken glass.

'Did you see the way people were staring at him?' asked Melanie. 'And those who didn't look made it just as obvious. You could have cut the atmosphere with a knife. They all think he did it, Laura. He's got away with murder and the whole world knows it.'

The lift stopped, they got out and walked down to where the porter had unlocked their adjoining rooms and was waiting with their luggage.

'I never thought I'd say this . . . but any other time or place I'd have been thrilled to have TV people interested in you, but not if it means you getting mixed up with that bastard again.' Melanie sighed. 'Oh, well, there are so many big names here, it probably won't make it on to the screen.' She paused. 'You believe he killed her, don't you? You wouldn't be so scared of him if you didn't.'

'I didn't say I was scared of him.'

'You didn't need to. You looked terrified.'

Because I was, but not because I think he's a killer. I was terrified because I wanted him so badly, thought Laura, and walked into the room at whose open door the porter stood.

He asked, 'Please, your case, which?'

'That one,' Melanie told him, pointing. He carried it to a stand at the end of Laura's bed, talking all the time in his broken English, telling them how to switch on the television, operate the air-conditioning, where to find the mini-bar.

Melanie stood at the door, her face clouded. 'Are you going to be okay? Do you want me to stay?'

'No, I'm fine.' Laura managed to hold her voice steady.

'Are you sure?'

Laura gave her a brief look. 'Yes.'

Reluctantly Melanie moved away. She called back, 'Have a shower, rest on your bed for half an hour, then we'll have a trip over to the city and do some window-shopping and sightseeing, okay?'

Laura tipped the porter, who bowed and murmured, '*Grazie tante, grazie*,' before leaving to show Melanie into her room next door.

Alone at last, Laura walked slowly to the window to gaze out at the sunlit view. Heat made the horizon dance, dazzling her eyes, making her head ache.

Her mouth was dry, her body burning; passion and fear darkened the sea and sky for her, blotted out the sun.

If she had known he would be here she would never have come to Venice.

When she had met Sebastian, Laura was working in London as a model and living in a flat in Islington, a large, northern suburb of the city. Her parents still lived in the old grey farmhouse just below Hadrian's Wall, which she missed intolerably in the cold, grey, dirty streets of the city. Her mother and father had not approved of her becoming a model: they had wanted her to go to college or get married, like her sister, Angela, who had trained as a nurse before she married Hamish, a doctor working in general practice in Carlisle. Somehow Angela managed to fit having children and running a home into a busy life as one of the nurses in the health centre Hamish worked for, and that was the sort of useful, satisfying life John and Lucy Erskine had wanted for Laura. A life much like their own.

She might well have ended up as they hoped, except that during Laura's last year at school she had met a man . . . As Bogart says in *Casablanca*, 'How many stories start with that?'

I met a man when I was young . . . Immediately you have forebodings, don't you? You imagine seduction, rape, the ruin of a life. But you would be wrong. Laura had met Bernie Piper on the Roman wall one bright spring day. She was there with a group from school, doing a sponsored walk to raise money for new computers for the science lab. Bernie lived in London, a busy, successful fashion photographer, but he was on holiday that week, exploring the architecture on the wall, since Roman history was one of his many interests.

Laura and her classmates walked past him in a brisk crocodile following the up-hill down-dale path while Bernie stood above the path, watching. He began to follow the girls, staring at Laura.

'Dirty old man,' her best friend, Ellen, said, loudly enough for him to hear, and the other girls giggled.

Laura turned salmon pink, as his eyes wandered from the top of her head, where her long red-gold hair was pinned in a neat bun, down over her distinctly skinny body to the legs that she privately thought looked like the roots of a plant, long and thin and pallid after the winter.

She was five foot nine, taller than anyone else in her class. Her height put boys off: who wants to go out with a giantess? Laura knew she was ugly and clumsy; she would have given her eye-teeth to be a demure five foot three, with a sexy, curvy figure.

The teacher shepherding them turned to give Bernie a cold, reproving look, and he pretended to be taking pictures of the view, his expensive camera raised, while the girls continued their walk for another half-hour before stopping to eat the packed lunch each had brought.

Breathless and overheated, Laura undid the top buttons on her shirt and tucked the hem into her bra to let the air get to her bare midriff. She was lying back, eating a cheese and tomato sandwich, when her friends nudged her. 'Hey, look – it's him again! He followed us. Well, followed you, anyway.'

Looking up, Laura blinked as Bernie took a rapid succession of pictures of her.

'What do you think you're doing?' The gym teacher Mrs Heinz, who was their chaperone that day, marched up to him, bristling. Short and muscled with crew-cut hair and a ginger moustache when she forgot to wax it, she was full of energy and often aggressive and overbearing. 'Stop that at once and go away, or I'll call the police!'

Bernie shrugged and went, but a week later he drove up to Laura's home with a pile of glossy photos.

When she saw them she was silent. Was that really her, that beautiful girl with pale breasts partially visible at the open neck of her shirt, lying back against a bed of long grass, her eyes half closed, languid and sultry?

Her face went bright red. She was so hot she could scarcely breathe, and she felt embarrassed, with her parents staring at the pictures then at her. What were they thinking?

Then she had wondered how he had made her look like that. And how he had got her name and address. That gave her a sense of Bernie's ominiscience, which never quite left her even when she knew him well and had discovered that he had asked one of the other girls which school they had come from. When he had processed the pictures he had gone there, had waited until some girls came out, shown then the photos and found out who Laura was that way. Simple when you know how.

It had taken her parents quite a while to get over their first view of those pictures. When Bernie had talked about a modelling career for Laura, her mother's reaction had been immediate. 'She's far too young. And even if she wasn't I wouldn't want her to get involved in that sort of life. She's going to college.'

Bernie ignored her and said to Mr Erskine, 'The camera loves her – I knew it would, the minute I set eyes on her. It's the bone structure. She could have a brilliant career as a model, earn a fortune.'

Laura's father was a shrewd, down-to-earth man who had had to work hard from dawn till dusk to earn his daily bread. 'What sort of money are we talking about?' he asked.

Bernie grinned, knowing that the fish had taken his bait. 'The sky's the limit, if she gets taken up by all the magazines and advertisers. She could be making a hundred thousand a year, or it could go up to a million.'

'A million?' Laura's father had been impressed, his eyes brightening. Then, catching his wife's angry, disapproving eye, he added, 'But she's still at school, you know, and we couldn't let her leave until she's taken her exams.'

Mrs Erskine interrupted angrily, 'She isn't going to be a model, now or later. She should never have posed for those disgusting pictures in the first place!'

'She's a natural, she didn't need to pose. I just took pictures of her as she was and look at the result! Stunning, isn't she? A beautiful girl. She takes after you, I can see that.'

He had wasted his flattery. 'She's too young and I won't have her going off to London!' Mrs Erskine snapped.

Bernie turned back to her husband. 'If you're worried I'll find someone to chaperone her. I'm a happily married man, Mr Erskine. I see beautiful girls all day long. I don't have to chase after them, they chase after me. I swear to you, your daughter will be as safe with me as if she was my own kid. I think it would be a crying shame if she didn't get her chance. She has terrific potential – I'm convinced she could get to the top and make a fortune.'

Laura had never had any self-confidence about her looks so she had never even daydreamed about being a model. She couldn't believe the startling metamorphosis Bernie had wrought in her, changing the gangling schoolgirl she knew from her mirror into a languid-eyed siren, but nothing would have stopped her grabbing Bernie's offer with both hands.

'I want to do it,' she said, an obstinate expression settling over her eyes and mouth. 'I don't want to go to college, I want to be a model, if he says I can.'

She had to finish her exams first, however, because neither of her parents would hear of her leaving before the end of that school year. Her mother hoped she might change her mind, and continued throughout those months to point out she was not a swan but an ugly duckling, clumsy, graceless, awkward.

'You'll never be pretty, so don't let that man pull the wool over your eyes. I don't know what his game is, but I don't trust him. Don't be a fool, Laura. Go to college, get a good education and a good job afterwards.'

But Laura was counting the days. She couldn't wait to leave for London and get away from her mother's drip, drip, drip of criticism.

When she began modelling, success came almost immediately and, with it, temptations of the kind her parents had feared, but Laura was always too tired to stay out late after working all day on her feet, and the clubs only began to swing at around ten or eleven at night. She wasn't attracted by smoky nightclubs, drugs or drink. She had one or two brief relationships with men, but they didn't mean much to her. She had fun with them, enjoyed their company, but never fell in love. Then, when she was twenty-one, she was chosen to be the 'face' of a famous perfume house for a year.

'You'll have to turn down any other offers during the run of the contract. We can't have your face appearing anywhere else,' she was told. 'That's why you'll be paid such big fees. You can't earn anything from anyone else. From now on you're ours exclusively.'

She didn't hesitate – the money involved was far too big and the coverage was saturating. Everywhere she went Laura saw her own face, huge and terrifying, barely recognisable at that size, staring down from billboards. She saw it on the backs of glossy magazines, alive and shimmering on television screens – you couldn't miss it unless you lived on a desert island. It made it impossible for her to go out alone.

She couldn't walk through the streets, take a peaceful stroll in one of the beautiful London parks, visit Harrods or Selfridges. She was driven everywhere, and suddenly acquired minders: big, muscled men with faces like scrubbed turnips who could toss people aside as if they were matchsticks.

The casual, light-hearted relationships she had had with young men, more friends than lovers, ended – the strain of being followed everywhere by the *paparazzi* made them irritable, and none of them wished to see themselves photographed with her and speculated about in the tabloid gossip columns.

'It's like being under siege! I'm sick of it!' she complained to Bernie.

'Go back home for a while, visit your family. It's time for some rest and recuperation,' he advised, and that was what she did. It felt strange, at first, to be back there, treated as a child again, with her parents, in the wild, green, lonely places of her childhood after the four years she had spent in London, but she gradually felt her pulse slow to the quiet beat of days that were always the same.

Since the moment when she had first met Bernie, Laura had believed in fate. You could call it chance, good luck, or pure coincidence, but whatever it was Laura believed some agency operated in her life that made the wheels of opportunity turn and directed her along the right path. During those days in the old farmhouse she felt as it she was drifting, waiting for a tide to turn and carry her onward. She didn't know what she wanted to do next, she simply felt that a future was waiting for her, to which she would shortly be directed. Meanwhile she read new novels, watched TV, helped her mother feed the animals and cook, went walking across the hills to gaze in breathless pleasure at the landscape, the heather moorland and green valleys, the bony hills, the clouds tearing overhead.

Sometimes she visited her sister in Carlisle, played with her little nephew and nieces, baby-sat while Hamish and Angela had an evening out. One day she took her parents with her. They had lunch with Angela and the children, and in the evening went to the local cinema to see *Back Streets,* a film about gangsters in Chicago, full of vice and drugs and murder. Mr and Mrs

Erskine hated the film, wanted to leave half-way through, but although it was so violent it was witty and melancholy, full of insight, and Laura was deeply impressed by it.

'Who made it, anyway?' demanded her father, as they drove home afterwards, along dark, mostly empty roads through remote villages.

'Sebastian Ferrese, Dad.'

'Who? An Italian. Well, it figures – he's probably in the Mafia,' he said in disgust.

'You can't say it was ever boring! And although it was violent at times, it seemed true to life.'

'Not my life.' He snorted, which made her laugh. He was so absolutely right. The Chicago they had just been shown was light years from the world her parents inhabited, but Laura had been to America now and had recognised some aspects of its modern city life in the film.

Her parents had never lived in a city. They worried about very different problems – sheep picking up one of the many diseases to which they were prone, ewes aborting if a dog got in among the flock and began chasing them, a sudden catastrophic drop in market prices, and the occasional scare about rustlers arriving with a lorry on a dark night, rounding up a whole flock and disappearing with them. The world Sebastian Ferrese's film reflected was utterly foreign to them, and made them uneasy. But Laura had not only recognised in it something of the underbelly of London life: the grasp of human weakness, the forgiveness, the film's wry elegiac tone had got right under her skin.

Ten days later Bernie rang and asked her to come back to London at once. 'Someone has asked to meet you.'

'Who?' she asked warily, hoping that she was not going to have a problem with one of the executives from the perfume house whose face she had become. It had happened to her before. Some men seemed to think that if you modelled for their firm you were available to them personally, and they weren't above trying to blackmail or bully you into bed.

'Sebastian Ferrese,' Bernie said.

Laura remembered thinking, Fate again. What else could it have been? Just when Sebastian was on her mind he turned up in her life. It had to be Fate; inevitable and inescapable.

She stared out of the hotel window at the hot blue Venetian sky and shivered at other memories: his mouth buried in her neck, between her breasts, his hands moving . . .

Behind her she heard a soft sound and turned in time to see a white envelope slide under the door.

It was from him, she knew it. She bit her lower lip, stared at it as if it were a snake. Then she walked slowly across the room to pick it up. Her name was printed on the front in large capital letters.

She tore open the envelope and found a sheet of hotel notepaper, covered in more printing.

GET OUT OF VENICE, YOU BITCH, OR I'LL KILL YOU.

Chapter Two

In his suite three floors higher, Sebastian Ferrese was standing by the window looking at the same view, absorbed in his thoughts. She had changed: he had known that from seeing her in the films she had made since they last met, but it was still a shock to realise that the sensitive, uncertain, gawkily beautiful girl he had met just four years ago had grown an outer gloss, an enamelled surface that had hardened to make her a guarded, remote woman. Four years ago she had had the unaware, vulnerable beauty of a flower. Now the flower had grown thorns to defend itself.

What had happened to her since they had last met? He knew what could happen to beautiful women in the film world: there were so many predators waiting in those deep waters to drag them down into the murky depths.

The air outside flickered in front of his eyes as if something had fallen through it.

Something – or someone.

She had screamed all the way down. Everyone for miles had heard her. People had stood and watched, as if it was a publicity stunt, not real. All the newspapers had commented on that. Even in her moment of death Clea had been performing, and in a sense that had probably been true, because she had always been conscious of being on display, night and day. Since she became a child star at the age of ten Clea's whole life had been one long performance in front of an audience.

Nothing in her life had been natural, spontaneous, truthful. Like the princess in the old tale, she had been endowed – by fairies, or Fate, or nature – with blonde curls, enormous eyes like violets, a beauty that could stop traffic. She was irresistible to every man she met – from the age of twelve when the powerful, wealthy producer who saw that she got the part she wanted made sure he got her in exchange.

Clea had yelled it at Sebastian when he asked her to marry him, the morning after the first night they slept together. 'What are you – crazy? You don't have to marry me because we had sex, stupid! Where've you been all your life? Oh, grow up. You think you're the first dirty bastard to fuck me? Don't kid yourself. Old Buck Ronay, remember him? The great studio boss, the family man who was so hot on old-fashioned moral values? Fifty years old, bald and sweaty, and he had me on the couch in his office before he signed my first contract.'

Sebastian could remember the shock of that moment. He was in love with her: she was so beautiful, with the face of the Madonna, a smooth oval, creamy skin, blue eyes wide and radiant, pink mouth an innocent curve. He could not bear to think about what she had just said.

She had delighted in his pain and disbelief: she loved to get a strong reaction to anything she said or did. She was acting even when she was hurt or sad, her quick, intuitive mind instantly working out how to express what she experienced and get a powerful response from an observer. Later, Sebastian decided that she could not feel anything, unless she had an audience. When she was utterly alone would she sag like one of the puppets in *Coppélia,* face blank and wooden, body collapsed? He only knew that she could not tolerate solitude, would ask the room-service waiter in a hotel to stay and drink with her if nobody else was around to talk to, would ring friends or acquaintances, anybody who would answer their phone, in the middle of the night, beg them to come over, there and then, never mind if it was three in the morning. She was moody, difficult, charming, enchanting, a world full of women wrapped up in one troubled human being.

That night, in response to his shocked face, her mood had changed. She had laughed at him, boasting, 'Sure! Old Buck always liked to try out the new kids on the block, and he liked 'em young. Twelve years old, never even had a boyfriend, because my mother wouldn't let me go anywhere she didn't come too. Buck told me, "Come, sit here by me on this couch. You're a pretty little girl. I hope you're a good girl and do what you're told," and I was dumb enough to say, "Yes, sir, I'll do whatever you want, sir." Well, that was what my mother had told me to say, so I did, and the next minute he was pushing me backwards and climbing on top of me.'

'Stop talking like that!' Sebastian had burst out, feeling sick.

'It happened! Why the hell shouldn't I talk about it?' she yelled back.

Then her voice became a soft dovelike coo. 'Gee, what's the matter, honey? You look green around the gills. Too raw for you? I guess you're the fastidious type.' Then she was snarling again. 'Well, buster, you'd better grow out of that if you want to make it in Hollywood. You're living in the gutter now, big guy. They may wear designer gear and have perfect teeth but they're predators, every one of them. Of course, I didn't know that when I was twelve years old. But my mother did and she let me walk into Buck's office alone.'

'But afterwards . . . when you told her . . .' He caught the sardonic look she gave him. 'You did tell her, didn't you?'

Clea had thrown back her head and laughed again. 'She knew, dummy. She knew exactly what he was doing to me in there that day – but she was desperate for me to get that part. So she shut her eyes and went deaf while that old bastard screwed me. I started working on the film a month later – and what do you know? Six months later I was a star.'

When Sebastian looked at her in horror and pity she had changed again, spun into one of her tantrums, which he was soon to recognise and even to predict. She shrieked, 'Don't you dare look at me as if I was something you'd found in the trash! I should never have told you, should I? Now you think I'm shop-soiled, huh? The engagement's off, is it? No white wedding for me.'

'Clea, my God, you don't imagine I think it was your fault?' he had stammered stupidly.

'You don't?' She mimed amazement, meek gratitude, and even as he hated it, he admired the skill of the born actress. 'Gee, are you sure? And all these years I've been thinking I was the one to blame. I thought I raped him, poor old Buck. I sat there in my frilly pink dress and white shoes, and forced that poor, weak old man to do those sick things to me.'

He had known how badly he was handling it, fumbling uselessly for the right words. 'Clea, God, what can I say? I'm sorry, so sorry it happened to you.'

Her lovely face was ugly with rage. 'Fuck you, mister. I wasn't asking you to be sorry for me, I was just telling you what my life has been like. It started the way it was meant to go on. Men have screwed me, one way or another, from that day on. But I've survived. I've damned well survived. Buck Ronay's been buried twenty years. He died in the back of his Rolls-Royce, having a quickie with a Beverly Hills teenage hooker.'

He had heard that story – everyone told it, laughing, loving the idea of the father figure of the film industry dying that way. He had thought it funny too. Not now, though. Now he just felt sick.

'Poetic justice, huh?' Clea said, laughing harshly. 'They cremated him in Beverly Hills. Pity they waited till he was dead. I didn't go to his funeral. I wasn't enough of a hypocrite. Everyone else went – there were huge crowds. Well, his two sons still have a lot of power. Afterwards they sprinkled his ashes over the Malibu coastline, from a plane. I watched them from my bungalow and laughed. I was still alive and a star, with more money than even I could spend, so to hell with Buck, in every sense of the goddamned word! If there's one man in hell it's bound to be Buck Ronay.'

He had been breathless with admiration of her courage. He had taken her hand and kissed it. 'You're wonderful. I love you and I'd be deeply honoured if you'd marry me. What we just did wasn't having sex, Clea, I was making love to you because I love you. I want to be with you for the rest of my life.'

Maybe she had meant to marry him all along. Had merely been showing him what he was really getting – not the icon of Hollywood, the great star, the goddess with the perfect body, but a woman who had been maimed yet was a survivor, with scars to prove it. She had told him the truth about herself, then waited to see if he would back off. Clea liked to set little tests for men, watch them jump through hoops for her. She manipulated everyone she met, but especially men – which, she once told Sebastian, was fair enough, considering what men had done to her in the past. He had seen the justice in that, even when it was him who was paying the bill for a guy he had never even met, who had been dead for years.

In those first months they couldn't have enough of each other. He still remembered the wildness and tirelessness with which they had made love. Clea always screamed when she came. 'Yes, yes, yes,' she would shriek, shuddering with pleasure, her smooth body arching in orgasm.

'No, no, no,' she had screamed, three years ago, all the way down to meet her death, while the busy traffic moved on and people below were quite unaware at first that she was falling towards them, like Icarus, burning from flying too high and setting the sky on fire.

* * *

At three o'clock that afternoon, the Venetian TV news began with images of the start of the film festival: the arrivals at the airport, snatched pictures of smiling, waving stars hurrying past, interviews with one or two better-known names, clips of the film for which they had been nominated. Then a reporter rapidly sketched in the gossip: who was in town, who had been nominated but had not come, who had not been nominated but had arrived anyway.

Towards the end of the item the scene switched to the lobby of the Hotel Excelsior. The camera skimmed famous faces, picked up the international babble, then Sebastian flashed into view. The viewers were shown him grabbing Laura's arm, saw her white, distressed face briefly, before she was tugged away into the lift.

The microphone hadn't picked up anything that was said – it had not been close enough – but it hadn't needed to: the faces said it all. The pretty, dark-haired reporter speculated excitedly, talked about the film Laura and Sebastian had made together, about the gossip surrounding them at the time. She reminded the viewers of Sebastian's Venetian birth, his marriage to one of the biggest stars Hollywood had ever known, then related the story of Clea's death.

'Nobody knows the truth of what happened that day, accident or suicide, or—' The girl broke off, gazing into the camera. 'Well, who knows? But Sebastian Ferrese is home again, after years in America, one of the biggest names in cinema today, a universally acknowledged genius of film, and it would seem fitting for him to win the award for best director here, in his own city.'

Many people in Venice saw the report: Sebastian, in his hotel room, bleakly regarding the screen, hearing all that the reporter did not actually say but hinted at; the members of his film crew, sitting in an American-style bar in the city; Melanie, in her room, talking on the phone to her office in London, with one eye on the TV. Laura did not see it: she was in her bath, listening to Puccini on her headphones and trying not to think about anything at all.

Sebastian's camera man, Sidney McKenna, drained his glass of whisky and called over to the barman to bring another round.

'Not for me,' Valerie Hyde said, nursing her Cinzano, her black eyes smouldering.

'Girlie, you look as if you badly need a few drinks.' Sidney rarely spoke much, but when he did he was usually blunt and incisive.

'Don't start on me, Sid,' she snapped. 'I'm not in the mood.'

'We can see that. You've been grim ever since she showed up. It was bound to happen one day – the film business is a small world.'

'She's bad for him. If he hadn't met her, Clea would be alive today.'

There was silence in their little group; people glanced furtively at each other, the bar so quiet that you could hear the slap, slap, slap of the water in the side canal on which it stood.

'Better not say that to anyone else,' Sidney said softly. 'Unless you want to destroy him. Is that what you want, Val?'

'Sod off.' She finished her drink and got up. 'I'm going for a walk.'

As she went out she met an American journalist who tried to stop her, giving her an ingenuous, open smile. 'Hi, there, Val, how're you? Let me buy you a drink.'

'Not today, Frankie baby,' she said, brushing past his detaining hand.

He let her go, caught sight of the rest of the crew at the bar and sloped over there, still smiling that cheerful, friendly smile, his stock-in-trade, the banner of his kind.

'Hi, guys! How're you all doing? I can see you're a few drinks ahead. Let me catch up – the drinks are on me.'

'Don't waste your money, fella,' Sidney told him kindly. 'None of us are talking to the press today.'

'Don't be so suspicious,' Frank Wiltshire reproached him. 'What story do you think I'm after? And I thought we were buddies.'

'You've never had any buddies, Frank. You know that. You only have victims and targets, and we don't intend to be either so stop trying to con us.'

Frank glanced up at the TV over the bar. 'You been watching that?' His eyes skimmed back to catch any betraying expression on their faces, but nobody answered or even looked at him.

Unsurprised, he went on, 'I've always wondered how much fire there was behind all that smoke. Did Sebastian have an affair with the girl? Did Clea find out about it? How *did* Clea die, exactly? The inquest just skated over the surface, didn't it? All the real questions never even got asked, let alone answered.'

Sidney slid off the bar stool. 'Got to go. *Ciao.*'

The others said, in a confused mutter, '*Ciao*,' and wandered away without looking back. Frank Wiltshire ordered another drink and sat alone for a while, contemplating just how to write the story.

Across the water, in the old city, others saw the news item too. In a high-raftered room on the first floor, a man in grubby dungarees and an old rust-coloured T-shirt turned, a small, delicate chisel in one hand, a matching-sized hammer in the other, to glance at the TV screen through the protective goggles he wore.

As the newscast ended, a door creaked open behind him and a woman walked in. She paused to look at the television, which was now showing a series of adverts. Chuckling children lifted spoonfuls of cereal to their mouths while a mother beamed approvingly behind them; then a cartoon mouse began to caper across the screen. The woman walked over, feet scrunching on flakes of chipped stone, and switched off the TV.

'You saw?'

'Sebastian on the news? Yes. Well, we knew he'd been nominated, didn't we? It was on the cards he would come. He was bound to come back here one day. I'm surprised it wasn't sooner.' The man turned back to his work, the muscles in his arm rippling visibly as he tapped the hammer against the chisel. 'Who's this Laura Erskine? Her face seemed familiar. Actress?'

'You know as much about her as I do – you heard what that girl on TV said. She was in one of his films. There were rumours that they'd had an affair, not long before his wife killed herself. Maybe that was why. She had to have a reason for throwing herself out of that window – or getting pushed out.'

The man frowned behind his goggles. 'You can't really suspect Sebastian of murder?'

'It's in his blood, treachery and cruelty.' The woman walked to the window, which ran from ceiling to floor and could be closed off with ancient, cracking wooden shutters from which the paint had long since peeled, stared out at the blue sky, her back to her son. Watching her, he thought how depressing it was always to see her in black. Didn't she ever yearn to wear something else? The world was so full of colour and yet she shut it all out, quite deliberately. It was an affront to God, rejecting the wonderful gift he had given the world.

'Oh, everyone is capable of cruelty. Even you, Mamma.'

She picked up the coldness in his tone, turned and stared at him. 'Don't say such things, even as a joke, Nico.'

His blows on the stone in front of him were light, quick, carefully controlled; he knew precisely what he was doing, what effect his chisel would have, where to strike, with what force, and what would happen in consequence. Sculpting was a science as much as an art: you had to understand stone to work with it, and he had chisels and hammers of every size and shape, lined up with great precision on a table behind him. As far as his tools were concerned, he had a passion for order.

A shape was emerging from the block: where once there had been simply a featureless square of stone you could now see a long, thin nose, angled cheekbones, hollowed eye sockets.

He stood back and pushed up his goggles to get a clearer view of what he had just done, blinking at the reflection of blue water rippling along the walls in dancing patterns of light. The sky outside was turning almost purple in the heat.

'It wasn't a joke, Mamma,' he said, absently. 'All human beings are capable of anything. That doesn't mean we'll do what we're capable of, merely that the potential exists inside us.'

A long silence followed. Then his mother said, 'That girl, the actress, her hair . . . did you notice? The same colour as his mother's.'

'Titian red. Of course I noticed. Gina had wonderful hair – I've never forgotten it, like fire in sunshine. The girl's bone structure is similar, too.'

Standing back, his head on one side, he ran a hand tenderly over the face he was carving, watching the way the strange light from the water flickered over it, making it look as if the mouth moved in a smile. He had read somewhere that Phidias, the Greek sculptor, had been able to carve stone so that it looked alive, real flesh that you could swear would move under your fingers. God, to be able to get that effect! 'Strange, what happens inside our heads, isn't it?' he thought aloud.

'What are you talking about now?' His mother watched him, frowning, her olive skin pale.

'I think we should invite Sebastian here while he's in Venice.'

'No!' The word came in a high sound, like the shriek of one of the gulls outside in the sky.

He pulled down the goggles over his eyes and lifted his chisel and hammer again. 'Of course we must. Don't be silly, Mamma. Will you ring his hotel? While you're at it, invite that girl, too.'

'I won't have either of them under my roof!'

'*Your* roof, Mamma? My roof, you mean. I want them both here, especially that girl. I want *her* here especially.'

'Nico, please . . . don't . . .' Her hands twisted together and she watched him with a fixed, anxious gaze.

'Don't keep arguing. Go and ring Sebastian now. You don't want to make me angry, do you?'

Laura spent ten minutes unpacking, hanging up her clothes, filling drawers, but only after she had sat Jancy, the doll she had had all her life and was never parted from, on the end of the bed. She had been given her for Christmas when she was four and Jancy had sat at the end of her bed ever since. Eighteen inches high, soft-bodied, with a smooth, pink porcelain face, delicately modelled little hands and feet in the same material, curly blonde hair and blue eyes that shut if you laid her down and snapped open again when you sat her up, Jancy had always worn the same knee-length pleated blue dress, with pearl buttons from her waist up to a rounded collar. Now and then Laura took her clothes off and washed them, the dress, the white slip, the lacy panties and the white shoes.

Melanie always teased her about Jancy. 'Aren't you too old to be carrying a doll around with you everywhere? I've heard of people who still keep their teddy bears – but a doll, for heaven's sake!'

'Call her my mascot. She's company for me when I'm alone in a strange hotel room.'

'Get a man!'

'Jancy's far less trouble.'

'That depends on the man. You choose the wrong ones.'

'So do you!'

Melanie couldn't argue with that and, anyway, Laura didn't care what she thought. Wherever she went in the world Jancy went, too, a constant reminder of her home, her family, a silent reassurance that she was still the same person. When your life changed as much as Laura's had over the past few years you needed that. There were so many temptations placed in your way that you had to build your own protective shell against the world's attack, and Jancy was part of hers.

It would have been easy to take drugs instead – they were always around: a joint of cannabis between sessions, cocaine cut on compact mirrors, at some parties, with tiny coloured straws to sniff it through, a dozen different pills if you were tiring and the photographer wanted to go on for another hour. Easy to let drugs take the strain of that life, but Laura never had.

She had had a lot to prove to the world, to her family, herself – she saw too many other girls going down the drain and it wasn't going to happen to her. So she clung to Jancy and photographs of her parents, her sister, her home, to keep her sane and above the dark waters of oblivion into which others sank.

At four o'clock that afternoon, she and Melanie took the hotel launch over to Venice, watching the well-known fabulous skyline appear through the heat haze, the lace-like white fretted stone of the Doge's palace, the spire-topped pink marble Campanile, the crumbling, pastel-painted façades of houses and hotels along the canal. Melanie began a travelogue in Laura's ear, a guidebook open in her hand.

'That must be the part of Venice called the Dorsoduro . . .'

'The what?'

'It means backbone, it says here. Venice's backbone, I suppose. Most of Venice is built up on wooden stilts but the Dorsoduro had a solid subsoil, it says. Anyway, that's where the Grand Canal begins. And that's the Dogana di Mare, the old customs house. The figure on top is Fortune standing on top of a golden ball and—'

'Mel, stop it, will you? If I wanted to read a guidebook I'd buy one.'

'How are you to know where you are if you don't have a guidebook? Look, that must be Santa Maria della Salute, that big church. It was built to celebrate the ending of some plague or other, and when ships came home from sea that was the first thing they saw, the dome of the Salute.'

Against the blue sky the dove-grey dome was massive, yet seemed to float, insubstantial as a dream, above a huge baroque church, ornamented with white stone statues, pediments and little cupolas. Beyond it, incongruously, Laura saw a dredger sucking sludge out of the canal. A speedboat whizzed past, making the hotel launch rock dangerously as it nosed into the landing-stage at San Marco.

Melanie swore furiously, brushing water spots off her aubergine linen pants and matching shirt. 'Look at that! I didn't bring many clothes with me. This outfit will have to be cleaned before I can wear it again!'

Laura considered the barely visible stain. 'Never mind, Mel, you can get it done at the hotel, and you know you're going to spend all your time buying new clothes here.'

Melanie eyed her pale green cotton skirt and T-shirt with disfavour. 'It wouldn't hurt you to buy some good gear. That is hardly chic, darling.'

Laura's eyes were invisible behind her dark glasses. 'I want to be anonymous, not chic. I don't want anyone recognising me.'

'Nobody will in that tat, honey.' A wistful look came into Melanie's eyes. 'I've had more calls from the press about you this afternoon than I've had for months – but all they want to talk about is Sebastian Ferrese and the way his wife died. It kills me to turn down all that PR but, just for once, it really wouldn't be good exposure. I don't want you tagged as the girl Ferrese killed his wife for.'

'I couldn't agree more. I am not talking to anyone about Sebastian.'

Melanie bit her finger thoughtfully. 'Although, mind you, that's a great shout-line – the girl he killed his wife for. A good PR firm could do something with that.'

'No, Mel! Don't even think about it.'

'I was only kidding!'

Laura wasn't so sure.

A moment later, Laura and Melanie were sucked into the enormous swirling crowds moving around the great square among the flocks of pigeons and stalls selling souvenirs. Laura did not know which way to look – there was too much to see.

'Napoleon said St Mark's Square was the drawing room of Europe,' Melarie read out, her guidebook held in front of her as she walked.

'Who?'

'Napoleon.'

'Who was he?'

Melanie did a double-take, realised she was being teased and snapped, 'Oh, very funny!'

Laura grinned at her. 'Well, stop reading me this stuff. I'm going to look at the basilica. Coming?'

'I've seen it, and the Doge's palace, when I was here on honeymoon.'

'How many years ago was that?'

'Never you mind!'

'And if you were on honeymoon I don't suppose you took too much notice of anything you saw, knowing you.'

Melanie gave a delighted, sensual smile. 'It was a great honeymoon – we had terrific sex in between eating three marvellous meals every day. That was pretty much all we did – fuck and eat. It was when we got back home that the rot set in. Turned out that was all he was good for – sex and food. But I'm not here to do any sightseeing – I want to shop until I drop this afternoon. I'll see you back here in half an hour, okay?'

Laura joined the throng of tourists slowly filtering into the Basilica San Marco and walked slowly around, staring up at the mosaic of Christ in Glory decorating the central dome. The whole enormous building was darkly mysterious, the ceiling and floors gilded, covered in elaborate mosaics.

Staring into the face of Christ in a Byzantine icon, Laura was shocked to find herself thinking of Sebastian – but; then, didn't most things remind her of him? She found herself thinking of him at the strangest times in the strangest places.

Yet this was different. There was a distinct resemblance to him in Christ's dark eyes, the bone structure of jaw and cheeks, the angle of the head, the curling dark hair – and it was not simply a physical likeness. The longer she gazed, the more she realised that there was something in the soul behind those dark eyes that spoke to her of Sebastian, a remoteness, a spirituality, another dimension that was god-like, and yet a gentleness and tenderness that was warmly human. It bewildered her that, at one and the same time, she could admit the possibility that Sebastian might have killed his wife and yet still see him in the body and soul of Christ.

To a believer that would be pure blasphemy, she thought. If she spoke her thoughts aloud people would think she was crazy, and they wouldn't be far wrong. There was, after all, madness in love; every poet said so. She knew so little about Sebastian – she couldn't even be sure that it had not been him who had sent her that scary little note.

Oh, stop it! she told herself. Stop thinking about him. Down that road lay true madness; total unreality. She wrenched herself away from the image of Christ and hurried on behind an American tour group, listening in to their guide's comments. It made everything she saw more interesting to know exactly what she was looking at, and the Italian-American guide spoke fluently, an expert, obviously, on everything Venetian. Laura became so interested that she paid the necessary sum to view the greatest treasure of San Marco, the Pala d'Oro, a heavily jewelled tenth-century altarpiece.

Half an hour later, Melanie found her still in the basilica so absorbed that she was half dazed with beauty. Grabbing her arm, Melanie hissed, 'What *are* you doing? I caught sight of you back there but they wouldn't let me join you unless I paid the entrance fee for this part of the cathedral, and I could see that if I yelled to you they'd throw me out. The guy on duty had that look on his face, a sort of just-you-try-it-buster expression, so you owe me, Laura. I'll put that fee on your next bill, and you'd better not query it!'

'Sorry, Mel, but you should have waited until I came out.'

'I have been, for ages, sitting in the square drinking a *frullato di arancia.*' She paused, watching Laura, who sighed.

'Okay, I'll buy it – what's that?'

Melanie grinned. 'Delicious, I can tell you! A mixture of chilled milk and orange juice. You must try it – I've never tasted anything like it! Come on! Haven't you seen enough of this gloomy old place?'

'You could stay in here for days and not see enough.'

'Not me, I couldn't. I'm not a great one for churches.' But Melanie stared incredulously at the magnificent Pala d'Oro. 'Is that real gold, do you think?'

'Absolutely, it's made up of two hundred and fifty panels of gold foil and precious stones.'

'You're kidding! Are they real? Do you think those are emeralds or just green glass?'

'Emeralds, and the red ones are real rubies.'

Melanie frowned suspiciously. 'How do you know that? I thought you didn't believe in reading guidebooks.'

'I listened in on a tour group.'

'I might have known you'd cheated.' Melanie held up one hand and considered her plump fingers, on which several rings gleamed. 'Imagine one of those big rubies in a ring! A heavy gold setting, of course – it would look ridiculous in anything else.'

Laura giggled. 'Come on. We'd better go before you try and grab one!'

As they walked out Laura looked at the large wicker basket her friend was carrying. 'What have you bought?'

'Some ravishing red Venetian glass, made at Murano. Do you know, they were making glass in the thirteenth century?'

'I hope they packed it well. You don't want it getting broken *en route*. I wouldn't fancy its chances bumping along the conveyor belts at Heathrow.'

'I'll carry it myself.' Melanie looked at her watch. 'Look, I don't want to hang around St Mark's Square all afternoon. I'm going to explore more shops.'

'What else do you want to get?'

'Some *prosciutto*, some squid-flavoured pasta – and you can get little bottles of pear and lime liqueur here that are supposed to be terrific.'

'You could buy all of that in Harrods,' Laura said.

Melanie gave her a furious look, her lower lip stuck out like a petulant baby's. 'It wouldn't be the same. And it would cost more. Imported food always does. Anyway, I like to buy stuff in the country of origin, it makes it special. When you eat it you can remember your holiday.'

As they emerged from the basilica Laura blinked in the fierce light of the sun. The enormous square was still crowded with tourists although it was now late afternoon. She put her dark glasses back on just in case there was a reporter or cameraman around. The sun poured down relentlessly, making her head ache after the cool shadows of the basilica.

'Coming with me?' asked Melanie. 'Shouldn't you buy presents for your parents, Angela and Hamish and the brats?'

'I can do that tomorrow morning, early, when it isn't so hot. Right now, I'm dying to sit down. I'll find somewhere nice and quiet in the shade. You can meet me again at that café under the arcade – it's bound to be cool. We don't want to sit outside in the sun, even if the tables do have umbrellas. And I think it's more atmospheric. I love those cloudy old mirrors on the walls.' Laura gazed across the square into Florian's, her eyes dreamy. 'You can't see yourself in them, but they seem to reflect other faces from long ago, strange shapes that keep changing, eyes that watch you. D'you know what I mean?'

'No, you're just crazy,' Melanie said with the impatience of the practical for dreamers. 'Now, don't get lost! Remember, anyone will show you the way back here, okay? And keep your eye on your watch. Five o'clock, okay? If you don't show I'm going back to the hotel without you.'

They parted and Laura tried to get a table at Florian's, but none was free. She wandered off into a quiet, shady square nearby, bought some postcards, then sat down at a street café under an awning, ordered iced tea and settled down to write to her family. She would go back to St Mark's at five o'clock.

Sebastian had come over to the city, too, but he had taken a *vaporetto,* which moved more slowly and stopped frequently, giving him a chance to reorientate himself in the city he found instantly familiar, even though nearly thirty years had passed since he had last seen it. Of course, he had been reminded of it over the years, on film and in books. The image of Venice was universal, a dream all men dreamt.

When he set out he had had no plans. As he stopped at the hotel desk to hand in the key of his suite, Valerie Hyde came up behind him. 'Going out? Want any company?'

He turned sharply to look at her. 'Oh, hi. Actually, I meant to leave you a message. Will you do some research for me? My mother died here and I've always meant to check up on the details. Can you go through the back files of the local paper for me?' He pulled a piece of paper out of his pocket. 'I've written her name and the date on here. If you can get them, I'd like photocopies of any news items covering the story, or the inquest.'

Valerie glanced at the handwritten note. 'What am I looking for?'

'Just the facts. She drowned. I want to know how or why and if anyone else was involved.'

She looked up and stared at him with narrowed eyes. 'It isn't always wise to dig up the past.'

'Just do it, Val,' he said curtly. 'See you later.'

On impulse he disembarked from the *vaporetto* in the Castello district, on the paved quayside called the Riva degli Schiavoni, at the landing-stage for the church of San Zaccaria Pièta. He did not want to get involved with the hordes of tourists that filled the further end of the Riva degli Schiavoni where it met St Mark's Square.

He had played with the idea of visiting Ca' d'Angeli that afternoon, but once he got off the boat his courage failed. He was afraid of what he would find, dreading that a child's memory would prove false, that the great golden palace of his dreams would be just another crumbling old house without any of the heartstopping beauty he remembered.

The Castello district was a less visited area of the city, although there were always tourists drifting about on the quayside, and stalls selling souvenirs and maps. As a child Sebastian had known this part of the city well. He walked now in a sort of trance, hardly knowing what he was doing, but along a route he had followed before, in another life, moving slowly through a narrow arch, along a shadowy alley, into a square in front of a great Renaissance church.

The weather was typical of the sweltering heat of an Italian August, the hot air so still that it moved not a leaf on the trees he walked beneath. Trees were rare in Venice, but this district had a park-like feel to it. The smell of the canals made his nose wrinkle in distaste. In Venice you were never far from water. The Grand Canal lay behind him and at one point he caught a glimpse of a small side canal; aquamarine sunlit water between crumbling, fading red-brick walls in which there were small, barred windows high up, with strings of washing hung out from one side of the canal to the other.

'Rio del Vino,' he said aloud, amazed to find the name coming up out of the past, and with it a memory of his mother telling him that name every time they came here.

'Why is it called the wine river, Mamma?'

'Because this is where wine was brought up from the docks,

Sebastian.' She had had a beautiful voice, sweet as honey, low and soft, intensely female.

He had looked across at the red-brick walls thoughtfully. 'Or maybe because the reflection of the walls sometimes makes the canal look like red wine?'

Mamma had laughed, throwing back her head, her long white throat throbbing with amusement. 'What ideas you come up with! Well, it's in your blood. I wonder if you're going to be an artist.'

'Yes, that's what I want to be. Would you like me to be an artist, Mamma?'

'I want you to be whatever you want to be.'

He had forgotten that conversation until now. Memory stung, like grasping nettles growing along some dusty, forgotten byway. He flinched and entered the church of San Zaccaria, leaving behind the heat and the dust of the square for the cool, deep shade within.

When his eyes were accustomed to the shadowy light he wandered around, absorbing it all slowly, until at last he stopped in the north aisle, in front of Giovanni Bellini's *Madonna and Child with Saints,* the exquisite altarpiece that radiated serenity, a soothing balm to a fevered spirit.

Sebastian felt the painting's calm invade his soul. He almost believed he could hear the music of the angel playing a viol while St Catherine, St Lucy, St Peter, and St Jerome stood around as he did, intent on the music.

Listening to that soundless music, his mind was absorbed in memories of his mother. She had brought him here on a fine spring day soon after his fifth birthday. He was already used to visiting churches and art galleries. Venice had so many of both and his mother loved pictures. She herself had painted, and knew everything there was to know about Venetian artists.

'It's by Bellini,' she had said. 'We've seen some of his paintings before – do you remember? No? Well, memorise his name, Sebastian. Giovanni Bellini. He was a great artist, you will see his work everywhere, and he came from a family of artists. One day you must learn to tell one from another. Giovanni is the great Bellini, of course.'

Sebastian remembered looking at the altarpiece, then up at her beautiful face, a fugitive gleam of sunlight in the gloomy interior turning her hair into a halo of gold and red, like the haloes of saints in missals and old paintings. The first time he saw Laura, on the cover of a magazine, he had felt a jolt of shock because, for a second, he had thought she was his mother: the shape of the face was so similar, the forehead, nose and jawline, and her hair was exactly the same colour as his mother's, that shade of red-gold which Titian loved to paint, the gleam of sunlight seen through a candle-flame, the colour of a halo in a Renaissance painting.

Thirty years had passed since the spring day when he and his mother had visited this church, but in front of the Bellini now he could remember every second of the time they had spent there together. He could even remember the weather, the peculiar brightness of the sun through the new leaves on the trees in the square, the light on the canal, the sound of birds flying back and forth, nest-building under the eaves of houses. At five years old, he couldn't remember last year's spring: to him this was the first spring he had ever noticed, a pattern for all springs to follow.

When she had died, just over a year later, it had been a snowy February.

Why was memory so fitful and selective? He had never been able to remember who else had been on the boat; he could see only his mother. But she could not have been alone on the boat that day.

She had vanished into the blizzard, and a few minutes later he had heard a confused noise somewhere out there, on the Grand Canal. He had never been able to remember just what he had heard, only that it had frightened him. A violent jab of pain made him shut his eyes and put a hand to his forehead.

Migraine. It must be the heat, and the disturbance of coming back here, after all these years.

Turning away from the altar, he walked out into the sleepy little square, turned left and began slowly making his way towards St Mark's. A few minutes later he stopped dead. There was Laura, sitting in a street café with a glass in her hand. A shock of joy hit him. She was so lovely. That gilded hair, that face, its serene, smooth beauty, a Madonna's face, pure and innocent – and below it a sensuous body that denied everything in the face, as Clea's had. As his mother's body had? Were all women the same?

You could never believe what you thought you saw. The eye is easily tricked, any film-maker would tell you that. Looking through the camera lense you could deliberately confuse the real with the illusory.

He stood, watching Laura, in the heavy, hot, somnolent Venetian afternoon. Flies droned past, footsteps echoed on the pavement, there was a dank odour from the canal. The smell of death.

All these years he had not wanted to return to Venice because he had known that death would haunt it for him. He had always had this uneasy feeling whenever he thought of the city: a brooding premonition as if doom awaited him there.

At times he had believed that he, too, would die here, that it was death that waited for him. How strange that he should find Laura again here, in this place. Even stranger that she looked as if she belonged here, had always been here, in this square, shade flickering over her face, her red-gold hair moving softly as she wrote postcards, bending over the table.

Sebastian began to walk towards her, his eyes fixed on her, but when he was a few feet from her table a hand grabbed his arm.

'*Signore!* Signor Ferrese! *Scusi, – mi dispiace . . .*' a rough, hoarse voice husked in his ear. Sebastian glanced round in surprise.

An old man, wearing the oil-stained navy blue jersey and

ancient trousers of someone used to working on boats, stared back at him, smiling with a mouth half full of blackened teeth. Nearly bald, his skin wrinkled and weather-worn, the old man's face had that slyness and secrecy which usually suggests a lack of any sense of right or wrong.

Sebastian gave him a wary, polite but distant nod. '*Signore?*' He looked around, too, in case others were close to him; gangs of pickpockets operated in most tourist centres and he would not have been surprised to find that this man was part of one such gang and was trying to distract him until the others made their move.

Still in Italian, the old man said, the Venetian dialect salting his words, 'You don't remember me, Signor Ferrese? Look harder. It's a while since we met, but you do know me, and I know all about you. I just want to warn you . . .'

Laura finished writing her postcards and pushed them into her handbag; the hotel would post them for her. Where was that waiter? When she had paid the bill she would have to rush, Melanie would be waiting.

Then, she heard Sebastian's voice. At first she believed it was inside her head, an echo from the past, until another voice answered in low, muttered Italian.

They were a few feet from her, standing close together, Sebastian in pale blue jeans and a thin white cotton T-shirt talking to an old man, who looked like a tramp.

A few scraps of their conversation reached her, but her grasp of Italian was not good enough for her to understand much. Just a few words leapt out at her.

'*Morte* . . .' That word she did know: it meant death. '*Morte violente* . . .' A violent death. She shivered. The old man must be talking about Clea. What was he saying? Her eyes riveted on Sebastian. She saw all trace of colour leave his face, his mouth harden, his face become a skull-like rigid mask.

'*Assassinio*,' the old man hissed, nodding insistently at Sebastian. '*Si, si, assassinio!*' Biting her lower lip so hard that she tasted blood, Laura thought he must be accusing Sebastian of murder.

Sebastian snapped back at him and the old man jerked away. '*Non vada in collera!*'

She knew those words – Don't lose your temper, the old man was saying, and he looked frightened.

Laura stood up and dropped money on the table, without taking her eyes from Sebastian.

He leaned towards the old man, his lips parting to snarl a muffled burst of words. Laura saw something in his face that she remembered from those terrifying, recurring dreams. She might love him but somehow she had picked up the violence within him; the murderous fury that showed now in his face. She didn't understand most of what he said, but she picked up the threat in his tone, in his face. '*I morti non parlano . . . un segreto . . . capisce . . .*'

God, why hadn't she learnt more Italian? She desperately wanted to know what he was saying.

The old man backed away, his hands held up in a plea. '*Signore, prego . . .*' He started talking faster, very softly; she picked up only one or two words she understood. *Moglie*. Wife – that meant wife, didn't it? Then again he whispered, '*Assassinio!*'

Laura couldn't bear to listen to any more: she turned on her heel and began to run, guilt poisoning her mind. If she had never met Sebastian, never fallen in love with him and let him see how she felt, would Clea have died? Life was like a soft-skinned fruit that bruises if you so much as brush it with a fingertip. Every little thing you do can have such far-reaching repercussions.

Had he killed his wife? *No!* Not Sebastian. He would never kill anyone, let alone a woman he had loved – and Laura knew that he had loved Rachel Lear when he married her. Sebastian would never have married at all if he had not been in love. He had told her that when he first met his wife he had fallen for her at once. Rachel Lear had been the sex goddess of her day and a lot of men went crazy over her. Sebastian had not been the first, or the last.

But even if he had fallen out of love, why would he kill Clea? If he wanted to be rid of her he would only have had to walk out, divorce her. But Sebastian was a Catholic, of course; he did not believe in divorce.

Clea did, though: she had already been divorced once so why not again, if she was tired of her marriage? Marriage was not something Clea took seriously. But had she been tired of Sebastian? She had been very jealous that day when she found her husband and Laura kissing. Laura remembered the look on Clea's lovely face; the black rage, the viciousness.

Next day Clea had sauntered on to the set and confronted Laura, who was sitting in a canvas chair out of sight of the camera, waiting to be called for a retake.

Laura had gone red, then pale, and had half risen. Clea had waved her back into the chair, had sat down beside her, crossed her legs – showing a lot of silky thigh in the process for the benefit of any men around – and yawned like a sleepy cat.

'Don't worry, darling, I'm not going to hit you. I'm quite sorry for you, actually. You don't really think a gawky, half-baked beanpole like you is going to hold him, do you? He may have taken you to bed, but he does that with every girl who chucks herself at him. It doesn't mean a thing. Take my advice, darling, get away from him fast. He'll only hurt you, he's a mean bastard.' She turned back the black lace collar of her dress, and gestured to her pale neck: a bruise showed up disturbingly. 'See what he did to me last night? He tried to throttle me. Those are his fingerprints. One day he'll kill me. He's so jealous of every man I look at. That's why he sleeps around – trying to make me as jealous as he is!'

She had laughed, a clear, light sound that did not match the expression in her famous, violet-blue eyes, and Laura had felt as if she was watching Rachel Lear in one of her films.

It was hard to distinguish her real life from her acting. How much of all that had been the truth? Oh, that Sebastian was jealous, Laura believed – what man, married to the most beautiful woman in the world, the modern Helen of Troy, adored and desired by millions of other men, would not have been jealous? He had possession of her, and yet he did not possess her. How could he when she constantly betrayed him, broke her marriage vows lightly – worse, enjoyed his pain, his frustration, his rage? If Sebastian had killed her, he had had good reasons for doing so.

Poor Sebastian. Laura knew how he must have felt. No other emotion was as corrosive: jealousy hurt, burned acidly in your stomach, destroyed your peace of mind, kept you awake at night and, when you did snatch a few minutes' sleep, tortured you with dark dreams. Laura knew all about jealousy now.

'Laura! Wait! Laura!'

His voice behind her made her panic. She ran faster but the path she was following now was so narrow that she was afraid she would fall into the narrow canal that wound beside it.

Sebastian caught her arm. 'Why did you run away?' He was breathless from running, or from the rage she had seen in his face when he was talking to the old man. She wished she knew exactly what they had argued about.

She didn't answer, tugging to get away from him, her eyes lowered to the surface of the canal, which sparkled in the late-afternoon sunshine, the gleam of petrol turning the water into a spreading rainbow.

'You've changed,' he said, almost as if it was an accusation.

She looked up into his face. 'So have you.' Her tone was heavy with sadness, a voice of mourning. 'Far more than me.'

He knew he looked older now than he had when they first met, and he felt older. Sometimes he felt like the oldest man still breathing.

'Far more has happened to me,' he said, in a harsh, smoky tone.

'Yes.' She took a breath, looked up, then plunged in. 'I was very sorry to hear of your wife's death.'

Their eyes held. 'You think I killed her, too.' Sebastian's voice was low and hoarse. 'Go on. Say it. You think I killed her, don't you? Everyone does. They don't come out with it but I see it in their faces. They all think I killed Clea.'

'Did you?' She stared at him, seeing the dark eyes glittering, the mouth hard and leashed. He looked capable of murder now.

In her head the old man's words ran like the words of a song. *Morte . . . moglie . . . morte violente . . . assassinio . . .*

Sebastian's tight lips parted. 'No.' The word grated though his teeth. His mouth said no, but his face contradicted what he said.

She could not stop staring at him, at the beauty of his face, the lustre of those great dark eyes, fringed by long, thick lashes, the powerful bone structure that told of strength and conviction, the stubborn, wilful jawline.

They heard footsteps behind them: an elderly woman with a shopping bag was walking along the narrow path. Sebastian's hands dropped to his sides and, freed, Laura turned and walked away very fast, towards the open waters of the Grand Canal. He followed and caught up with her.

'Have you been sightseeing?' His tone was politely distant, the voice of a stranger making small-talk.

She nodded without speaking, sick with desire, miserable with guilt.

'Where have you been?'

'The basilica.' Her throat was ash-dry – it was hard to speak at all. She forced herself. 'Breathtaking, isn't it?'

'I haven't been there yet.'

Her green eyes opened wide, startled, instantly suspicious. 'You told me you were born here. You must have visited it some time.'

'I was six when we left.'

Slowly she said, 'Yes, of course. I suppose you don't remember much.'

'Not much.' Too much, he thought, yet not enough. It was like seeing in flashes by a flickering candle in a high wind. 'How long are you staying?'

'Only a couple of days. Have you finished the film you were shooting in South America?'

'Yes, I wrapped it up the day before yesterday, just before we hit the deadline. Are you working at the moment?'

'No. I just finished filming in Ireland with Ross Kintyre. An Irish novel, *The Grey Pebble*. A small part, but the money was good, and he's a wonderful director. It was great experience.' How easy it was to slip into shop-talk, avoiding anything personal. Easy, but unreal.

They were not talking at all, were they? Not aloud, anyway. Their bodies spoke, but not their minds, which were shut to each other, shuttered rooms full of . . . what?

'Work lined up?'

She was hot at the moment: soon producers would be beating down her door to offer her work. He watched her eyes, very green against that delicate pale skin, and her pink mouth, warm and sensitive and unbearably sexy. Did she know how desirable she was? When he first met her she had not had any idea what her body could do to men, but she moved differently now, with grace and control. She knew precisely the effect of her body. He had dreamt of being the one to teach her and hated to imagine her with some other man.

Laura shrugged. 'I've been turning stuff down. Melanie's getting cross with me. I keep getting offered parts that are dead ringers for the girl in *Goodnight, World, and Goodbye*. Why are so many people copycats? Why don't they ever take chances, try something new or different? I don't want to keep playing the same part over and over again. What about you? What are your plans?'

She was afraid to stop talking shop in case he moved on to something more personal, less safe.

'I want to make a movie here, in Venice. I've had one in mind for years and I think I've even got a backer.'

'How exciting. Who's doing the script?'

'At the moment I am. I've had a couple of people working on it, but I haven't been pleased with anything they've turned in. The present version has something of the atmosphere but it needs sharpening up.' They passed a gondola idling on the edge of the Grand Canal and Sebastian asked, 'Have you been in a gondola yet?'

'No. Mel said they're a rip-off.'

'Well, you can't leave Venice without having been in a gondola. It's too special an experience.' He hailed the gondolier who, silently moved closer to the edge of the path.

Alarmed, Laura said, 'I have to go, I'm meeting Melanie at Florian's.' Floating around Venice in a gondola, alone with Sebastian – the idea was too dream-like, marvellous. She was afraid.

'I want you to see Ca' d'Angeli.'

Her heart turned over. 'The house where you were born?' Was it real, after all? Were there angels and ancient, faded tapestries on the walls, family portraits, echoing marble floors, a reflection of water on the ceilings?

'I'd love to,' she said wistfully, 'but I can't. I have to find Mel.'

Sebastian curled a hand around her arm just above the elbow and, without looking at her, spoke to the gondolier in Italian.

'Ca' d'Angeli?' the man repeated, staring. '*Si, Signore.*' The man contemplated the sky, thought, named a figure.

'A hundred thousand lira?' Sebastian laughed scornfully and began to argue, shaking his head.

'I really must go.' Even to herself, Laura sounded helpless, weak-willed. She should pull free and walk away, but she was paralysed, torn between her fear of getting involved with

Sebastian again and her desire to see Ca' d'Angeli, to be alone with him for an hour or two.

The bargaining ended abruptly. Sebastian jumped down into the gondola, still holding Laura's hand.

She tried to move away, but he gave a little tug and tightened his grip. She uttered a faint, bird-like cry of alarm, her foot slipped on the wet edge of the crumbling canal path, and she lost her balance, toppling forward into his arms. Sebastian held her, while the gondola rocked to and fro on the petrol-streaked water.

Clutching him, she breathed in his familiar scent, eyes closing. Hadn't she dreamt of this many times? Venice, the canal, a gondola, herself and Sebastian, floating towards the palazzo and the carved stone angels? He pulled her down on to the dark red padded seat, and the gondolier began to pole his way slowly into the Grand Canal.

Chapter Three

She picked up the telephone twice before she finally dialled. The operator's distinctly Venetian voice was automatic, briskly polite. 'Hotel Excelsior.'

'*Posso parlare col Signore Ferrese?*'

'*Un momento, per favore.*' A pause, then the girl said, '*Non rispondono,*' and told her that Sebastian had gone out an hour earlier.

A moment's hesitation – should she leave it at that? Nico had asked her to ring; she had rung. She did not want Sebastian under this roof. A shadow passed over the sun as she stared out of the window, but there was no cloud in the hot, blue sky: the darkness had been inside her eyes.

'Hello?' the operator asked, impatiently.

'Would you take a message, please? Ask him if he would be so kind as to ring Contessa d'Angeli.'

The girl's tone changed, warmed. She was Venetian: she knew this house, this family. '*Si, certo,* Contessa.'

'*Grazie.*' She replaced the receiver. Sometimes she tired of this city, yearned for cooler, northern skies, for the bustle and buzz of her own city . . .

Milan, 1932

Contessa Vittoria d'Angeli had not been born in Venice, but in

Milan, the commercial centre of Italy, modern, busy, industrious. It was the most significant time for Italy since 1861, when the scattered states had been unified as one kingdom. Mussolini had come to power in 1922, after which everything began to change for the better; not only were the trains running on time, as everyone joked in Europe, but Italy was being brought up to date in every other way. She was developing a large, modern navy, she had new factories, which were working flat out; medicine was improving, too, and new hospitals were being built. The old medieval Italy had gone for ever; a modern state was taking its place.

By the time Vittoria was born, in 1932, Mussolini's grip on Italy was total although not everyone was happy with how he ran the country, or his foreign ambitions. He had signed a pact with Ethiopia only four years before, but now he was building up arms and moving his army over its border. Why should he do that unless he planned to annex it? people asked each other, behind locked doors, in the privacy of their homes, or in bars when they were drunk.

In 1932 none of the Serrati family were in the army; the new baby's half-brothers were all too young, and their father too old and too important to Italy's economy. The atmosphere in the house that day was of elation and excitement; the little one was healthy, her mother had had an easy time and was delighted to have her slender figure back.

The Serrati family gathered to toast the health of its newest member. Champagne corks popped, people chatted and laughed, and in her swinging cradle the baby slept, oblivious of the changing panorama of faces that moved above her head. She had been born into a large, extended family of three generations and many were gathered here to welcome her: two grandmothers, a grandfather, uncles and aunts and her half-brothers.

The four boys did not dislike their young stepmother but they still mourned their mother, who had died two and a half years ago. They were not easy at this party: they felt it would be disloyal to enjoy themselves too much.

Their father glanced at them occasionally, his slightly bulging eyes urging them to look cheerful, then he would look back at his second wife in the low-necked white silk nightdress, which showed him how her breasts had ripened since her pregnancy. She was more desirable than ever. How long would it be before he could have her again? She wouldn't let him near her while she was pregnant; claimed the doctor had said that sex might endanger the baby. Not that he had gone without all those months: his appetite was voracious, and had always driven him to others as well as his wife – servants, women who worked in the factory, or whores, although he used them as a last resort. With them, there was always that element of risk: you might end up with the clap or worse. He had been caught like that before and it had been no joke: the cure was almost as painful as the disease.

He frowned thoughtfully. With all these young men in uniform and away from home, there was bound to be far more need for such treatment. He had had a chemist working on research for a couple of years, getting nowhere. Time to put more men on the quest for a less painful but more effective cure. Maybe he should offer a bonus. They would make a killing if they succeeded.

Anna Serrati leant back against her pillows, smiling happily at the prospect of being able to go shopping again and buy lots of new frocks. Sickening to have been as fat as a pig for months. She wasn't getting pregnant again in a hurry – she would see to that. Anna had a shrewd idea of how her husband had solaced himself while he was forbidden her bed, and she would be quite content if he went on getting his fun elsewhere. Anything, as long as he didn't bother her too often. His weight was no joke.

'Isn't she sweet? Look at these beautiful big eyes,' the nurse said, taking the baby, in her long, white lace-trimmed gown, out of the cradle and holding her up for them all to admire.

Leo Serrati stared dubiously at the child's round, red face. Look at that big nose and the double chin. She reminded him of someone but who?

Anna Serrati considered her child, clear-eyed and cynical. Too bad she was no beauty – Well, she looks like him so let's hope he takes to her. He isn't getting any more from me!

'It's an ugly little bug,' the eldest boy, Carlo, whispered to Alfredo, a year younger.

'Looks like Papa,' Fredo mouthed back, and the two other boys, Filippo, who was eight, sturdy as a young pony, and Niccolo, the youngest, with great dark eyes and a skin like polished ivory, shook with smothered giggles.

Their father didn't hear any of that exchange. 'We'll have the biggest christening party Milan has ever seen,' he announced. 'We'll invite everyone who is anyone. We have a lot to celebrate. We have a wonderful future to look forward to, and Milan is going to be the heart of the new Italy.'

The baby yawned, pink gums glistening. Outside, church bells rang and the pink apple blossom showered in a soft, spring breeze.

Four years later, the Italians had achieved what they were assured was a great victory: Il Duce had taken the capital of Ethiopia. However, many people hoped secretly that that would be the end of Il Duce's territorial ambitions and that their men could come home. Few had any idea where Ethiopia was, but they had been told that the Italian army had been welcomed there as liberators. They had not been told that their army had occupied only a tiny fraction of that vast country, or that Mussolini had decreed that Ethiopian prisoners-of-war should be executed as rebels.

Vittoria Serrati was unaware of all that as she watched swallows darting in light zigzags around the stable-yard of her home on the Via Marsala in Milan.

It was a bright May morning in 1936, her fourth birthday.

She had just been placed on the broad back of her first pony and clutched the edge of the saddle with both hands, staring up at the flickering fork-tailed birds through her straight, dark fringe, paralysed with terror, certain that at any minute she would be thrown off on to the cobbles below. It seemed such a long way down to the ground.

'Relax, Vittoria, for heaven's sake! No need to be nervous. The pony's as good as gold. You'll see! She loves children.'

Her father was in one of his better moods because it was her birthday and he believed her to be overjoyed at his present – as she might have been, if only she had not been so scared. She had wanted a pony but it was so big and, standing beside it, Vittoria had felt very small.

If only she could have had time to get used to it, but her father never had time. Not a patient man, he was always in a rush to get away to work – or pleasure.

Without warning his strong square hands had seized her round the middle, lifted her up and dumped her on the pony, and now he was irritated because she hadn't set off around the stable-yard.

'Off you go! Don't just sit there!' he scolded. 'Giorgio, you'd better lead her.'

The groom clicked his tongue. He was a short man, bow-legged, lined and wrinkled from working in the sun and wind, grey-haired because he was over sixty. These days, you couldn't get young men for domestic service: they had all been called up. He led the pony a few steps and Vittoria gripped tighter at the saddle, helplessly jogging back and forth.

Leo Serrati shook his head in disgust. 'Sack of potatoes! Look at her! No give at all. She'll never ride as well as Carlo.'

He shot a look at the gold watch he wore on his dark-haired wrist. 'I have to go. We're having a board meeting this morning. Must get those monthly figures up. We can't afford to fail to meet our quota.'

His wife, Anna, tall and slender in a white dress made in

Milan by one of the top designers, leant over to give his cheek a cool brush of her lips. 'You won't. You never fail at anything, you know that.'

His firm had even succeeded in coming up with a rather more effective, less painful cure for venereal diseases, although it was not yet perfected. The army was trying it out on soldiers and the results looked good, not that he had talked about *that* to his wife. It was not a subject you mentioned to ladies.

But her praise made him puff up like one of the pigeons strutting on the stable roof. He stroked a hand down her back. 'I'll tell the works committee you said that. It will put new heart into them. You know, Il Duce is right about the laziness of the people – they just want to have a good time and sit around in the sun. They have no stomach for work or war.'

Anna's face clouded. 'You don't really think he'll get us into war with the British, do you? Why can't we just leave it to Germany? What has it got to do with us?'

'You don't understand, Anna. We have to show we're Germany's friends. Hitler is the sort of man who thinks you're either with him or against him. Don't worry too much, the Germans can't lose. The British won't fight, nor will the French. Hitler invaded the Rhineland because it's German territory. And he's got away with it – nobody stopped him, they don't dare. They won't dare attack us because we're helping Franco, either. They're old dogs without teeth.' He looked at his watch again. 'I must go. Now that Vittoria has a pony she can ride with you every morning, but take Giorgio with you, I don't like you riding alone.'

She didn't argue, not that she meant to obey him. '*Si, certo. Arrivederci.* Don't work too hard, have a good day, *caro.*'

Vittoria watched them glumly. If only she looked like Mamma, fine-boned and elegant, long legs and narrow, aristocratic feet, beautiful, wide eyes and a mouth like a red rosebud!

Why had she been born so short and dumpy, with a face that always seemed to scowl because of her heavy black eyebrows and round black eyes? Girls were supposed to take after their mothers, weren't they?

Leo Serrati hurried back into the house without saying another word or even looking at his daughter. Tears pricked at her eyes.

Her mother bit her lip ruefully. 'Don't cry, sweetheart. Papa isn't cross with you. It isn't your fault if you aren't a natural rider. I don't think we can hope for much, do you, Giorgio? Poor baby, she doesn't have a clue how to sit a horse.'

'Not like you, Signora,' the groom said adoringly. Summer and winter alike. Anna Serrati rode every morning for an hour. Her seat on a horse was famous and much admired; she had hunted in the winter when she was younger. Now she rode very early then returned, changed out of her riding clothes and came downstairs to take charge of the house, which she had to run with just a few of the old servants who had been with the family for years. Young women wanted jobs in factories where they could earn far more than they ever had before; they laughed at the idea of domestic service.

Luckily, the old servants knew their jobs inside out and were used to working long hours; especially as they all lived in the house and Anna Serrati had organised a rota, like the one used in her husband's factory, so that work and rest time were equally divided. So far the house was as spotless as ever, the panelling highly polished, as was the *art-nouveau* furniture made for Leo Serrati's father at the turn of the century. The food was as well cooked, the kitchen filling every day with the scent of bread baking and the strong aroma of garlic, wine and herbs.

When this house was first built there had been other medicinal, smells in the air, of herbs, carbolic and tar, eucalyptus, menthol and liquorice, because the factory had originally occupied one wing, but now both it and the laboratory were in a new complex, half a mile away. The old premises had been pulled down to make room for this stable-yard.

Vittoria was unaware that anything had changed, of course:

to her, the world had always been the same. She was oblivious of the talk of war, the tensions beneath the apparently smooth skin of daily life here in Milan.

She was just discovering that her family were part of what people called the *capuccio*, the cream of Milanese society. Leo Serrati's pharmaceutical firm was important to the country; the drugs he manufactured were needed now more than ever and he grew richer every day. People were eager to be friendly with his family, especially as Anna Serrati was so beautiful.

Sometimes she took her small daughter out shopping with her, or to have coffee with her friends, and Vittoria was petted and made much of by smiling women who kept saying how pretty she was, what a sweetie, wasn't she a little doll? Their eyes told her that they lied, said that she was plain, not pretty, just as her mirror did.

'Have you had enough, Toria? Take her off, Giorgio.' Anna Serrati bent to kiss her cheek. 'Run in to Nurse, darling. I'm going for a ride.'

Vittoria's legs felt wobbly now that she was safely down on the ground, but she ran back into the house, through the winding corridor to the back stairs the servants used, and began the climb up to the bedroom floor.

Her nursery lay at the back of the house, overlooking the stable-yard, but when she paused at the top of the steep, narrow staircase breathing hard from the effort of the climb, she heard sounds from her mother's bedroom at the other end of the landing. It was her father's voice! Eagerly, Vittoria ran towards the open door only to stop dead. When the nurse wasn't looking after the child she had other duties in the house. Once she would have refused to do anything but take care of Vittoria, but with Italy girding herself for war she had bowed to the inevitable. Every morning she made beds and dusted furniture upstairs. She was doing Anna Serrati's elegant nineteenth-century bed now, with deft, quick movements.

As she leant over to plump up the pillows Leo Serrati

watched the way the girl's short lavender cotton print uniform slid up those slightly plump legs. He moved forward and ran his fingers up under the skirt.

The nurse straightened with a gasp. 'No, please, don't, Signore.'

He grabbed her by the waist and jerked her towards him, bent his head.

The girl wriggled in his arms, her head pushed back by the onslaught of his full, wet mouth. His free hand roamed over her buttocks, pulled her closer, then ran up to fondle her full breasts under the stretched cotton. She struggled uselessly.

He took a step, then another, still kissing her, pushing her backwards in front of him until she toppled on to the bed. He went down on top of her, fumbling underneath the full skirt. He pushed it up and Vittoria watched him pulling down white cotton knickers.

'Don't, oh, please don't,' the girl whispered, crying in husky, choked breaths, pushing at Leo Serrati's fat shoulders.

Leo Serrati didn't answer. A second later the nurse opened her mouth to scream, but the man on top of her put his pudgy hand over it and pushed himself down between her spread legs. Her naked white bottom writhed on the bed.

Grunting, panting, Leo Serrati was going up and down as if he was riding one of the horses in the stables. The girl had stopped struggling and just lay there with her eyes shut. She was making a funny little moaning noise, like one of the pigeons in the yard crooning to itself, and she was moving, too, her legs jerking.

Vittoria felt sick and frightened. She didn't know what her father was doing but she hated the way it made her feel. She was trembling and sweating. She wanted to run away, but couldn't move.

With a long, thick groan Leo stopped riding the girl and fell on top of her, while she writhed under him, one leg thrashing about as if she was having a fit, making a high-pitched whining noise.

'You see, you wanted it,' Leo Serrati muttered, his dark-haired hand caressing the girl's thigh.

Vittoria began to scream. From that instant events moved too fast for her to remember just what happened. Her father leapt off the bed and began to fumble with his open trousers. The girl scrambled up, too, pulling up her knickers and bursting into tears.

'Shut up! Stop that noise, you nosy little bitch!' Leo Serrati yelled, slapping the child's red, tear-stained face.

'What the hell is going on?' said Anna Serrati from the doorway, and then she stood, staring at them all, contempt flooding her eyes. 'I see,' she said. 'I don't care if you sleep with every one of the servants, but not on my bed, you bastard! Don't ever bring one of them in here to fuck them, especially when my child is likely to walk in on you.'

He ignored her as if she hadn't spoken, walked out of the room past her without a word or a glance.

Vittoria was crying in violent gasps, her cheeks burning from the vicious blow her father had given her.

Icily, Anna Serrati said to the nurse, 'Take my daughter to her room, wash her face, comb her hair and get her out of those riding clothes.'

Vittoria never forgot her fourth birthday. She never rode the pony again and did not care when, years later, it was shot and eaten because food was scarce in the shops and many Italians were starving.

Venice, 1997

The sun was very low, far out across the misty reaches of the lagoon, as the gondola negotiated the crowded waters of the Grand Canal, slipping between water-taxis, refuse barges, private boats, *vaporetti*. Leaning against the padded back-rest, languorous with heat, the green cotton T-shirt sticking to her back, Laura stared up at the palazzi they passed; some had become hotels, or housed institutions others had been divided into apartments. Only a few were private homes. From the outside, though, they were still ravishing. The images of Venice are so familiar, even when seen for the first time: they are embedded in the European consciousness, their beauty timeless, unforgettable.

She and Sebastian sat side by side, their shoulders touching, but neither of them spoke or looked at the other although Laura was intensely aware of him. Miser-like, she had treasured every tiny contact they had ever had – at one time she would tell them over to herself in bed at night, how once he had run a finger along her face, from her temples to her mouth, a track of fire that burned long after he had moved away. Once he had smiled into her eyes while he explained softly what he wanted from a scene they were about to shoot, and her heartbeat had quickened until she could barely breathe. How tiny, how infinitesimal, were the gestures that could feed obsessive love.

Don't think like that! she told herself sharply. She had no business loving him, any more now than she had had three years ago. The man who had married Clea might be guilty of her murder – had she ever had the faintest idea of what sort of man he was? Even to admit the possibility that he might be a murderer was to allow that she had thought herself in love with a stranger. She was still half in love with him and, knew that desire was dammed up inside her waiting for his touch to release it and drown her in a tidal wave of passion.

Deep inside she relived the shock of hearing how Clea had died, the terror when that old man with the blackened teeth had shouted, '*Morte, morte violente!*' and '*Assassinio!*' Sebastian had turned pale, looked haggard and haunted. Why would he have looked like that if he had not killed his wife?

Had Sebastian sent her that card this afternoon? GET OUT OF VENICE, BITCH, OR I'LL KILL YOU.

Looking sideways secretly, Laura tried to read his face, but that hard-edged profile gave nothing away, merely shut her out and made her feel young and stupid. What on earth had ever given her the idea that he might feel anything for her? They were light years apart. She had been a silly fool to let herself dream. Clea had been unforgettable, magnificent, a star of the first magnitude; the world was full of men who had adored her. No man who had been her husband would look twice at any other woman, let alone at one who was in many ways Clea's very opposite – gauche, shy, with legs that were too long and clumsy, a skinny body, too wide a mouth, without sophistication, sex appeal or charm.

'What are you thinking about?'

'Nothing,' she said hastily. 'Why? What do you mean?'

'You looked upset.' His eyes skimmed her face. 'You have an extraordinarily revealing face, you know. That's why the camera loves you. You show the tiniest change of mood without speaking or even moving a muscle. It's a rare gift – try never to lose it.'

The compliment made her look down, moved. A moment later she felt the muscles contract in the arm touching hers. Sebastian had leant forward, was staring ahead. Laura followed the direction of his gaze and there it was. Ca' d'Angeli.

She knew it instantly by the figures on the façade: cherubs, small, plump, naked children with folded wings, which Sebastian had told her were called *putti*, made of plaster, painted white and pink, playful, coy, faintly erotic, as they gambolled among the tall, grave archangels, with folded hands and precisely chiselled wings, who kept watch over the house.

Silently the gondola drew closer to enable its passengers to step out on to the landing-stage. The sinking sun suffused the ornate carving on the upper floor of the palazzo in golden light and Laura was so dazzled that she shut her eyes. Was she dreaming? She slid her fingers into the canal. The touch of cool water on her hot skin was a sensuous pleasure so intense that she knew she had to be awake.

Opening her eyes again with a sigh she saw Ca' d'Angeli reflected on the rippling surface of the canal, and reached out to touch the gold and pink of the mirrored stone. At her touch the reflection dissolved. The incandescent house sank down, down, into the Grand Canal, the stone angles, the delicate lacework balconies, the ornate trefoil grilles in the walls – which, she discovered later, were there to allow light to penetrate the windowless dark corridors within – and the finials on the roof that were called crockets Sebastian said, or crochets, but did not look like musical notation to Laura. They resembled nothing so much as leaves fluttering on the edge of the roof.

Other reflections crowded in: the faded, crumbling cloud castles of other palazzi along the Grand Canal were stirred by her fingers and sank down into another, secret Venice far below the water.

The gondolier spoke in rapid Italian. Sebastian nodded, stood up, balanced carefully for a second before he jumped out and bent to offer Laura his hand. She got up and felt the gondola rock.

The gondolier gripped the edge of the landing-stage to steady them. She reached quickly for Sebastian's hand, with a dream-like sense of leaping into his childhood to find him. If anywhere, she would find in this place whatever had made him the man he was: innocent or guilty.

As they turned towards it, the dark shadow of the house fell on them and Laura shivered. If she had been superstitious she might have thought she was getting a warning, a premonition of danger, but she had a basic common sense, in spite of her sensitivity to atmosphere, that told her she was imagining things.

She was tired: she had flown from London that morning, had not slept well last night, and she had had the emotional shock of seeing Sebastian again. This had been a long, punishing day. The colours of sunset would soon be draining out of the sky and the August heat of Venice would evaporate in dew.

'Who lives here now?' she asked, in a whisper. 'Is it your

family?' There were so many questions she wanted to ask, but he had a way of evading answers, which she remembered all too well.

He laughed, in a strange, angry way. 'Good God, no. I'm not one of them. My father worked for them.'

Eyes opening wide, she said, 'Oh, I see. What did he do?'

Sebastian's face was dark with pride and defiance. 'He was the gardener.' The answer was curt, harsh.

Her breath caught in comprehension. Was that why he had been so reluctant to talk about his childhood? Was he ashamed because his father had been a gardener here? The way he had talked about Venice, about Ca' d'Angeli, had left her with the distinct impression that he had been one of this aristocratic family with roots going back into medieval Venice.

A grating sound made them both start and swing round to face the house. The heavy wooden front door, studded with iron nails whose heads were shaped in the sign of the Cross, slowly opened and a woman in black appeared, exactly dead centre below the round stone arch above the door.

There was something archetypal about her: the black clothes of widowhood and bereavement, the hands folded at her waist – you saw women like this all over Europe. Black for death. The hair rose on the rape of Laura's neck. In spite of the heat she was icy with fear, but fear of what? Of this woman? Of Sebastian? Of memories of Clea?

Beyond the woman was a shadowy vista of cracked marble walls and floors, pale pink and grey, high plastered ceilings, a great empty, echoing space, with no furniture whatever, only a flight of wide marble stairs going upwards.

Glancing nervously at Sebastian, Laura saw that he had turned back into a figure of stone, like the angels above them, eyes hooded, features rigid. His fingers tightened on Laura's until she caught her breath in pain.

'Sebastian!' she gasped, and he looked down as if he had only then remembered she was with him. 'You're hurting me!'

'Sorry.' He let go of her and looked back at the other woman.

'Who is she?' Laura whispered.

'La Contessa herself. Contessa d'Angeli.'

The Contessa had a regal air, an enormous sense of her own importance, yet physically she was far from beautiful. A short woman, plump, with big dark eyes, lids purpled with eyeshadow, she wore her thick, lustrous hair, once obviously jet black but now streaked with silver, pinned up at the nape of her neck, showing the fullness of her throat and faintly sagging jaw.

Her hands were weighed down with rings: a ruby, in an elaborate gold setting; a big, square-cut emerald. A brooch on her dress blazed with gold and rubies. She were ruby earrings, a cascade of small blood-red drops, which swayed as she moved her head. Laura was no expert, but she felt sure that everything the Contessa wore was genuine and very valuable: it had a depth and fire that was unmistakable and must mean that the family were still very wealthy, because when rich people lose their money the first thing to go is jewellery. It is so easy to sell without anyone noticing: you just make excuses, say, 'Oh, my pearls? They're in the bank, the insurance people insist,' or, 'They're being re-strung,' or 'cleaned'. Or you simply claim that you're afraid to wear them in case you lose them. Laura had known Hollywood stars who wore fake jewellery and made all those excuses about their real ones, long gone, pretending they still had them.

She came towards them, her full mouth curving into a smile as ambiguous as the smile on an Etruscan carving or on the Mona Lisa. 'Sebastian!' She spoke in English with a strong Italian accent. 'This is a coincidence. A few minutes ago I rang your hotel, but they told me you had gone out. We saw you on the television news, Niccolo and I. That was when we discovered you were in Venice, and Nico said we must get in touch, invite you to the palazzo.'

'How kind,' Sebastian said, in that curt, harsh voice, but the

Contessa did not appear to notice his tone or the frown on his face. If anything, she smiled even more.

'It is a pleasure to see you again, and so grown up! You were only six when we saw you last. Of course, we've followed your career. Oh yes, we know everything you've done! We've seen all your films from the very first one, and it is such a pleasure to have you back in Venice at last. Welcome home.'

She held out her hand. Laura saw Sebastian hesitate before he took it and bowed to kiss it with a formality she had never seen him use before. The woman had invited that response by the way in which she spoke and moved. The Contessa knew who she was and her smile had a tinge of condescension, a self-assurance that expected respectful attention from everyone she met. Laura realised that both Sebastian and the Contessa were aware that Sebastian was not 'coming home', as she had put it. He was visiting a house where his father had been a servant, and the woman was reminding him of that with every syllable, for all her sweet smile, her well-bred voice, her queenly air.

'How is Niccolo?' Sebastian asked.

'Very well, as always, thank heavens. He will be pleased to meet you again. He's a fan of yours, he admires your films, especially the way they look. You know, the set designs, costumes, the backgrounds you choose. That's what interests him in the cinema, not the acting or the plots. The look of things. If he wasn't a sculptor I suspect he would love to be a theatre designer.'

'A sculptor?' Sebastian looked up at the house. 'Does he work in the old studio?'

'Of course. Where else? He went to art school in Florence and I hoped he would paint, like his father – it's in his blood, after all – but from the beginning it was sculpture that obsessed him.'

Sebastian's smile froze.

Why did he look like that? There was some subtext to their conversation, but Laura had no clue to its content, only that it disturbed Sebastian. 'What sort of sculpture?' she asked, to distract the older woman, who looked at her quickly, laughing with a shrug of those plump shoulders.

'Don't ask me! He says he represents the human form by what he sees in the personality. Not that I can see what he's trying to do, but the critics seem impressed with his work, so I have learnt to say nothing. I'm old-fashioned, he tells me.' Her voice was complacent; if her son did call her old-fashioned she seemed to take it as a compliment. 'I expect his father would have understood what he was trying to do. I'm a strong believer in heredity. Aren't you, Miss Erskine?'

Laura could still feel Sebastian's tension. What on earth was all this? Something to do with the Count? Had the Count been unkind to him when he was a child? The Contessa spoke about her husband in the past tense, which indicated that he was dead, but childhood terrors could haunt you all your life.

'I've never thought about it much, but no doubt you're right.'

'Oh, I am right, *certo*! No question.'

The Contessa had the absolute certainty of one who has never doubted her own beliefs or decisions. Laura wished she had a fraction of that assurance.

The dark eyes scanned her face. 'Sebastian directed your first film, didn't he? I remember it, a very exciting début! We saw you on television, too, this afternoon.'

Suddenly Laura remembered the TV camera filming her and Sebastian during their tussle by the lifts, and flushed. What had they made of that, this woman and her son?

'Really? We were on the TV news? My agent will be delighted with that. Publicity is so important in our business.' She knew her voice sounded very English, which it rarely did now. Living in the States you picked up their intonations, phrasing, without meaning to, especially if you found it easy to mimic the way people spoke, and actresses usually did: it was an important part of their technique. Suddenly, though, she was speaking in clipped English, retreating into formality and reserve in self-defence.

'I know nothing about the film industry, I'm afraid, except what I read or see on TV.' The Contessa's smile was smug.

Laura smiled back. 'Your English is terribly good, which is a relief. I'm afraid I know very little Italian. I must try to learn some more before I come to Italy again.'

'I was taught English at school as a girl. I have kept it up since – there are so many English and Americans living here – one is always meeting them at parties – and they speak such bad Italian that one has to speak to them in their own language.' The Contessa chuckled dismissively, then offered Laura her hand. 'Sebastian didn't introduce us. I am Vittoria d'Angeli.'

Although she must have been in her sixties, her skin was smooth, unlined, her fingers plump but strong, yet Laura had to fight a desire to pull herself free. Something in the woman's touch chilled her, like touching a snake, she thought. Yet the Contessa seemed friendly enough. Laura told herself her imagination was working overtime.

'Now, you must both come upstairs, to the *sala*. Niccolo is up there.' The Contessa turned her head upwards to where pale pink columns stood along the first floor with a terrace behind them. The sound of Mozart drifted out from an open window hidden somewhere at the back of the shadowy terrace. The pianist played a false note and stopped for a second before beginning again.

Startled, Laura said, 'I thought it was a recording! Is that your son playing?'

The Contessa nodded, smiling.

'But he's brilliant!'

'Yes, he is good, he could have been a concert pianist if he had been prepared to work at it, but he is too talented. He can paint and write songs too, and doesn't work at them, either. Sculpture is the only art form he cares about enough to work at.' She looked at Sebastian. 'I hope you will both stay to dinner. It will be nothing special, I'm afraid, a simple supper – pasta with a plain pesto sauce, and *calamari ripieni* – that's squid stuffed with garlic, tomato and anchovies. It has a strong flavour, but it is delicious. Then Lucia has made a little *zuppa Inglese*. Sebastian, do you remember Lucia?'

He looked blank. 'Lucia?'

'Our cook – she has worked for us for forty years. She makes such delicious *zuppa Inglese*. You loved it when you were a little boy.'

'Soup?' queried Laura.

Sebastian laughed shortly. 'Trifle – they call it English soup here, their idea of a joke!' Why was he so sombre, so brusque? She wished she knew more about his early life here, the reality of his relationship with this aristocratic Venetian family – the way the Contessa talked it was hard to be certain how she felt about Sebastian.

'Lucia soaks the sponge cakes in amaretto,' the Contessa said. 'Do you know amaretto, Miss Erskine? It is almond liqueur, delicious. She makes her own custard, and on top of that puts whipped cream, sprinkled with pieces of almond. Sebastian, you remember how you and Nico used to fight over who got the last spoonful from the dish?'

'I remember,' Sebastian said, his eyes distant, fixed on the past, perhaps.

He would have seen far more of the cook than of the Contessa, thought Laura. Had the reminder been deliberate? Or was the Contessa genuinely unaware that she was treading on delicate ground when she spoke of his childhood, his father's position in this house? Vittoria d'Angeli smiled a good deal:

whenever you looked at her that bland smile was on her face, but what was behind it?

'You must go down to the kitchen and talk to her later, after dinner, about old times,' she said, and again Laura wondered if that was a subtle reminder that the kitchen was where he belonged, in spite of his fame, his success, his money. She could see nothing in Sebastian's face to betray what was going on inside him but Laura picked up an echo of pain, anger, and felt an instinctive urge to protect him from the soft, smiling murmurs of the Contessa.

Her mother had often said she loved drama too much, put more of it into daily life than was really there. She hoped she was overreacting: she would hate to see Sebastian – or anyone else – get hurt.

'I'm afraid I have to get back to the hotel, Contessa,' she said, politely. 'I would have loved to stay for dinner but it is impossible. Someone is waiting for me.'

The dark brows made a half-moon of amused query. 'Ring him and ask him to join us.'

Laura knew she had flushed and was angry with herself. 'She's my agent, and we are having dinner with some important people this evening. I have to be there.'

The Contessa pouted like a child. 'Oh, but you could change the time. Meet them later. You know, we eat very late, in Venice – you could eat a little pasta with us, then have dessert with your important people.'

Sebastian drawled, 'I'm afraid I have to get back, too. My whole team are waiting for me. We are planning a celebration meal after finishing our last film, I can't back out.'

'Nico will be very disappointed,' the Contessa said reproachfully.

'I'm sorry, some other time, perhaps. But I know Laura would love to see something of the palazzo before we have to go.'

'Of course, please, come in – ah, here is Antonio.'

The man had appeared silently in the doorway: very thin, slight, in a black waistcoat and white shirt, black trousers, giving the impression of a uniform. He had grey hair, olive skin and dark eyes.

'You remember Antonio, Lucia's husband, Sebastian? He, too, has been working for us all his life. He remembers you, don't you, Antonio?'

The man smiled faintly, bowing. '*Si, si, già,* Contessa.'

Sebastian shook hands with him, spoke in rapid Italian. Laura picked up a touch of frost in him, sensed that he did not much like this man, and she could understand why: Antonio had secretive, cold eyes behind those heavy lids and black lashes. He kept them veiled most of the time but when you did catch sight of them they betrayed a chilly subtlety, which made you shiver.

'Some wine, Antonio, *per favore.*'

'*Si,* Contessa, *subito.*' He vanished and the Contessa waved Sebastian and Laura after him, into the house.

'My husband's family is one of the most ancient in Venice, Miss Erskine. Ca' d'Angeli was built in fourteen thirty-five, during the reign of the great Doge, Francesco Foscari, who was a cousin of the man who built this house, Simeone d'Angeli.'

Laura explained apologetically, 'I'm afraid I know almost nothing about Venetian history.'

'No, of course, how should you? It means nothing to anyone but a Venetian.'

'And your own family?' Laura asked. 'Are they Venetian too?'

The question fell into a silence, cold as marble, frosty as winter. 'No, we are Milanese,' the Contessa answered at last, and walked quickly towards the open front door to close it.

Laura gave Sebastian a look of enquiry, raising her brows. He shook his head, but she saw cold amusement in his eyes. Maybe he would explain later.

As they passed through the ground floor, the Contessa

leading the way, Laura asked, 'Why is this floor completely empty?' then hoped she had not touched on another delicate subject. Maybe the family couldn't afford to furnish the whole house.

But the Contessa answered casually, and without resentment this time, 'So that when the tide floods in over the door-sill, as it does with every really high tide, nothing will be ruined. If you look at the wall you'll see tide-marks from years back. Here, in Venice, we're used to flooding. We clean the marble once the water level falls again but you never quite get rid of the stain. The mixture of salt and grime sinks in – it is very destructive to this marble. But that's why most houses in Venice have an empty ground floor. We all live on the upper storeys of our homes.'

The stairs were steep and Laura clutched at the banisters, afraid of slipping on the marble. At the top they emerged into a wide, dark room running from the front of the house to the back, hung with tapestries over marble walls. The floor was marble too; the ceiling decorated with cartouches containing paintings, each framed in gilded plaster. Laura stared up at plump ladies floating on pink clouds, looking sensually inviting, surrounded with more cherubs like those on the palazzo's façade, but painted this time, each carrying a cornucopia from which flowers and fruit cascaded into the laps of the smiling women.

'Do you remember the ceilings, Sebastian? Or have you forgotten everything about Ca' d'Angeli?' The Contessa's dark eyes watched him intently.

'I remember very little. I was so young when we left.'

'So you were.' The Contessa walked on. 'This is the main floor of the house, the bedrooms are above, but the salon is down here.'

The long, dark room was sparsely furnished: here and there gilded chairs with bow legs had been arranged against the walls between elegant bureaux and several tables on which stood delicate little objects, of ivory, silver or glass. A high window at each end gave some light but the hall was still shadowy and the air had a mustiness that told you the windows were never opened, even at the height of the summer.

From an open door on the left came the sound of Mozart, clear, precise drops of music. They walked towards it into a large, high-ceilinged salon where two comfortable yellow silk brocade sofas faced each other in the middle of the room, placed on faded but clearly old and probably valuable Turkish carpets; nearby stood a table piled with leatherbound books, and around the room smaller tables supported lamps with Venetian glass shades in deep, dramatic colours, rich burgundy or dark blue, leaded like Tiffany glass to form the shapes of flowers and leaves. Next to them were silver-framed photographs, a gold clock and delicate porcelain figures, which looked like Meissen.

The panelled walls were hung with paintings and tapestries and a massive white marble fireplace, carved with figures, men's faces, animals, birds, flowers, reached almost to the ceiling. Laura felt suddenly out of place, a clumsy creature in this exquisite world.

As they entered, the man playing the piano looked across the room at them, his fingers stilling on the keys. Laura felt a bewildered recognition as if she had met him before, but knew that it must be merely the Italian colouring, the black hair, olive skin, dark eyes. He had an aquiline nose, a long jawline, high cheekbones and a mouth with a firm upper lip but a full lower one, suggesting passion and sensuality.

His mother bustled towards him, gesturing with her plump little hands. 'Nico, look who's here! While I was ringing his hotel he was on his way to see us.'

The pianist rose. He was taller than Sebastian, more than six foot, slim-hipped, narrow-waisted, yet with broad shoulders and a deep, muscled chest, the figure of an athlete. It seemed strange that he was wearing jeans, thought Laura. He should be in the dress of some other century, another culture. He did not have a modern face. Her eyes wandered from him to the shabby, ancient tapestries on the wall behind him, filled with men in doublet and hose, riding big horses, with dogs milling around them, confronting a stag at bay, or in a timeless Italianate landscape of cypress and olive trees with red-brick houses and churches in the distance. The faces were all Italianate – any of them could have been the living man at the piano – but there was a far more striking resemblance in a portrait hanging on another wall. of a man, full-length, in sombre red satin. It could have been a painting of Niccolo d'Angeli, and had to be one of his ancestors: the family face was unmistakable, that curved, predatory nose, the same sensual mouth, smouldering dark eyes and angular jaw.

Sebastian went towards him. They stared at each other, then began talking in rapid Italian, shook hands, smiled.

It was a shock to Laura to see how alike they were, at least in their colouring and build, both of them tall, dark men of much the same age with similar faces. They could be brothers.

Her breath caught. Brothers. She slid a furtive look at the Contessa, who was intent on watching them and did not catch Laura's stare. Sebastian couldn't be this woman's son, too? Could he? He had never spoken about his mother to her, except to say that she had died before he left Venice at the age of six. It would explain so much.

Then her common sense reasserted itself. No, it couldn't be. She had only just met the Contessa, but there was no mistaking the pride and arrogance in that face under the bland smiles. This was not a woman likely to have had a love affair with one of her own servants. She mustn't let her imagination run away with her.

She was so busy staring at his mother that she missed the moment when Niccolo d'Angeli turned in her direction and suddenly found him standing in front of her, looking intently at her with those liquid dark eyes so like Sebastian's.

He was saying something, but his Italian accent was so strong that for a moment she didn't realise he was speaking English and gazed at him without understanding, only thinking that he was much taller than herself – which she always noticed because she was often conscious of being taller than some of the men she met. They always hated that: you saw it in their eyes, in their reluctant, sulky smiles. Men liked women who were smaller than they were, little women they could feel protective about, pet, patronise.

'Delighted to meet you,' she heard, and then he reached out, took her limp hand and lifted it to his mouth, the kiss so soft and brief she could hardly believe it had happened until he had released her hand. Then she felt herself blushing.

'How do you do?' she mumbled, looking down, in the old child-like belief that if you didn't meet someone's eyes they couldn't see you.

He smelt of a strange mixture of fragrances: turpentine and paint, woodsmoke and a fresh, astringent pine aftershave.

'I recognised you at once from your films, and you were a model, weren't you? The camera loves you – it's those high cheekbones and that wonderful mouth.' He lifted one long index finger and brushed it along her lips, making her shiver. Sebastian had done that once; the gesture had been identical, her own sensation too.

'Please,' Nico said, in his deep, foreign voice, waving a hand towards the yellow sofas. 'Shall we sit down? Will you have a drink? Some wine?' He walked to a tray standing on a table near the piano, pulled a bottle out of a bucket of ice and held it up to the dying light from the window. 'This is a very good Soave, from Verona, not far from here. I know the vineyard it comes from, it is last autumn's vintage, and you know, they say with white wine drink the youngest wine you can – I can promise it is good.' It was pale yellow with a green tinge to it. He poured glasses, handed them to his mother and Laura, who had both sat down, then to Sebastian, who still stood as if he couldn't wait to get away, his brows creased in a faint frown.

Raising his glass in a toast, Niccolo said, '*Cin cin . . . salute!*'

Laura took a sip. It tasted faintly almondy, quite pleasant. She took another mouthful, self-conscious under the two pairs of eyes, wishing that Niccolo and his mother would stop staring at her.

'How long are you staying in Venice, Miss Erskine?' Nico asked.

'Please, call me Laura.' The formality of the house was unnerving enough; having him use her surname made it worse. 'Just two days, we leave the morning after the award ceremony.'

'Do you have to? Couldn't you stay a little longer?'

'I'd love to, but our flight is booked.'

'Have you been to Venice before?'

She shook her head.

'Then you must change your flight and stay a few more days – it would be a crime for you to leave so soon. There is so much to see here that a month wouldn't be long enough, let alone two days. I would love to show you my city, a guided tour of some private houses as well as the usual tourist places.'

'That's very kind but I have to get back.' Laura jumped as something moved behind her on the sofa. She twisted her head to look and broke out into laughter as she saw a tiny black kitten curled up on one of the cushions. 'Oh, how sweet!' She put her wine glass on the floor, then turned to pick up the kitten and put it on her lap, stroking the small head with one finger; a slender crimson leather collar encircled its throat. 'I didn't see it there. How lucky that I didn't sit on it. I might have injured it, as it's so small. How old is it?'

Niccolo knelt down beside her and caressed the kitten too. 'Just six weeks, his mamma is our kitchen cat, a stray who wandered in here one day.' She was beginning to understand his English now that her ear had grown accustomed to his strong accent, or perhaps she was so interested in the kitten that she was listening more intently.

'Lucia adores cats, and she has a soft heart, but my mother was not pleased when these kittens arrived. One died and we've managed to find homes for two, but not for this one yet.' He smiled into her eyes. 'If you would like him we'd be very happy to let you have him.'

Her face fell with regret. 'Oh, I wish I could take him back with me, but we have such strict laws about animals coming into Britain. They would insist on him staying in quarantine for six months and that would be cruel to such a very young cat.'

'Yes, too cruel, I agree. Well, while you're here you can visit him whenever you like, then,' Nico said softly, and his long, sensitive fingers brushed against Laura's as they both fondled the kitten. A prickle ran up her arm, awareness, attraction, a rare sensation for her.

She looked round involuntarily and found Sebastian watching them, a smouldering anger in his eyes, a darkness she had seen before.

Glancing back hurriedly at Nico she said, 'Your mother told us you are a sculptor. I would love to see some of your work.'

'Nothing easier. Come along to my studio now.' He got to his feet and Laura did so, too, still holding the kitten.

'I'm sorry. We don't have time. We have to get back to the hotel for dinner,' Sebastian said, abruptly.

Laura looked at her watch, sighed, put the kitten down on the sofa and said regretfully, 'I'm afraid he's right, I can't be late.' She smiled at the Contessa. 'Thank you for letting me see your lovely home, and for the wine, it was delicious.' Risking a little Italian she added shyly, '*Grazie, tante grazie, lei e molto gentile.*'

The Contessa smiled. Her son said, '*Benissimo!* So you do speak some Italian?'

'A few words, that's all,' she said ruefully.

She began to walk towards the door and Nico caught up with her while Sebastian was saying goodbye to the Contessa.

He said quickly, 'What about tomorrow? Could you come for lunch and see my studio? Would you pose for me? I have an idea – I won't tell you about it now, we can talk tomorrow.'

She would have loved to, but she had to say, 'I'm afraid I'm busy all day.'

'Try. Come for lunch – we'll eat out in the garden. You know Sebastian's father was our gardener? His pride and joy were the lemon trees. We still have their descendants – the ones Giovanni planted all died during a very bad flood. They drowned in their pots, or withered with salt-burn, but luckily we had taken cuttings, which were inside, on the upper balcony, and they survived.'

'Did you know Sebastian's mother?'

They had reached the end of the long, shadowy hall and started down the marble stairs. Laura heard the Contessa's dress rustling and looked back in time to see her coming out of the salon alone, walking across the hall into another room and vanishing. Sebastian came out of the salon, too, hurried after Laura and Nico. He looked angry. What had the Contessa said to him?

She suddenly caught what Nico was saying, and her eyes opened wide. 'Didn't Sebastian tell you? Gina was my wet-nurse when I was a baby. Sebastian is a few months older than me. My mother had a bad time in labour, she was ill for a while afterwards and her milk dried up. She couldn't breastfeed me, but Sebastian's mother had enough for both of us so she took care of me along with her own baby. She and Giovanni had rooms on the upper floor at the back, a private little apartment. One room was a nursery for me and Sebastian. I saw more of Gina for the first few years of my life than I did of my own mother. Mamma was always so busy running the house, visiting people.'

Standing at the door of the palazzo Laura looked out into the soft dusk at the gleaming waters of the canal. The gondola that had brought them was no longer tied up at the painted poles of the landing-stage. Sebastian was running down the stairs and Laura swung round to look at him, her head whirling with what she had just discovered. She had realised at last why Sebastian had always thought of Ca' d'Angeli as home. He had spent his first six years upstairs in it, in his parents' apartment.

'Sebastian, the gondola has gone! How will we get back?'

'The Contessa is ringing for a water-taxi now.'

They walked out on to the landing-stage. Nico said, 'Will you come tomorrow?'

Sebastian looked sharply at her. She avoided meeting his eyes, and said, 'I'm afraid my agent may have fixed up meetings for me. As so many important film people are here, you see, it is a chance to make valuable contacts. Can I let you know? I could ring you.'

'I'll ring you—'

Sebastian interrupted, 'Why don't you come to us? Have breakfast with us at the hotel, Nico, in my suite – around eight?'

'But I wanted to show Laura my studio and some of my work.'

'Of course, but tomorrow will undoubtedly be difficult for her. I have an idea I want to talk to you about, and it involves Laura.'

Nico stared at him. 'Idea? What sort of idea?'

'I'll tell you tomorrow. Eight o'clock at our hotel, then.'

A motor launch chugged towards them, slowed, and drew up beside them. Nico took Laura's hand and kissed it again, then helped her down into the boat. 'Until tomorrow morning, then.'

She nodded, sat down, and Sebastian joined her. Laura waved goodbye to Nico as the boat moved away slowly from Ca' d'Angeli and he waved back, his black hair ruffled by a faint breeze. She put her hand down into the water, as she had when they arrived; the sun had set now but there was still plenty of light, and the reflections of the palazzi floated along beside the boat.

Something else floated there, too. For a second she didn't

identify the wet black fur, and then she gave a stricken cry as she noticed the crimson leather collar around its neck.

'Nico's kitten!' She leant over the side making the boat rock, and just managed to touch it, but the instant she did she knew it was dead.

Chapter Four

Melanie was furious. 'Where on earth have you been all this time? I waited around for hours and then decided I'd missed you somehow, so I came back to the hotel, thinking I'd find you here. I was worried stiff. I thought you might have got lost. I was just about to get the hotel to ring the police and organise a search for you.'

'I'm sorry, I ran into Sebastian.'

As she had expected Melanie exploded at the news. 'You're kidding! You've been with that bastard? Are you crazy? No, don't bother to answer that, I know you are. What have you been doing with him all this time? No, don't answer that, either – I suppose you've been in his room.'

Laura felt herself go scarlet and was angry enough to snap back, 'We weren't here at the hotel and we weren't alone. He took me to see the house where he was born.'

Melanie blinked furiously, her shoulders moving as if she was ruffling feathers, which made her look like an agitated parrot. 'You mean he really was born here? And I always thought that must be a myth he invented for himself. Film people are always doing that, building their own legend because the truth about them is really pretty ordinary. So, what was the place like?'

'Extraordinary. He hadn't exaggerated by a hair, honestly. It was what he said it was, a palazzo, right on the Grand Canal, medieval. They call it Ca' d'Angeli, the house of angels, because the outer walls are covered with them, such beautiful carving, little cherubs and tall stone archangels with these wonderful wings – it took my breath away.'

'I thought nothing would ever surprise me again,' Melanie said. 'But it seems I was wrong.' Her eyes narrowed. 'Hang on, did you actually go inside? I mean, how do you know he wasn't just spinning a line? How do you know he really was born there?'

'You're so cynical! We did go inside. I met the people who own it, the d'Angeli family. They've always lived there, since it was built, they're Venetian aristocrats. His father worked for them – Sebastian isn't one of the family. He just lived there with his parents.' Laura saw the curiosity stirring in Melanie's shrewd eyes and knew what questions were coming next so she hurried on before her friend could interrupt. 'I met the two who are left, the Contessa d'Angeli and her son, Niccolo. He's fabulous-looking, tall, dark and very sexy. He's a sculptor. You should see the rooms, full of the most wonderful antiques and paintings and tapestries. Priceless, all of them. I was afraid to touch anything in case I broke it.'

'I wish I'd been able to see the place,' Melanie said discontentedly. 'I suppose you just forgot you promised to meet me.'

'I know, I'm sorry. I didn't mean to go with him but Sebastian kind of kidnapped me. I bumped into him and he persuaded me to go for a gondola ride with him and we ended up at Ca' d'Angeli, which wasn't what I'd intended at all.'

Melanie stared at her. 'Laura, have you forgotten what happened to his wife? Do you want to end up the same way?'

Luckily they were in Laura's room with the door shut, but Laura couldn't help looking nervously around in case Melanie's raised voice could be overheard. She lowered her own, scolding softly, 'Mel, you mustn't say things like that! Whatever you suspect, the inquest cleared Sebastian—'

'On the evidence of that creepy secretary of his! She wouldn't think twice about lying for him, you know that. I wouldn't believe anything she said. No. He chucked his wife out of that window – everybody thinks he did it.'

Agonised, Laura cried out, 'Don't *say* that! You know, if anyone overheard you and repeated what you'd said Sebastian could sue you for every penny you've got!'

Luckily, the prospect of losing money had its usual effect on Melanie, who sighed and subsided. 'There's no justice. But it's just as well I didn't know you were with him – I'd have been far more worried and I might have said a damn sight too much in the bar while I was waiting. Stay away from him, Laura. If your sense of self-preservation doesn't stop you, at least think of the bad publicity! People will talk, you know.' She met Laura's derisive eyes and had the grace to go a little pink, muttering, 'Well, what can you expect? You don't want people believing that you were the reason why he did it, do you?' She held up her hand as Laura stirred angrily. 'I know, I know, he's as innocent as a newborn lamb. But that isn't what people believe. So, promise me you won't see him again.'

'I'm having breakfast with him tomorrow,' Laura told her flatly.

'You're what?' Melanie went bright red.

'In his suite. Nobody else will see us so you needn't worry.'

'I don't believe I'm hearing this! You need a full-time minder – do you know that? You are not meeting him, Laura. I won't let you get involved with him again. In any case, I've already fixed a working breakfast at ten o'clock with Sam Beethoven – he never gets up any earlier, it was quite a concession he made in agreeing to be up by ten – and he could do so much for your career. He's the most powerful producer at the festival. It shows how hot you're getting that he wanted to meet you. And at half past eleven we're having brunch on the terrace with some people from Hollywood. I'm not sure what's behind their interest but they have a lot of clout and we don't want to offend them. So you can ring Sebastian Ferrese and tell him your date with him is off.'

'I can't do that! And it isn't a date, exactly, anyway. I'm meeting him at eight o'clock and it's business.'

'Oh, sure! Pull the other one, Laura. Sebastian Ferrese is a genius at mixing business and pleasure where women are concerned.'

'Mel, he has a new project, a film he wants to make in Venice. Do you remember that big bestseller, *The Lily*, by Frederick Canfield? Set in Italy in the thirties and forties? It's about a rich Italian family with two sons who both fall in love with the same girl and become deadly enemies over her.'

'Never heard of it, but the storyline is as old as the hills.'

'The difference with this book is that one brother is a Fascist and the other is a Communist, who later joins the partisans on the outbreak of war. The Fascist brother is captured by the partisans at the end of the war, and it's his own brother who executes him.'

'Sounds a jolly little tale – typical storyline for Sebastian Ferrese,' Melanie muttered. Her stomach rumbled and she swore. 'I'm dying for my dinner – get ready and let's go down.' She walked over to the mini-bar and opened it, studied the contents, chose a packet of potato crisps and a can of Diet Coke.

'Oh, for pity's sake, Mel, don't stuff that crap into yourself,' Laura objected, as Melanie tore open the crisps. 'You'll ruin your appetite.'

'Fuck off. And hurry up, will you?'

Laura went into the bathroom, peeled off her sweat-slick clothes and dropped them into the laundry basket. The Italian heat was exhausting – why did they have the festival in August? Watching films in this appalling temperature, even in air-conditioned theatres, was no picnic, and walking about today she had felt as if she was in a sauna.

She turned on the shower and stood under the jets of

water. First an ice-cold sting her muscles, her nipples, her tensed shoulders and face, then the water changed gradually to lukewarm. She relaxed under it, eyes closed, breathing with delight as the moisture trickled down her hot body, oozed between her naked breasts, crawled down her flat midriff, the curve of her abdomen, along the creases of her inner thighs, down her legs to her toes.

Laura turned slowly to sluice every part of herself in blissful sensuality. You never appreciated water until you were in a very hot country.

That image was suddenly replaced by another: Niccolo's dead kitten in the oil-slicked water of the Grand Canal. She had looked up at Sebastian, tears in her eyes. 'I left it on the sofa in the salon. How could it have got into the canal?'

'Its neck looks broken – it must have fallen out of a window.' He sounded so offhand, but there was a darkness in his eyes that frightened her. Clea had fallen out of a window. Was that what he was thinking about?

How *had* the kitten died? Nobody would want to kill a kitten. It must have been an accident. It must have climbed up to the window and fallen out.

She had stared back at the palazzo vanishing into the dark blue night, lamps lit on the walls of the landing-stage, the upper windows of the salon glowing gold and pink. They were all closed, to keep out the mosquitoes and moths. The kitten couldn't have fallen out.

The kitten had been so small and soft; she thought of the fast beating of that tiny heart under her fingers, the stare of those milky blue eyes, and tears burned in her own.

Sebastian said abruptly, 'My mother died out here. She drowned, too. Soon afterwards we left Venice, my father and I, and went to the States.' He looked round at her. 'I want to make a film here. On location at Ca' d'Angeli. It may exorcise some ghosts. And there's a major role in it for you, Laura . . .'

* * *

She heard Melanie bellowing from the bedroom for her to hurry and switched off the water, wrung out her hair and pinned it up deftly at the back of her head before she stepped out of the shower.

She towelled herself dry rapidly and put on clean underclothes she had laid out in the bathroom cupboard, before she went back into the bedroom to find something to put on.

Mel was turning Jancy upside down so that her dress fell over her head. 'I see you still go around with this doll. When are you going to grow up?'

Laura took Jancy away from her and put her gently in her accustomed position at the foot of the bed. 'She's the best friend a girl ever had. She never argues or criticises, just listens to whatever you want to tell her and nods sympathetically.'

'Nods? What the hell is it with you? It's a bloody doll! How can it nod?'

Laura picked up Jancy and said, 'She's dumb, isn't she, Jancy?'

Jancy nodded.

'See?'

'You did that! I saw your finger at the back of her neck, moving her head up and down.' But Melanie was grinning; she had enjoyed the joke. 'I have to admit, I could do with someone like that in my office. A silent nodder. Wonderful.'

'I'll buy you a doll on your next birthday.'

'Diamonds would be better.'

'Dolls cost a lot less.'

'Skinflint.'

Barefoot, in a lace-trimmed white silk bra and matching lacy camisole, Laura went over to the wardrobe and flicked through her clothes while Melanie watched her.

'The white dress, Laura. White always looks good on you – cools down all that red hair.'

Laura took down the ankle-length silk dress, classic in style, with a halter neckline and low back, and let it slither down over her head, the folds clinging softly to her body as it fell almost to her feet.

She stood back to survey the result. The dress gave her a very feminine line, emphasised every curve of her body, from her long neck to her breasts and on, down her shapely legs.

'You look great,' Melanie assured her.

Laura smiled, sat down at the dressing table and blow-dried her hair into its accustomed style, then started on her foundation. She brushed a dust of the lightest gold glitter on her eyelids, curled her lashes with mascara.

'Get a move on,' implored Melanie, but Laura was not going to hurry because she did not want to start perspiring again. In this sultry night heat, you were wise to move as slowly as possible, especially if you were wearing a white silk dress that would show every tiny stain.

'There's plenty of time yet. Men expect women to be late. I haven't finished explaining about Sebastian's film. He wants to shoot some of it in Ca' d'Angeli. He needs the Count's permission, which is why Sebastian invited Nico to breakfast.' She looked wryly into the dressing-table mirror at Melanie's disapproving face. 'You see? I'm not being set up for a seduction scene. I'm needed to help Sebastian persuade the Count to co-operate on this film.'

Melanie sniffed scornfully. 'He's using you, in other words. As usual. And what's in it for you?'

'A starring role in a major film! That's what we've been waiting for, isn't it? He wants me to play the girl the brothers fight over, the one they call the Lily. She's the central character and a lot happens to her. She's raped by German soldiers, almost shot by partisans, her heart gets broken. You must see that this could be the break I need.'

Melanie had that blank, fixed expression, which meant she was thinking intently. 'Maybe,' she mused. 'It's true, we're looking for a big break for you. Your career has gone very well so far but if you're ever to be a star you need to get a major part in a big commercial film, and this could be it. Okay. But if it means you getting involved with Sebastian Ferrese I'm not sure that the price isn't too high. There's an atmosphere around that man. I always have the feeling he's bad luck, and not just because of his wife's death. The man himself has an aura.'

'A lot of directors are pretty weird. It's a strange profession. Like acting. I know some truly crazy actors.' Laura grinned at her teasingly. 'And as for agents . . . I know one who should be certified.'

'Yes – for having an idiot on my books who won't listen to a word I say!' Melanie grumbled. 'Don't come to me to complain if he chucks you out of a window next week.' She marched to the door. 'There's no time to talk this through. Come on, we've got to get downstairs. It doesn't hurt to keep men waiting, but I want my dinner. Now, be nice to these men! They could do a lot for you, and even if they don't, making friends in high places is always a wise policy.'

One eye on her watch, Valerie Hyde sat in her own room waiting impatiently for her mini-printer to finish churning out pages of notes she had earlier tapped into her lap-top computer.

It had been easy enough to get permission to search the local newspaper files and, as she knew the month and year of the accident, she had had no trouble in finding the reports of the inquest on Sebastian's mother. She had been given permission to use her lap-top to take notes, expecting it would take just a few minutes to transcribe the news reports. She certainly had not anticipated uncovering what increasingly began to look like an unsolved murder.

She had continued to comb though months of files in the hope of discovering further information, but in vain: there was no report of anyone being arrested or even questioned, let alone charged or convicted of the death by drowning of Gina

Ferrese. Valerie had considered approaching the Venice police for information, but had decided against that until she had had time to discuss the idea with Sebastian. He must have had some idea that there was a mystery attached to the way in which his mother died to have asked Valerie to go through the newspaper files. Perhaps it would be wiser not to probe too deeply yet, in case Sebastian already knew who had done it and wanted to keep it quiet.

His father could have been behind the death – who else would have had reason to kill Gina Ferrese? Valerie knew Sebastian had been devoted to his father: he might go to great lengths to protect the memory of the dead man, and, after all, what would be the point of digging up a long-forgotten mystery when everyone concerned was now dead?

When the printer finally stopped chattering, she collected the pages, put them in order and quickly read through her notes yet again.

Did Sebastian know exactly how his mother had died? He had only been six. Had he known who died with her that day?

He had rarely talked about his childhood or his background, and Valerie's curiosity had been strongly aroused when she read the name of the man who was in the boat with Gina Ferrese. There was a lot more to this story than she had yet discovered – that much was certain – and, whether Sebastian wanted it or not, Valerie was determined to dig deeper.

Sidney McKenna lifted his head to watch the latest arrivals in the bar, his eyes narrowing to slits. He had a throaty, whisky voice after years of sitting around in smoke-filled bars drinking and shouting to make himself heard above the clamour.

'There's Laura. You know, she's growing into her looks. When we first found her she was a gawky kid, like a young foal, all big eyes and long legs. Look at her now.'

Sebastian had seen her long before Sidney did – he had felt

her walk into the bar, the tiny hairs on the back of his neck bristling.

Sidney was right: she had lost the heartbreaking vulnerability of the very young girl, which had moved him so deeply when he first met her. There is something about very young things that touches a chord in the heart as nothing else does.

After living with a woman who swore like a trooper, was belligerent, a street-fighter, very sure of herself, the hidden tenderness in Sebastian's heart had loved the things about Laura that were the opposite to Clea – her shining innocence, the wide-eyed uncertainty, the way Laura never quite seemed to know where to move her hands and feet, the sudden scalding blushes that swept up her face.

She was a woman now, far more aware of herself, poised and cool, moving with calm grace in a dress that flowed down her body in a silky wave.

What had happened to her? He would never know. Clea threw the truth at you as if it was mud that she hoped would stick to you. Laura's reticence was part of her natural defence system: she would never tell. He could only hope it hadn't been as bad as Clea's experiences in this filthy business.

'She should cut that hair. I'd like to see it almost down to stubble, just a head full of tiny, tiny curls, like a baby.' Sidney propped his elbows on the bar table and rested his chin in his palms, his long, sensitive fingers forming a frame through which he gazed at Laura. 'Yes, that would look good. The hair's too ordinary like that. She can challenge convention, she's a one-off, she should exploit that. Of course, she's too young to understand what she's capable of – that will come, once she's fully mature.'

'Can we go and eat? I'm starving, and when this lot finally get through drinking themselves stupid every table in the dining room will be taken,' Valerie said, her black eyes burning with resentment.

She had not yet given Sebastian the notes she had typed

earlier. She wanted to get him to herself first, so that she could watch him read the pages, decipher his expressions, the look in his eyes. She knew him so well. Better than anyone. Yet Sebastian was like an iceberg, with large areas of his personality and thought processes buried beneath the surface. What was hidden was probably far more dangerous than anything you could see with the naked eye.

Sidney smiled sleepily at her. 'Aren't we in a temper? I wonder what tweaked our tail. Or do I? No, not really, it's pretty obvious what's eating you up, Val, I'm afraid.'

'Screw you.' Valerie turned red and glanced at Sebastian, who was totally unaware of her, his eyes fixed on Laura.

Sidney crowed, 'Is that an invitation? Here and now? Or shall we go upstairs? What's your favourite position, darling? I've often wondered. Missionary? You don't look the adventurous type.'

'Do I have to listen to this crap?' she demanded of Sebastian, who blinked at her and suddenly woke up to the conversation.

'Let her alone, Sid. Your idea of humour isn't the same as hers.'

'She hasn't got a sense of humour! She hasn't got much sense at all. If she had, she'd stop baying at the moon. She's a sad case, nearly as blind as you are.'

Sebastian looked blank. Absently he said, 'What are you babbling about?'

His eyes moved back to Laura, who was laughing at something Melanie had just said to her. He watched the pale curve of her throat, the way the sensuous, elegant white silk gown clung to her body. His mouth went dry. Heat burned in his groin.

Valerie's long nails curled into her palms and she dug them in, deliberately, to stop herself screaming at Sidney. He would love that. It would give her away in front of Sebastian and cause a scene, and Sidney loved to cause scenes. She admired and liked Sidney: he could be thoughtful, affectionate, sensitive – if she was ill or in trouble there was nobody she would rather go to – but he could also be spiteful and mischievous. His nature was strongly tilted to the feminine, which explained his intuitive instincts where film was concerned. Sebastian said he was a great artist, using the camera instead of a paintbrush.

Most people in the business agreed, and Sidney was one of the most respected men in his profession. He had a wall full of awards and could pick and choose what he did. But when he was in one of his wicked moods, Valerie felt like scratching his eyes out.

'Tomorrow morning they're screening that French thriller *Ecoute et Regard* at the Palazzo del Cinema,' Sebastian said, sliding a hand inside his white dinner jacket. He rarely dressed formally but tonight he looked unusually elegant. He pulled out an envelope and proffered it to Sidney. 'I got four seats. I can't come, I've got an appointment, but you said you wanted to see it.'

Valerie's head swung towards him. 'I don't remember any appointment. Who's this with?'

He ignored her.

'Thanks, guy,' Sidney said, taking the envelope and pulling out the tickets to read them. He looked at the others of the crew around the bar table. 'Who else wants to come?'

'Are there sub-titles?' Fred, the sound man, asked. 'I don't speak a word of French.'

'Sure there are – in Italian!' said Sidney, grinning.

'Valerie, I'd like you to go, and give me a report on it later,' Sebastian told her.

'Won't you need me to take notes during this appointment you have?'

'No, it isn't business. I'm having breakfast upstairs in the suite.'

'How mysterious,' Sidney said. 'Male or female?'

'He and I shared a mother,' Sebastian said, in the soft voice of someone who knows he is dropping a bombshell, and watched them to see how they would react.

Their faces froze incredulously. For a moment they were unable to speak.

Sidney was the first to get over the shock. 'You have a brother?' His voice was careful, testing the ground. Every piece of publicity Sebastian had ever had stressed that he had been an only child whose mother had died when he was very young.

They would all have sworn they knew everything about him: they'd worked with him for years, on and off, spent months with him in the enforced and unreal intimacy of the film crew on location, far from home, sharing bad food, dull hotels, uncertain weather. Suddenly they watched him as if he had become a stranger, as they had just after Clea's death, when they weren't sure what to believe, when they were waiting for him to reassure them, tell them he had had nothing to do with it. Sebastian knew precisely what was going on inside their heads.

He laughed shortly. 'No, he isn't my brother. I meant literally that we shared a mother. My mother. His mother couldn't breastfeed, but my mother had enough milk for two, so she fed both me and Nico.'

Sidney whistled. 'You're kidding! What was wrong with bottle-feeding?'

'Nico was premature and very small. They thought he would have a better start if he was breastfed, less chance of infection.'

'How very earthy and primitive. It sounds like Dickens. Remember *Dombey and Son*? There was a wet-nurse in that,' Sidney said, raising his eyebrows. 'Did she feed you both together? It conjures up very sexy images – a baby at each breast. She must have had big ones to do it.'

Sebastian got up and walked away.

'You're talking about his mother, you creep!' Valerie spat at Sidney. 'And she's dead! Well, you really did it this time. He's furious with you.'

'And that's made your day!' sneered Sidney.

He and Valerie, the whole crew, were always in competition

for Sebastian's attention and approval, like dogs in a pack permanently fighting to lie next to the leader.

Valerie ignored him and hurried after Sebastian while Sidney sauntered behind, looking bland and amused, an expression that sat naturally upon his face because his bald head and large ears gave him a comic expression without his needing to try. He hoped that Valerie wasn't right, that he hadn't deeply offended Sebastian.

'Shit,' he thought aloud. 'Me and my big mouth.' He should have remembered that a man was always sensitive on the subject of his mother, especially if she had died young. Shit, shit. 'Sidney McKenna, you're a fool,' he told himself scathingly.

For Laura the dinner dragged on and on; she smiled and nodded like a doll, listening to the male American voices, aware of eyes wandering over her like sticky hands, trying not to yawn, trying not to look as bored as she felt. Melanie did most of the talking, as always; she oozed film gossip, laughed a lot, asked questions, listened as if fascinated, and clearly enjoyed the meal – which was just as well as Laura had no appetite. It was too hot and she was on edge; her mind kept drifting away to Sebastian. She had seen him in the bar, with Sidney and Valerie and the others; she was aware of him now, eating on the other side of the beautiful dining room.

'Are you going to the showing in the square tonight, Laura?' one of the men asked, and she blinked at him, lost for a second, not having been following what was said.

Melanie saved her. 'She's too tired to stay up late and she'll be going to bed. Tomorrow is going to be a very busy day, and even if she doesn't win she has to look good.'

The men laughed, staring at Laura. 'I'm sure she will,' one said. 'The company are thrilled that she got this nomination. It'll be a big boost for the film around the world.'

'Wonderful,' Melanie said enthusiastically. 'I think I'll go along tonight. It sounds marvellous. I've never seen a film in a setting like that – it's a brilliant idea, showing films in St Mark's Square, right out in the open under the stars, a damn sight more pleasant than watching them in a cinema. Oh, I know they're air-conditioned, these days, but when the place is packed with people it still gets hot and stuffy. It would be a pity to miss one of the latest films while I'm actually at the Venice Film Festival.'

'I'd love to go, too, if only I could stay awake long enough,' Laura said, stifling another great yawn. She caught the eye of one of the men and smiled an apology. 'Sorry, I'm dead on my feet. I had to be up terribly early this morning to fly here.'

The waiter brought liqueurs and strong black coffee. Laura felt her gorge rise. She had eaten such a weird mixture already, since Melanie had insisted on letting the men choose the food. They had picked a dish each: a risotto coloured black by the cuttlefish ink used to flavour it, followed by guinea fowl cooked with mushrooms and lots of cream, both accompanied by far too much wine, and then a pudding with a strong almond flavour and masses more cream. Laura rarely ate much and the peculiar mix of ingredients was turning her stomach – it felt like something resembling a washing-machine.

'Not for me, thanks,' she said, her face pale. Her eyes implored Melanie. 'I'm sorry, would you mind awfully if – I think I really must go to bed—'

She got up, stumbled, and the men rose, too, concerned.

'Are you okay? Would you like someone to come upstairs with you?'

Fat chance! she thought. What an opportunist – but then most men are! Aloud she said, 'No, no, please, stay and have coffee with Mel. I don't want to spoil the evening for you.'

Melanie stayed resolutely in her seat. 'A good night's sleep is what you need,' she said, with a smile pinned to her face but a look in her eyes that told Laura she would be in trouble tomorrow for running out.

'See you in the morning.'

As she left Laura kept her eyes from the corner where Sebastian was sitting, yet was still conscious of being watched from there, aware of a coldness, as if someone had opened a refrigerator door and released a wave of chilly air. Every nerve in her body tingled with dread. Oh, God, she thought, that isn't just coldness. It's hatred. Her temples began to throb with distress, as if she heard the brazen sound of a gong being beaten. Somebody wanted her dead. Somebody wanted to kill her. From across the room, that dark intention beat on and on, and she knew it must come from Sebastian. Had Clea felt that death-wish beating on her before she died? Laura had assumed that either she had jumped or was pushed – but now she saw that Clea could have been driven to her death by that relentless hostility.

She hardly knew how she got out of the crowded room, across the even more crowded lobby, to the lifts. Her body moved automatically, her mind submerged and drowning beneath waves of shock.

It wasn't until she was back upstairs that the faintness and sickness began to subside. She went into her room, closed the door and staggered to the bed, which had been turned down by a maid who had left a bedside lamp switched on, making a gentle glow. Laura sat there for several minutes, trembling and breathing thickly, before she had the strength to move again. She undressed and washed, put on a cream silk nightdress, which the maid had left out on the bed, and was about to slide under the covers when there was a tap on the door.

Melanie! she thought, tempted not to respond, but the tap came again, louder.

Laura went to the door. As she opened it a crack and looked out, she saw Sebastian. Her heart constricted in her chest, and she tried at once to shut the door, but he had his foot inside and forced it back, pushing her with it. Laura leant her whole strength on the door, but so did he, and he was bigger, stronger.

The struggle was silent, despairing. She knew she must lose but wouldn't give up until, with one last thrust, Sebastian sent her flying.

She sprawled on the carpet, aware of him closing the door and kneeling beside her.

'Have you hurt yourself?' His eyes were anxious, his face pale, but she remembered what she had sensed coming from him in the dining room, the desire to hurt, the hatred.

'Leave me alone!' she said hoarsely. 'Go away or I'll ring downstairs and get hotel security to come and chuck you out.'

'I just want to talk to you for a minute.'

'I don't want to talk to you, especially alone in here. I don't feel safe around you. I don't want to end up the way your wife did.'

His expression changed. The concern vanished and a blackness invaded his eyes, a burning resentment and hostility. That was what she had felt in the dining room, but it wasn't quite the same now: the feelings she had picked up earlier had been bitter, a hatred like black ice. This rage was hot, gushing up from deep inside the body. Not a desire to kill. A very different desire, which made her throat close up in fierce shock.

'Don't touch me!' she cried, scrambling to get up and away from him, but she didn't move fast enough.

He took hold of her shoulders, forced her back down on to the carpet and held her there while he climbed on top of her, his knees on either side of her waist, holding her silk-covered body rigidly between them.

'You think I'm going to kill you, do you?' he muttered. 'Thanks for the vote of confidence. I'm beginning to think I should do just that. At least it would get you out of my head. I spend too much time thinking about you.'

'Well, don't! I don't want you thinking about me.'

His temper flared again. 'I don't give a damn what you want! What about what I want?' His eyes travelled over her slowly. 'You know what that is, don't you?'

She looked up at him, her mouth dry, her body pulsating suddenly with wild sexual awareness. Sebastian stared down at her, his black pupils glowing and dilating. His lips parted to suck in air audibly. The hands pinning her shoulders relaxed slightly and slid caressingly down over her bare skin, peeled back the silk that was half covering her breasts and his warm palms cupped the soft, smooth flesh he had exposed.

He bent his head slowly and she watched him as if hypnotised, unable to move, her throat beating with passion and fear, so much on edge that she thought she might scream. At the same time she ached, with a deep physical need, to feel his mouth on the bare breast he held. When his lips parted around her nipple her body jerked into an arch, and a harsh, low cry of pleasure came from her.

Sebastian lifted his head slightly to look down at her again. 'Like that, do you? Funny. So do I.' He moved his head to her other breast and took the nipple of that into his mouth, sucked softly, his fingers playing with the warm flesh, fondling and stroking the way a baby does as it takes milk from its mother. Laura felt her breasts swell, felt, too, the flesh between her thighs burning, moist and open with arousal.

Terrified of her body's response, she said shakily, 'Don't, Sebastian, please don't. Go away, please.'

He ignored her pleading. Without taking his mouth from her nipple he ran his hands lingeringly down her body and she quivered, eyes half shut, heat following the track of his touch on her skin, as she fought to regain self-control, struggled to find the will-power to get away from him before it was too late.

Sebastian pushed her nightdress upwards until she was bare to the waist, slid his hand up over her smooth thighs into the warm cleft between, his fingers probing, exploring, making her gasp and shudder.

'Oh, God,' she groaned, eyes tight shut. 'Oh, God . . . please stop it, I can't, I mustn't . . .'

'Don't lie to yourself, Laura. You want it as much as I do.'

His fingers slid backwards, forwards, the friction agonisingly pleasurable. 'I can feel it, here, and here,' he whispered. 'You want me badly, you're so hot you're melting, and so am I.'

She stopped thinking then: he was right, why try to lie to herself? She wanted him. She waited in piercingly sweet agony for him to enter her, to complete the electric circuit between them.

Ever since she had seen him again in the lobby when she and Melanie arrived, this was what she had ached for: the ending of years of longing and frustration. While they were working together their feelings had been a guilty, secret passion that had ended almost as soon as it had begun, leaving her with this smouldering, unsatisfied need.

Breathing hard and raggedly, Sebastian was pulling off his clothes and it could only have been a matter of seconds before she felt the roughness of the hair on his legs and chest rubbing against her soft skin as he came down on top of her between her parted thighs. He slid his hands underneath her buttocks and lifted her legs into the air; Laura caught his waist with her knees and held him, her arms closing round his back. As he drove up inside her, her whole body jerked in anguished pleasure and, without even realising what she was doing, she drove her nails into his back with the clutch of ecstasy.

Clasping him, with arms and legs so that they were almost one creature, she arched to meet his deep thrusts, their sweat-slick bodies clinging, parting only reluctantly and coming back together again with frantic haste.

She was in orgasm a moment later, a pleasure so intense it was almost pain, her head flung back, her neck and face tortured and rigid, her mouth open as she cried out wordlessly like an animal, jerking and shuddering underneath him as if she was dying. Sebastian drove on faster and faster to his own climax. When it came, he collapsed with a long groan on top of her, his body pumping fiercely, his throat vibrating with deep sounds of ecstatic satisfaction.

Afterwards they lay for a long time without moving or speaking. Laura was cold, on the point of tears. She felt them behind her eyelids, then a few began to trickle out down her face. Only a little while ago she had been thinking of death, convinced that Sebastian wanted her dead – had he been thinking about doing this to her, all the time?

Death and sex were so close, after all. The intensity of desire followed by that spiralling downward into emptiness . . . wasn't that a sort of death? The reverberation still beat inside her body, but now she was as chill and limp and lifeless as a corpse. As the kitten in the waters of the Grand Canal.

Sebastian slid off her, stood up. Then he bent down, picked her up, carried her over to the bed and slid her between the sheets. 'I need a drink,' he said, and walked across to the mini-bar.

Laura's teeth were chattering. She stared at his long, naked back, the deep division of his spine visible as he bent to pour the contents of two miniature bottles of brandy into glasses. There was a feathering of dark hair above his buttocks; they were paler than the rest of his tanned body. He spent most of his time out in the open air when he was filming, and back in the States when he wasn't working he was often still out under the hot California sun, half naked around a pool, studying scripts and working out storyboards, or lounging on the sand below his bungalow on the coast.

He brought the drinks over to the bed, got in beside her and offered her a glass.

She shook her head, icy cold and still trembling. Sebastian put an arm under her, lifted her up, held a glass to her lips. 'Don't be stupid, you need it as much as I do.'

Her teeth hit it with a clink, the liquid flowed into her mouth and she had to swallow, her throat stinging. She gasped and more went down; she felt warmth growing inside her. Sebastian laid her back against her pillow, swallowed his own brandy, put both glasses on the bedside table and came under the bedclothes with her, his arm covering her, heavy on her shivering body.

'Go to sleep,' he whispered, pulling her close to him.

She shut her eyes, grateful for the heat of his body, but she remembered her fear and was afraid to relax. Somehow, though, she couldn't stay awake. Sleep engulfed her, and that night she had no bad dreams.

When she woke up Sebastian had gone. She might almost have believed he had never been there, except that the other side of her bed was still warm where he had lain beside her all night. By the golden dawn light she could see the impression of his body. From the dampness and heat between her thighs she could feel him there, too. It had not been another of her passionate dreams.

She turned over towards the imprint of him in the bed and felt something brush her cheek. Sitting up, she saw a white envelope on the pillow. Her name stood out in black capitals on the front.

Laura heart thudded. The printing was familiar. She sat upright and tore open the envelope. There was one sheet of hotel writing paper inside with more capitals written on it.

SHE DESERVED TO DIE. SO DO YOU, YOU WHORE. THIS IS YOUR LAST WARNING.

Hands shaking, Laura read it twice more. It could only be from Sebastian. How else could it have got on to her pillow while she slept? And he must have sent her the other note, the one that had been pushed under her door soon after she arrived here. There couldn't be two anonymous letter-writers here.

Her head swam as if she was going to faint. My God. My God, why? If he hated her that much, why had he made love to her with such passion? She remembered the feelings she had picked up last night in the dining room: the cold, black hatred. It must have come from Sebastian. This note proved it. He might desire her, but he hated her too, just as he had obviously hated his wife. SHE DESERVED TO DIE.

Clea. It must mean Clea. He was telling her that he had killed Clea.

Desperately her eyes darted around the room, looking for an escape route. What was she going to do? Seeing the clock on the bedside table, she flinched. Seven already. Soon it would be time to get up and go to his suite to meet him for breakfast. How could she face him now?

What sort of man was he, this man who had made love to her, got into bed and slept with her in his arms all night, seeming so tender and loving, but who, before he went, wrote such a terrifying threat to her and left it on the pillow beside her sleeping head?

He must be mad. What other explanation could there be?

What about you? she mocked herself angrily. Aren't you mad too?

She had been determined not to see him again, and she certainly hadn't intended to let him make love to her, yet last night he had had a walkover. She had been easy. How he must have laughed. 'Don't touch me,' she had said one minute, and the next she had been burning up underneath him, out of her head with pleasure.

She crumpled up the note and threw it across the room. No, that was stupid, she must keep it, it was evidence. She had always laughed at people who threw away menacing letters without showing them to the police. She wasn't going to make that mistake.

She scrambled out of bed and picked it up, smoothed it out and hid it in a drawer in an antique table by the window, under a little pile of paperback books she had put in there when she unpacked.

Now that she was up she might as well stay up, she thought, so she picked up her crumpled nightdress and put it out to be washed by the hotel, then walked into the bathroom. The window was open and she stood beside it, naked, gazing at the crenellations of the roof in black shadow on the lawns, breathing in the salty air, glad of the cool of morning.

People were already on the beach and in the distance she saw heads bobbing in the water, early-morning swimmers. Laura leant over to watch them and felt dizzy. She clung giddily to the window-sill. For a second she had almost fallen, had wanted to let go, to give herself up to the emptiness of space and death.

That was what Sebastian had done to her: he had made her yearn for death as an escape from the pain of loving him and fearing him, swinging helplessly between the two agonising extremes.

Had Clea ended her life because she couldn't bear the pain of loving Sebastian any more?

Chapter Five

Nico d'Angeli had never cared much for the Hotel Excelsior. Like many of his friends, he had made fun of it as a young man, sneered that it was far too over the top, camp, an extravagant film set dreamt up by Hollywood – all of which made it the perfect place for the film festival headquarters. Every year they flooded into Venice: actors, directors, producers, camera men and sound men, set and costume designers, the accountants and executives of film companies – and they loved the Excelsior. It was their idea of high style, and as it had been built at the start of this century to Americans it was an antique, they thought it classy.

Nico hadn't been there for some time and found himself quite looking forward to seeing the place again as he came over on his own launch from Ca' d'Angeli. He was beset by memories of the hotel: summer days when he and his friends, or girls he was dating, had come over to play golf or tennis after lunch in the splendid dining room, or to swim off the private beach with its Moorish beach huts, so luxuriously furnished that you would have been happy to spend the day down there without ever going up to the hotel itself – except that the food was so marvellous that you couldn't miss the chance to sample it. Nico found the sediment of years stirring, resurrecting his own past, making him feel distinctly middle-aged.

As he arrived the doorman stopped him, judging him by his wind-blown black hair and well-washed old clothes.

Most of the time Nico barely noticed what he was wearing, and that morning he had simply put on the nearest clean clothes – pale beige cotton pants and a dark green shirt, clearly neither designer style nor expensive, and worn with grubby trainers. The doorman needed to take only one glance to place him as a workman. Nico was muscular, broad-shouldered, deep-chested, and his body bore the badge of his work: healed scars on his hands and face where he had been caught by flying chips of marble, rough skin on his palms, a toughness about him that spoke of manual labour.

'Where do you think you're going? Back door for trade.'

Nico grinned. 'I'm meeting one of your guests. I'm Count Niccolo d'Angeli.'

'Yeah, and I'm Michael Jackson,' the doorman said. '*Ma va là, amico!* Round the back!'

Without shifting an inch, Nico said, in the deep-accented Italian of the streets, '*Sta attento, amico!* Just watch yourself, my friend. You're making a mistake. The manager is a friend of mine – ask him to come down and identify me.'

The man's eyes flickered uncertainly, but he wouldn't back down. 'And get myself sacked for wasting his time? Oh, yeah, I'll do that.'

Nico looked past the man's broad shoulder. 'There he is now!' He waved, and the hotel manager came over to greet him warmly.

'*Come sta,* Nico? It's a long time since we saw you over here. What are you doing here so early in the morning? Playing golf?'

The doorman had paled, his face tense. Nico met his pleading eyes and shrugged. He decided not to bother to complain: he would feel guilty if the man lost his job.

'No, I'm not here for golf. I'm having breakfast with Sebastian in his suite.'

The manager's face changed. 'Of course, I'd forgotten, he's . . . His mother was . . .' He paused, looking self-conscious, asked, 'Have you seen him yet? Has he been over to Ca' d'Angeli?'

Nico nodded. 'Yesterday.'

The other man seethed visibly with curiosity but was too discreet to ask direct questions. 'He had dinner here last night, with his crew. Of course, we're packed at the moment, full to the rafters. The festival brings in so much business. And tonight we have the prize-giving – the biggest event of our year! Everyone who is anyone in the film world will be here. My staff are buzzing with excitement.'

'Good business for you, and this is the perfect hotel for the festival,' Nico said, as he walked towards the lift.

'Wonderful business, and it spreads our name, worldwide, with all the TV and other media people here. The hotel is on the news in a lot of countries every year, great free publicity. You should visit us more often, Nico – we haven't seen you for a long time. Don't you play golf any more? You used to come over to our course every week.'

'Too busy for golf these days, I'm afraid.' The truth was, he had lost interest; if you permitted it, golf could take over your life and although Nico was a good player he had better things to do with his time than tramp around a golf course following a little ball.

'A pity. You're good, and you'll lose your handicap if you don't play.'

'That won't keep me awake at night.'

The manager laughed uncertainly with the air of a man who does not appreciate jokes about golf, his own personal religion. He played whenever he had a spare minute. He said, 'I guess you don't have time. I know you're becoming a big name in the art world. I read the rave reviews in the local newspapers of your pieces in the Esposizione Internazionale d'Arte Moderna here last year. They really loved your stuff. I meant to try to get to the exhibition but I never had time. The papers said you were selling your sculptures all over the world these days. Congratulations.'

'I'm doing okay,' Nico agreed. 'I've even got one here, in the Galleria d'Internazionale d'Arte Moderna in Ca' Pesaro. A mother and child, not very big, but I got a good price for it.'

Now the manager did look impressed. 'I'd no idea! You must do something for us, something special that will fit in with our décor.'

Nico glanced around, his brows lifting in disbelief. Something that fitted in with all this turn-of-the-century kitsch? But the lift arrived before he had to answer. '*Ciao*,' he said, then as the doors closed he began to laugh.

A few floors up the lift stopped, the doors opened and Laura Erskine walked in. He looked at her with real pleasure: she knew how to dress, this girl – he admired the white cotton tunic she was wearing. The simplicity was perfect for her: elegant, sophisticated, exciting, with that Titian hair in soft coils around her face and her long, long legs beneath the white cotton, touchably smooth in sheer stockings. Few women had that height, even fewer the ability to carry it off, with head held high, moving with cool grace, the touching vulnerability of a foal.

'*Ciao*,' he said softly, and for a second saw a freezing rejection in her face because she hadn't yet looked at him closely. Then she did a double-take, her features unlocked and she smiled shyly.

'Oh, hello, it's you. I didn't recognise you for a second.'

She was pale this morning, he noted, her beautiful green eyes underlined by bluish shadows on that delicate skin, and there was a faint quiver on the wide, generous mouth. What bone structure! He traced it from the high temples to the fine jawline. Wonderful.

Had she dined here last night, with wine flowing freely? She looked as if she was suffering from a hangover.

'Oh, we're all linguists in Venice,' he said. 'We need to

speak most of the major European languages. People are our business and we can't expect our visitors to speak Italian.' He grinned. 'Late night?'

A warm pink flush ran up her face, delighting him. It suited her better, that glowing colour. 'Yes.' Her voice was husky and self-conscious.

She wouldn't blush like that over a mere dinner party. What had she been doing last night? And with whom? Nico found himself interested in the questions, even more so in the answers.

'You are going to sit for me, aren't you?' he asked, his brain busy with suggestions and conclusions. How involved was she with Sebastian? Newspaper gossip had reached them here, but how much fire was there behind all that smoke? 'I have an idea for a piece. It's vague at the moment, and I'm not sure how it will go when I actually start work, but I was thinking of doing you as David.'

She stared blankly at him. 'What?'

'A female *David* – you know, Michelangelo's statue in Florence.'

Still baffled, she nodded slowly. 'Of course.'

'And there are many others, of course.'

'Many other what?' She was watching him as if he was talking in riddles.

'*Davids*. He was always a popular subject for artists through the Middle Ages, the little man who takes on a giant and wins. And it occurred to me that this is the age of feminism, of women taking on every aspect of man's world so it seems to me time to have a female *David*, a very young *David* taking on the world of men in what appears to be a hopeless struggle. What do you think? Now, be honest! If you think the idea is crazy, say so.'

'Oh, no! I didn't get what you meant at first, but I love it,' she said, as the lift stopped and they got out. 'What a brilliant idea! It's amazing that nobody's thought of it before. What would I wear?'

He laughed – every woman who ever sat for him asked that question. 'Don't worry, I won't ask you to pose in the nude.'

Her colour deepened to a lovely glowing rose. 'I didn't think you would!'

'No?' His eyes were faintly cynical, a little mocking. 'Most women think of that right away. They assume artists always want to get their clothes off! But, actually, I'd ask you to wear more or less what you're wearing now. A simple tunic ending above the knees, and your hair just like it is today. Those curls are oddly similar to the way Donatello's *David* wears his hair, you know.'

'I only know Michelangelo's.'

'You'll find Donatello's *David* in Florence, too, but in bronze not stone, a slender boy, very camp, with a lot of curves, wearing a hat over long hair.'

'A hat? What sort of hat?'

'Just like one you would see at Ascot today.' He grinned. 'A charming little hat, you'll love it. Women always do. The Donatello is very different from the Michelangelo statue – that *David* is stern and frowning, with a lot of muscle, very grave, very masculine. Donatello's has one hand on his hip in a provocative pose – yet he's holding a massive sword in one hand – you can't believe he could ever lift it to cut off Goliath's head!'

They walked along the corridor and paused to ring the doorbell of Sebastian's suite. Nico propped himself against the wall, arms folded.

'I see you in exactly the same position as the Donatello, but holding out the head of Goliath.'

She shuddered. 'How horrible! No, I couldn't do that, don't ask!'

'You wouldn't really be holding a head – I'd need you to hold something, to give me the muscular contraction, but I could work on the head itself later without needing you to be there.' He caught her hands, moved closer. 'Say you'll do it! Don't stop to think – say yes!'

The door of the suite opened. Sebastian looked from one to the other of them, eyes razor-sharp as he took in their linked hands.

In what she knew to be a defensive voice Laura said quickly, 'We met in the lift coming up here,' and pulled her hands free.

Nico shot her an alert glance; she avoided his eyes. He saw too much, was far too aware, and she had things she wanted to hide, from him as well as from Sebastian. Her heart was awash with terrifying memories; the note she had found on her pillow this morning and which could only have been put there by Sebastian, the intensity of their love-making last night, Clea plunging to her death from a high window, his tenderness, the warmth of his body as he held her all night, close and secure, as if he loved her, the kitten that had somehow died in the Grand Canal after she had left it on a cushion in Ca' d'Angeli.

She couldn't make sense of any of it. Sebastian was a divided soul, moving between night and day, darkness and light, and so were her emotions: love and fear fought inside her without either winning.

'Come in,' Sebastian said coldly, just as a rattling of dishes on a table being wheeled along the corridor proclaimed the arrival of their breakfast.

He had opened the high windows of the sitting room, which led out on to a balcony. A cool morning breeze blew through the elegantly furnished room: soft gauzy curtains rustled and flew up, and the distant salty smell of the sea filled the air.

'*Buon giorno,* Signorina, Signori,' the waiter said, negotiating the table through the open door of the suite. Sebastian directed him towards the balcony, then asked the others, 'Okay with you if we eat out there?'

'That would be wonderful, it's so cool at this hour, after that hot night.' Laura was afraid to meet his eyes. The words he had written in that note kept echoing around her head. Why did he want her dead? Especially after last night. They had begun with a struggle and anger, but after they had made love there had been a deep peace between them.

Sebastian had his back to her, was speaking to the waiter. She walked out on to the balcony, only to stop dead, a fluttering of panic in her breast as she saw how high up they were.

Hands screwed into fists, gulping air as if she was suffocating, she stood by the open french windows.

She had never suffered from vertigo before – the first time had been an hour ago when she had looked out of the bathroom window and felt she was going to fall out. Now the same terror had her by the throat again. She was afraid to move in any direction.

Neither of the men seemed aware of what was happening to her. The waiter was moving things around on the white-damask-covered table, putting out orange juice in white-capped glasses set in silver bowls of ice, baskets of hot rolls, croissants, little cakes, silver pots of coffee and hot milk.

After glancing over the table to check that they had everything they needed, Sebastian tipped the waiter, who bowed and left. Nico walked to the rail and gazed down over the green trees to the golden sands. Laura wanted to cry out to him, 'Keep away from the edge!' but she was pressed against the wall, unable to move or speak.

'Sit down, Laura,' Sebastian said, watching her with those dark wells of eyes. She stared back at him, like a rabbit hypnotised by a snake, seeing death dancing in front of it but unable to escape.

Was Sebastian silently willing her to throw herself off the balcony? Was this why Clea had thrown herself to her death? Laura remembered vividly how she had felt the power of Sebastian's will when they were working together. She had obeyed him as if she had no will of her own.

'Come and have breakfast.' Sebastian walked over to her and took her arm. He looked startled. 'You're freezing! Why are you so cold? Are you ill? What's wrong?'

His touch, the words, broke the spell. She blinked, her pallor was invaded by a rush of red, and she stammered, 'No, no, I'm fine, just . . . I don't like heights.'

His eyes sharpened into scalpels that probed her face. 'I don't remember that. How long has it been going on?'

Nico had turned to watch them. Laura was staring up into Sebastian's face, seeing there the remembrance of Clea's death. She was still between them.

Jealousy made a bitter taste in her mouth and she swallowed, jerked away her head and was suddenly able to move. 'I'm fine now.' She walked away from Sebastian and sat down at the table, her back to the view of the hotel grounds, the rail and the long drop to the ground. She picked up her glass of chilled orange juice and took a sip.

Nico sat down beside her. 'You have promised to pose for me, haven't you? I'm very excited by my idea. I think it will be a sensation.'

He took a croissant, tore off a piece and chewed it, his teeth very white, charmingly uneven, against his tanned olive skin.

'What idea?' Sebastian poured coffee, black and fragrant. Its scent filled Laura's nostrils. Every tiny impression seemed too intense this morning. She felt as if this might be the last morning of her life – everything meant so much.

What is the matter with me? she asked herself, watching Sebastian drink his coffee while he watched her in turn with eyes that were full of questions.

'I don't want it talked about in case somebody else steals it,' Nico said. 'You know what the art business is like. A new idea is like gold dust – everyone is on the look-out for one, and I don't work fast. I like to take my time, get something absolutely right. If anybody knew what I was doing, somebody who worked faster than me could come out with their piece, and mine would be worthless.'

'I'm intrigued. But when is Laura going to sit for you? She leaves tomorrow.' Sebastian kept his eyes on her.

She didn't answer, so he shrugged. 'Well, if you don't want to talk about your idea, we'll talk about mine. I've got an option on *The Lily,* that Frederick Canfield book set in the Second World War. Do you remember? I've had it in development for a year or so. We've got a script, of sorts, and a storyboard. The money should be okay, if I get the right casting.'

'I've read it several times,' Nico said, tense with interest his face golden in the morning sunlight. 'A brilliant novel. Are you going to cast Laura as the girl?'

'I'm hoping she'll agree. She'd be perfect, and it would be a wonderful role for her, at this stage of her career. She has to move up a step or two and what she needs is a big box-office success. This film would be it.' He was talking to Laura rather than Nico, watching her. He finished his orange juice and pushed the glass back into its bed of melting ice, turning it round and round so that the ice clinked and groaned.

'Which brings me to what I wanted to discuss with you.' He talked rapidly, barely taking a breath between sentences, to make sure Nico didn't interrupt him. 'If your mother would agree, I'd like to use Ca' d'Angeli for some of the location work. I'd probably need it for a month or so. You and she could take a holiday, leave a servant to keep an eye on the place, make sure we didn't do any damage. You've no need to worry, I assure you. We wouldn't make any structural alterations, and probably wouldn't change the décor at all – it fits the book perfectly. Antique furniture is fine for any period and, if you remember, the house in the book is very much like Ca' d'Angeli. Even the garden is perfect. But do you think your mother will agree, or not?'

'I wasn't expecting this!' Nico said. 'I own the house so it is my decision, but I'd have to consult my mother, for courtesy's sake, and she may not like the idea.'

'It would pay very well – I don't suppose sculptors make a fortune, do they? And the house must cost a lot in upkeep. Think of what you could do with the money!'

Nico looked sideways at Laura. 'Would you stay with us at Ca' d'Angeli while you're in Venice making this film? Then, when you aren't needed for a scene, you could pose for me.'

She heard Sebastian shift in his chair, felt tension in him, carefully didn't risk looking in his direction. Cupping her hands round her coffee cup, she nodded. 'Okay.'

After all, what difference was there between posing for a photographer and posing for an artist? What you were doing was basically the same: a matter of training in patience and response, giving the photographer or artist what they wanted. Certainly a photography session involved lots of movement, using props, changing mood – smiling, being serious, looking tigerish or sweet, playing up to the camera as if it was a man you loved – and when you were posing for an artist you had to keep still, not move a muscle, hold a pose for ages. She could imagine that that would be exhausting, and probably tedious, if it went on for too long. But it would be fascinating to watch Nico working: she had never known a sculptor before and she would have plenty to think about while she was modelling for him. No doubt he would give her a break every so often.

'If I do the film, that is,' she added. 'This is a chancy business. Projects fall through all the time, or take years to get into production. This film may never get made at all, or I may not be available on the date they start shooting. But if I do get that part, I'd be happy to pose for you whenever I have any free time.'

'You aren't likely to have much. This part would call for you being on set most of the time,' Sebastian said.

She smiled at Nico. 'I'm bound to get one day off a week, at least, so don't worry.'

'We have a deal?' he said, getting up. 'Well, I'll talk to my mother and let you know our decision, Sebastian. Now, I'm afraid I have to get back. I'm at work on something important. Thanks for the breakfast. I normally just have coffee and some fruit – a touch of luxury is always welcome. And it was a very useful meeting, for both of us.'

Laura got up to leave, too, but Sebastian stopped her. 'Don't go yet. I want to talk to you.'

When the door had closed on Nico and she and Sebastian were alone, she pulled free. 'I've got another appointment at ten, I can't be late.' She hadn't meant to say anything more to him, but suddenly her anger flared. 'Why did you write that note to me this morning, Sebastian? Why are you threatening me?'

'Note?' He looked mystified. 'What are you talking about? Which note?'

'Oh, don't play stupid games! You know what I mean! The note you left on my pillow.'

'Oh, that! I didn't write it, I found it by the door. Someone had obviously pushed it underneath—' Sebastian stopped. 'What did it say?'

She stared at him, trying to read his expression, not sure whether or not she could believe him. The envelope she had received soon after she arrived had been pushed under the door, and it had been from the same person.

Could Sebastian be telling the truth?

'What did it say?' he insisted.

'Never mind.'

'I do mind. If you thought I might have written it, then presumably it was anonymous. What sort of filth is someone writing to you? It must be pretty nasty or you wouldn't have looked at me that way. I want to see it, Laura – I'll come down to your room and get it. You should tell the police if someone's sending you junk like that. Have you rung them?'

'You know I can't speak Italian and, anyway, what could they do? Both of them were printed—'

'Both?' he exploded. 'There was another one?'

She could have kicked herself. 'Oh, forget it!'

'Are you *crazy*? How can I forget something like that? One

threat was serious enough – but two? What did the other one say?'

'Same sort of thing.'

'You still haven't told me what they say!'

'Threats,' she muttered. 'Get out of Venice or else . . .'

'When did you get the first one?'

'Just after I arrived yesterday.'

'Let's go to your room. I want to see them. You *must* go to the police, Laura! You're taking a silly risk not showing them these notes.'

'I'm only going to be here one more day, then I'll be on my way back to London. What's the point? Stop shouting at me! Forget I mentioned the notes. I've torn them up and flushed them down the lavatory.'

He swore. 'For God's sake! That was a damn stupid thing to do! You should have kept them, They're evidence. Come on! What did they say?'

She couldn't tell him without mentioning Clea and she couldn't bear to repeat what the note had said, the words stuck in her throat. 'Whoever wrote it doesn't like me very much. That's all.' She reached for the door but Sebastian stepped in front of it.

'Which made you think it was from me. After last night?' His voice was harsh. 'Well, thank you, Laura. That tells me a lot.'

'No, I didn't mean – You're jumping to conclusions—'

'Isn't that what you've done about me? Not very nice conclusions, either.'

'I'm sorry. But I did find that note this morning on my pillow and only you could have put it there. What else was I to think?'

He stared down at her pale face. 'Okay. You say it's from someone who doesn't like you. What does that mean? Why won't you tell me exactly what was said? Is he threatening you?'

'I don't want to talk about it.' She looked away, her mouth a stubborn line.

'Why are you so damn stupid?'

She laughed humourlessly. 'I can't help it, I suppose.'

'Don't sound so pleased with yourself!' There was a brief silence. Then he asked, 'What's going on between you and Nico?'

She felt herself flushing, knew she must look guilty. 'Nothing. You heard what he was saying – he wants me to pose for him.'

'With or without clothes?'

The biting sarcasm hurt, but she answered, chin up, defiant, 'More or less what I'm wearing now, actually, but with boots and a hat.'

'Boots and a hat?' Sebastian's eyes widened, his brows met. 'Is this a statue, or does he intend to paint you?'

'I can't tell you. You heard him – he doesn't want anyone to know his plans. It seems the art world is as competitive and treacherous as the film world.' She looked at her watch. 'Please, I must go, I have a very busy day ahead of me.'

'Do you know yet which table you'll be sitting at tonight?'

'Mel knows, I haven't checked.' He moved away from the door and she turned the handle, saying, with relief, 'Well, see you.'

'What time are you leaving tomorrow?'

'The first flight, I think, mid-morning.'

'If you like the script I'll be in touch in a few weeks in London, to draw up contracts for the film.'

'Not with me, Sebastian, with Melanie. She deals with the business side, you know. I can't make any deals without her agreement. You have to talk to her about the contract.'

He grimaced. 'I know. But if you want to do it, don't let her talk you out of it. You're the client, remember, she's just the agent.'

She giggled, 'Don't tell me that, tell Melanie. 'Bye, Sebastian,' then hurried away down the corridor towards the lift, relieved to have escaped.

'I'll send you the latest version of the script as soon as I get back,' he called after her.

She waved without turning round. 'Okay, I'll look forward to reading it.'

'And be careful!' he yelled. 'Don't take any risks. If you get any more anonymous letters, take them to the police.'

She waved again, without answering, and walked into the lift. She was not as disturbed by them now that she was almost sure Sebastian hadn't sent them. People in the public eye received notes like that all the time and most of them meant nothing. She had only had them since she came to Venice . . . which must mean that they were from someone here at the moment, or someone who lived here all the time and had access to this hotel – maybe someone who worked here. It could be anyone. She didn't care who it was, so long as it wasn't Sebastian.

Of course, it wouldn't be wise for her to accept this role in his new film: she had sworn never to work with him again, and last night had shown her that she was as vulnerable to him as she had ever been: emotionally nothing had changed.

But that role might be a real chance for her. She hadn't even read the script yet but she sensed that this was going to be a major film. She couldn't turn it down or she might never get another break like it: very few people were given such an opportunity.

It would mean coming back to Venice, too, and she had fallen in love with the city. Being here was like living in a waking dream – what other city had that magic? She loved the idea of spending weeks here, maybe months, especially if she was staying at Ca' d'Angeli, which was the loveliest house she had ever seen. She couldn't believe that she was going to be living under that roof, with the Grand Canal flowing past the front door, and all those extraordinary, beautiful objects surrounding her day and night. The tapestries, the bronzes, the paintings were like nothing she had ever seen before, and she couldn't wait to see Nico's studio – was that where he would be working on this statue of her as a female David? That was another reason why she couldn't refuse: it was such a wonderful idea that she couldn't bear to miss out on it.

Who are you kidding? she asked herself, knowing that she was just making up a string of reasons for doing what she badly wanted to do. She would give anything to work with Sebastian again. He was as mysterious as Ca' d'Angeli; a maze of winding corridors, secret, full of shadows and angels and reflections that bewildered her. She knew so little about him and what she thought she knew could all be an illusion. So much of the film world was illusion, and even though she was inside it now she still hadn't fathomed what really went on in it.

But if Sebastian hadn't sent those notes, who had? Her skin crept. What if he was right and she had somehow become the target of someone who might not stop at notes? Who might be serious about wanting to kill her? Who might follow her to London and try there?

Chapter Six

Nico's favourite possession was his boat; it was his escape when life got difficult. He could get into it at any time, day or night, and zoom away into the misty reaches of the lagoon, or even out into the waters of the Adriatic, Italy's own private sea, leaving behind everything that got on his nerves and made life unbearable. That usually meant the summer, when the city was torrid and airless, the narrow streets crammed with tourists and stinking with the smell of stagnant water. It was why he had given the boat the name *Angelica*. It was a joke about his home, Ca' d'Angeli, of course – that was how everyone took it – but it was also a secret code for himself because the boat could take him to heaven, far out where he would switch off the engine and drift in silence and emptiness, through mists or clear blue waters, alone for hours with only the cry of sea birds, the slap of the waves on the hull, the rhythmic rocking, the wind blowing. He had painted the hull midnight blue, which could look black on dark days, when no light reflected, although when the sun came out the colour took on a brighter sheen, like a blackbird's wing. The name was painted in gold, and above it was a pair of golden wings made of delicate fretted wood.

He had bought *Angelica* second-hand and repaired her himself; he enjoyed buying something cheaply and working on it to give it a much higher value, whether it was a work of art or a boat.

That day he came back at speed from the Lido, automatically steering his way through the other craft, past water-taxis, barges carrying freight, a builder whose boat was laden with bricks and tools, hotel launches full of arriving or departing guests. These were crowded waters and you needed sharp wits and eyes.

Nico slowed as he came in along the Grand Canal, watching the ripple of water on ancient walls up side canals. That was what you grew up with here: the sound and sight of water moving around you, as much your environment as if you were a fish.

Reaching Ca' d'Angeli, he switched off the engine and carefully steered *Angelica* into the boat-house alongside the palazzo. There was little room in it: a clutter of old disused boats, some of them antiques, most just crumbling or ruined, piled on top of each other, took up most of the space at the back in the same way that Ca' d'Angeli itself was crowded with the debris of centuries. Nobody in the family had ever thrown anything away, they just pushed it into cupboards or put it up into the attics. When a boat was past repair they cannibalised any useful parts of it, and chucked the rest into the corners of the boat-house to decay, wreathed in cobwebs, riddled with woodlice and woodworm.

Once upon a time, the d'Angeli family had had some of the most elaborately decorated, the grandest, Venetian launches. In this watery city, boats took the place of cars and every family was expected to have the best they could afford. The d'Angelis had always spent extravagantly on these status symbols.

Nico often browsed among the jumble of boats, looking for anything he might find useful. On most of them the paint had blistered and peeled off; the gilded ornaments like *Angelica*'s angel's wings, had all been carefully forced off and used again on newer craft. Nico was ruefully aware that his current launch did not have the elegant lines, the speed, the sheer style of the older boats.

Something like that would cost the earth today and he couldn't afford to pay a first-class designer, or even the craftsmen to turn plans into reality. Once the family had been among the richest in Venice; today they managed on a private income left by his maternal grandfather, who had headed a big pharmaceutical company now no longer under family management. Without that money, the d'Angelis might have had to sell up and leave Venice. Maybe that would have been the saving of them. Hanging on here, in decaying grandeur, on a gradually shrinking income, had been a strain for years.

Nico turned away towards the private staircase built in an angle of the house wall that wound up to the studio. His grandfather had had it built sixty years ago so that he could come and go as he chose without needing to pass through the house. In the beginning it had led to his bedroom, and the visitors he brought in had been whores or friends who had enjoyed those secret little parties.

Nico's father, Domenico, had also had secrets to protect, visitors he smuggled in and out of the studio as his father had, but not the same sort. He had never used whores: he had had just one mistress all his life. She had been more like a wife than a mistress, but Domenico could never marry her: she was not of his class; his family would never have allowed it.

Nico had no visitors by that route: he used it to slip in and out without being noticed by his mother, who watched every move he made. He knew she loved him, and he loved her, but her eternal vigilance made his life complicated. It was unbearable to have to explain everything he did and said, to have no private life, to have her trying even to guess what he was thinking.

The stairs were narrow and spidery since the servants were forbidden to come here – his mother had accepted his order without too much argument, even though she did point out that the boat-house and the stairs should be cleaned from time to time.

'I'll clean them.'

'You?' She had laughed. 'I can't even imagine that.'

'If I think they need it I'll see to it,' he had insisted stubbornly, and she had let the matter drop, although he wouldn't be surprised to be told that she sent someone secretly to sweep and dust when he wasn't around.

Nico unlocked his studio door. The high-vaulted room was shadowy, the shutters closed because he had been working in here last night very late. He opened them and daylight burst into the cluttered interior. Little spirals of dust rose into the light, floating golden particles like tiny glittering spiders on invisible strings being drawn upwards to the beamed ceiling.

He watched them with pleasure, as he always did, before going over to strip the dust cover off the shape waiting in the centre of the room.

Once he was in his studio his mind was immediately taken over by work: he forgot everything else as he put on his protective leather apron, his gloves, goggles and a cap to cover his hair against the dust in the air, and prevent fragments of stone embedding themselves in his scalp. All the time he was staring at what he was working on, seeing it as a lover sees the beloved first thing in the morning, a revelation of beauty, an endlessly renewed surprise.

An hour later his mother tapped on the door; Nico did not hear her. She came into the room and moved to where he could see her.

Sighing, he stopped work, hand raised, chisel poised. 'Yes, Mamma?'

She was sweetly reproachful – he remembered that tone from his childhood. 'I've been waiting for you to come and tell me what happened.'

He had been so engrossed that he couldn't understand what she was getting at. 'What are you talking about?'

She did not believe in his bewilderment. 'At the hotel this morning.'

'Oh, that! Sebastian wanted to talk about a film he plans

to make on location in Venice. He asked if he could use Ca' d'Angeli – he'd pay us a small fortune in rent, he said.'

He chipped lightly along a plane: a delicate flake flew off and he saw the angle he was looking for. Ah, yes, he thought. There it is: smooth as a young girl's behind, a slatish blue shining in the late-morning sunlight, like a pigeon's wing, dark grey irradiated by colour, a streak of white, a wild pink, a phosphorescent green, flashes of black. Like an opal. When you looked hard at anything for long enough you saw colour hidden in what, at first, seemed monotone. People simply did not use their eyes enough. They saw what they expected to see.

'No!'

Nico had forgotten she was there and almost jumped out of his skin. His chisel slipped and gouged along the stone with a high-pitched squeal like a cat having its tail pulled. He swore. '*Merda*! Christ! How many times do I have to ask you not to come in here and chatter at me while I'm working? See what you've made me do!'

She was pacing to and fro, not listening to him. 'I won't have it, Nico! How could you even consider letting him use Ca' d'Angeli?'

Bending forward, he blew the dust away from the site of the gouge, pushed back his goggles to get a clearer view of the damage. It didn't look as bad as he had first thought. He wet his finger and rubbed gently, looked round for his little bottle of water, which was topped by a spray, found it on a table, came back and aimed, watched the jet spread out over the stone, darkening it, blotting out all those delicate colours, making the edges black, showing up precisely where his blow had struck. A sigh of relief. No, not beyond rescue.

'Nico!' His mother was shouting now.

He looked at her. 'Luckily for you, it isn't as bad as it looked.'

'Never mind your work!'

His scowl cut deep lines into his forehead. 'Get out of here, Mamma, before I really get angry.'

She ignored his flash of temper. 'He can't come here. You didn't tell him he could, did you? I'm not having him in my home for weeks on end. I won't have it, however much he offers!'

Nico's eyes chilled, black and lightless. 'Ca' d'Angeli belongs to me, not you. I decide whether or not Sebastian rents it, and if he offers enough I'll take his money. It's the sort of windfall that only comes once in a lifetime – and if his film is a big hit, who knows? We may start getting more money from visitors who want a tour of the house. We've never been on the tourist trail, but no reason why we shouldn't start out on it. We can pay someone to act as a guide, if you don't want to do it.'

He saw her white face and fixed, intense eyes, and felt a spurt of bitter glee. She shouldn't have walked in on him when he was working, interrupted him at a crucial moment. He had been pleased with how the piece was looking, now he would have to spend most of the next hour repairing the damage she had caused. She had disobeyed the only rule he ever made – that nobody should come into the studio without his permission. He had let her get away with too much, that was the trouble. She thought she could do just as she liked, but she was wrong.

'In any case, it will be fun having a film made here, I'm excited by the idea.'

'You can't be serious, Nico! Strangers cluttering up the house, touching my things, shifting them around, taking down our pictures, no doubt, putting furniture out of sight to change the way rooms look – I know these film people, they take liberties, everyone says so. Why, when Berta Rossini had them in her place they broke some of her Meissen and it took her years to get the money out of them. I won't have my things touched.'

'*My* things, Mamma,' he reminded her. 'It all belongs to me. None of it is yours, not the tapestries, not the portraits, not the furniture. It is all mine, and if I want to earn money by letting the house to strangers, I will.' She always behaved as if Ca' d'Angeli belonged to her, and normally he didn't mind, but she had made him angry this morning – not least because if Sebastian did not come neither would Laura, and Nico was determined to do that figure of her. His mind had been racing with excitement ever since he thought of the female David. Nothing must stand in its way.

The Contessa bit down on her full lower lip, her chin trembling. 'Nico, don't you understand? I couldn't bear to have him in this house every day, walking around as if he belonged here, owned it – him, of all people! Seeing him in the flesh hurt more than I'd bargained for. I hadn't realised how much he looked like—'

She stopped dead and Nico stared at her, saw her throat move as she swallowed.

'You've seen dozens of photos of him!' he protested.

'It's different, having him standing in front of you. Then you can see it, really see . . . the colouring, the way he turns his head, the way he moves his hands . . . No, you can't do this to me, Nico.'

Obsessed with his image of the female David, remembering the firm column of Laura's throat bearing that delicately chiselled head, Nico found it hard to follow what she meant. 'What the hell are you talking about now, Mamma? Oh, I know you never liked his mother, but I wouldn't have said he looked like Gina.'

She gave a gulp of laughter and put her hand over her mouth.

Nico wished she wasn't given to these sudden bouts of hysteria, which had erupted from as far back as he remembered. The façade of placidity she showed the world would crack and you would glimpse something disturbing inside, a wild streak, a clamour and fury, an emotional inferno. Then, just as rapidly, the surface would smooth back and you would be left wondering if you had imagined the whole thing.

Her hand still over her mouth, she walked away to the window and looked out, her back to him, her black-clad shoulders shaking, although she was making no sound.

She couldn't help her temperament, any more than he could – maybe he had inherited more from her than he realised. He had always told himself there was nothing of her in him, yet now he began to understand something in himself that echoed something in her. She had always been two people, he thought, the sweetly smiling, serene woman who ran this house, gave dinner parties for a small circle of friends, always the right people, well-bred, admired. And then there was the other, secret one – the woman obsessed with the past, with his family history, his father, this house, the woman consumed by that internal fire you rarely glimpsed.

Nico felt very sorry for her. What sort of life had she had? Widowed so young, left alone to bring up her child . . . Why hadn't she married again? She must have been a tempting prize, with her private fortune from her own family – but although over the years several men had shown signs of interest she had never responded. She had never worn anything but black, or purple on special occasions. She had buried her youth with her husband. Now her dark hair was silvery and she had put on quite a bit of weight; she was an old woman.

Contrite, he said, 'I know it won't be easy for you to put up with a lot of strangers in the house, it's bound to be messy and tiresome – they'll have wires and equipment everywhere, and the servants will complain – but we can do with the money, Mamma.'

Although she still had considerable capital it had been carefully tied up in a trust fund by her father before he died. Now, she and Nico shared the income, which would, in turn, pass to the succeeding generation. Leo Serrati had been a shrewd, hard-headed businessman. He had not intended his fortune to be frittered away after his death.

'We can manage – we always have!'

'But, Mamma, it would be fun to have a little windfall, wouldn't it? We could take a holiday, be extravagant for once. And, anyway, I'm curious about the film-making process, I'd like to have a ringside view of how it's done. I could learn a lot from camera techniques, how to look, how to see what the naked eye cannot.' He did not tell her that he wanted Laura Erskine to model for him and that this was the only way to get her here. There were some things he had learnt not to talk to his mother about – women, above all. She had a puritan attitude to sex, he suspected it revolted her, yet she loved gossip and scandal, especially sexual innuendo and rumours about people she knew. Women were odd creatures, contradictory and baffling. Like cats.

She was staring at him as if she was trying to see into his head. Her hands hung by her side, screwed into fists. She was rigid, her plump body reminding him of a wooden toy he had once had, Mrs Noah, who stood on the deck of the Ark she inhabited, among the carved wooden animals, staring straight ahead fixed for ever in a defiant pose.

He had loved that toy passionately. His father had made it for him, carved the wooden pieces, painted them himself. He still had it, somewhere, the colours faded, some of the animals missing. Old Noah, with bold black eyes and gold buttons down his bright blue coat, Mrs Noah with red cheeks, which came off on your hands on humid days, the tawny giraffes, sandy lions with bared white teeth, battleship grey elephants with long, swinging trunks you could actually move because his father had hinged them, two proud black horses with wild manes, two curly white sheep, one with horns, two ostriches lovingly painted to show their feathers soft as thistledown, birds of paradise, eagles, swallows and doves. How many hours had he played with it, making up adventures for them all, feeling the life in those wooden figures as he stroked them so that the wood warmed in his hands? He could almost have sworn he had felt them breathe and move under his fingers.

It had never occurred to him until now that that might explain why he had chosen to be a sculptor: his Ark had shown him that you could create life out of seemingly dead wood and stone. How much small things could affect your entire life without you being aware of what was happening!

'Why does he want to make a film in Venice?' his mother asked. 'Why in this house?'

'He wants to make *The Lily*, that bestseller everyone was talking about, remember? You read it, didn't you?'

Her olive-golden skin was set rigid across the heavy bones of her face. 'Canfield's book?'

Nico remembered suddenly. 'Of course, you knew him once, didn't you? I'd forgotten. Didn't you meet him before the war?'

There was a long silence, then she nodded. 'Yes, he taught my brothers English and French until the British were ordered out of Italy by Il Duce.'

Milan, 1940

Vittoria did not know what to make of the Englishman. He was taller than her father, with lots of floppy light hair that kept falling over his eyes; it fascinated her to watch him raking it back only to have it fall forward again. His eyes were bright blue, like shiny glass, and his clothes were casual and faintly shabby, old grey flannels and a white shirt, which had been neatly darned. It was obvious even to the child that the Englishman was poor, yet his cool, assured manner puzzled her. He did not behave in the way she expected poor people to behave: there was something different about him. Maybe it was simply that he was a foreigner.

'What's he doing in Italy, living hand-to-mouth like this?' her father asked her mother, over a lazy Sunday lunch. 'I'd suspect he was a spy if I thought he had any brains, but all he does is read books and talk nonsense.'

Anna Serrati sighed. 'How many times do I have to tell you? He's a writer, in Italy because he admires Italian art. He's learning our language, and writing a book.'

'He climbs,' little Niccolo said, secretly feeding scraps of fatty meat to the spaniel under the table.

Leo Serrati glared at his youngest son. 'Climbs?'

'Mountains.'

Carlo said, 'He goes off to the Alps all the time. He said he would take us one day.'

Leo's voice grew hoarse with excitement. 'That means he could cross the Swiss border without anyone being the wiser! That area is lousy with British spies, always has been – they come across the lakes at night. What did I tell you? He's spying on us! And you pay him to come to our house!'

'What military secrets do we have?' Anna said. 'Don't be silly, Leo. Do you really think the British want to know how you make your laxatives?'

Leo shouted, 'Don't talk about such things in front of the children!'

'What things? The castor oil they take when they're—'

'Be quiet!' he snapped, getting up from the table. 'You have no decency. My mother would never have talked the way you do. And next time that Englishman comes here, throw him out.'

'It's important for the boys to speak other languages. If the firm keeps growing you'll be selling all over Europe one day, and whoever is running it will need to speak French, German, English.'

Leo's eyes brightened at the idea of a company that sold its products all over Europe. 'Well, watch him whenever he comes, and remember anything he says about politics.'

'He never talks about politics,' Carlo put in. 'Only art or literature. It's very boring.'

Carlo took after his father in looks and nature yet the two were always arguing, but Leo was a man given to angry outbursts over nothing, and he never backed down or even admitted he might be wrong.

'The English are mad!' Anna heard him say a week or so later, when Frederick Canfield joined them all in the garden for what she hoped would pass as English tea – tiny sandwiches of thinly sliced country ham or cheese, a rich chocolate cake and cups of milkless tea, heavily sugared.

Frederick accepted a sandwich and a cup of tea, smiling at Anna as he took them while to her husband he said calmly, 'I won't argue with you, Signore, but, if I may ask, why precisely do you think we're mad?'

'What else explains it? Why don't you make terms with Hitler? He's offered to come to an agreement, and you'll have to sooner or later. You know your people don't have the will to fight – look at the way all the students voted not to go to war! And you have no tanks or planes, you aren't ready for war. All our newspapers agree about that. Hitler will crush you.'

To Vittoria's amazement the Englishman laughed. 'The British never want to fight, Signore. They look for other ways of resolving problems, diplomacy, discussion, because they're sane. Only crazy people want to kill or be killed. What good is that for trade? But if we are forced into war . . .' He shrugged cheerfully. 'Well, we haven't lost one for a thousand years, you know.'

Reddening, Leo barked, 'You haven't fought us yet!'

The Englishman's bright blue eyes smiled and his mouth curled up at the edges. He did not seem worried or frightened by Leo's temper. His manner was always the same, calm, friendly, faintly amused. 'True, not since the days of the Romans, but you haven't been fighting many wars, have you?'

For some reason that remark made Leo's face stiffen with rage.

Frederick turned to Anna. 'These are delicious sandwiches, Signora. I've not eaten ham as good as this since I left England.'

'It comes from a farm up in the hills. They breed the pigs

themselves. Their cured ham is expensive, but it is the best in Italy.'

'I've never tasted better.' He turned to look down into Vittoria's eyes. Nobody else had noticed her, sitting silent as a mouse, very small and still, next to her mother, nibbling at a slice of cake and catching the crumbs in her palm to lick them off quickly before they melted. 'Do you still remember the little poem I taught you last week?'

Blushing as everyone around the table stared at her, Vittoria nodded. She was always both nervous and elated when she attracted any attention, especially in front of her terrifying but wonderful father.

'Will you say the first verse for us?'

She hesitated. Her mother took her hand. 'Yes, say it for us, darling.'

She hung her head.

'What's the matter with her?' Leo Serrati boomed. 'Do as you're told, girl!'

Vittoria began in a rush, 'I have a little shadow . . .' afraid she would forget the words, but she managed to finish the verse without a mistake.

'Well done!' Frederick congratulated her. 'Your daughter has a good memory, Signore, and a head for mathematics. You must send her to a modern girls' school when she's old enough.'

Leo Serrati scowled. 'Girls don't need an expensive education. I don't intend her to be a typist or to work in a shop. She'll marry, of course. The convent school is the best place for a girl – the nuns will teach her all she needs to know to make a good wife.'

Frederick looked at Anna, who gazed back at him, her pink mouth ironic.

A week later over breakfast Leo Serrati waved a newspaper at his wife. 'See? Il Duce has ordered the British out of the country. Your wonderful Englishman will have to go, too. He needn't think I'll lift a finger to save him.'

Ignoring him, Anna helped Vittoria to a warm brioche with some of the home-made black cherry jam from last year. Vittoria bit into it, wishing she dared ask why the British were being sent away.

Later that morning Frederick Canfield arrived while Leo Serrati was at work, the boys at school and only Anna and Vittoria at home. They were sitting by the window, in the gentle sunlight of early summer, sewing with the radio on. As soon as she saw him, Anna leant over to switch it off.

'You're leaving?'

He nodded. 'I've come to say goodbye.'

Vittoria was startled to see tears in her mother's eyes. 'What a terrible world this is! This time next year we could all be dead.'

The child sat up straight and pale, frightened. What did her mother mean?

Frederick knelt down by Anna's chair and took her hands. 'Don't despair, my dearest Anna. This evil thing must end one day. We'll have good times again. Won't you take me for one last walk through your lovely garden so that I can remember it when I'm back in England?' He lifted the hands he held to his mouth, kissing each one on the palm with the reverence people showed to the statue of Our Lady in the church.

Anna Serrati looked at her daughter. 'Signor Canfield and I are going to walk in the garden. Stay here, Vittoria, and get on with your sewing. I won't be long. You'll be able to see us from here, don't worry.'

Obediently Vittoria stayed where she was, sitting on her chair, her short, plump legs stuck out in front of her, like a doll's, and went on primly with the handkerchief she was making. There were spots of blood here and there where she had pricked her finger with the needle, and smudges of dirt from when she had once forgotten to wash her hands before beginning work but her sewing was improving. Mamma said she would soon be good at keeping the stitches small and neat.

Now and then she looked out of the window. Her mother and Signor Canfield were walking away from her across the lawns. Their hands hung loose at their sides. Vittoria's plump pink mouth opened in a gasp as she saw the fingers brush, entwine, break free again. Her mother had held hands with the Englishman. Vittoria felt uneasy, the way she did when she was going to be sick from eating too many honey cakes.

The garden looked at its best in early June before the sun grew too hot and the grass dried into pale, rustling hay. The roses were in full bloom; golden brown bees hummed drunkenly around those great pink flowers whose golden hearts left pollen on your finger if you touched them. Vittoria loved their heady scent, it made her head swim. She watched disapprovingly as Frederick picked a new, tightly closed bud. Papa would have been very cross if he'd seen that. Then the Englishman kissed the rosebud, before offering it to Mamma, who kissed it, too, then slid it down inside her neckline so that it lay hidden against her breast.

Vittoria didn't understand what was happening, but she was frightened. She wanted to scream, call her mother back, as though Anna was being taken away from her.

Her head filled with images she always tried to forget – the things that had happened on her birthday. Papa pushing her nurse down on to Mamma's bed and doing those strange, frantic things to her. She didn't really understand what she had seen but she knew it had been bad. Was her mother . . . Had her mother . . . done that with Signor Canfield? Or was she going to now?

Vittoria shut her eyes and deliberately stuck the sharp point of the needle into her finger, then screamed, holding up her hand, blood spurting.

With sick relief she saw them turn. Even from a distance she could see sadness in their faces and didn't understand that, either.

A moment later her mother hurried into the room. Vittoria sobbed, 'The needle went in my finger!'

Anna looked at the blood, 'Oh, *poverina* ...' She gently wiped it away with a clean handkerchief. 'We must put some disinfectant on it, darling.' To Frederick she said, 'She's always doing it. Look at this poor handkerchief! When it's finished it will have to be washed and washed to get the blood out.'

He smiled. 'At least this blood will wash out.' He was always saying baffling things. Vittoria looked at him with hostility, and he bent to kiss her forehead. 'Be safe, *bambina,* I hope I'll see you again one day. We must all pray for an end to this war. Give the boys my best wishes.'

Vittoria stayed obstinately silent, glowering. She wasn't going to pretend she was sorry he was going away: she did not like the way he looked at her mother, or the way her mother looked at him.

When Anna told the boys that Signor Canfield had been at the house to say goodbye, Carlo scowled. 'Lucky he's going. At school they say Il Duce is going to put the English in prison if they haven't gone by the end of the month.'

'Probably going to shoot them,' little Niccolo said, with bloodthirsty glee. 'I never liked him.' He mimed machine-gunning. 'You're dead, Signor English,' he shouted, capering about.

Anna slapped his face. 'You stupid little boy! You don't begin to know what war is about. Soon you won't talk so cheerfully about killing people.'

Niccolo's eyes filled with tears and Carlo glared at his stepmother. 'Don't you hit my brother! He's right – we've put up with too much from the English over the years. They've talked down to us and laughed at us for the last time. Let them try it now, after this defeat in France. In a week or two they won't have an army. Hitler will smash it to smithereens, and when he's finished taking over France, he'll invade England. This war will be over by Christmas. I want to get into it while I can.'

Carlo should have gone to university in the autumn of 1940, but once Mussolini had declared war, on 10 June that year, every able-bodied young man was expected to join one of the services as soon as he was eighteen.

'We have to be there, fighting side by side with Hitler before he grabs the whole of Europe for the Germans,' Carlo said. The next day he joined the army and vanished off to officer training, as did so many other young men.

Alfredo, who was still only sixteen, ran away to join up, too, not wanting to be outshone by his elder brother. He gave a false name to make sure his father could not stop him.

Leo Serrati tried to track him down, even getting Carlo to ask questions of every soldier he met, follow up every whisper of a clue, but Italian men were being drafted in every direction and it was impossible to get answers out of the overworked, muddled bureaucracy of the army. Leo came back, looking worried and angry.

'They won't, or can't, tell me anything. When I do find that boy, I'll kill him myself!' It was later that he burst out, 'You know what I heard in a bar in town today? They say thousands of Italians who joined up were sent to Germany, not into the army, to work as slave labour for the Germans. Some of my workers have vanished, you know. They just disappear without saying a word. I'd assumed they were going off to fight, but now—' He stopped, his face drained of colour. 'It can't be true. Il Duce wouldn't allow it.'

No word came of Alfredo until a year later when his father received an anonymous letter from Germany, from another Italian. He and Alfredo had joined up together. They had been put into a cattle truck on a train and sent off to Germany where they had been forced to work as cleaners in an army training camp. After a few months Alfredo had tried to run away. He had been caught and shot as a deserter, as a warning to other Italians not to do the same.

Leo Serrati tried for months to find out the truth. He pulled every string he had without success. They never heard anything of Alfredo again.

He was the first of the Serrati boys to die. Carlo fought in the Balkan states and every so often they got a letter from him, telling them as much as he could. Men died around him every day, dirty, bloody and screaming in agony, but somehow Carlo survived to be sent to North Africa for yet another hopeless fight. In the desert he was so seriously wounded in the back and legs, when a shell exploded right beside him, that he was sent home on a stretcher in June 1941, a few days before the news broke that Hitler had attacked Russia.

After a year in various hospitals Carlo came home, paralysed, knowing he would never walk again. For him the war was over, except as a civilian facing food shortages and spiralling inflation. By then even bread was rationed, although a rich family like the Serratis could buy anything on the black market: millions of forged ration cards were in circulation, and stolen food was available, too, if you knew where to go. The Serrati family did better than most, especially at first.

Anna had always spent her days gracefully performing social duties, working in charity committees, sewing, running the house, choosing clothes, shopping. Now she was up at first light to hurry off to nurse, part-time, in a service hospital, doing jobs the trained nurses felt they could delegate to these society women whom they openly despised as 'playing' at their profession.

On her way home, she would stop to buy whatever she could find in the shops, then cook lunch for Leo and Carlo, the two younger boys and Vittoria. She gardened in the afternoon, since now they had to grow most of their own vegetables, mixed the food for the hens and ducks they had begun to keep. Vittoria loved feeding the pig, who lived in a little sty and ate any scraps left from their own meals. Carlo had to guard the animals at night, with his service revolver, because black-market gangs were always on the look-out for home-raised animals.

As the war went on, life in Italy became worse. People were starving in some parts of the country, while it was said that in

Rome all the classy, expensive restaurants were packed with rich people eating their heads off. The newspapers did not report any of this, of course, it was all rumour and gossip – but, as everyone said, there's no smoke without fire. Some of the whispers had to be true: Mussolini had lost control; Il Duce was dying; people who saw him that winter said he was pale, haggard, losing weight.

Leo Serrati knew many of the top medical men in the country and soon had the truth. 'Poor man, suffers agonies from dysentery. Picked it up in Africa when he went there in July.'

'One of the other nurses told me she'd heard he's having an affair with some whore who's given him syphilis.' Nursing had changed Anna Serrati: she had seen and heard things that made her view life without rose-coloured spectacles.

Leo bristled. 'Will you stop talking like that? Ears, remember, ears!'

Anna looked at her daughter, apparently absorbed in nibbling her rough brown bread and a tiny piece of cheese, made from their own goats' milk. 'She isn't listening – and if she was, she wouldn't know what I was saying.'

'And I don't want her to! It's a lie, anyway! These pains he gets are all in the abdomen, some internal problem ... Cancer, maybe?'

'This war is responsible for many terrible things.' Anna looked sad, and Vittoria, watching her, remembered the Englishman, whose face was beginning to fade in her memory now. That was how Mamma had looked as she walked with him in the garden that day. Where was he now? Fighting the Italian army somewhere? Maybe it had been his shell that exploded near Carlo in the desert. She had never loved her half-brother, had never even liked him much. Carlo could be cruel, teased and pinched her, pulled her hair. But she had hated Frederick Canfield from the first moment she saw him, because she loved her mother.

* * *

Venice, 1997

At eight years old Vittoria hadn't quite understand what was going on or how she felt. Years later when she read Canfield's book *The Lily* she realised how much she had sensed without knowing it, and she hated him far more, recognising how much of the book was based on her own family and the way they lived, the society they had inhabited, self-indulgent, thoughtless, amoral to Canfield's eyes; a world that had vanished for ever, about which she, herself, felt wistfully nostalgic.

It had amazed her to discover that Nico loved the book, admired the style, the smooth, flowing prose, the descriptions of an Italy still as it had been for centuries.

A country of glorious, golden sunlight, where men lived so close to nature they were almost one, full of laughter, warmth, generosity, winding medieval streets, a land of lakes and mountains, of great art, gardens, church bells, remote villages, street cafés where small bands played and sang old folk-songs under the stars while you ate pasta and drank rough red wine. Nico had read the early part of the book, where Canfield first found Italy and fell in love with it, and excitedly told his mother she must read it. Vittoria enjoyed that part, too, until she began to recognise incidents, descriptions, characters that stripped the veils, one by one, from events in her own past that she had either forgotten or misunderstood.

She had never told Nico – he must not see his grandparents, his family, his country, through those alien eyes – so she could not explain now why she did not want a film of that book made in their own house.

She told him instead, 'My father always said he was a spy, Nico, and Papa was right. Canfield was a British agent. He lived among us, pretending to be our friend, and all the time he was betraying us. His whole book is a betrayal.'

'I thought it was a brilliant book, Mamma. It isn't hostile to Italy. What on earth makes you think it is?'

'I suppose he never . . . Nico, did Sebastian say he ever met Canfield? You mentioned that he had been planning this film for years. Canfield only died four years ago. *Did* they meet?' Her eyes were dilated, black saucers of shock. 'What did Canfield tell him that isn't in the book?'

'What are you talking about?'

'That's why he wants to make the film here! It makes sense now. Why didn't I see it? He's another Canfield, pretending to be friendly while all the time he's scheming to destroy us! But I won't let it happen! He isn't conjuring up those ghosts in my house. If he tries, I'll kill him.'

Her son was horrified by the venom in her voice. She hated Sebastian, hated him in a way that Nico found deeply disturbing. There was something unbalanced in her face, her voice. What on earth was behind all this?

Laura flew home from Venice in a flat, depressed mood. She had not won an award and she had not been able to talk to Sebastian at the ceremony, had seen him only from a distance because their tables had been miles apart. She'd had a couple of glimpses of him in evening dress, among his film crew, but with Valerie Hyde always between them, leaning forward with one elbow on the table, a bare shoulder turned, as if deliberately to block Laura's view of him.

Laura had drowned her sorrows in wine. She had drunk far too much, at first to calm her nerves, then to comfort herself because she hadn't got the award. It was odd: she'd convinced herself that she was cool, it didn't matter whether she won or lost – yet when she heard the announcement, and knew that one of the others had won, her stomach had dropped away through the floor. Shit, shit, she thought, I really wanted the damned thing, and was ashamed by the strength of her own feelings. Was it her English upbringing that made it so hard to admit she wanted anything that much? That kept telling her it was shameful and embarrassing to care whether she won or lost? That Kipling poem kept coming into her mind . . . 'Treat those two imposters just the same . . .' Win or lose, succeed or fail, you were supposed to laugh merrily. Well, she couldn't. Oh, in front of Melanie and everyone else in the world she pretended she didn't care, but she knew she did.

After all that wine, she had slept heavily last night, and in the morning when she packed she could not find Jancy. The doll had been on her bed before she went down to the award ceremony last night – she had kissed her for good luck before she left her room.

Laura had searched her room, and the bathroom, had rung for the floor housekeeper and questioned the maid who had turned her bed down last night, but both women had denied any knowledge of the doll. Miserably, Laura had had to leave for the airport without finding Jancy, and Melanie had not been sympathetic.

'It's only a doll, for heaven's sake! You can buy another one back in London – and much prettier than that one was too. Look, tell you what, I'll buy you one myself. How's that?'

'Jancy wasn't just a doll.'

'No, of course, she was magic – she could nod her head. I'd forgotten. Grow up!'

Afraid she might burst into tears, Laura dropped the subject. Thank God none of the *paparazzi* had recognised her as she and Melanie walked through the airport. She'd put on dark glasses, not to disguise herself from fans, this time, but to hide her red eyes, the bruise-like shadows under them. She had looked into the mirror before she left the hotel, groaning. She looked like shit. Looked the way she felt: dull, let-down, empty, close to tears.

What on earth could have happened to Jancy? Someone must have stolen her. But why would anyone want a shabby, much-handled doll? Jancy wasn't an antique – twenty years isn't old for a doll – and she hadn't been made by a famous company, nor had she been expensive when she was new.

Laura felt too sick to eat. She refused the food the stewardess brought, just took the orange juice, which at least was drinkable, and black coffee, which she hoped might wake her up.

She would probably never see Jancy again ... unless ... could Sebastian have taken her, as a tease? He must have seen Jancy the other night, when he left her room before she woke up, and he had known all about her doll anyway. Jancy always came to work with her. If Sebastian had taken her, she could be sure of seeing Jancy again ...

Maybe he would use the doll as an excuse to visit her flat in London to give her back. He'd said he would send her that script – but had he been serious about offering her this part? Yesterday Melanie had talked excitedly about the offers they might get if she won the award. Her value would go up instantly and directors would start clamouring for her – but would anybody want her now that she had lost? Would Sebastian? Once she started on that gloomy, downward path she couldn't stop.

'You're very quiet. What's bugging you?' Melanie asked, drinking free Italian wine as if it was water. She turned to yell at the stewardess, 'Hey, can I have another little bottle of this stuff? It isn't bad.'

Already several rows away, with her clinking, rickety cart, the woman smiled tightly and came back with one. Melanie always made sure she got her money's worth on a flight, just as she had filled her suitcase with every freebie from her own and Laura's bathrooms, the shampoos, shower gels, body lotion, plastic shower caps and tiny bottles of mouthwash. It was a wonder she had had space to pack all the presents she had bought, and the food and clothes. Her case must be as heavy as lead.

'I was thinking, Mel. As I didn't get that award, maybe Sebastian won't want me for his film.'

Melanie had that cynical look she wore when she was talking business. 'If he ever gets the money together we'll hear from him, and if we don't, well, there are other directors. You are going to be a big star, I'm certain of that, with or without Sebastian Ferrese.'

Taking a long swig at the red wine in her plastic glass, Melanie's eyes gleamed with wicked amusement. 'And he didn't win, either, did he? The great Sebastian Ferrese got beaten by an old guy for what is probably going to be his last film. I bet that hurt.'

'Everyone knows it was a sympathy vote, the poor man's dying of cancer, after all, and he's made some great films in the past. I've seen all of them and he was a genius. I don't suppose Sebastian will grudge him a last triumph.'

Mel showed her teeth in a sardonic grin. 'Sweetie, nobody likes losing, even to an old man dying of cancer.'

'But Sebastian's half his age, he has plenty of time to win awards, and I'm sure he will. He's a great director, too. I learnt a hell of a lot from him.'

'I bet you did,' Melanie muttered, hailing the stewardess again to ask for a brandy.

Laura flushed angrily, but didn't snap back, tried to be calm and reasonable. 'You said yourself it would be good for my career to work with him on this film. I'm going to read *The Lily* again.'

'You're only taking the part if he comes up with a serious offer. However good the script is, he has to pay our price this time. You're no beginner now so he isn't getting you for peanuts.'

Laura didn't argue but her face set obstinately. If Sebastian offered her that part she was going to take it, whatever Melanie said, in spite of her reservations about him, about the threats in the notes pushed under her door.

All of that weighed nothing in the scales against the heart-stopping prospect of working with Sebastian. He got the best out of everyone on a film – even if you didn't get paid at all it would be worth doing, just for the sake of what you learnt about your craft.

A little voice in her head added, 'You mean you can't wait to sleep with him again!'

Her lips clamped together. No. She knew now that she was as weak as water where he was concerned but she wouldn't let him seduce her again. He wouldn't get the chance to catch her alone, for one thing: she would be careful and, staying at Ca' d'Angeli, he couldn't force his way into her room – he wouldn't dare risk a scene under that roof. But then her mind filled with confused and sensual images, his hands, his mouth, his knees nudging her thighs apart . . . her body as he'd forced her down on the carpet, throbbing with desire for him, burning inside, needing the rhythmic massage of his hard flesh to soothe that terrible yearning.

Even if he did get in touch, send the script, make a deal with Mel, how long would it be before they began filming? She knew how interminable these negotiations could be. It might be months, years, before they shot a scene. So much could go wrong – and probably would, with her luck.

The script might have to be rewritten, Sebastian might have to wait to get the right people. There were sound stages to book, sets to design, props to collect, other locations to choose – she was sure the hero of the book had travelled around Italy during the 1920s and 1930s, had been in Rome at one time, Milan at another, always on the move from job to job. And even if all that could be worked out, the money might be a problem. Backers were notorious for changing their minds, pulling out of a film, sometimes for other projects they thought less risky, sometimes because they didn't like the director's intentions.

The stewardess took away their trays and Melanie yawned. Suddenly she pointed over the shoulder of a man sitting in front of them. She strained forward to a newspaper he held open. He became aware of this and looked round, irritated.

'If you want it, take it!' He thrust it into Melanie's hands and opened another the stewards had given him when they had boarded the plane.

'Thanks,' Melanie said, unruffled by his tone, and spread the paper on her lap. Laura glanced at it curiously, then gasped as she recognised the photograph at the top of the page – of herself and Sebastian in the hotel lobby the day she and Melanie had arrived in Venice.

'What do they say?'

'The usual innuendo,' Mel muttered, closing the paper. 'Don't bother to read it. It will only upset you.'

'About Clea?' What else? That was all that interested them, wasn't it? Rumours of sex, violence, drugs, murder – what else did they have to fill their newspapers? They knew what the public wanted.

'Ssh,' Melanie hissed, keeping her voice low so that none of the other passengers could hear her. 'Of course. Don't worry, it's only the same old stories. They just about stay within the law of libel. The only new one is about you and Sebastian meeting up in Venice. It's given them a chance to speculate about whether or not you're going to make a film together, and if you do, will the affair be on again?'

'We hadn't seen each other for years!'

'What do they care? It makes good copy, sells papers.'

Laura turned her head away. Clea had been dead for three years but the press kept writing about how she had died, rehashing old gossip. Why couldn't they let her rest in peace?

Hypocrite! You don't want peace for Clea, she thought bleakly, you want it for yourself. And you want Clea's husband for yourself, too.

London, 1997

Two weeks later a parcel arrived at Laura's London flat. It was not very heavy, wrapped in brown paper, stamped with a London postmark.

Laura's heart lurched with excitement. The script at last! She had been looking out for it ever since she got back from

Venice. She tore off the brown paper and found a cardboard shoe-box. She took off the lid and peered inside, then made a high-pitched, keening noise.

It was Jancy, come back to her. Jancy, with her face smashed in, one bright blue glassy eye dangling on a spring, her nose a jagged crater, her pink rosebud mouth deliberately beaten down inside her head.

Her blue dress had been ripped down the front, her underclothes torn and dirty, as if she was a rape victim.

Pinned to her chest was another of those notes, printed in capitals.

YOU'RE NEXT.

Chapter Seven

Within a week Sebastian had sent the script of *The Lily*; Laura found it heavy-going, too static, wordy, scenes telegraphed too far in advance, as though the writer believed the audience couldn't follow the storyline without heavy hints about what was coming. One night he rang to ask what she thought.

Laura was truthful. 'I'm sorry, but it stinks. It's more like chunks from the book than a film script.'

'Yes.' He groaned. 'I know. The trouble is, the book's so long, so much happens over more than twenty years, and if we leave half of it out the audience will miss the nuances – and all the really important stuff goes on inside the heads of the characters.'

'You need a narrator.'

'That's an alternative, but first I need a new writer. Each script I get is an improvement, believe it or not. You should have seen the one I did myself. The sets are finished now – all the pre-production stuff is going like a dream. I just can't get the script right.' He laughed. 'So what's new? Story of my life.'

'How are you going to get a unit base anywhere near Ca' d'Angeli?' She had been wondering about that ever since he first broached the idea of using the palazzo. All the ancillary services would need to be set up near the location – catering, the master production computer, somewhere for everyone to meet and talk about work, the wardrobe, makeup, not to mention all the electrical capacity for cables, lighting, cameras.

'We've managed to hire an old warehouse not too far away, which should take care of the heavy stuff, and we're renting a house behind Ca' d'Angeli, to take Wardrobe and Makeup.'

'When do you plan to start shooting?' She hadn't yet allowed herself to believe this film was going to happen.

'The early location work ought to be done in February, during the Venice Carnival – that's the atmosphere I want. To re-create it for the film would cost a fortune in extras and costumes. I'll set up cameras in the streets and just shoot what goes past – free and spontaneous action, as unpredictable as life itself, can't be beaten.'

'Won't it be cold in February?'

'Very. And wet.'

'Cameras always seem to seize up in really cold weather. They're more delicate than human beings.'

He laughed. 'True, but Sidney has a few tricks up his sleeve to cope with that. We'll have to live with it.' A pause, then he asked her, 'How are you?'

'Okay.' She took a deep breath, then plunged. 'Although I miss Jancy.'

'Who the hell is Jancy?' His voice grew rough, as if he was angry. Or was it guilt?

'You know. My doll.'

'Doll?' he echoed, his tone changing. 'Oh, I thought this was some guy you were talking about. My God, that doll! I remember it. You've had it for years, haven't you? What do you mean, you miss her? Have you lost her?'

'In Venice.' She could not believe him capable of the violence, the viciousness, that had destroyed Jancy.

'Have you rung the hotel? They may have her in their lost-property box.'

'I don't need to. Somebody sent her back to me – with her face smashed in.'

She heard his sharp intake of breath. 'Christ.' There was a long silence, then he asked, 'Was there a postmark? Was the parcel sent from Venice?'

'No, from here, London. And whoever sent it knew my address, which isn't common knowledge, is it?'

His voice was deep and harsh. 'That's worrying, Laura. Have you told the police?'

'What? That somebody stole my doll and battered its head to pieces? It's hardly a hanging offence, is it?' It can't have been him, she thought. He isn't an actor, he sounds genuinely worried. 'There was a note pinned on her, Sebastian. Now, *that* was scary.'

'What did it say?'

She told him.

'Tell the police, Laura. *You must.* And tell them about the notes you got in Venice, too. These days, you hear so much about stalking – that's what this could be, some lunatic fixated on you in a very dangerous way. Tell the police at once and get some protection.'

'I doubt they'd have time to give me a police guard night and day.'

'Promise you'll at least talk to them about this. I wish I could be around to keep an eye on you, but I'm off to South America early tomorrow morning to do some retakes.'

'You're still working on that film?'

'You know how it is – it isn't over till it's over. I guess I rushed it, to get to Venice and see you.'

Her breath caught.

He went on, 'Well, I still have to pack. You must ring the police, Laura. You could be in danger. Promise me you'll do it?'

'Yes, I will. Take care, Sebastian, have a good flight.'

When he had rung off she stood for some time with her hand on the phone, trying to nerve herself to ring the police, but what was the point? They would listen politely, pretend to take her seriously, but until whoever had smashed Jancy came back to do the same to her there was nothing they could do.

A shiver ran down her spine. From now on she was going to keep looking over her shoulder, wondering who was behind her, what might suddenly spring out of the dark. She looked out of the window but the street below her flat was empty, except for parked cars; nothing was moving in the shadows or the yellow circles of light around each lamp-post. Not even a cat, although you often saw them walking along walls or sleeping on window-sills in the morning sunshine.

How many people did she know in this street? One or two neighbours in other flats whom she greeted when they got into the lift or when she was collecting post from the boxes downstairs. This was the anonymous London of small flats and single people, who led quiet, dull lives, ate out at local restaurants, perhaps, but shopped in supermarkets near their work, in their lunch-hour, not in any of the corner-shops near here unless they ran out of something. Faces changed frequently: you saw them for a few months then one day you realised you hadn't seen them for a year.

She had never grown used to living in London – she still missed the quiet, windy green hills below Hadrian's Wall – but she couldn't go home. She was working on a three-part TV thriller throughout the autumn, too busy most of the time to be able to think about anything but work. Up at dawn on cold rainy mornings, collected by the taxi company the TV people used, and coming home the same way at night, too tired to do anything much. She always had a long hot bath, a light supper in bed watching TV, before reading through her script for the next day's shooting. By ten every night her light was out and she was asleep.

Sebastian was busy all that time, cutting and rearranging scenes from his last film, but he still managed to stay on the tail of

Jack Novotni, the scriptwriter he had hired to do a better job on *The Lily*. Jack had read the book several times when it first came out, and was enthusiastic about it, which was a plus. His experience and razor-sharp mind were what Sebastian needed. Jack wouldn't hesitate to junk everything that wasn't essential, cut down major scenes to make the film move faster, or even leave them out altogether. He wouldn't let himself get bogged down in overlong dialogue. Respect for a text could go too far and film worked visually: what you saw mattered more than what you heard. In some ways, Sebastian hankered for silent film: words could get in the way.

In between editing sessions, he and Valerie worked on the plans for the Venice February shoot, which was coming uncomfortably closer as the year rushed onwards. He relied on her to do much of the booking and researching in Venice: she never let him down, her mind clear, cool and uncluttered. He had only to give her an instruction then leave her to fulfil it.

Late one night he leant back in his chair, yawning, and said, 'Let's stop, shall we? That seems enough. Thank God I'm almost at the end of editing. Tomorrow can you ring Jack and see how the script for *The Lily* is coming along?'

'Oh, I spoke to him today. He says he'll be finished by the end of the month.'

Sebastian's tired face lit up. 'That's great. I can start work on that once I've finished here.'

'You need a holiday,' scolded Valerie, watching him with those intense dark eyes.

'I'm fine. Being busy's good for me.'

'Huh!' She snorted.

He looked at his watch. 'Time for some sleep now or I'll never have enough energy tomorrow.'

'Have you read those notes yet?' she asked, as he got up, stretching.

'Notes?' He looked blank.

'On your mother's death.'

'Oh, that. Yes, I read them. You did a good job, but in the end what do we really know for sure? It could be suspicious, or it could just be incompetence on the part of the police, but it all happened too long ago. The trail's cold.'

Carefully, Valerie said, 'I think the trail ends in Ca' d'Angeli, don't you? After all, it wasn't just your mother who died in that accident, it was the Count, too. Surely it's more likely that he was the target, if it was an assassination. Who would want to murder a housekeeper?'

'Why would anyone want to kill either of them?'

'I suppose he wasn't involved in the Mafia?'

Sebastian rubbed a hand through his tousled hair. 'Poor old Mafia – they get blamed for everything that happens in Italy. No, the idea's ludicrous. The family are wealthy and influential, with hundreds of years of history behind them. Why would they get involved in anything criminal? It must have been a simple accident. The police would have looked deeper if they had suspected murder.'

'So you don't want me to hire a private detective to sniff around some more?'

He hesitated. 'Wait until we're in Venice in February. I'll let you know what I decide. God, I'm tired, I must get some sleep.'

She walked with him to his car. 'Would you like me to drive you home? You're in no state to drive yourself.'

'I'm perfectly sober.'

'But exhausted. That can be just as deadly.'

He felt the weight of her concern, her caring, and sighed. 'I'll be fine. Goodnight, Valerie.'

She watched him drive away, and he felt those dark eyes burning through his skull. One day he would have to do something about her. She was his right hand, he needed her, but she knew too much about him and never took her eyes off him day and night. He had to get rid of her. The question was: when and how?

* * *

It wasn't until the start of December, after Laura had finished work on the thriller, that Sebastian sent her a new version of the script. She recognised the name on the front, that of a screen-writer with a high reputation, who commanded equally high fees. He was worth his money: the script was now faster, clearer, with shorter scenes and half the dialogue; a cinematic script that let the camera do a lot more of the work, and Sebastian had taken up her suggestion of a narrator, which gave the script an added depth, an elegiac feel that echoed the original book.

Two weeks later Sebastian rang her. The sound of his voice on the line made her heart turn over, but if hers affected him he didn't show it.

'Hi, Sebastian here,' he said tersely. 'Get the script?'

'Yes—'

'Read it? What did you think?'

'It's brilliant! What a difference! He's terrific, Jack Novotni. I was riveted all the way through.'

Sebastian came in again before she had finished speaking, the way people do when they're phoning from the other side of the world, an echo behind them.

'He was the first writer I approached but he was too busy with other projects. Luckily, one fell through and he suddenly had a few weeks free so I snapped him up at once. I think he did a marvellous job, too. So, will you play Bianca?'

'Yes—' she began, and was interrupted again, before she could hedge her agreement with the proviso that he had to talk to Melanie first.

'Good. This film is going to be important – for both of us.' A pause, then he asked, 'What are you doing over Christmas?'

'What I always do. I'm going home. We always have a big family Christmas. What are you doing?'

'Working, I'm busy editing at the moment – this film's a

pig to cut. I'll probably have a nice quiet Christmas Day here, in my beach-house. A California Christmas, very different from yours.' Then he said, 'But the really good news is that I've got the money and we're all set. I'll be talking to that agent of yours tomorrow.'

Within a week, Melanie had had a meeting with the contract manager of Sebastian's film company, who flew to London to talk to her and hammer out an agreement. Laura signed in early January, and was told that she would be needed in Venice within five weeks.

'So soon?' She was startled: that gave her a such a short time to get used to the idea of working with Sebastian again.

'Apparently, all the pre-prod stuff is done, they're ready to go. They're shooting some key scenes during the Venice Carnival, and they have to have you there.'

'And after that?'

'The entire crew moves back to Los Angeles to finish the picture in the studio.' Melanie shivered dramatically. 'Brrr! Venice in February – Don't ask me to come this time. You'll need lots of warm clothes, and don't forget your wellies! St Mark's Square will be under water, even if it isn't snowing. It's amazing the place hasn't sunk altogether.'

Venice, 1998

The snow started during the first week of February, a few days before the film crew were due to arrive. The Contessa stood at the high windows of Ca' d'Angeli, watching great white flakes blowing past in the keening wind, dancing in the air, blinding her so that she could not see the snow-encrusted roofs on the other side of the Grand Canal.

It was so cold that she was wearing a woollen vest under her black dress and two thick cardigans over it. They still used open fires to heat the great, barn-like rooms because they'd been advised that central heating could cause serious damage: it would dry out the medieval wood, opening great fissures, and might make the marble crack.

In weather like this the only way she could keep warm in the evenings was to sit hunched over the fire with a rug over her knees. During daylight hours she kept busy, and there was always plenty to do, especially since Nico had insisted on letting Ca' d'Angeli to Sebastian.

The Contessa and the servants had been hard at work from morning to night getting the house ready for the invasion. They were leaving the tapestries and furniture in place since Sebastian wanted the atmosphere of the palazzo to be intact during the filming, but everything breakable or particularly valuable had been hidden away upstairs in locked rooms or in a bank vault. The Contessa saw no reason why she should risk having one of her beloved possessions broken or stolen, however much the film company were paying and however good the insurance. Money would not compensate her for the loss of something she loved.

Most of the film people were staying in small hotels nearby, but Nico had invited Sebastian and Laura Erskine to stay with them, which was something else that was preying on the Contessa's mind.

She was his mistress, obviously: the whole world believed it. Would they do it under her roof, in the bedroom Nico had picked out for the girl, overriding all protests, all pleas?

No, no, she must have that room, the best in the palazzo, the master bedroom, Nico had said. That red hair of hers would burn like a forest fire among the green and gold of the bed-hangings, the tapestries, the floor-length curtains.

The Contessa ground her teeth, a jagged, icy pain inside her, a pain that had been with her for many years. Was the anguish and humiliation never to end?

It had been her husband's bedroom – but she had never shared it. She had been given another room, on the floor above. After Domenico died, she had moved into his room but after one freezing, sleepless night in it she had fled back to her own room and never tried to sleep in his again.

Outside the window, the wind howled like a wolf – if her own sense of dignity were not so great she would have howled, too. The patterns of her life kept on repeating, as if time was a record stuck on one note, shrieking it over and over again.

She was so cold: her breath froze on the air in front of her. Draughts blew under the heavy wooden doors, down the long, endless corridors, bringing her memories of other, even colder, lonelier winters.

Venice, 1942

The winter of 1942 had been terrible, not so much because of the weather as because they had little food or fuel to make it bearable. The Italian army was defeated in the battle of El Alamein, and people in the streets wept openly, for their sons, their brothers, and themselves. Grief was hard enough to bear, but hunger made it worse, especially when they were always cold. People burned anything they could find: trees, shrubs, driftwood, old shoes, the wood from attic floors, books. Beds were piled with coats, and to save fuel everyone retired early, kept warm like moles, by tunnelling through the bedclothes with shutters closed over the windows.

Carlo slept downstairs so that he could be wheeled out of his bedroom to the kitchen, where he insisted now on working, preparing vegetables, cooking, washing up.

By then they had only one servant, who had stayed on because she was too old to get work anywhere else. Leo Serrati had been furious when Carlo first suggested that he worked in the kitchen.

'My son will not be a servant in my own house.'

'At least that way I can be useful.'

'If you want to be useful, come and work in the factory for me.'

Carlo's face took on that grim, mutinous look, which signalled one of his angry moods. 'And have them all staring at me and whispering behind my back? You know how men despise cripples. They wouldn't respect me – and they wouldn't take orders from a man in a wheelchair.' He stared at his father. 'Would you, Papa?'

Leo went red and walked away without another word.

Carlo began work the next day. At first he was clumsy, kept breaking things, but slowly he got used to it, and soon he could be heard all over the house, singing Italian opera as he cooked.

Just before Christmas that year Anna collapsed with pneumonia and overwork. She was kept in hospital for several weeks, then sent home with orders to stay in bed until she was completely recovered.

The only servant they had left, old Agnese, nursed her, but had no time to do much else. Carlo couldn't cope with a lively child as well as the other household jobs he was now doing, so it was decided to send Vittoria to Venice to stay with her mother's aunt, an old woman of seventy who lived in a small house in the maze of streets behind San Marco.

'I don't want to go away! I want to stay at home with Mamma,' Vittoria sobbed.

Carlo patted her heaving shoulders roughly. 'We all have to put up with the way things are. Mamma is sick, she needs a rest. Be a brave girl and stop crying. Tears do no good. When Mamma's better, we'll send for you.'

The journey by train was long and frightening. Vittoria travelled with a neighbour, Signora Rossi, who was visiting her daughter whose husband had just been killed in North Africa, leaving her with two children and another on the way. They had to be up at dawn and the station platform was packed with people. The train was hours late, and when it finally set off it jerked and dawdled through the countryside, the compartments crowded with soldiers and sailors, who drank cheap wine from bottles they passed around, laughing, shouting, growing ever noisier the more they drank. Signora Rossi became tight-lipped and angry. Even the corridors were full of people standing up, crammed together like sardines.

Vittoria was crushed into a corner of a compartment beside Signora Rossi, who had achieved a seat by pulling a young man out of it, glaring ferociously at the other people, daring them to say anything. At intervals she fed Vittoria furtive titbits of unappetising food produced from a large carpet bag while the other passengers watched hungrily.

'Like seagulls at a picnic,' muttered Signora Rossi, in Vittoria's ear. Vittoria was too unhappy to eat, especially under those fixed, ravenous stares. If the other people had been seagulls she would have thrown her food to them just to get rid of it and stop them watching her. But she was afraid of Signora Rossi.

When, at last, the train drew into the nineteenth-century railway station of Santa Lucia, it was dark. They could see nothing of Venice but the outline of a huddle of roofs pierced here and there with spires.

Vittoria's name had been pinned to her coat, printed on a luggage label, but Signora Rossi felt she had to stay with her. She danced from one foot to the other, eager to go to her daughter, yet duty-bound to look after the child. The noisy, echoing railway terminal filled and emptied with people as trains arrived and left, while the Signora impatiently watched the clock over their heads.

At last a young girl ran towards them, panting, red, out of breath, staring at Vittoria and trying to read her label. 'Are you the little girl? From Milan? Oh, thank heavens – I thought I might have missed you, and then the Signora would have killed me.' She looked apologetically at Signora Rossi. 'I'm sorry, I left in good time but I didn't know the way and kept taking wrong turnings.'

'Have you some proof that you have come from the little

girl's family?' demanded Signora Rossi, still holding Vittoria's shoulder as if expecting to have to fight for her.

The girl pulled a large card out of her coat pocket, with Vittoria's name printed on it. 'I'm Rosa Bonacci. I work for Signora Bari – she sent me, she's very old, you know. She lives just off the Frezzeria and she cannot walk this far.'

Signora Rossi bent down and kissed Vittoria. 'Be good, do whatever your aunt tells you. I'm sure you will soon see your mother.'

As she was taken away Vittoria began to cry silently, with Rosa clutching her hand tightly to make sure she didn't get lost.

'Don't cry, *la Signora* is very kind and I'll look after you. But don't cry, because we have to hurry, to get in before the curfew.' Rosa squeezed her hand comfortingly, but Vittoria went on crying. She was so tired she could scarcely walk, her head ached, she wanted her mother, and her own home. She was afraid she would never see either of them again.

An hour later, after a bowl of hot onion soup and a chunk of new-made bread, she was tucked up in a narrow little bed, with a heavy old quilt piled over her, Her stomach full, her body warm, sheer weariness made sure she slept soundly all night.

Next morning she had her first, dazzling glimpse of Venice by winter sunlight when Rosa took her out to a street-market to buy whatever they could find.

Carlo had told Vittoria that Venice was a city of water and reflections, of canals instead of roads, of ancient houses and churches, a magic city, she would love it – but how could she have imagined what she saw that first time? Silvery herring skies, slate-blue roofs, crumbling, fading pink brick, a watery sun mirrored in the winding canals, the forest of black poles at which gondolas were tied up, bobbing on the water. Vittoria remembered the fairy story her mother had often read her: she felt like the little girl who was flung into a well and came out in another country down below the water, a country so beautiful she wanted to stay there for ever.

While Rosa bought onions, cheese and oranges, Vittoria wandered around the square in which the market had sprung up overnight: green-canvas-topped stalls with green baize under the fruit and vegetables. She paused to stare at heaps of nuts on one stall and tears came into her eyes. To her nuts meant Christmas, and Christmas meant home – and Mamma.

Sobbing, she turned away, only to freeze in shock at the sight of grey German uniforms. Two soldiers in peaked caps, guns on their hips, were strolling across the square, pausing now and then to eye the market produce. They bought lemons and oranges, a bottle of wine, and walked off laughing, their German voices making everyone turn to stare.

Vittoria ran back to Rosa, tugged at her skirt, pointing. 'Rosa, look! German soldiers!'

Rosa was calm. 'Don't be scared. They come here for a holiday. We aren't at war with them, you know. And they have lots of money. Now that the English and the Americans can't come we need German money more than ever.'

Aunt Maria was a quiet, gentle old woman, with thin, fine white hair, plaited on top of her head; her eyes were pale and dreamy, her brown skin wrinkled, weatherbeaten. 'You will be safe here, child,' she promised. 'We had a bad time in the First World War – we were bombed then, and they sent the horses away to Rome—'

'The horses?'

'The four bronze horses of St Mark – you'll see them above the central doorway of the cathedral but they're not the originals. Those are safely hidden away inside.'

'We stole them,' said Rosa gleefully.

Vittoria stared at her. 'What do you mean?'

Her aunt intervened. 'Rosa means we seized them from Constantinople, centuries ago. That wasn't stealing, the horses were prizes of war. But in this war I'm sure we'll be safe. They've put up air-raid shelters everywhere, just in case …'

'They look like little hats, all over St Mark's Square,' Rosa said.

'But they will never be needed,' Aunt Maria insisted. 'After all, we aren't a military target. Venice is too precious to be attacked.'

Vittoria's life soon settled down into a busy, comfortable routine. Every morning Rosa got her up, gave her breakfast, of whatever they had, then walked her to the convent school a few streets away. Later, and for the first couple of months Rosa met her and walked her home but after that Vittoria was allowed to make her own way back.

They lived in a dark, narrow little street off the Frezzeria, a street that took its name from the *freccie,* the arrows, that had once been sold there in the Middle Ages.

Vittoria loved to wander at her leisure on her way home, gazing into the shops, breathing in the smell of herbs and spices from one, salty fish from another, new-baked bread from the next. Even in Venice, food was rationed, but people here seemed to eat better than they had in Milan since the war began. There was always plenty of sea-food: crabs and clams, squid, prawns, mussels, as well as every type of fish that swam in the sea beyond the lagoon. They ate plenty of game, too: hare, rabbit and wild birds from the marshes. Aunt Maria had taught Rosa to cook and expected Vittoria to eat whatever was put before her.

'Hunger is the best sauce,' she said, if Vittoria tried to refuse anything. 'Think of our soldiers, dying for you. They would give anything for a plate of this squid in tomato and clam sauce.'

But Vittoria could not force down the squid. It tasted like scraps of the boots she wore on rainy days when the tide sloshed over from the canal and ran through the streets.

She quickly made friends at school – Gina, the daughter of a grocer who lived a few houses away, and Olivia, whose family lived in a great house on the Grand Canal to which Vittoria and Gina were never invited.

The girls dawdled on their way home, sometimes visited Gina's family in their dark little apartment above the shop. Gina was two years older than Vittoria, and far more sophisticated. She was already a beauty, having inherited red hair and fine, pale skin from her mother, a Florentine who had once been head parlour-maid in a big, aristocratic house.

Signora Cavani doted on her only child and spent hours curling Gina's hair, making her pretty clothes, showing her how to walk and sit down gracefully, sew neat, straight stitches and, most important of all, she said, how to speak Italian with the right accent. 'We are not peasants!' Signora Cavani would say. 'We're not like these shop-keepers, even if we live among them. You must keep up your standards, Gina. Act like a lady and people will treat you like one.'

Vittoria observed that Signora Cavani lived by the standards she preached: she treated Olivia with flattering warmth because Olivia came from an old-established Venetian family, but towards Vittoria she was coldly offhand, hostile. All that changed when she discovered that Vittoria's family, although undoubtedly in trade, was also very wealthy.

Sometimes the girls went back to Aunt Maria's house, where Rosa fed them dried figs and hot rolls, with some of their precious home-made black cherry jam, and told them ghost stories or sang them the latest songs.

At first, Vittoria thought the tall, thin terraced house was poky and gloomy: the rooms were much smaller than those in her own home, the furniture old and shabby. The ancient wooden stairs creaked, as did the floorboards, even when nobody walked across them.

At night, lying in bed, she felt as if she was in a very old ship: even if there was no wind the house lurched and cracked around her. And mice lived under the floorboards and the eaves, their pattering feet seeming very loud: they stole crumbs from the kitchen and ate into vegetables in the wooden rack. The noise made her nervous – perhaps they would climb on to her bed and run over her face while she was asleep – but she didn't tell Rosa or Aunt Maria in case they set one of the traps kept in the kitchen, fearsome-looking objects that would cut a little mouse in half with a sharp snap, Rosa said.

Bats flapped about in the roof space making a noise like a wet fish in the bottom of one of the fishing-boats she watched unloading, down on the fish harbour. On summer nights they streamed out of the eaves like black smoke, and vanished into Venice to feed on the insects swarming above the oily waters of the canals. Olivia was scared that one would get caught in her hair, or bite her and suck her blood, like one of the vampire stories Rosa had told her. Rosa knew a thousand folk-tales, and believed implicitly in ghosts, vampires and goblins. On dark winter nights, Vittoria found it easy to believe in them, too.

At first, Vittoria expected every day to hear from her parents, and letters did get through now and then from her mother, with news of the family. That was how, in 1943, she heard that Filippo had run away to join the partisans, who had begun to gather in the mountains, refusing to fight for Mussolini, occasionally making sorties to attack convoys driving through the valleys. 'Communists!' everyone at school said. 'If they're caught they're shot without a trial.' The nuns were fiercely opposed to Communism, and were always talking about the horrors inflicted on priests and nuns during the Spanish Civil War by Communist forces. Nuns had been raped, priests tortured, then killed, their churches burned to the ground.

Vittoria hated the thought of Filippo being shot: she was fond of him, he could be fun – although Nico was her favourite brother, the one closest to her in age. It didn't seem real, though. She couldn't believe it could happen – people of her age didn't get killed.

Her mother's letter was hard to read, it was so scrawled and blotchy, as if she had cried as she wrote it. Vittoria had to work it out line by line before she understood it all.

> He is so young, I am terrified he will be killed. Of course, your papa calls him a traitor, says he'll never forgive him. People blame us, although what we could have done to stop him I don't know. These boys have their heads filled with wicked Communist talk at school. Carlo is very angry, too. He says if he sees Filippo again he will shoot him, but I don't think either Papa or Carlo mean it, they are just afraid of what could happen to him, and all of us. These are bad times, my darling. Be good and do whatever Aunt Maria tells you. It is so kind of her to take you in and look after you. We miss you but you must stay there. At least I know you are safe.

Vittoria knew then that nobody would come to take her home: she was going to have to stay with Aunt Maria for the rest of the war. How long would that be? It seemed to have been going on for ever – she could barely remember a time when they had not been fighting.

As she grew older she began to understand more of what was happening in her country, how the war was going. News was talked about openly in Venice, in the cafés, streets and squares. It was at her little school that Vittoria first heard that some cities were being bombed by the British, whom newspapers described as barbarous war-mongers who had forced Italy into a war she did not want.

Aunt Maria read the newspaper aloud over dinner each evening, her voice quavering. If Italy lost the war, they were constantly warned, the British and the Americans would force Italians to work for them, they would become slaves. The Allies would burn down their factories, seize all their food, steal all their art treasures, shut the schools and universities, kill all the men and rape all the women, including the children.

The newspaper Mussolini had founded, the *Popolo d'Italia*, went further: it wrote that if Britain won the war the Italian people would be ruthlessly exterminated.

Looking up, Aunt Maria would say, 'But I've known so many English. They came to Venice all the time in the old days. Such kind, such charming people – I cannot believe they would be so cruel and wicked.'

Vittoria remembered Frederick Canfield and was silent. The English could be treacherous: she knew that from her own experience.

By mid-1943 the rumours swelled as the tide of war turned against the Fascist forces. Il Duce was seriously ill, might be dying; the demoralised Italian army joined the partisans in the hills. There were worrying rumours that the Germans were poised to invade, but it was the Anglo-American force that arrived first, from North Africa, on the island of Pantelleria, which Mussolini had believed impregnable.

By July the Allies were moving rapidly up Italy. 'They won't come here, they wouldn't destroy Venice – the English love Venice as much as we do,' Aunt Maria said, her stiff, gnarled fingers fumbling with her old ivory rosary, whose beads were worn, yellow with age and use. She lapsed into prayer, which sounded to Vittoria more desperate than confident.

Not long after that news that Mussolini had been arrested spread like wildfire. A sense of wild relief and hope filled everyone. Fascism had collapsed. Surely now they could get back to normal and end this war.

Within days of that the Allies bombed Rome. The Holy City, was burning, street by street, and waves of panic swept through the country. Aunt Maria spent hours on her knees in prayer: all the churches in Venice were crowded with terrified people whose murmured prayers swelled to a sound like groaning. Some wept, others were white and silent, staring at the altar, at the statues of Our Blessed Lady and the saints, as if hoping for a miracle that never came.

Vittoria never forgot those days: it was like living through the end of the world. Every night you went to bed not sure that you would be alive in the morning, and every morning began with fresh news of disaster and death.

On 3 August the Allies bombed Milan. Thousands of civilians were killed in their own homes. From miles away, people could see the houses burning and crashing to the ground. Even the statues on the cathedral were blown to smithereens and La Scala was half destroyed.

Vittoria heard the news at school. Reverend Mother came to her classroom, her rosary clinking in agitation and sympathy. 'They have bombed Milan,' she told the class, but looked at Vittoria, who was blanched with terror at her desk. 'Vittoria, you may go home now, and be brave, whatever the news. We will pray for your family, child, that God has been merciful and they are all safe.'

As Vittoria made her way shakily to the door, Olivia and Gina put out their hands to touch hers. 'I'm sure they'll be safe,' Olivia whispered.

Gina said, 'I'll pray for you, Vittoria.'

She ran home so fast that she tripped on the way and hit her cheek on the edge of a pavement, arriving home with blood running from the cut. Her head beat with terrifying questions: what had happened to her mother and father, to Nico, to Carlo, to their home? Rosa met her at the door, swathed in a white apron far too big for her, flour on her nose and on her hands.

'You poor little mite,' she said, hugging Vittoria.

Vittoria burst out, 'What have you heard? Are they dead?'

Rosa looked horrified. 'Don't say that! It's bad luck to say things like that out loud. We don't know anything yet. Your aunt tried to telephone but all the lines are down in Milan.'

It was a week before Vittoria heard that her home had been destroyed. Her father had been killed outright when his factory was hit. Her mother and Carlo had survived because they had taken shelter in the cellars, from which they had emerged later, bruised and in shock – half deaf from the explosions but alive. Anna wrote a long description of the raid, told her that Papa had been buried, that she, Carlo and Niccolo were in no danger, they were living in the ruins of their house on whatever food they could get. It was even more imperative that Vittoria stay in safety in Venice.

Vittoria went back to school in black, filled with anguish and hatred. After a while, though, she realised that she was only one of many other children at the school who had lost brothers and fathers, killed on the battlefield or in the bombing raids. At first you cried, but even grief did not last long: fear was stronger, and prayers, she now knew, were useless. God was deaf, people said openly. God was dead, one or two dared say, angry and defiant, hating Him for having failed them. The churches were still full: most people prayed harder than ever – but not Vittoria. She told herself she would never pray again. God had let her father be killed.

It was at that time, wanting to comfort Vittoria, that Olivia first invited her and Gina to her home. Few people in Venice had gardens – the houses were mostly crammed together with no land between them. Vittoria had had no idea what Ca' d'Angeli looked like for nobody had warned her what to expect, but she knew it was thought one of the loveliest houses in the city and she was eager to see it. They walked the long way round, through dark, narrow alleys and quiet, dusty, sunny squares, and entered through the rear gate into a magic kingdom of clipped box trees and gravel paths, statues of naked men and women, lemon and orange trees in huge pots, a curtain of purple wisteria over the high red-brick walls.

'We'll play out here. I'll ask someone to bring us cakes,' Olivia said, loping off to the door, her smooth black plaits bouncing on her shoulders.

'She's not going to ask us into the house. I knew she wouldn't,' whispered Gina. 'Her family wouldn't allow it, because we're not of their class. We're trade – my father's a grocer and yours sold drugs – and the d'Angeli family never mix with tradespeople. If it wasn't for the war Olivia would have been sent away to boarding school where she wouldn't meet girls like us.'

Olivia came back with a maid in a black dress and white apron, whose hair was piled up behind her head under a lacy white cap with long streamers, which fluttered as she walked. She brought them a tray of little golden cakes and glasses of home-made lemonade, which she laid out on a table beside a splashing fountain in the centre of the garden.

'Let me know if you want more lemonade, Signorina.' The maid glanced at the other two children and gave a disdainful little sniff. 'And, you two, don't touch anything! La Contessa will be very angry if you pick any of her flowers or make a mess.'

As she walked back into the house Olivia put out her tongue and the other two giggled. They each took a cake and had a glass of the lemonade, which had hardly any sugar in it and made your tongue fizz. In the shade of the lemon and orange trees the sun was not too hot, and they sat lazily, nibbling cakes, listening to the trickle of water. Then they played hide-and-seek. Vittoria hid behind a hydrangea bush, whose blue flowers reminded her of her own garden in Milan. The colour made her want to cry. Olivia soon found Gina but although they peered into every corner neither of them could see Vittoria.

'We give up! Come out, come out, wherever you are,' called Olivia, at last. 'You win.'

Vittoria appeared just as a tall boy came out of the house facing her. The sun was in her eyes the first time she saw Domenico; like a halo, his black hair framed his face, which was so beautiful she couldn't breathe, just stood and gaped at him.

'What are you up to?' he asked Olivia.

'Why are you home so early?' Olivia sounded edgy.

'It's her brother,' Gina said softly. Vittoria had not even known that Olivia had a brother but, then, she was an outsider in Venice, she knew almost nothing about its society or the old families, and Olivia had always been careful not to mention hers.

That reticence betrayed something that Vittoria only then understood: that, however friendly she might be with them, Olivia did not think of her schoolmates as existing in the same world as herself. At school she was the Olivia they knew – but what was she at home?

One thing was immediately obvious: physically, she was very like her brother, tall, slim, with the same colouring, similar features. In the boy, though, they added up to a heart-stopping, angelic beauty, while Olivia was merely striking, not pretty so much as interesting.

'How old is he?' Vittoria whispered to Gina, thinking that it was typical of Gina to know so much about Olivia's family. Signora Cavani loved to chat with anyone who came into their shop, lingered outside the church after Mass to exchange gossip with any woman she knew, read all the society pages in magazines and newspapers – avid to find out as much as possible about important Venetian families.

'Sixteen,' Gina said, without a second's hesitation. 'Mamma said the other day that, by the end of the year, he will have to join the army. He's still at school now. When he's seventeen he'll be called up like everyone else – their money doesn't save them.'

'I hate this war, I wish it would stop!' Vittoria cried, close to tears.

Olivia and her brother heard this, and broke off their half-whispered conversation to join the other two girls.

'Well, it's a pity we ever got into it, I agree,' Domenico d'Angeli said, looking down at her curiously. 'But we're in it now, and we can't get out. We just have to take what comes and pray to God that it's over soon.'

'I don't believe in God,' Vittoria said fiercely.

'Toria! That's wicked!' Olivia was very conventional, especially in her religious beliefs. The nuns had a responsive pupil for their teaching.

'God killed my father!'

The other girls fell silent. Gina's father, the grocer, was still alive, and Olivia's father, Conte Niccolo d'Angeli, had been shot on his horse in the First World War. He had limped ever since so he had not been called up. He didn't live at home, however, because he had accepted a post in Mussolini's government, first as a diplomat and then, since the war began, based in Rome, dealing with foreign affairs.

'He was in the army?' Domenico asked quietly, watching her.

'He was killed when the English bombed Milan.'

'What was he doing in Milan?'

'We live there. He ran our factory. I'll never forgive God for letting him be killed. Our home isn't there any more, either.'

'God didn't make this war,' Domenico said. 'Governments did. Men did.'

'Then men are stupid and so are governments.'

'You're very violent in your opinions,' he said, and laughed suddenly. 'But I admit I don't entirely disagree. What's your name? And what are you doing in Venice if your family live in Milan?'

'My mother sent me here to my aunt. She thought I'd be safer. My name is Vittoria Serrati.'

He frowned. 'Serrati . . . That's a familiar name, I'm sure I've heard it before.'

'Her father makes pills,' Gina said, with a sting of spite that made Vittoria flush. 'Every chemist sells them.'

'Oh, *that* Serrati. Of course!' Domenico laughed again, then did a sort of double-take. He was staring at Gina, silently taking in the way she looked: her apricot skin, huge eyes, red-gold Titian hair. The other girls watched, recognising the effect thirteen-year-old Gina always had on men. She was precocious for her age: her mother had seen to that, dressing her in the latest fashions, teaching her how to pose, look through her eyelashes, smile invitingly. Signora Cavani wanted her to marry well, catch a man with money, and Gina was already an expert fisher of men. Men of eighteen or eighty-five who passed her in the street always turned to gape after her. Schoolboys followed her, making chicken noises and whistling, and even the priest, who came to hear their confessions and teach them their catechism, flushed when Gina bent over his desk to point out something in her exercise book, her hair straying against his cheek. And she knew what she was doing. Gina was already aware of her powers.

'And you? Who are you?' asked Domenico, at last.

'My name is Gina Cavani.' She did not smile. Her oval face was clear and cool, an exquisite cameo, her lashes flickering against that warm, smooth skin.

He went on staring, saying nothing. From the house someone called, 'Domenico? Come in, you have a visitor!'

'Coming!' he shouted back. '*Ciao,* girls.' But it was at Gina that he took his last, long look before he went.

Afraid that he would become a bargaining tool in peace terms with the Allies, the Germans searched for Mussolini, but the new Italian government had moved him up into the Appenine mountains to an isolated skiing resort, which they hoped would be easy to defend. However, it did not take long for the Germans to bribe someone to betray his whereabouts.

On 12 September 1943, a commando unit made a daring landing, in a plane, right on the mountain peak and Mussolini's guards gave him up without resistance.

Then Il Duce was back in power, a puppet whose strings were now pulled by the Germans. The reprisals he took against those he felt had betrayed him were bloody and ruthless – even his own son-in-law, Ciano, was shot, and hundreds of others soon followed, many of them denounced in secret letters. Italy was disintegrating into madness.

Few letters got through now to Vittoria, but she heard whispers of what was going on. Milan was in turmoil; there were a dozen Fascist squads in the city. They competed against each other, fought over territories, ran protection rackets, burgled empty houses, looted after air-raids, arrested anyone they suspected might be anti-Fascist.

Mamma and Carlo were still living in the ruins of their home. Carlo had taken over the running of what was left of the Serrati factory – everyone needed drugs – and he survived by paying one group to protect him and his factory against all the others. Day and night armed guards were at the gates of his home and his workplace. The bombed section was left to fall down and the firm operated in the untouched sheds. Life in Milan was hell, Anna wrote to her daughter. Niccolo disappeared one day, either ran away to join Filippo in the mountains, or was abducted by Germans or one of the Fascist gangs – although if it had been the latter they would have sent a ransom demand for him, and none had come.

Olivia's brother celebrated his seventeenth birthday by going off to join his father's regiment. Within a month he had been wounded and after that he disappeared. All his mother and sister could do was hope that he was alive somewhere, in a prisoner-of-war camp or with the partisans, and one day would come home.

'Mamma says it's better that we shouldn't hear,' Olivia said. 'Not knowing if he's alive is better than knowing he's dead. At least we still have hope.'

'Of course you do,' said Gina, putting an arm round her friend's waist. 'Don't worry, Livy, he's safe, I know it. He'll be back when the war is over.'

Vittoria shivered. What would life be like when the English and the Americans came? She was afraid to think about the future.

In the spring of 1945 Vittoria's mother wrote to her aunt.

> I have just heard that Filippo was shot by the Germans in a reprisal for the partisans blowing up a train. Nico

> sent me word, a scrap of paper was pushed through the door the other night. A letter from Nico – at least he's still alive, poor child. But what sort of childhood has he had? He's still just a boy, and he has been killing men for months. I wish he would come home but he is staying up in the mountains with his group, he says they will take revenge for Filippo, and then I suppose the Germans will kill Nico, too.

Aunt Maria crossed herself. 'Those poor brave boys. Oh, this is a terrible world we live in.'

'What else does Mamma say?' Vittoria asked.

Aunt Maria continued, in her wavering voice, '"God bless you, thank you for taking care of my little girl. Kiss Vittoria for me and say that as soon as it is safe she shall come home. It makes me happier to think that she is not in as much danger as her brothers."' Aunt Maria folded the letter, sighing. 'Amen to that. We are lucky to be in Venice, Vittoria.'

Those last months of the war were an endless nightmare. The Allies swept up through Italy, with the Germans giving way in front of them and the Italian army disintegrating.

In April 1945 Mussolini was persuaded to talk to the leaders of the partisan movement about his future. The most they would offer was that he should have a fair trial. Realising he had no hope, he tried to escape, but within minutes had been stopped by the 52nd Garibaldi brigade of partisans. His fate was sealed.

There was no time for a formal trial – the Americans were only hours away. The partisans executed him and his mistress. The bodies were driven in an open truck to the Piazzale Loreto in Milan where they were strung up by the heels, and left there, upside down, like pigs in a slaughter-house, while the crowds jeered and threw things at them.

Italy fell apart. Italian fought Italian, Communist against Fascist, and in some parts of the country bodies littered the streets. But Venice was still quiet, a little oasis of peace. At last, the Germans fled back into their own country and the English and the Americans occupied Italy.

Walking home slowly from school one summer day, Vittoria heard English spoken for the first time in years. She stopped in her tracks and turned, heart pounding behind her rib-cage. A group of khaki-uniformed men were standing on a corner with a map in their hands, staring down at it.

One was Frederick Canfield. He looked different in uniform, older, thinner, tougher, but it was him. Why were they here, these English soldiers? Had they invaded Venice?

When she got home, Rosa rushed her in to see her aunt, who held out her arms. Vittoria flung herself on to her knees and clasped Aunt Maria round the waist.

'Oh, Aunt—'

'Toria, I have such news for you!'

'I know, I saw them! English soldiers have got here – what will happen to us?'

Aunt Maria pushed Vittoria back so that she could see her face. 'What are you saying? I was talking about your mother.'

Vittoria looked up at her aunt no colour in her face. 'My mother? Is she dead?'

'No, no, child, she's here. Upstairs. She was so exhausted by the journey that I sent her to bed, but you'll see her very soon. Let her sleep for a few hours.'

Vittoria looked up the dark, narrow stairs. 'Which room is she in? Can't I just go and peep at her? I won't make a sound.'

Aunt Maria brushed her dark hair back from her forehead. 'No, darling. Be patient a little while longer. Did you say you saw English soldiers? Oh, the saints have mercy on us! I wonder what that will mean for us all?'

That evening, Frederick Canfield arrived at the dark little house. Rosa almost fainted with fright as if a devil was at their door.

'Signora Serrati?'

Rosa fell back without answering. It was Vittoria who met him at the door of the tiny parlour, confronted him, chin up, eyes full of loathing. How had he found out that her mother was here?

'Toria?' he asked, incredulous. 'Is it really you? The last time I saw you, you were just a baby. You've been growing up while I've been away. But you still don't look like your mother, do you?'

His voice was so familiar, so English and cool, that she hated him even more. 'What do you want, Signor Canfield?' she asked icily.

'I have come to see your mother, Toria,' he replied.

'You can't. She is very tired. She has only just arrived from Milan.'

He gave her that languid, mocking smile she remembered so well. 'I know. I escorted her here in my Jeep. There was no other way she would have got here safely from Milan – the roads are still very dangerous and the partisans kill on sight without bothering to ask questions.'

There was a creaking on the narrow little stairs and he looked over Vittoria's head. His face lit up. 'Ah . . . Anna, there you are.'

He walked towards her, holding out his hands, and Vittoria watched bitterly as her mother took them. She saw him kiss Anna's hands, while she smiled at him, her mouth a passionate curve.

They were lovers. Vittoria knew what that meant now. She was thirteen. She knew all about what went on between a man and a woman. But, then, hadn't she known from the moment when, at only four years old, she had seen her father on the bed with her nurse and had heard the ugly noises he made? Hadn't she known when she saw this man with her mother, in the garden in Milan? Oh, then she had not fully understood what she now knew; she had only glimpsed it through a veil of uncertainly and fear.

Now she knew everything. Frederick Canfield had taken her father's place in her mother's bed. Vittoria felt sick, hating both of them. Even more, she was frightened. What could happen to her if this Englishman took her mother away with him?

Chapter Eight

'You look grisly,' Melanie said with her usual bluntness, leaning forward across their table at the Ivy to peer myopically at Laura's pallor and the shadows under her eyes. 'What's wrong? You sick?'

'I'm just a bit edgy.'

Melanie nibbled a piece of Melba toast. 'Edgy about what?'

Laura hesitated, then admitted, 'Going to Venice.' She played eyes down, toying with her glass of sparkling Malvern water, watching the ice bob and chink.

Melanie exploded, 'Why didn't you decide that before I signed the fucking contract? You can't say I forced you. In fact, I warned you not to accept that part, but you didn't listen, did you?' Half satisfied that she had been right, half irritated that Laura had come to see that too late to get out of the contract without paying a hefty cancellation fee, Melanie then asked, 'And what do you mean you're edgy? Are you scared you'll find the part difficult? Or scared of Ferrese? You don't think he's going to push you out of any windows, do you?' She laughed, but something in her face wasn't amused.

Wishing now that she had kept quiet, Laura lied, 'No, of course not, don't be ridiculous. I guess I'm just nervous about this part. It's really going to stretch me and I only hope I can pull it off.'

The waiter arrived with their first course: houmous with chick pea relish for Melanie and tomato and basil galette for Laura.

'You'll be great,' Melanie said, picking up her knife and fork, voice thickened by hunger. 'I haven't eaten a thing since yesterday lunch time, my stomach thinks my throat's cut.'

Laura hadn't eaten much for days, she rarely did, lived on salad and chicken or fish, but didn't say anything. Melanie would take it as a personal attack: when she was dieting her temper was always on a short fuse, she resented anyone who seemed to her to be boasting that they ate less than she did or had lost more weight.

They talked about several other projects that had just come up on offer for the future. 'Since word got round that you'd got the lead in *The Lily* the phone hasn't stopped ringing. You are *hot,* girl. If this film does big box office, I'll be able to name my own price for the next job. You can take a few scripts with you to Venice and let me know which one you like, and it had better be one with a big price tag!'

'I don't want to think about the future. I've got enough problems right now.' Laura played with the Thai baked sea bass in front of her; it was served with fragrant rice, scented with lemon grass and lime leaves.

'Isn't that any good?' Melanie was visibly enjoying her escalope of veal Holstein, which she had chosen to have with a green salad.

'It's delicious, I'm just not hungry.' Her stomach was like a washing-machine, the contents tumbling over and over. She would be flying to Venice in two days and as the time got closer her fear grew stronger. What was waiting for her there?

'Oh, lucky you, then,' muttered Melanie, greedily eying the fish. She had finished her food and was still hungry, but refused a pudding. 'Just a black coffee,' she told the waiter as he took their plates away.

When she and Laura parted, an hour later, Melanie said, 'Bring me back some Venetian goodies, don't forget – some amaretti and a bottle of *grappa* would be great.'

'I won't forget.' Laura wished she could talk to Melanie honestly about her fears, but Melanie wouldn't understand: she was far too down-to-earth. Go to the police, she would say. Get some protection. Don't ever be alone with Sebastian Ferrese. But Laura was afraid to tell anyone. That might be disastrous, might precipitate the very thing she most feared. It might drive into a frenzy the shadowy figure who had sent those notes and destroyed Jancy, who had threatened to destroy her.

Venice, 1998

Sebastian was already in Venice. The day after he arrived, he met the police adviser on the film, Captain Saltini of the Vigili Urban, the Venetian municipal police.

The Vigili Urban were in charge of local bylaws and traffic control; their co-operation was essential if the film-making process was to be trouble-free, so Sebastian had invited the Captain to meet him for lunch at the luxurious Hotel Europa, on the Grand Canal, a short walk from San Marco. He wanted to talk through the script and discuss the problems involved in shooting outdoors in Venice.

'At this time, with all this snow, not so many worries with sightseers, just the *paparazzi*,' the policeman promised. He spoke in English and his accent, though thick, was perfectly comprehensible. 'Until the carnival starts mid-week, and then there will be a whole bag of students and tourists arriving. It's always bad weather here in February, not a good time for being out in the streets, but that doesn't seem to bother anyone, even when the Piazza San Marco is several feet under water and it's snowing.'

Sebastian laughed. 'Don't you wish you were twenty again? I know I do.'

Captain Saltini, a tall, commanding-looking man with a swarthy skin and greying dark hair, gave a wry smile. 'Don't we all?'

Sebastian picked up his script. 'It's the carnival I'm here to shoot, the dancing, the costumes, outdoor scenes. I want to capture the atmosphere by using the actual crowds in the streets.'

'Yes, yes, I understand, and that's okay, so long as they agree to let you film them – but you mustn't film anyone who objects.'

'You'll be on hand to talk to them for us?'

The policeman, in his immaculate dark blue uniform, gave him a cynical smile. 'Sure, sure, that's my job, but I'm not leaning on anyone for you. I don't want to find myself falling foul of the Carabinieri.'

'I wouldn't dream of asking you to,' Sebastian said. 'They're tough boys and we don't want any trouble with them.'

The armed officers of the Carabinieri, in their navy blue uniforms with red-striped trousers and peaked caps, were responsible for public law and order, and separate from the Vigili Urban. No doubt there was occasional friction between the two forces when their jurisdictions collided. The last thing Sebastian wanted was to upset either of them.

'Please, just be around when we need you,' he asked Captain Saltini, as the waiter removed their cheese plates. 'Shall we have some brandy with our coffee? Or do you prefer another liqueur?'

'Brandy for me, *grazie*.'

A few minutes later, holding his brandy up to the light and staring out at the snowlit Grand Canal through the glass, Sebastian said casually, 'My mother drowned out there, in the canal, you know.'

The other man nodded, eyes sympathetic. 'I remember.'

Giving him a sharp glance, Sebastian asked, 'Were you a policeman then?'

Another nod. 'Only just – it was my first year and I wasn't sure I liked the job.' Saltini grinned, showing yellow teeth. 'I'm still not sure. I'd have liked to be a film director.' He laughed, to show it was a joke, and Sebastian laughed, too.

'In some ways the jobs aren't so very different,' he said. 'You need to be observant, quick-witted, a bit ruthless, and pretty tough to do either. Tell me, would the file on my mother's accident still be in existence, or do they trash old files after a certain time?'

'These days, no, everything is on computer. But thirty years ago we put everything on paper and files do get lost. But I could look for you, if you like?' The policeman gazed out of the bar window at the snow-veiled canal. 'Not my department, of course, but my brother's a senior officer in the State Police. They deal with serious crime, and I think the accident was handled as a possible murder. I'll ask if he can get me a photocopy of the file on your mother's death. After all this time the file may have been destroyed, though.' His eyes were shrewd. Lowering his voice, he murmured, 'You know, there was something fishy about that case, but as they never found who was in the other boat they never came up with any answers. In the end it was put down as an accident and the file was closed, but I remember a lot of whispering.'

Sebastian kept his own voice low, and watched Captain Saltini closely. 'The other day someone here told me that people thought somebody wanted the Count dead, that it *was* murder, not an accident.'

'*Si*, I heard that, but nobody knows who or why and, after all these years, well . . .' The policeman shrugged. 'No chance of any new answers.' His dark eyes surveyed Sebastian thoughtfully. 'If that is what you're looking for?'

He was smart, thought Sebastian. 'I'm just curious. I was only six at the time and my father never talked about it, so I really know nothing about what happened, and I'd like to find out exactly how my mother died.'

'That's natural,' Captain Saltini agreed. 'In your place, so would I.' He glanced at his watch and pushed back his chair. 'I'm sorry, I have an appointment at three, I must go. I'll try to get a copy of that file for you and let you have it tomorrow.'

Sebastian shook hands with him and walked him to the hotel door, said goodbye and went back into the bar. He stood at the window, watching curled flakes of snow flying past like goose feathers.

The weather had been exactly like this on the day his mother had died. As he continued to stare out at the Grand Canal, he could almost hear the crashing, the screams, the splash. He closed his eyes, feeling again the terror and misery he had felt all those years ago as he stood on the landing stage in front of Ca' d'Angeli, listening to his mother die while the Contessa watched and listened above his head.

Suddenly he realised he had always blamed the Contessa, without ever thinking about it. As a child of six he couldn't have put it into words but, instinctively, he had feared and disliked La Contessa.

He still did.

By the time Laura flew into Venice the production crew had already been at work for some days. Ca' d'Angeli was littered with equipment, cables snaking across the floors, the great arc-lights, under their hoods, waiting to be put into position. A carpenter was busy laying a hardboard track on which they could nail the camera dollies, so that the marble and parquet floors would not be scratched, broken or marked in any way. A girl in a tracksuit and big, bulky sweater went backwards and forwards with an automatically rewinding tape measure, checking distances and scribbling notes in her spring-backed pad, while Sidney and Sebastian stood beside one of the gilt-framed mirrors, so absorbed that they didn't notice Laura's arrival.

She had been met at the airport by a tall, skinny girl in black ski-pants and a scarlet sweater under a black leather jacket speckled with snow, who took her case from her and hustled her out to a waiting launch. 'I'm Carmen, assistant director on the film.' Then she made a face. 'Sounds good, but there are five of us! There are three units working out here. Sorry to rush you, but I have to shoot a street scene once I've dropped you back at the house.'

Laura had felt sick throughout the flight, partly because of turbulence over the Alps, but also from a foreboding that kept her nerves jangling.

The chilly, snow-laden wind outside the airport was another shock to the system. It had been quite mild in London. Keeping her head down, Laura dived into the launch and collapsed on to the seat in the tiny cabin. Carmen joined her and the engine started a second later.

Pulling a walkie-talkie out of her pocket, Carmen said into it, 'Hallo, Mama San? Carmen here. Carmen. Can you hear me? You're breaking up a bit. Oh, that's better. Okay, I found her. We're just starting back.'

Pocketing the walkie-talkie, she subsided with a sigh. 'I never seem to stop running. My feet are twice their normal size, I swear it.'

'But you like the job?'

Carmen glowed. 'Oh, *yes!* It's so exciting, especially working for Sebastian Ferrese. He's wonderful, I've been very lucky.' Then she gave Laura a funny sideways look, and flushed, as if remembering something. Laura could guess what.

'Isn't it cold?' Laura changed the subject. 'I was here in August and we had a heatwave then.'

'The weather's been bitter ever since I got here. I'm beginning to feel like a polar bear.'

'You don't bite like one, I hope!' Huddled inside her tweed

jacket Laura pulled up over her head the thick wool scarf she had been wearing around her neck: she didn't want her hair blown to hell when she got out of the boat. 'It was almost spring-like in London when I left, but snow was on the way there too. You said you were shooting a scene today? I didn't think production had started yet. How many other actors are here?'

'You're the first. We aren't expecting anyone else for a few days. We're using local extras to dress up the scenes, but that means finding dozens of costumes. Wardrobe and Props have been having nightmares.'

'They always do!' Laura stared out of the window, which was glazed with snow and white spray. Grey sky, grey sea. The launch bounced over high waves, flinging her about. 'Lovely weather for filming!'

Carmen laughed. 'The director of photography's mad as hell about the weather. We have to have umbrellas over the cameras to keep them dry, and that casts a shadow, but if we get snow inside one we'll lose that camera while it's being dried out and maybe even a day's shooting.'

'Sidney's a perfectionist.'

The odd look came again. 'Of course, you know him.'

'We worked together before.' Laura avoided the girl's curious stare. This was going to be even more difficult than she had expected. It was hard enough to be working with Sebastian again, but it looked as though she was going to meet avid curiosity from everyone else on the production. It would be a nightmare. Even without the added fear of knowing that, somewhere out there, somebody dangerous was watching her and planning . . . what?

She wished she knew. Acid flooded into her throat, the bile of terror and dread.

'Tell me what you did before you got this job,' she asked Carmen, to give herself something less worrying to think about.

It always worked: people loved nothing better than to talk

about themselves, and Carmen was no exception. During the rough boat-ride she took Laura through her training at film school, the dozens of letters she had written in search of work, her amazing luck in finally getting a job with Sebastian as a runner on a film he made eighteen months ago.

'They paid me peanuts and I was on my feet eighteen hours a day most days, but I learnt a lot and worked like a dog, which is why Sebastian gave me this chance as an assistant director. I'm the lowest of the low. All the others are more experienced than me, but it's pure luck to get a chance to show what I can do.'

Laura smiled. 'He took a big chance on me in my first film – I knew absolutely nothing about acting or making films. Everything I know I learnt from him.'

Carmen went pink, and averted her head. That look again.

Laura had had a vivid picture of the palazzo in her mind ever since she had first seen it, in August, but as she stepped on to the landing-stage and looked up she found that the reality was even more powerful than she remembered it, although the great archangels were now robed in folds of snow, the little cherubs half obliterated by it.

'Isn't it gorgeous?' But Carmen was in a hurry to get inside, out of the blizzard, and urged her towards the entrance.

Face stinging with cold, lashes wet with snow, Laura stumbled inside the empty ground floor, and climbed the great marble stairs into the upper hall – to be met by a scene of utter chaos, which was comfortingly familiar.

Then she saw Sebastian in the middle of it all, talking to Sidney. He was too preoccupied to notice her, but Valerie Hyde, standing close to him, making notes on everything he said, lifted her head and glanced sharply towards Laura, nose beaky, eyes fierce, as if warned of her presence by the instinct with which an owl, hunting in the dark, picks up the invisible fieldmouse hiding in deep grass.

She really hates me, thought Laura. And loves him. Does

he know? Jealousy stung in her throat like heartburn, a physical pain, as if she was going to be sick.

Carmen touched her arm. 'You know you're staying here? Will you mind? It isn't exactly the Hilton, although it's so grand. No central heating, but they've had an electric heater in your room for hours. The bathroom's a frozen waste, I'm afraid. Oh, a magnificent tub with gold feet and bronze fittings – it should be in a museum – but without heating it must be like Siberia. You'll have to warm the room before you can take your clothes off, I expect. We're picking up the tab on their electricity while we're here, so keep your heater on as long as you like. Sebastian told me to make sure you were comfortable. I'll take you up to see your room now. It's very beautiful – it could be a set for one of those Hollywood epics about the Borgias or whatever.' She laughed, and Laura pretended to laugh, too.

'It will be an experience, anyway.'

Carmen nodded. 'Come on, then. If we walk round the wall we won't get in their way.'

Skirting the busy film crew, Laura followed her until the sounds faded and they were in the part of the house kept exclusively for the family.

Stopping at a door at the far end of the great hall, Carmen tapped and waited. 'These rooms are out of bounds to everyone who isn't on a special list.'

'Who is on it?'

'Sebastian, you, Valerie, Sidney, the heads of the production team. It's essential that Sebastian has a room he can use during the day as well as at night, so that he can talk to us quietly in private. But the house is crammed with antiques and the insurance is astronomical. If anything was damaged or stolen we'd be out of a job, I should think.'

The door opened and she stopped talking, her face glowing with excitement as she smiled at the man who stood facing them. 'Oh . . . I hope we didn't interrupt you. This is Laura Erskine – she's just arrived from London. Could she see the room you've given her?' Carmen made a confused introduction. 'Count Niccolo d'Angeli . . . Laura Erskine.'

'Hallo, Nico,' she said, holding out her hand with the same sense of pleasure she had felt the first time they met.

'Oh, you know each other already, then,' Carmen said, watching them with the same curiosity she showed every time Sebastian's name came up. Film companies were always hotbeds of gossip.

Laura had forgotten how tall Nico was: she had to tilt her head a little to meet his eyes. There was something so familiar about his long face, olive skin, dark hair and eyes – seeing him again, after this long gap, made his likeness to Sebastian seem stronger, irrefutable.

He took her hand and kissed it lingeringly. '*Ciao*, welcome back, Laura, I've been waiting impatiently for you.' He gave Carmen a smiling nod, '*Grazie*, Carmen,' then drew Laura through the doorway, closing the door on the other girl, who looked distinctly glum at being excluded. She obviously fancied him – and who wouldn't? thought Laura.

He asked, 'Did you have a good flight? What was the weather like in London? When do you have to start work on the film?'

'The flight was trouble-free and it was much warmer in London. I don't start work here until tomorrow.' She had the impression that he barely listened to her polite replies.

Eagerly he asked, 'Then will you have time to sit for me today? I'll have to push ahead at once, and if I could just take some photos of you to begin with? It wouldn't take long.'

They were moving through one tapestried room after another. Laura gaped at the ornate furniture, the high, painted ceilings, the gilt on ormolu clocks glittering under the crystal blaze of chandeliers, highly polished walnut and satinwood tables and chairs, rich brocade sofas, paintings of landscapes, Venetian scenes, portraits of the family.

She recognised Niccolo in some paintings and in the fading

tapestries; that face of his, which looked as if it came from another period, like the horsemen in those sixteenth-century landscapes with their frozen stares, their sense of life stilled, men going somewhere, busy with killing animals, riding home, or going off to war. He did not belong to today, he came from the past.

The snow blowing outside the windows made strange reflections on ceilings and mirrors. The rooms had the unreal beauty of a troubled dream she had had. Laura felt she was being led through a maze to a place she had known in another life.

'This is your room,' he said, opening a door and standing back to watch her face.

Her first impression was that she had wandered into a hall of mirrors: they hung all around the room on the rich green-silk-covered walls, with sensual, blatantly erotic paintings of naked women hung between them. The mirrors were of all sizes, gold-framed, some ornate, some a plain gilded wood; they reflected the snowy light from the high windows, and, as she and Nico walked right into the room, reflected them, too, back and forth, like an army of shadows flowing through the chamber.

A huge four-poster bed, with baroque carving on the oak columns supporting the canopy, dominated the room, the green-silk hangings around it drawn back to show the matching coverlet. The canopy had a pleated edging of dark green silk but its main fabric was delicate white lace that cast a dappled light over the coverlet.

'That's unusual. I've never seen a lace canopy over a four-poster bed.'

Nico gave her an odd look. 'Once there was a mirror on the ceiling above the bed.'

Laura looked startled, then giggled. She studied the sumptuous bed and imagined what that mirror had once reflected – scenes like those depicted on the ceiling above, where gilt cartouches held pictures of gods and goddesses making love, a bearded Jupiter with dark, slanting eyes kneeling between the thighs of a full-breasted Juno.

'Really? Well, I'm glad you had it taken down before I moved in. It would have made me very self-conscious.'

'Oh, it came down years ago.' His face had a sombre shadow across it. 'I hope the room's warm enough now. It was like a refrigerator a couple of days ago, but we've had a fire going since this morning and electric heaters, too.'

She walked over to the huge, carved white stone hearth in which a great pile of logs burned spitting resin and giving off a scent of pine. Holding out her cold hands, she sighed with pleasure as warmth invaded her for the first time since she had arrived. 'Oh, that's wonderful. Lovely to have a real fire, on a day like this. You're very thoughtful.'

'I wish I was a painter, to capture the firelight on your skin,' Nico said. 'It makes your skin almost transparent. I can see the blood moving through your veins.' He walked over to a white, serpentine-fronted, dressing table in a corner of the room, the thin, elegant legs gilded, ending in tiny bird-like feet. He picked up a little pile of clothes that lay on it and came back to Laura. 'Could you put these on now so that I can take a roll of film of you?'

Laura looked at the pale cream straw hat, a wreath of pink and yellow flowers around the base of the crown, the calf-length boots made of bronze leather, which had a fringe around the top, the thin gauze tunic.

'That looks transparent!'

'I've seen photos of you wearing less.'

She couldn't deny it. 'That was years ago, when I was a model.'

'In a British film I saw, you wore just bra and panties! Black lacy ones, very sexy.' His eyes were wicked; she couldn't help giggling. 'Oh, what you are wearing now is elegant . . .' He stared at the jade green sweater, the warm, chocolate brown woollen pants. 'But you'll look gorgeous in this tunic. Please put it on.

The Donatello *David* is naked – Renaissance statues generally are – and this tunic will show me the shape of your body.'

'Yes,' she said drily, but took the pile of clothes and looked around the room. 'Is there a bathroom?'

He gestured to one of the long wall hangings. 'Behind there. While you're changing I'll set up my tripod. First I'll take a few Polaroids to check the lighting and background, then we'll get down to work. Oh, yes. I nearly forgot – here's Goliath's head.' He held out a string bag.

'Well, at least it isn't a real one!' Laura said wryly. 'I won't be a minute.'

The bathroom was as ornate and splendid as the bedroom, and as chilly as a tomb. It had a high ceiling, an arched window, looking down on to a deserted back canal, a white marble floor and green marble walls. The free-standing bath was enamelled dark green with gilt taps, gilt legs and gilded lion's feet.

An oil heater stood in one corner but it looked so old-fashioned that Laura was reluctant to switch it on in case it blew up, so she stripped off quickly, shivering, and put on the tunic, the boots and the hat.

When she went back. Nico was adjusting his camera on the tall tripod. He straightened to look round, eyes bright. 'Ah . . . yes . . . perfect . . . Pity your hair isn't longer, but never mind. Maybe it's better short, to underline the symbolism.'

'That bathroom is a morgue. After two minutes in there I feel like a corpse!' Laura said, accusingly, and rushed over to stand in front of the hearth.

'My God, if *only* I was a painter,' Nico said, as he had earlier. He wandered over to her and put out a hand to smooth down the hem of the tiny tunic. His fingers lingered on her upper thigh for a second too long. 'The firelight is making that tunic totally transparent – your body's perfect. You look wonderful standing there with your Titian hair and those cat's eyes spitting temper at me.'

'It's my cat's claws you need to watch out for, if you

touch me like that again,' she warned him, but he merely smiled at her.

'Film directors never come over to shift your position, when you're working on set?'

'Well, yes . . . but—'

'And when you modelled, you never allowed the photographer to push you into poses?'

'Is that what you were doing?'

He nodded. 'Put this hand on your hip.' He watched her, shook his head. 'No, like this.' He adjusted her wrist, then took the football out of its string bag, knelt down, lifted her right foot and placed it on the ball. 'Yes, that's about it. Now I want you to bend this left knee, hitch your right hip a little, camp it up – yes, that's the look I want. Tilt your head slightly, half close your eyes, half smile, a sleepily triumphant look. Great. Now, don't move.'

He backed away, picked up a camera and took some Polaroid shots from different places in the room.

After a minute or two, Laura began to feel the heat of the fire burning her right side. 'Can I move soon? I'm too close to the fire.'

'Okay. I've got enough of these.' He inspected the photos, and Laura walked away from the fire and climbed up on to the bed to sit, her hands clasped around her smooth, bare knees, the tiny tunic showing most of her long legs, reflecting on how alike he and Sebastian were. Was it just that they were both Italian – or something more?

The idea had been on her mind ever since she had first seen Niccolo, but she didn't dare bring it up – how could you phrase such a question?

He walked over to her, dropped the handful of Polaroids on the bed. 'What do you think?'

She picked up the pictures and looked at them. The gauze tunic in firelight concealed nothing. She might as well have been naked. Nico sat on the bed beside her, staring over her shoulder.

'You are so lovely. What a body! I can't wait to make it.'

She looked sideways through her lashes. 'I hope you're talking about your statue. You won't make *me*, Nico. Get it into your head that I'm not here as a plaything for you.'

He ran a hand up her sleek, bare leg, fingering the muscles in her calf, her thigh. 'You go to a gym regularly? I can tell – you've got such good muscle tone.' He slid his hand down her spine, like a violinist practising his fingering. 'Your bones are terrific. I love them.'

She laughed. 'Will you stop that? I'm not a doll.' Then she flinched.

'What is it? Are you ill?'

'Oh, nothing . . . A ghost walked over my grave.'

'Oh, this house is full of ghosts. Any house as old as this would be, and my family were pretty violent over the centuries. Murders, suicides, natural deaths – every room has had a death in it, and this room more than any other.'

She shuddered and slid off the bed, saying, 'Shall we shoot the rest of your pictures now, then?'

'So professional,' he mocked, but with warmth in his eyes. 'Okay, let's go. This time I want you to hold this.' He turned and picked up a sword, which had been leaning against the wall. 'Be careful, only hold it by the pommel. The edge is sharp.'

She was reluctant, but warily let him put it into her hand. Her wrist gave way under the weight as she tried to lift it. 'It's very heavy.'

'Lean on it, make it part of your pose, okay?'

'Like this?'

'Beautiful! The Donatello statue is androgynous, faintly perverse. Can you get something of that in your expression?

'I'll try,' she said, amused. 'You don't ask much, do you?' She felt weird, modelling again, but she fell into it without difficulty and hardly noticed half an hour go by, unaware when Nico switched cameras and went on shooting more film of her, in the transparent gauzy tunic, the boots, the flower-decked hat, leaning on the heavy sword.

They both jumped at a tap on the door.

'What the fuck is going on?' Sebastian exploded into the room towards them, face rigid, skin an angry red.

Nico said coolly, 'What does it look like? She's posing for photos I can work with while she's acting – I told you I wanted her to model for me.'

'You didn't tell me it would be porno stuff!'

Nico's eyes were contemptuous. 'Look at her again, you moron! She's dressed as the Donatello *David*. Surely even you recognise that?'

'She looks pretty undressed to me!' Sebastian's eyes raked over her body in the flimsy tunic, which showed everything from her breasts to the curly red-gold hair above that cleft between her thighs.

'The hat's cute, though,' Laura tossed at him, so furious she wanted to hit him but hiding it under a bright, phoney smile. 'And the boots are very sexy.' She put one foot up, posing. 'Don't you think so?'

Without looking at Nico, Sebastian said, through tight lips, 'Get out of here before I smash that camera. She's under contract to me and I need to talk to her. When I need her, she can't work for anyone else.'

'This isn't work, it's fun,' Laura said, offering the sword back to Nico.

His eyes smiled. 'You're wonderful.'

'Get out, will you?' Sebastian grated.

Ignoring him, Nico told Laura, 'I'll take the sword, but keep the rest of the costume up here for the moment. Let me know next time you have a few free hours to work with me.'

He began to dismantle his equipment without hurry; Sebastian watched, eyes smouldering, and opened the door for him when he left, carrying his tripod over his shoulder, cameras strung around him.

Laura walked towards the bathroom, intending to change out of the costume, but Sebastian caught her arm. 'What was really going on in here before I arrived?'

'I was posing. He was taking pictures.' She looked down at the curled fingers around her arm. 'Will you let go of me? And don't grab me like that again. I'm not some piece of meat and I'm not your property. If I want to pose for Nico, I will.'

'He wants you! Are you blind? If you let him into your bedroom he'll be in your bed next.' His mouth twisted into a sneer. 'Or is that what you want? Do you fancy him, too? And I thought you were different!'

She hated the way he was looking at her. It made her feel dirty. Pulling free she tried to run to the bathroom, but he caught her again before she had got to the door, his hands on her waist.

Her hat fell off and she struggled helplessly, but he lifted her into the air and carried her to the bed where she sprawled, heart beating so fast that she was gasping for breath. Sebastian got on to the bed and knelt over her, taking her face between his two hands and gazing down at her.

'Don't sleep with him, Laura, don't. I'd have to kill you,' he muttered. Then he began to kiss her hungrily, and her body responded as it always did to him, melting, trembling, turning to wax under his caressing hands. He could do anything with her and to her, and she would never stop him; the pleasure of his touch was too intense, she needed it with an ache she had never felt for anyone else.

Her eyes closed, her arms went round his back, she lifted her legs to enfold him, groaning with pleasure as he stroked her breasts, her thighs, his fingers sliding inward, finding the soft, moist, hot centre of her body and making her gasp with desire.

Sebastian lifted his mouth and looked at her with half-closed, gleaming eyes. 'I've been waiting months for you – it's been torture.'

She was desperate to have him inside her, she couldn't pretend. 'Sebastian ...' She groaned, clutching him, arching against him.

'Laura ... God, Laura, you're unbelievable,' he said, tearing off his clothes with hands that shook visibly.

'I ought to take off these boots!' Laura said, laughing wildly.

He gave her a look that made her insides turn to water. 'I love them. They're the sexiest things I've ever seen. With that beautiful body naked and those boots, you have no idea what you're doing to me ...'

Her head tilted back and she stared up through the lacy canopy above the bed, then froze in shock. Eyes were staring back at her from the painted ceiling. Not the painted eyes she had noticed earlier, these eyes moved, flickered. She saw light reflecting back from the glassy black pupil.

Someone was up there, behind the ceiling, watching them.

Chapter Nine

A scream tore from her throat. Sebastian started violently. 'What the hell— What is it? What's wrong?'

'Eyes,' she whispered. 'Eyes – in the ceiling – watching – Somebody's up there, watching us!'

He shot a glance upward. 'Where? What are you talking about?'

'Her eyes – Juno's eyes – she's watching us. Well, not her, of course, but somebody. There's somebody behind the ceiling, I saw the eyes move.'

He was staring at her now as if he thought she was mad. 'Well, they're not moving now. All I can see is painted eyes. For God's sake, Laura!'

She pushed him away and rolled off the bed, looked up at the ceiling. He was right. The eyes were painted, flat, lightless.

Naked, Sebastian got off the bed and reached for her. 'Have you taken anything? Smoked a joint?'

'No!' she screamed, pushed him away and ran into the bathroom, bolting the door behind her. In the mirror her face was bleached white. What was the matter with her? Sebastian had asked. Laura wished she knew. All that was certain was that she had seen those painted eyes move, had seen light glinting off their shiny surface, but they weren't shiny now, they were the same dull, flat painted surface as the rest of the ceiling.

She had imagined it.

No! she thought, remembering the way the pupils had flickered. She hadn't imagined anything. This house was full of secret passages and hiding places. Nico had told her of a back staircase from the boat-house up to this room. He had laughed, saying he often used it to come and go without his mother seeing him. Couldn't there also be a false ceiling though which people could watch what was happening in this room? Secret panels and two-way mirrors were commonplace in brothels. Someone had been watching her and Sebastian making love. Who could it have been?

Nico? No, it was totally out of character. You'd have to be sick to do that, and Nico wasn't sick, he wasn't a voyeur.

How do you know? she asked herself, uncertainly. She buried her face in her hands. She didn't want to think about it any more.

Hurriedly she pulled off the *David* costume and took a quick shower, then dressed in the clothes she had been wearing when she arrived and went back into the bedroom. Sebastian was standing at the window, fully dressed too, in jeans and an olive sweater with leather patches at the elbow. The sagging, cloudy sky was heavy with snow.

He glanced at her over his shoulder. 'I heard your shower running. They're more efficient than I'd expected. Feeling better?'

She was still too choked to speak.

His eyes narrowed. 'You must be very hyper. Starting a new film is always an ordeal, but you have to calm down, Laura, or you won't be fit to work. Look, we're all going out into Venice to have a drink in St Mark's Square, and then a meal together. Come along with us. You know most of the crowd and talking to them will help you relax.'

Her voice sounded rusty, like old bellows. 'When are you going?'

'Now, right away. I rang Valerie on the walkie-talkie, and

told her to gather everyone together for a two-hour break. We've been working since first light and we need a rest.'

'I want to unpack and settle in first. You go ahead and I'll see you all down there.'

His brows jerked together. 'You can't walk around the city on your own!'

She snapped back hotly, 'I'll wrap up warmly. A hood and thick coat will be some sort of disguise and I'll be careful.'

'Don't be so damn stupid! Do you want to get mobbed? Anything could happen to you.'

'Look, I need some time alone. And I walked around Venice when I was here at the film festival,' she said, with a touch of desperation. 'I'll be fine. Please, you go on, I'll see you in the square – Florian's?'

He said grimly, 'Well, it's your life.'

The words hadn't been idle. Something in his face told her he was warning her. But about what?

He picked up a leather bag which he had had in his hand earlier and flung on to a chair. Unzipping it, he pulled out a script, dropped it on the rumpled bed. 'Here, I brought you the latest draft. I've tagged the scenes we'll be shooting here over the next week.'

'Have there been many changes?'

'No, just tinkering, sharpening up. You won't have any new lines to learn for this location, so just check your cues. I'll mostly be doing background shots and crowd scenes with you in the foreground. But have a read through it, and let me know if you think it's an improvement.'

Sebastian stood, silently staring at her, a thin dark man with flashing eyes. She waited for him to say something but he just turned and slammed out of the room. Wincing at the crash of the heavy door, Laura almost called him back, but in the end decided not to. She really needed these precious moments alone.

She picked up the script, to the front of which was clipped the pink pages of the shooting schedule starting with day one.

Sebastian planned to shoot four pages every day while they were here, she noted. He was optimistic. She flicked through it. Under the title was typed the fact that this was the 15th draft. She wasn't surprised. Sebastian was a perfectionist.

The first page was almost entirely scene-setting, just four lines of dialogue between herself and someone called the Old Chestnut-seller. The following pages also revealed scanty dialogue. No problems there. She could learn the lines as she went along.

She dropped the script and began to unpack, putting her clothes away in musty-smelling closets and chests of drawers. She had brought a few lavender bags with her and laid these among her undies before she closed the drawers. It didn't take long. She was now an experienced packer and unpacker: she had her own routine, every move worked out to save time.

When she had finished, she put on a thick, padded green anorak with a black hood, slipped black sunglasses on her nose, put on gloves and knee-length black leather boots and studied herself in the mirror. Nobody would recognise her, surely. The *paparazzi* had been at the airport, snatching pictures, but they hadn't bothered to pursue her to Ca' d'Angeli, and they wouldn't hang around to catch sight of her in this weather. She was wearing something entirely different, her fiery hair was out of sight under the hood, every strand combed back from her face so it wouldn't show.

As she left the private apartments she walked past the Contessa, who was talking to several of her servants.

'*Buon giorno,* Contessa,' Laura said politely, and got a faintly surprised, but perfectly friendly, smile.

'You are going out?' the Contessa asked, and Laura nodded.

'It will snow,' she warned.

'I'll be okay.'

Laura walked out into the long gallery, picked her way through the film equipment strewn everywhere, higgledy-piggledy, like the abandoned baggage of a retreating army.

There was even a corpse or two: younger crew members stretched out on rugs to snatch an hour's rest while Sebastian was elsewhere. They didn't even look at her – they were too tired to take an interest in anything that happened around them.

'Laura!' It was Nico's voice. He took in her outdoor clothes. 'You aren't going out, are you? It could blow a blizzard any minute, from the look of the sky.'

'I have to. I'm meeting some of the crew in St Mark's Square for a drink, and a few prelims.'

He was baffled by the word. 'What?'

'Preliminary shots. Sebastian needs to decide which angles to choose, which views to get in, what he'll want on the final shot. Apparently we're shooting a lot of stuff out in the streets, to get the carnival atmosphere. How do I get to St Mark's? Walk?'

'You can, but I'll happily take you along the canal. My boat's outside. Come on.'

Watching the flicker of his dark eyes, she remembered that moment in the bedroom when she had seen eyes staring down at her and Sebastian. Once again, sickness rose in her throat.

'No, that's okay, I think I'd rather walk,' she said unsteadily. 'I want to explore this part of Venice before the snow starts again. I may not get another chance for a few days.' She turned before he could argue and walked quickly towards the stairs, but he ran after her.

'Go the back way, then – I'll show you the short-cut. It will take you to St Mark's Square by the quickest route.'

Nico took her down some narrow, winding stairs to the dark kitchen quarters and out through a corridor into the formal garden, which she had not seen before. He walked her along the maze of gravelled paths, through the snow-decorated topiary, which had a surreal look, as if it came out of a painting. When they reached a gate in a high wall he unlocked it with an ornate brass key he took from his pocket. It creaked as he pushed it open. 'You turn to the right, walk to the far end, turn left, over the bridge, straight on along the back canal, the next right turn, and then take a left-hand fork into an alley. You'll see the piazza at the end of it.' His face crinkled in a grin. 'Do you think you'll remember that, or shall I come with you?'

She smiled back, liking him more every time they met. 'Don't forget I'm an actress. I have a good memory. Repeat it, slowly.'

She closed her eyes and listened intently, then opened them and repeated what he had said, word for word.

Surprised, he nodded. '*Bene*. You do have a good memory, don't you? If you get lost, though, no problem. You'll find a black arrow painted on corners, pointing either to San Marco or the Accademia. And if you still get lost, most Venetians speak English.'

She thanked him and hurried off, avoiding the eyes of anyone she passed, keeping her hood pulled forward. On one side of the bridge she had to cross she saw a little group of art students in pink body-stockings. They were busy painting each other in gaudy swirls of colour, zigzags of red, yellow and black. One of them, a boy with short black hair cut razor-style and greased to make it stand up in spikes, shouted at her.

'Sorry, I don't speak Italian,' she said.

'American?'

She let him think so, knowing it was probably a mistake to talk to anyone, but finding the ordinary human contact reassuring.

'Aren't you cold, wearing just a body-stocking?' she asked.

'No, is fun. The *carnivale* is fun. You here for *carnivale*? Got a costume? I can hire for you.'

She shook her head. She knew Sebastian had hired one for her and for everyone else in the cast and crew.

'You want I paint your face?' the student asked. 'Only forty thousand lira.'

'You're kidding! Forty thousand . . .' Her brain wasn't working fast enough.

'Thirty dollars American.'

She had brought out a pile of lire with her, having locked her credit cards, cheque book and cash in a cupboard in her room at Ca' d'Angeli. She was sure she had enough.

'Okay,' she said, and his olive-skinned face split open in a wide grin.

'Half money now, half when I finish?'

She slid a hand inside her anorak and pulled out some cash, counted it into his hand and hoped he wouldn't just run off with it, but he put it away carefully into a bum-bag and gestured at a stool.

'Please. Sit.'

She sat on the low wooden stool, feeling the chill wind at her back, blowing off the Grand Canal straight from the lagoon. Any second now it would snow – and heavily.

The art student sat down on another stool, and indicated his palette of colours. 'Please, choose. What you like?'

She ran her eyes over the range, chose a delicate mauve, a very pale green, silver and black.

'Is good,' said the boy, and a second later took her dark glasses off her nose.

His other hand came up to push back her hood but she grabbed it and held on firmly. 'No, leave my hood!'

That surprised him but he didn't argue: there weren't many customers around in this weather. 'Okay, okay,' he said. 'Now close your eyes, please. I start with them.'

She did so obediently and felt the soft hairs of his brush begin to glide over her skin. Laura sighed, enveloped in the strange calm that always descended on her when she was in makeup.

It was so soothing to have someone touching you, soundlessly, gently, making no demands on you. She always felt at those times that she sank deep inside herself, leaving her mind free to wander. Today she thought about her parents, to whom she had talked before she left for Venice. They had told her that in Northumberland the weather was far worse than it was here, snow making the narrow, winding roads along the Wall impassable, imprisoning the family for days at a time. Yet she wished she was there: she loved the silences, or the sharp wail of the wind through bare thorn trees, the blue, blue sky on really cold days, the frosted white of the fields.

The art student said, 'Okay, finished, you look now.'

He was holding up a mirror in a hand-painted wooden frame. Her eyes were framed now in triangles of silver and black, her forehead and cheeks seethed with mauve and green wavy lines, with dots of black here and there, the design continuing down to her chin.

'Terrific!' she said, then grasped for her few words of Italian. '*Bella, molta bella, grazie tante.*'

He beamed. 'You like?'

'I like.' She got up and hunted in her pocket for more of her Italian banknotes. She gave him a tip on top of the rest of the agreed fee, and he thanked her eagerly, delighted.

'*Ciao!*' she said, flipping her fingers at him.

'See you, baby,' he said, in an exaggerated American drawl.

Laughing, Laura walked away, following the side canal, watching the first drifting flakes of snow falling, melting on the surface of the dark, oily water. Lights from windows high up in blank, brick walls were reflected there, too, shimmering, rippling, dissolving, never still, always changing, while up above in the late-afternoon sky a faint wraith of the sun gleamed between those heavy clouds. There were very few people about. No doubt they were all in St Mark's Square, listening to music she could vaguely hear.

The winter wind blew across squares, made flagpoles rattle on hotels, tumbled Coke cans across the stone pavements, set up eddies of dust and paper in doorways, down narrow alleys. As she turned a corner she heard whispers in the dark, laughter from open windows, balconies. Someone was singing in a gondola on the Grand Canal: the sound echoed from stone walls and up from the secret depths of the water.

It was a longer walk than she had realised: she was getting tired and cold. She would have gone back but she had forgotten the way. Every time she turned a corner she hoped to see St Mark's, but she never did. She was lost.

It reminded her of a disturbing dream she sometimes had, in which she was always lost, afraid, running without ever finding whatever she was looking for.

A second later, someone came out of an alley. Laura was confronted by a white-painted face, cut in half by a black mask over the eyes, hair hidden under a black tricorn hat. The figure was ambivalent too: a swirling black coat hung to the feet hiding gender, shape, age.

Nervously Laura forced a smile. '*Buona sera.*'

The eyes glittering through the holes in the mask showed no reaction.

Not Italian? There were a lot of Americans in Venice at the moment.

'Hi,' she offered instead. 'Excuse me, but could you tell me the way to St Mark's? Silly, I know – but I seem to be totally lost.'

Below the scalloped line of the mask a red-painted mouth curled in a smile.

From under the cloak a hand emerged, holding something Laura recognised a second too late. The knife flashed down.

Chapter Ten

When Sebastian walked into Florian's café in St Mark's Square there was no sign of the crew. They had asked for a chance to do some shopping before meeting up and he had expected to find them scattered like confetti all over the square, but he hadn't spotted them among the crowds in the dusk, hair deckled with snow, faces ruddy with cold. Where was Sidney? Valerie? They should be here by now – he was late himself.

The snow wasn't deterring tourists any more than they had been driven off by the rising tide. Duckboards criss-crossed the square; people trod along them, the wise ones wearing boots, children sloshing through the puddles, shrieking and giggling.

A green tarpaulin-draped stage had appeared: there would be concerts every night during carnival week, rock bands blasting away, the crowds dancing, and sometimes classical music with audiences seated in rows as in a concert hall, or sheltering under umbrellas if the rain came down.

Thank God he wasn't staying in one of the nearby hotels; the noise would be hideous. Most of the students here would sleep by day and party by night, so it wouldn't bother them.

'Signore?' A waiter had materialised beside him.

'*Un bicchiere ... vino rosso.*' This was red-wine weather; Venetians would say it warmed your blood.

He hadn't been specific enough for the waiter, who suggested, 'Valpolicella? Bardolino?'

'Bardolino, *si*.' Sebastian always enjoyed the local Veneto dry red, on its own or with food, especially *fegato alla Veneziana*, thin strips of liver fried with onions in a wine sauce. A flash of memory brought a picture of himself sitting at the kitchen table in his childhood home, his mother cooking liver in a large, black pan, the smell of wine and onions, the red blood oozing from the thinly sliced offal, his mother's creamy skin as she stirred the sauce, her cheeks pink from the heat against the fire of her hair.

The waiter still hovered. '*Cichetti*?'

Sebastian came back to the present. 'No, I won't have a snack just now.'

But the waiter brought him a saucer of pistachio nuts, anyway. He would pay for them, of course, they weren't free, but he accepted them. He sipped his wine and lost himself in the cloudy mirrors lining the café. He loved their blistered, quicksilver surfaces. They no longer reflected truly, the light too diffuse to give back an unbroken image. Instead it flickered with movement, part of a face here, a hand there, as if you were looking into a world you could not see clearly, perhaps peering back at the past.

His mother had brought him here sometimes. He could almost believe he saw himself, and her, in the mirrors – he tousle-haired, just at the level of the tables, big-eyed, taking in everything around him but even more aware of his beautiful mother, her gorgeous clouds of red hair and those entrancing eyes, her generous smile. Men at other tables tried to catch her eye – even as a young child Sebastian had been aware of the attention she attracted, and of her amused, sidelong glances, acknowledging men's interest. She had enjoyed male attention, just as Clea had.

Once, on a hot summer day, he had been eating vanilla ice-cream with chocolate wafers, resenting the way men stared at his mother. He had looked up and seen the crowds outside, floating like coloured clouds in the mirrors behind the reflection of him and his mother.

Could he use that image in the film? A scene was set in Florian's at the end of the Second World War ... His mind quickened. A double image – yes, first the German soldiers going by, in the mirrors, not goose-stepping or carrying rifles, but off-duty, laughing, whistling at local girls, a fade, then American or English soldiers. Not original, okay, a pretty standard switch, but it would save time, time he needed to save: he had so much to cram into this film. He'd talk to Sidney about it. The book contained quite a long passage about Venice, just after the war. When Sebastian had read it he had imagined much of it happening in Ca' d'Angeli, although the palazzo was given another name.

Canfield had been a private man, reluctant to talk to either the press or the literary beavers burrowing away in his work. If he had visited Ca' d'Angeli the Contessa would know, thought Sebastian. He must talk to her. He had been putting it off because he disliked her so much, and knew that this was mutual.

For months now Sebastian had been digging inside himself to find the essence of the film, not quite sure in places what Canfield had intended. He couldn't switch off, day or night, had to keep focusing on the film; it was exhausting, but necessary. It was the only way he knew to make a film work. He had to give it everything, couldn't spare time or attention for anything else.

Making love to Laura just now had been a brief respite from that intense absorption. For a little while he had broken free, back to the real world, to sensuality, human contact; touching her warm breasts, her smooth thighs, poised to plunge into her, desperate to reach that little death, which came at the height of pleasure.

And then she had shattered the moment. Had she really seen eyes watching them from the ceiling?

With any other actor he would have thought nothing of it – they took drugs like kids eat popcorn. But he'd have bet his life on it that Laura wasn't into that scene. He hated drugs because you lost your mind, became a stranger to yourself. Oh, he'd tried them, when he was younger, tried everything during those years with Clea – until he grew out of it, hating himself for ever having been such a fool. But Clea had had good reasons for wanting to lose her mind, her memory, herself.

When he first met Laura he had known she was a virgin; she was as shy as a fawn, trembled when he spoke to her, even though her eyes and mouth had told him she was aware of him: his desire for her was mirrored in her face. He had burned to touch her, but held off all those weeks while they shot the film, because he loved knowing that she was untouched. He wanted her innocence like shot silk in every scene.

Clea hadn't been so lucky, or so sensible, however you liked to look at it. She'd been used, abused, passed around like a joint at Hollywood parties. The whole world knew the famous story of the party to which she had gone naked, except for a fabulously valuable black mink wrap, to save the men the trouble of undressing her.

'I'm your birthday present,' she told her host, pivoting on one toe. 'No need for a bed. Just lay me down on the the floor.'

By the time she arrived the guests had been stoned or drunk. They had stood in a circle, clapping and shouting encouragement, as their host had pushed her down on to the marble floor, spread the mink as a mattress, and fucked her while she screamed with laughter until she went into wild, convulsive orgasm, excited by the audience as much as by the sex itself. Clea had always loved to be watched, whatever she was doing.

He closed his eyes, pushing away the image. She was dead. Gone. For ever. But he couldn't forget her. He tried hard enough, God knew, but nobody would let him. The media brought up her name every time he was mentioned. Clea,

Clea, Clea. He was sick of having it all dragged up, sick of the guesswork, the hints and implications, the guilt trip laid on him without any of them knowing what had really happened the day she fell.

No, no, no.

He could almost hear her scream the words again, as she tumbled like a dying bird, down through the bright air to the hard, unrelenting earth.

Had Laura felt that Clea was up there, looking down at them?

He felt a stir in the café and opened his eyes. Customers at other tables were staring out of the misty windows into the square because people were running past, shouting, pointing, away from the canal, to the far end of the square. Sebastian craned his neck.

Laura! he thought. Someone must have recognised her. Hadn't he told her not to walk here, all alone, from Ca' d'Angeli? Didn't she know the Venetian papers had been full of the fact that she was going to star in *The Lily*? As the book was set largely in Venice everyone here was fascinated by the filming of it. Her picture had dominated the front pages ever since the first of the film crew arrived.

Leaping to his feet he dropped some money on the table and hurried out, only to walk straight into Sidney, who clutched his arm and blurted out, 'Laura – she's been—' He was breathing hard as if he had been running and, for a second or two, couldn't finish the sentence.

'What? *What?*' Sebastian demanded. 'Where is she? What's happened?'

'St-st-stabbed,' Sidney got out, and another fleeting image of Clea falling, screaming, flew into Sebastian's mind. Of his mother dying in the misty waters of the Grand Canal.

He was suddenly icy cold. I'm cursed, he thought. Everyone I ever love dies suddenly, violently.

'Is she—' Dead, he thought. She's dead. She has to be.

Sidney was almost in tears. 'God, Sebastian, there's blood everywhere, poor girl. Why would anyone do that to her?'

Sebastian began to run through the hazily lit square, following everyone else. Sidney followed him, his breathing shot to pieces.

'Turn – l-left, down the alley – as if you're going to San Moise, that church – amazing gargoyle of a place,' he panted.

'You'll have a heart attack if you keep talking and running at the same time,' Sebastian yelled, over his shoulder. 'Stop for a minute, get your breath back.'

A second later, he saw the crowd, huddled together, like sheep, not knowing what to do.

A couple of Carabinieri were pushing back the crowds. He heard their raised voices. '*Prego . . . prego, signori . . . Non spingete . . . Passare avanti, signori . . .*'

The chugging of an engine made the crowd stir, then comment noisily, 'They're coming . . . the ambulance . . .'

It was in sight on the back canal: faded cream paint, a sandy brown stripe along the side, the ambulancemen in their orange jackets at the wheel.

Sebastian put on speed to get to Laura before the ambulance did.

The Carabinieri moved to push him back, then recognised him, permitted him to go through, to kneel down beside Laura's body.

He gasped when he saw her face. 'What the hell is that?' It hadn't been painted silver, mauve, green and black when he left her in Ca' d'Angeli – how long ago? Half an hour? Three-quarters?

The zigzags of colour made her look like an alien, a beautiful, strange creature from another planet – if he had passed her on the street he might not have known her. Her eyes were shut, the lids pale green, her breath coming through lips so colourless they were almost white under the sheen of silver covering them, except for spots of blood where she had bitten down and torn her flesh.

Sebastian drew a short, choked breath.

Look at all that blood. Sidney had said there was blood everywhere and he was spot on. Sebastian thought, as he had the day Clea fell to her death, that blood was redder than you expected it to be. Such a bright colour, puddled here like spilt wine, on the broken paving stones, on her clothes, her face, her neck. There was blood everywhere.

Was she dying, right here, in front of him?

He groaned, and at the sound her eyes opened wide, fiercely green in the light of the street-lamp. They had the glare of a wild cat's eyes when it scents danger.

'You're alive . . .' He couldn't believe it. His eyelids felt hot and as if they were full of sand. He bent closer, put out a hand to stroke her cheek.

She shrank away, and he read fear in those glowing eyes.

The Carabinieri saw it, too. One of them took his shoulder and pulled him to his feet just as the ambulance boat tied up and the men on board leapt out.

'Dr Garrieri? They didn't say you were here. That was lucky. How bad is she?' Someone asked a grey-haired man in a camel-hair coat.

Sebastian strained to hear the reply but the doctor lowered his voice, conscious of the listening crowds.

A stretcher had been set up, the two ambulancemen lifted Laura gently on to it and covered her with warm red blankets. Then, each took one end of the stretcher and carried it to the boat swaying on the water.

'I want to go with her.' Sebastian tried to free himself but the policeman's grip tightened.

'No, I'm sorry, Signore. No.'

The other policeman was using a walkie-talkie, his head turned away so that Sebastian couldn't hear what he was saying. When he had finished, he turned back and said politely, 'We would like you to come to the station with us, Signor Ferrese. There are some questions we need to ask.'

Sebastian saw in their eyes that they wouldn't let him refuse. He saw, too, that they thought he had done it. They'd seen her fear and drawn their own conclusions.

His mouth twisted. Of course, they would start by suspecting him. He had been here before. Here we go again. The same old merry-go-round. Questions, answers not believed, long, frozen silences, more questions, more disbelief. Guilty, even if they can't prove it.

Sidney had arrived, still panting, his face red from the exertion. 'Is she . . . How is she? Did she say anything? Tell you who did it?'

'Go with her in the ambulance,' Sebastian curtly told him. 'You know my mobile number. Ring me at once if – if anything happens.'

The story led the late news on television that night. Nico saw it in his studio where he was working on a clay model with blown-up photos of Laura propped in front of him. He rarely watched TV, but tonight he had switched on just in time for the news. He missed the first few words, but caught the end of the sentence.

'. . . attempted murder of film star Laura Erskine . . .'

His fingers skidded down the soft, moist clay. Attempted *murder*?

He wiped his hands automatically on a damp cloth, intent on what the announcer was saying.

'Film director Sebastian Ferrese is helping police with their enquiries . . .'

Nico could hardly believe his ear. They'd arrested Sebastian. He picked up his mobile phone and rang the hospital, but the operator told him curtly that Laura had only just left the operating theatre. There was no news yet.

'How badly hurt was she? Is she going to survive?'

'We cannot give any further information,' he was told, before the operator cut him off.

In her private sitting room Vittoria d'Angeli saw the same news broadcast, her plump hands laid on her black-skirted lap, small feet planted close together, stiff-backed, bolt upright, on a shabby, faded, but still elegant eighteenth-century cream brocade sofa, whose design made it impossible to slouch.

The newscaster hadn't said the girl was likely to die.

She must. Vittoria's fingers clenched. She couldn't bear to have her under the roof for even one night, sleeping in that room, with him ... their moans of pleasure, of echoes the same sighs and groans, the smooth flesh sliding together, thigh on thigh, rising and falling, those sounds ...

She bit the fleshy mound of her thumb. Everything came back, like the dead on the Day of Judgement, the drowned faces floating up from the dark waters of Venice, green and white ...

Green eyes, cloudy red hair, that full, sensual mouth, the white skin ... reminding her of what she longed to forget. Was there never any peace?

The police had been quick, arresting him. How had they done it so soon? And on what evidence? Of course, they had a reputation at stake. Murder was rare in Venice. Venetians were proud of their city being called the safest in Italy – and it probably was, for all sorts of reasons. Surrounded by water, and without any roads, it was hard for criminals to make a fast getaway, and the local population knew each other too well for anyone to get away with crime for long. The city was full of eyes and ears, awash with gossip.

Vittoria had had to learn to live with gossip, to accept that people she scarcely recognised, or might never even have met, knew her private life as intimately as she did – better, at first, because she had been naïve. She hadn't guessed, suspected, understood anything. When you're young you can be deceived by surfaces; you believe what you see.

It had been one of the gossiping, treacherous friends of the d'Angeli family who had told her – one of the worst moments of her life. She had sat there smiling, while inside she ripped apart. She had wanted to die of pain and humiliation. For a time, she had thought of throwing herself into the Grand Canal from one of the upper windows of Ca' d'Angeli, as others had down the centuries. But she was made of tougher stuff. She had learnt to survive however hard the struggle, to plan however remote the future seemed, and Vittoria had vowed calmly to take revenge. One day she would make them pay.

And she had. In the end. She had been the victor at last, no longer the victim. She had had to wait, but she had learnt patience and tenacity as a child. That was why the Jesuits had said, 'Give us a child until it is seven and it is ours for life.'

Milan, 1945

She had been just in her teens when her mother took her back to Milan. She hadn't wanted to go and had cried bitterly at parting from Aunt Maria and Rosa.

'You're going home, you'll be happier, now,' Aunt Maria had said, trying to look cheerful in spite of the tears in her tired old eyes. Vittoria had wanted to believe her, but she knew nothing was as it had been before she went to Venice. Three of her half-brothers were gone, so was Papa. Life would be different at home, and in Venice she had been happier than she had ever been in Milan before the war. She couldn't even remember Milan – it was all so long ago and far away.

'I don't *want* to go,' she had sobbed.

'You must,' Aunt Maria said, patting her heaving back. 'We'll miss you. The house will be so quiet, without you running up and down the stairs, chattering to Gina and Olivia.

But your mother needs you at home now and you must go.'

They returned to Milan in Frederick Canfield's Jeep. Squashed into the back with the luggage, Vittoria had pretended to sleep, but from under her eyelashes she had silently observed her mother and the Englishman. They talked quietly to each other, looked at each other and smiled, the intimacy between them evident even to a girl of thirteen. Vittoria could never remember her mother looking at her father that way.

Had Mamma ever loved Papa? Had her father loved her mother? She had seen him kissing her, putting his arm round her, as if he did, but if he loved Mamma why had he done ... *that* to her nurse?

They had left Venice at first light, but it was dark by the time they reached Milan, and Vittoria was genuinely fast asleep as the Jeep pulled up. Drowsily she stirred and her eyes opened. Disorientated, she stared out at lighted windows, at a shadowy building that rose up very high.

Frederick Canfield got out and began to unload the luggage. Her mother whispered to him, 'Stay the night. There are plenty of empty rooms.'

'No, I have too much to do tomorrow,' he said, just as Carlo came out to welcome them.

Vittoria stumbled out on to the gravel driveway.

Carlo stopped dead. 'My God, are you Vittoria? Last time I saw you you were just a baby.'

'You've changed too. You look—' She couldn't finish the sentence, not knowing how to say what she was thinking.

Last time she had seen him he had been a slumped body in a wheelchair. A man like a sack, except for the arms that had developed great muscles from having to propel the wheelchair. Since then he had taught himself to walk using two sticks, swinging along on them at an amazing speed, his lean, wiry body seeming weightless between them.

He had lost so much weight that he looked taller and

younger, his arms, shoulders, chest powerful. His thick black hair and black eyes reminded her of her father, but Carlo was better-looking, with a determined, tenacious air about him. Pain had etched itself into his face; his eyes burned with it. He had been to hell and back, and it showed.

Her mother had already told her how brilliantly Carlo ran the company. He was, Mamma said, a better businessman than their father had been, perhaps because he had suffered so much, had had to learn to adapt and to cope with whatever life threw at him.

'I'm okay,' he said, grinning suddenly. 'Life's been hard, these past few years, but it's going to get better now.'

'Oh, I hope so! It can't get worse.'

He crossed himself. 'Don't say that! It's tempting God.' He had not always been so religious – perhaps that was something else the war had taught him.

Mamma said, plaintively, 'Why are we standing around out here in this cold wind?'

'Of course,' Carlo said hastily, 'come inside. You missed dinner, but it won't take ten minutes to throw some supper together. There's minestrone, and you can have pasta and tomato sauce. Our new cook's food is pretty basic, but it's always eatable.'

'I'm starving,' Vittoria confessed, and followed him, as a thin, black-haired young man came out to take the luggage into the house.

'This is Antonio. He was in the army until a few months ago and now he's working for us,' Carlo told her. The young man gave her a faint bow and a brief glance from slanting eyes like wet liquorice.

Vittoria smiled at him. 'Hallo,' she said shyly, noticing that the white shirt he was wearing was far too big for him. Suddenly it occurred to her that it had belonged to her father: she could see it was well tailored, still in good condition, way beyond a servant's means. It hung on his skinny shoulders and ballooned as he stretched to pick up the cases.

She wondered if Carlo, too, was wearing her father's clothes. That shirt fitted him, but the quality of the material was so good that it couldn't have been bought lately. You simply couldn't get shirts made of such cloth, so generously cut. Everything was skimped, of poor fabric and hard to come by. Well, it had been in Venice. Perhaps Milan was better off.

A little later, they sat down to supper in the high-ceilinged kitchen, by candlelight, a mean little fire in the hearth. As they ate the thick minestrone, Carlo told Vittoria at length about his plans for a new, even more magnificent house to replace the home that had been destroyed in the bombing.

She looked around the shadowy room at the copper pans hanging on the walls, the closed wooden shutters on the windows, the huge fireplace that gave out so little heat.

'Mamma said you were renting this place?'

'Yes, it's convenient, close to the factory. A rambling old place, I know. It has fourteen bedrooms! The owners fled in 'thirty-nine to live in Switzerland with their banker son in Geneva. Dirty cowards!'

The contempt in his voice made Vittoria jump.

'As you'll see in the morning, most of the houses around here were destroyed in the English bombing raids. This one wasn't touched. Some people think the English left it alone because the Escali family were spies. It's a strange coincidence otherwise.'

'Was much saved from our old home?' Vittoria asked.

'Most of the furniture was smashed, but we rescued a few things. We had to move fast to get them out before the looters arrived. As if being bombed out of your home wasn't bad enough! We had to contend with ghouls searching the ruins for anything worth having. I shot one bastard I caught trying to make off with an armful of Papa's clothes.' He gestured at himself. 'I'm wearing one of the things he was trying to steal.'

'Did you kill him?' she whispered.

'A bullet right through the heart,' he told her grimly.

'What did the police do to you?'

'The police?' He laughed shortly. 'They shot looters if they caught them – they had to. Milan was overrun with them then, living in the ruins of houses like rats living in the sewers. They stole, killed, raped. Mostly they were army deserters, armed and dangerous. This was a terrified city in those last months of the war.'

That first evening, Vittoria was low-spirited. She would miss the sound and gleam of water all around her, not to mention her friends, Gina and Olivia, and the nuns at the convent school. That night she dreamt about Venice, and the dark little house off the Frezzeria, and cried in her sleep. It was to be months before she stopped dreaming of Venice, and for days she felt lost in the wandering corridors and high-ceilinged rooms of her new home.

That first evening, Carlo had told her he was about to get married; Vittoria had been brought back to be a bridesmaid.

'You and I, we're the only ones left,' he said heavily, and she nodded. It was so long since she had seen the others that she had nearly forgotten what they had looked like.

His face lifted a little. 'Rachele is only going to have you as a bridesmaid because, of course, she's been married before. She doesn't want the wedding to be too formal, this second time.'

Carlo's bride was no blushing young virgin. He had chosen the widow of Captain Lensoni, his platoon commander, who had saved his life in Africa only to die later of his own wounds.

Rachele Lensoni, was nearly forty, a sultry creature, charged with frustration and passion, raven-haired, olive-skinned, ripe-breasted and broad-hipped. She was built to be the mother of a large family, but her only child had died during the worst months of the war. Half starved, weak, the little boy had contracted pneumonia in the winter of 1942. There had been no medicines available for the civilian population then; in desperation Rachele had come to Carlo for help, although they had never met. But he had written to offer his condolences after the death of her husband, and Rachele knew that he manufactured drugs. He had given her what she needed, but her son had died anyway. The medicine had come too late for him.

'That's how they met,' Anna told Vittoria next morning, after Carlo had left for the factory and they were eating breakfast together; black coffee and hot rolls with home-made black cherry jam. Food was still scarce, and people ate sparingly even now. 'Carlo offered her a job in the office and soon he was taking her out to dinner and bringing her home. I could see how the wind was blowing. It was time he married, anyway, and I like her, I must say. She'll be good for Carlo.'

'But she's so old. Could she still have children? I'd have thought Carlo would want them.'

'Oh, I think she has a few years yet!' Anna said, laughing. 'Forty isn't that old, darling.'

Her bright eyes reminded Vittoria that her mother wasn't forty yet. Was she going to marry the Englishman? Her stomach lurched.

Thoughtfully, Anna went on, 'The question mark is over Carlo's capacity, not Rachele's. He told me he's talked to his doctors and they say he could father a child.' But she looked doubtful. 'Let's hope they're right, for Rachele's sake. I don't think Carlo will care much, either way, or he would have married long ago. But Rachele is desperate to have another child.'

Vittoria burst out, 'Mamma, are you going to marry the Englishman?'

There was a silence. Then Anna said flatly, 'He's married already, Vittoria. He got married while he was in England training for the work he is doing.'

Vittoria could scarcely breathe in her relief. She swallowed and cleared her throat before asking, 'What work *is* he doing?'

'Translating, assessing the situation here in Italy . . .'

'Spying,' Vittoria thought aloud. 'Papa was right. He's a spy – he was always a spy.'

Mamma looked angry. 'No, that isn't true! He wasn't spying – he isn't now. You don't understand. Spying is one thing, intelligence work is another. He knows our country so he can see just how much it has changed since the war started and he can advise on what help we need – we do need help, Vittoria. We're in a mess, brother fighting brother, Communists fighting Fascists. The hills are full of people who are still at war, hiding out there. Freddy knows so many people, he can find out what Italy needs if it is ever to recover. He's liaising with the Americans, too. They're the ones with the money and they will help us far more than the British can. I think Britain will be in a pretty bad way, too, after these terrible years of war.'

Vittoria had lost interest in what her mother was saying. Her mind was working along other lines. 'Is his wife back home in England?'

Mamma sighed. 'Of course. Where else would she be? They have a child, a little boy, two years old. His mother worked for the army before he was born. She was driving Freddy while he was working in London – that's how they met – but she had to give up her job to take care of the baby.'

'And he will go back to them? To England?'

Her mother nodded without speaking.

'Soon?' Vittoria insisted.

She got a weary, impatient look. Her mother did not want to think about Canfield going back to England.

'Why do you keep harping on about it? One day he'll be sent home, but until then he's here.' Here with her, her eyes said.

'The war is over now, they'll send him back home soon, I expect. He won't be able to refuse, will he?' Vittoria's voice throbbed with satisfaction. She wasn't going to pretend she liked him, even to comfort her mother.

Anna said sharply, 'No, he can't refuse to go. He's in the army so he has to obey orders. We're none of us free, Vittoria, you'll understand that one day. Italy has lost the war. We can't help ourselves so we have to accept what happens to us.'

'We don't have to accept anything!' Vittoria bristled. 'This is our country! We don't have to let the Americans or the British tell us what to do!'

'You're too young to understand. We let Il Duce take us into that war, on the German side, and now we shall have to pay for losing. We need all our friends, like Freddy, now.'

'He's not my friend!' Vittoria got up and ran out of the kitchen. Canfield had taken her father's place in her mother's bed even though he was married and had a child of his own. She hated him. Sometimes she felt she hated her mother, yet she loved her, too. She was in such a muddle: she could never sort out what she really felt or why. She was like a piece of seaweed carried back and forth on the irresistible tide, torn from its roots, helpless, lost.

Carlo's wedding was quite an event in Milan society. The austerity years were coming to an end, people were eager to have a party, dress up, enjoy themselves. It was so long since they had had any fun, but now the greyness of the war was past. Blue skies were back, hope, happiness; they had a future again.

There was no chance of Rachele getting a new wedding dress, so she wore her mother's, which had been laid away in tissue paper in an attic in her family home. It had been rediscovered after her mother died in 1943 during an Allied bombing raid. Rachele had gone through the dead woman's clothes. Nobody threw anything away during the war. Everything was potentially useful.

Old biscuit tins were used to keep food fresh, or to store needles and thread, old clothes were made into rag rugs or cut down for children. When Rachele found her mother's heavy creamy satin wedding dress, she had sat in rapture for a long time, stroking it, feeling the weight, the beauty, the irreplaceable lustre of that marvellous material. It had been rewrapped in the crumpled, yellowed tissue paper in which it had been packed, then hidden again. Rachele couldn't bring herself to cut it up or use it for anything else; nor could she bear to sell it.

It didn't fit her, of course: her mother had been tiny, not above five foot, and as flat as a boy, while Rachele was very female with those full breasts, bigger waist and curvy hips. Luckily, the style of the period had meant that there was lots of spare fabric in the skirt. The seamstress had done a good job of inserting panels in the back and at the waist, to accommodate Rachele's rounded body. Originally the dress had been designed to sweep the floor as the bride walked, but as Rachele was so much taller than her mother the hem ended just below her ankles, which was much more sensible, made it easier to walk up the aisle.

Vittoria wore an old pink silk ball-gown from her mother's first year of married life. Anna remade it, with puff sleeves, a plain round neckline, long skirt, and the dress was a dream. Vittoria loved it. She had never had anything like it before. She felt beautiful.

The wedding breakfast was crowded with people, many of whom Vittoria had known before she went to Venice. They all looked older and shabbier than she remembered, and there were many noticeable gaps in families: sons, brothers, fathers, uncles gone. Nobody talked about that.

Everyone was determined to enjoy themselves and forget what they had suffered, forget what they had lost. Anna and Vittoria wanted to forget, too, but Vittoria was haunted by the ghosts of Alfredo, Filippo and Niccolo. For her they would always be children; it was hard to believe they were gone for ever.

She caught sight of Frederick Canfield moving among the guests, talking, laughing, tanned and slim in his British uniform, his brown leather belt tight around his waist, his buttons highly polished, his brown hair slicked down. Some people were polite, some openly hostile, more to his uniform than to him, but after a few minutes that charm of his softened most of them, especially as his Italian was fluent. From time to time he looked towards her mother with that intimate, secret glance Vittoria had seen them exchange often before; and each time her mother's eyes met his in the same way, completing a magic circle of love, which was almost visible.

Vittoria hated Canfield so much that she could barely eat any of the wedding breakfast. Every time she saw him with her mother she felt their love betray her, shut her out.

The war might be over, but Canfield was still her enemy.

After the wedding, life sank back into the exhausted depression of that bitter, post-war time. Going around Milan on the old bicycle Carlo had managed to buy for her, Vittoria hated everything she saw – the blitzed city was a desert of gutted houses, broken stones, shattered glass and tiles, gardens thick with weeds.

The once magnificent centre was a wreck: the Piazza del Duomo, linked by the Galleria Vittorio Emanuele to Milan's pride, the great opera house La Scala, had been reduced to mountains of rubble after the bombing raids. Even the cathedral had been hit, although by a miracle most of it still stood, some parts shored up with great wooden piles. The streets had been cleared now, traffic flowed again, horses and carts, a few vans and cars, most workers riding battered bicycles like hers – but when would the old beauty of Milan be restored?

Vittoria couldn't believe what had happened to the great glass-vaulted arcade where her mother had so often taken her. She remembered the beautiful, chic women in elegant hats, wandering in and out of the expensive boutiques, drinking coffee and eating rich cakes in the famous Milan coffee-houses. The Galleria, once the envy of Europe, was now roofless, shattered. Everywhere in Milan you saw the price Italy had paid for entering the war, and the more she realised what had happened to her beloved city the more she hated Frederick Canfield.

Over the next few months Canfield came and went all the time, but Vittoria was back at school in Milan and able to stay out of his way. It meant she did not have to pretend to be polite to him.

One day when she came in from school she found her mother in the kitchen preparing a simple evening meal of pasta with basil, garlic and pine kernels.

'Mmm, that smells good! Is it just us tonight, or are Carlo and Rachele eating with us?' The newly-weds had their own suite of rooms on the second floor: Rachele cooked their meals in a tiny, makeshift kitchen that had once been a maid's bedroom.

Without looking round Anna said, 'Freddy is coming to dinner.'

Flushing angrily, Vittoria said, 'Well, I'm not eating with him! I'd rather have dry bread in my room than eat with the Englishman. I wish to God he would go back to his own country.'

'Oh, don't worry, Vittoria. You can be happy now – he goes tomorrow.'

Vittoria felt as if a bird sang inside her. He was going. Going.

But her mother sounded so miserable that she flung her arms round her, hugged her. 'Don't cry, Mamma! I'm sorry. I hate you to be unhappy.'

She couldn't keep the triumph out of her voice, though. Her brain raced. He would have to stay in England with his wife and his child. Please, God, keep him there, never let him come back to Italy, she prayed, as she went upstairs to her room, taking a sandwich of bread and honey with her. This would be their last evening together. She would stay out of their way. Now she could afford to be generous.

The following day, Frederick Canfield left, and six months later Anna Serrati gave birth to his son. Mother and child died within forty-eight hours.

* * *

Venice, 1998

In the police station Sebastian sat with two officers in a chilly, cream-painted room, wrapped in a blue blanket since everything he had been wearing had been taken away for forensic testing. He stared across the table at the policeman who had been interrogating him for what seemed days. Captain Bertelli. Big, sallow, with a waxy black moustache above a full, red mouth. He kept taking a small carton of thin cheroots out of his pocket, looking at them, then sliding them back out of sight.

'Do you smoke, Signore?'

'No, but go ahead if you want to.'

'I'm trying to give up. It isn't easy, especially when you're working on a case. Habit. Smoking when you're questioning a suspect.'

'How can I still be a suspect?' Sebastian erupted. 'Have you talked to the people in Florian's? They must have told you I was there for half an hour before my camera man ran there to tell me Laura had just been attacked. I had nothing to do with the attack on her. I was never anywhere near where it happened.'

Bertelli regarded him stolidly. 'You say she has been receiving anonymous letters, death threats. Why didn't she take them to the police in England?'

'I told her to, but she said she had burned the letters. She wouldn't even tell the police about the doll.'

The policeman looked down at his notes on the table. 'Ah, yes, the doll that was sent back to her, broken . . .' He sounded amused, as if he didn't take it seriously.

'Don't laugh! It wasn't just broken. The bastard had smashed it into smithereens,' Sebastian growled. 'I told her to talk to the police, show them.'

'But she didn't?'

'She said it would sound stupid – after all, it was only a doll. But there was a note pinned to it saying, "You're next!" I thought someone very nasty was behind it and Laura ought to take precautions.' He ran a shaky hand over his face. 'Obviously, I was right. It must be the same guy.'

'Which guy?'

'I don't know. Someone she knows, obviously. Someone who had access to information about her, where she lives in London, how much she loved that doll – she'd had it from childhood, she never parted from it, took it everywhere with her. He must have known that or he wouldn't realise how upset she'd be to see it smashed like that. And how did he get into her hotel room to steal it before she left?'

The policemen listened in brooding silence. Then Bertelli took out his packet of cheroots again, opened the lid, delicately slid one out, rolled it between finger and thumb, lifted it to his nostrils and inhaled with a sigh of need.

'For God's sake, smoke one of the damned things!' Sebastian snapped, and Bertelli gave him a smile, which was somehow triumphant, as if by provoking Sebastian into rage he had won some battle against him.

'You know, I think I will,' he purred, putting the cheroot between his tobacco-stained teeth. The other man produced a lighter, flicked the top with his thumb and a little flame appeared. He held it to Captain Bertelli's cheroot and the policeman inhaled deeply, his eyes half closed in something like ecstasy.

I must remember that look, Sebastian thought, the half-closed eyes, the funny little sigh. It will focus attention on the actor lighting his cigar, whatever else is going on. Could be very useful in that scene where . . .

Then Bertelli asked sharply, 'Are you sure you don't know who he was, this man you're talking about? Did she have a lover? An ex-lover? She's an actress – they have admirers, men hanging around them. Was it someone like that?'

'If there was anyone like that around, she never told me. I don't have a clue. I've seen very little of her over the past few years. I only met her again during the film festival here.

We spent a couple of days together, I've called her a few times since, and then she arrived . . .' He looked at the faded, blistered face of the old clock on the wall opposite him. 'It was only today, around lunch-time, that she got here. It seems like weeks.' Sweat stood out on his pale skin. 'Look, can you ring the hospital again and find out how she is? How bad her injuries were. It's hours since she was taken in. They must be able to tell us how she is. I need to know! I'm going crazy, not knowing whether she's alive or dead.'

The policeman's face betrayed no reaction. He didn't respond by look or word, just blew smoke into a ring above his head, while he watched through those heavy-lidded, half-closed eyes every flicker of expression that passed over Sebastian's face.

Stone-faced and hostile, thought Sebastian. Bastard. Doesn't he have any feelings? He must know . . .

He drew a harsh, painful breath. Of course he must know. What wasn't this bastard of a policeman telling him? Was Laura dead?

Chapter Eleven

Laura was running barefoot through winding corridors, through shadowy rooms, in a house like a museum, richly furnished with old, old things grown shabby with time. Tapestries, faded and mysterious, blew about as she ran past, a high, ornate cabinet's doors flew open, spilling black lace, a white carnival mask, a string of pearls – and then a knife. She heard it clatter on the tiled floor and shuddered, ran faster. A clock chimed on a highly polished octagonal table.

What time is it? Where am I? she thought, but did not speak aloud because she was afraid that the sound of her voice would echo up and down the dark maze and someone might hear her – find her.

Kill her.

She couldn't hear footsteps, but she knew he was somewhere, might at any second spring out.

He . . . Who? She tried to remember, and felt only the pain. It burned like a hot iron in her flesh. She ran faster, fighting not to groan. He mustn't hear her! He would find her! Who? Who was she running from? She knew but couldn't remember.

On and on the corridors wound, now upwards, now on a steep incline down. The walls on either side arched to meet overhead. They were different now, white, blindingly white. She began to think she would never get anywhere, never get out, and at that second she saw ahead an opening, a round window, from which light streamed.

A giant eye stared in at her.

Gasping, she shut her own eyes, but found she could still see. How was that possible?

Because the eye was hers! She was outside, looking in at herself, could see that the white corridors were the winding interior of a skull, the window at which she had halted was an eye socket, the walls and floors were bone, white bone.

Dreaming. She must be dreaming. This wasn't . . . couldn't be . . . real.

Terrified, she opened her eyes again and the eye was still there, shining at her.

'*Come sta?*'

Laura didn't understand what had been said – but the giant eye was a torch. A face loomed behind the beam of light. Hair, a cap, a pale circle of a face.

'*Come sta? Si sente meglio?*'

'What? Who are you? Where is this?'

'You don't speak Italian? Don't worry, please. You are in hospital. But you will be okay. Water? You like?'

'Yes, please.' Her mouth was so dry. Thirstily, she watched the other girl pour water into a glass. The nurse bent over her, slid an arm under her shoulders, to lift her higher on her pillows, and Laura gave a thick, involuntary grunt of pain. 'Oh . . . God, that hurt . . .'

'*Le chiedo scusa! Non volevo*—' The nurse broke off, sighing. 'Sorry, sorry. My English, she is not so good, okay?'

'Better than my Italian,' Laura told her.

The nurse laughed and held the glass to Laura's cracked lips.

Sipping carefully Laura winced at the flow of cold liquid into her mouth.

The nurse laid her back gently on the pillows.

'What have I done to my shoulder?' Laura trid to look

down sideways but could see only white bandages under the loose gown she was wearing.

'Is not serious, please, don't worry,' the other woman said soothingly.

But Laura's memory flashed her the image of a knife. She began to shake. 'He stabbed me. He tried to kill me!'

From the outer darkness of the shadowy room a shape emerged, another face, a different uniform.

'Who stabbed you, Miss Erskine?' the policeman asked urgently. 'Who was it? Did you recognise him?'

She shrank back. 'Where did you come from? I didn't see you.'

'I was sitting beside the door. Tell me what happened, Miss Erskine. Do you remember who it was who attacked you?'

'I don't know. He had a mask on his face. He was wearing a ... sort of cloak ... one of those black carnival cloaks ... It came right down to his feet.' She began to sob. 'He tried to kill me. And he smiled! His mouth was so red. He smiled and then the knife came out and – and – he stabbed me!'

The nurse spoke urgently in Italian but the policeman gestured her away, answering in the same language, tersely, sharply.

Then he sat down beside the bed, produced a small tape-recorder. 'Could you tell me everything you remember, Miss Erskine? From the moment you left Ca' d'Angeli.'

'*Aspetta un momento!*' the nurse told him angrily, and ran out of the room.

'What's going on?' Laura asked, turned her head painfully to look after the nurse.

'She is a silly girl. She goes to find someone to stop me asking you questions, but they have to be asked, you know. We have a man at the station. We need to know if he is the man who attacked you.'

Laura stared at him, eyes stretched so wide the skin around them hurt. 'Who?'

The policeman didn't answer, but she saw his eyes. What he was thinking leapt across to her. She bit her lower lip.

'Sebastian? Is it Sebastian?'

Eagerly, the man leant forward, holding out the tape recorder. 'Are you saying it was Sebastian Ferrese? Was it him, Miss Erskine? Did you recognise him?'

Sebastian was lying on his back, an arm across his eyes to shut out the electric light that stopped him from sleeping, but he still didn't sleep. How could he when he didn't know if Laura was alive or dead? Why wouldn't they tell him?

That was obvious, wasn't it? They were trying to trip him up, catch him out. If they kept him in suspense long enough they hoped he might make a mistake. Policemen were creatures of habit and routine, liked the obvious, played the percentages. They fixed on a prime suspect, the obvious one, the most likely one. Then they went through their bag of tricks to get him to betray himself. Because often enough the obvious suspect turned out to be the murderer.

And this time it was him. He was the obvious suspect. With his past, who else would they pick? He had never been charged, but everyone still thought he had killed his wife.

'Your wife died in mysterious circumstances, didn't she, Signore?' he had been asked. 'Tell us about that.'

'Nothing to tell. She jumped out of a window and was killed. Nothing mysterious about it.'

'You were in the room with her, though, weren't you?'

'Yes.' They must know all this. 'Haven't you had the files sent over from the States yet?'

Bertelli didn't answer that, but Sebastian saw his eyes shift. Yes, they had been faxed a report. He was sure of that. Well, of course, that was the first thing they would do, ask for information from the American police.

These days the Internet made the transfer of information

simple, almost immediate. At the touch of a switch the stuff went speeding down the line. Instant evidence, your past open to inspection. No hiding place any more. Your whole life was on a computer somewhere and Interpol despatched it to any police force that wanted to scan it.

'Where were you standing when she jumped?'

'I wasn't standing. I was sitting, at a table, writing.'

'Writing what?'

'Notes.'

'Notes for what?'

'The film I was planning.'

'And your wife was by the window? Was it open?'

'She opened it.'

'You saw her open it?'

'I heard her.'

'And you didn't get up to find out what she was doing?'

'I knew what she was doing. She told me. "I'm going to jump," she said, and opened the window.'

'And you didn't try to stop her?' The policeman's voice was cold, critical; he stared at Sebastian with that look he had seen in the eyes of the policemen who had interviewed him after Clea's death.

'You don't understand,' Sebastian said wearily.

'Explain, then, tell me how it was.'

'Have you ever lived with a hysteric? She threatened to kill herself all the time. Throw herself out of windows, out of trains, out of cars doing eighty miles an hour down a motorway.'

Bertelli's heavy black brows twitched upwards. 'Do you always drive that fast, Signore? If you do that here, you will find yourself in trouble.'

'I haven't even got a car at the moment. I don't need one, in Venice, do I?'

Bertelli surveyed him. 'You were telling me about your wife.'

'She was always threatening to kill herself,' Sebastian

repeated. 'She fought with me to grab the wheel of my car: "I'm going to kill us both," she'd scream. "I'm going to jump out." And then there was the gun. She kept a little handgun in her purse. Lots of women do in the States, for protection when they go out on the street. Clea was always waving it about. "I'm going to shoot myself," she'd yell. Or she'd pick up kitchen knives and say, "I'm going to cut my throat!"' He lifted his heavy head and looked at the policeman, his eyes lightless black. 'That's how she was. She threatened to kill herself all the time.'

'And you never believed her?'

'Oh, at first, yes. She terrified me. I didn't dare leave her alone at times, in case she did kill herself. Her therapist told me people like that never do. If they keep saying they will and don't, they never will. It's an attention ploy. "She wants your attention," he said. "She needs to know you care." Well, I was sick of giving her my attention at the end. I was so tired of her scenes and tantrums. So that last time I ignored her. Took no notice at all when she opened the window, climbed on to the sill, screamed at me, "I'm jumping, I'm jumping". "Go ahead, you stupid bitch," I said, without even looking round. "Jump, give me some peace!" And she did. Okay?' His voice hoarsened. 'That last time she went ahead and fucking did it.'

And fell screaming, 'No, no, no,' all the way down while he had run to the window and had frozen in horror and panic.

He looked at the policeman with eyes that burned. 'So in a way you're right. I killed her. She died because I wouldn't give her my attention. And if you want to know if I feel guilty – of course I fucking well do. If I had had any idea that that one time she would really do it . . .' His voice broke. 'Oh, go to hell,' he said, putting his arms on the table and his head down on them.

They left him alone for an hour or so after that. He lay down and tried to sleep. He was so tired he was hallucinating, seeing images of his mother screaming in the blizzard over the canal, of Clea falling, crying out all the way down, of Laura . . .

The door opened. His nerves jumped. They were back. 'Leave me alone, I'm not answering any more questions,' he said, not moving from the bunk.

Bertelli walked towards him. He had a large plastic bag dangling over his arm. In it was something wet and black. A coat?

'Do you recognise this, Signore?'

Sebastian shook his head.

'Stand up, please.' The man's voice was curt.

Sebastian almost refused to obey, but what was the point? They would pull him to his feet. So he swung his legs off the bunk and got up. The policeman held the plastic bag against him. Adjusted it. Stared.

'What's going on?' Sebastian asked. 'What is this?'

'It was found floating on the canal, close to where Miss Erskine was attacked. It fits the description of a cape she says her attacker was wearing.'

Sebastian stepped back involuntarily, away from the cold plastic bag and what it contained.

'I told you, I was nowhere near there, I was in Florian's, I never saw her.' He drew a long, audible breath. 'I wouldn't harm a hair on her head. If I knew who stabbed her, I'd kill the bastard.'

'That wouldn't be very clever, would it?' Bertelli frowned, yet his dark eyes were not unfriendly. 'We'll find him, don't worry, Signore. And the law will deal with him when we do. We would like you to sign a statement. We talked to the waiter who served you in Florian's, and the other customers. You were in the café when the attack took place. And you're too tall, anyway. Miss Erskine said the cape came down to feet of the attacker. I can see it would only come midway down your legs.'

'So you believe me now?' Anger choked Sebastian's throat, his voice sounded slurred. 'Well, thanks for nothing. I told you I didn't do it. You've kept me here all this time, grilling me, when you should have been out there looking for whoever really did do it.'

'Oh, we've been following up many other leads, don't worry. I'm sorry, Signor Ferrese, but you want us to catch the man who tried to kill Miss Erskine, don't you? We need to know everything we can about her – how else can we be sure whether it was a random attack, or one aimed specifically at her?'

Sebastian asked, 'Have there been other attacks?'

'No, this is an isolated incident – so far. But we have to check every avenue. Tell me, to your knowledge, has Miss Erskine any enemies? Male or female?'

'I told you about the threats—'

'Yes, but did you suspect anyone you knew?'

Sebastian bit out, 'No!'

'When your wife jumped, Signore, were you alone with her? Just the two of you, in the room?'

A silence, then Sebastian said, 'No, my assistant was there. Valerie Hyde. What are you getting at? Who have you been talking to? You know what it's like in any organisation – people get jealous, resentful, envious, they jockey for position, they bitch about each other in private. Valerie has her enemies, just as I do. You don't want to take any gossip too seriously.'

'I am only interested in hard evidence, Signore, don't worry.'

'Have you talked to Valerie?'

'Not yet. I will do that tomorrow.'

'Go easy on her. She's not a happy woman. She's alone in the world, she has very few friends. Her work is her life.'

'You like her very much?' The man watched him closely and Sebastian wondered what his face was betraying to the policeman's shrewd, clever eyes. He tried to look as blank as Bertelli did, but he hadn't had the training for it. The policeman gave almost nothing away; his emotions must be in the deep freeze. Sebastian wished his own were.

He said, 'I'm sorry for her. And I like her – of course, I do, but if you mean more than that, no. There was a time, years ago, when we had a brief fling, but that was all it was. She isn't my type. Since then, *niente,* zilch, zero. She works for me. That's all there is to our relationship. And anyway—' He broke off.

Bertelli considered him, staring into his eyes. 'What were you going to say?'

Heavily, Sebastian said, 'Look, I think I may have to fire her and I feel guilty about it, okay?'

'Why are you going to fire her?'

Sebastian didn't want to talk about it: he felt disloyal, discussing Valerie behind her back, but he had opened this can of worms by a slip of the tongue, and he knew Bertelli wasn't going to let him close it again.

'She – she's too . . . obsessive. She's on my case day and night. I can't move without tripping over her. I find it uncomfortable.'

Bertelli listened thoughtfully, scratching his chin. Sebastian sensed that the man knew he had left a good deal unspoken.

'So, she's in love with you? When you had this . . . what did you call it? . . . fling? What does that mean, I wonder? Just one night, or a little more than that? Hmm? Well, whatever, it meant nothing on your side – but she was more serious? You knew it at the time? That she was in love with you? Or did you realise it later?'

Red in the face now, Sebastian said, 'Maybe. I don't know for sure how she feels. Look, it was a long time ago, and it wasn't even really an affair, just a . . .'

'Fling!' nodded Bertelli. 'I understand. But she went on working for you afterwards. You say it is years since you slept with her. Why do you suddenly feel you must fire her?'

'I suppose I feel guilty about her. I've come to realise I'm all the life she has and I've begun to feel claustrophobic around her.'

'What sort of woman is she? Beautiful?'

'No. Too thin for that. She's energetic, quick in everything she does. Black eyes, dark hair, dresses well, but her face and body are bony, angular. Not very feminine.'

Bertelli smiled. 'And you like feminine women?'

'Don't most men?' Sebastian looked defiantly at him.

Bertelli shrugged. 'I suppose. Okay, I'll have a written statement of what you've told us typed up. Read through every word, then, if you accept that the statement is an accurate reflection of what you said, would you sign it at the bottom on the last page?'

'Are you releasing me?'

'For the moment, but you must not leave Venice. We may need to talk to you again.'

Urgently, Sebastian asked, 'Laura . . . Is she – how is she?'

There was a faint sympathy in the policeman's eyes now. 'You are in love with her, aren't you?'

'Did I ever deny it? I've loved her from the minute I met her.'

'You were still married then, though?'

'Yes.' Sebastian's face was weary. 'Oh, yes, to the most beautiful woman in the world, Captain Bertelli. Clea was the biggest star in films, and breathtakingly lovely, even at the end.'

'Yet you fell in love with Miss Erskine on sight?'

They stared at each other. After a silence, Sebastian said, 'Laura was shiningly innocent, Captain, a very young girl with eyes as pure as the sea. If you had known my wife you would understand why I found Laura irresistible. And still do. She still has that sweetness and purity, even now. I love her more than life itself. Literally. If she died, I'd want to die too.'

'She's in no danger, Signore. She was stabbed several times in the upper arm and shoulder – her attacker was undoubtedly aiming for her heart, but Miss Erskine put up her arm to fend off the knife. That saved her life. Luckily, someone came round the corner before the murderer could stab her again, and the man – if it was a man – ran off. Miss Erskine has had an operation and is heavily sedated, but we were able to talk to her while she was conscious.'

'Can I visit her?'

'Not tonight, Signore. Perhaps tomorrow. I'll send you back to Ca' d'Angeli in one of our boats now.'

Sebastian looked at the plastic bag and what it held. 'Are you sure that's what he wore?'

'Yes. Forensic has found Miss Erskine's blood on it.'

'The bastard . . .'

'We've taken a lot of other samples from it. We have his DNA. We'll find him. As you know, we've taken your DNA, and we'll be testing it, and tomorrow we'll ask every member of the film crew to give us a DNA sample.'

'You really think it was one of us?'

'Don't you?' Bertelli smiled at Sebastian.

'It seems pretty likely,' Sebastian conceded unwillingly, thinking of his friends, colleagues he had worked with for years. Sidney? It couldn't be. No, not Sidney.

'Just the men, at first.'

'At first? You surely don't think it could be a woman?'

'It was someone short. And a knife is as much a woman's weapon as a man's. And . . . there are other reasons.'

'What other reasons?' Sebastian remembered the questions about Valerie. Surely to God they didn't suspect her? No. No, he couldn't believe it.

'I can't say. But, please, make sure nobody from the film company leaves Venice until I say they can go.'

The film crew went to bed late that night. They sat about in a gloomy silence all evening in a little bar along the Rio San Barnaba, one of the many canals bisecting the Dorsoduro, the peaceful residential area directly opposite the San Marco district, where the Accademia, Venice's greatest art gallery, was to be found.

Sidney was staying in a pretty little *pensione* in Campo San Barnaba Square and had become infatuated with this part of

Venice. He loved to walk around the tiny narrow streets, called *calle*, or along the canals, absorbing everything he saw. He was fascinated by the houses behind high walls, windows shuttered against prying eyes, an air of mystery hanging around them with the white mists of the lagoon. He was crazy about the great churches, the open, windy squares, the elegant little bridges with their shimmering reflections on the water below their perfect bow shape.

'What's it mean?' asked Carmen, the junior assistant director, her young face pale, her hair loose and tousled, staring a little unsteadily out of the window at dimly lit buildings on the other side of the narrow canal.

'What's what mean?' Sidney asked, looking in the same direction but seeing nothing to explain her question.

'Dorsowhat's-it,' she muttered.

'Dorsoduro. It means "hard backbone".' He leant over, refilled his glass from one of the copper jugs of wine standing along the table at which, much earlier, they had eaten dinner, a simple meal of bean soup followed by *risi e bisi* – the traditional Venetian dish of rice and peas sprinkled with grated Parmesan. They had all skipped dessert and gone on to coffee, but none of them wanted to leave yet.

'Did you know Venice is made up of over a hundred tiny little islands?' Sidney asked.

Nobody seemed interested, but he didn't let that put him off. 'All built over now, of course, but once, long ago they were islands, made up from soil that washed down from the Dolomites. That's what Venice started from.'

'Why did they want to live out here in the middle of the sea?'

'Protection, I guess. Living on an island made it harder for enemies to get at them and life was dangerous a thousand years ago, especially in the Med, with pirates and bandits roaming around. Fear makes people do the damnedest things. That's why they built Venice here. It couldn't have been easy. First, they had to drive wood piles into the lagoon bed, rows and rows of them, all very close together. On top of that, they laid a single row of bricks, then a band of Istrian stone, a sort of marble, and then they made their homes on this platform.' He paused to drink some of his luscious, glowing red wine.

'Sidney, Sidney, you've been reading books again,' the Camera Operator mocked him plaintively. 'How many times d'you have to be told? You'll go blind. It's a nasty habit, give it up.'

'Look, the girl asked me for information, I gave it to her. We don't all want to talk about football, you know.'

'You don't know zilch about football. That's why you don't want to talk about it!'

'Moron!'

'D'you want a punch in the mouth?'

'Oh, for Christ's sake, shut up, all of you!' Valerie snarled, and everyone in the cramped, smoky little bar turned to look at her.

'It's okay, Val, we're just having fun. We're all friends, aren't we, Joe? You look shattered, though. Why don't you go back to your place and get to bed?'

Sidney's voice was gentle but she glared at him, her intense, black eyes all pupil, in her white face. The red scar of her mouth made her look like a crazy clown.

'Why don't you mind your own fucking business?'

The others looked down into their glasses.

Sidney said, 'The strain's getting to you, you won't be fit for work tomorrow.'

'Are you so stupid you don't know this picture is dead in the water now? There won't be any work to do tomorrow.'

They avoided each others' eyes. Sidney said flatly, 'Of course we know – why do you think we're drinking ourselves stupid? There's nothing we can do but wait and see what happens.'

'You're ostriches, the lot of you!'

'Go on back to your room, Val, and get some sleep. If the

police let Sebastian go, he'll want to get on with the schedule. We still have to shoot some street scenes.'

'Don't you realise? With her out of it, there's no picture. He won't recast, he'll just junk the whole project.'

'She may recover sooner than you think—' Carmen began, but Valerie almost screamed at her, 'She won't recover. She can't. She'll die. She's probably dead already, she has to be. There was so much blood—'

They all looked at each other, their eyes startled, wide. Valerie got to her feet and blundered out into the dark of the Venetian night.

Carmen whispered, 'You don't think . . . ? She's so fixated on Sebastian. She wouldn't – It couldn't be her, could it?'

Sidney looked round the circle of faces. 'Where was she when Laura got attacked? You were all in the area, around St Mark's Square, and those shopping streets beyond it. Did any of you see her?'

'No,' Carmen said. The others shook their heads one by one.

Sidney got to his feet. 'She doesn't strike me as the murderous type. Don't let your imaginations run riot. Leave the detection to the cops. And now I'm off while I can still just about make it to my *pensione*. I'll pay the bill – it can go on expenses. In the circumstances, I think it will get through. You lot can stay here and drink – but from now on it's on you. Night, everyone.'

Sidney paid with his credit card, and tucked it and the receipt carefully into his sheepskin-lined wax jacket, which he zipped up to his throat before walking out of the bar into the chilly night air.

The snow had long stopped falling. The sky was alive with stars, as bright as if they were almost within reach. They and the Victorian-style street-lamps were reflected in the dark water of the canal. The narrow streets were empty, silent, every window shuttered.

'I'll walk along with you, Sidney,' said Carmen, who was also staying at his *pensione*. 'I think I may be a bit tipsy.'

'Me, too,' Sidney said, linking his arm with hers in a friendly way. 'I hate the middle of the night, don't you? Three in the morning especially. Depresses me, especially when I'm alone.'

'Me, too,' she said, swaying and bumping her shoulder against his.

Sidney looked down at her sleepy young face, wishing he was her age again. 'You're gorgeous, Carmen – you know that? Why don't we share a bed tonight? Keep each other warm and safe.'

'Fuck off,' she said, without resentment, but smiled, flattered by the pass. She might not fancy Sidney, but he was almost god-like in her eyes. She had known his name, seen his films while she was still at school, and she couldn't believe she was here, walking arm in arm with him, talking so easily to him.

'Okay, fair enough,' Sidney agreed amiably. A look of relief passed over Carmen's face at his cheerful acceptance of the brush-off. The last thing she wanted to do was offend him.

He said, 'Darling, remember, I'm old enough to be your father, but I know a thing or two about women, and how to please them, which is more than most guys your age can say. If you change your mind, just whistle. You know how to whistle, don't you?'

She put on an American drawl. 'You just put your lips together and blow.' And demonstrated but only came up with a faint whisper of sound.

They laughed at each other.

'Did you think I wouldn't get that, Sid? I love Bogart and Bacall films.'

'Who doesn't? I've noticed you're a movie buff, Carmen. See everything you can, good, bad or indifferent – the more you see the more you'll learn.'

'I do, I always have. At home I have a wall full of videos.' They wandered on and paused outside the *pensione*. 'Sid ...' she began, and stopped.

'Uh-huh?' he encouraged, smiling down at her.

'Valerie?'

His face changed, froze.

'Just now,' she went on. 'Didn't you think – well, wasn't she weird? All that about the blood, I mean. You don't think? Well, anyone can see she hates Laura. The way she looks at her. Sends a shiver down my spine. And she hangs around Sebastian day and night, tries to keep everyone else away from him. Dead jealous, if you ask me. I know you said she didn't seem the murderous type, but she is definitely a bit psycho.'

'We all are,' Sidney replied. 'In our own way. Some of us more so than others. Sebastian, especially.'

She looked up at him. 'Do you think it was him?'

'No. He was in Florian's – I saw him there as I walked past before I found Laura, and she'd only just been stabbed when I got to her. It couldn't have been Sebastian.' He got out the front-door key of the *pensione*. 'Let's get out of this horrible weather and try to thaw out with a hot-water bottle – if you won't help me get warmed up any other way!'

The Contessa lay awake in her high, cold room listening to the soft murmur and slap of the tide along the canal, the faint echo of music from somewhere in one of the grand hotels nearby, the hum of electricity that told her that her son was still up, working no doubt, in his studio. He had always kept strange hours: a sculptor did not need daylight to work by, as a painter did. Her husband had often been up before the sun rose, in his studio, preparing his paints, blocking out canvases, or just standing by the window gazing at the miracle of Venice in the first gold gleam of light, wrapped in a fur robe in winter but on hot summer days often naked, his beautiful tanned body gleaming as he stepped back from his easel to consider his work.

Suddenly she heard a sound in the room below her own, a creaking that told her somebody was in there, in her dead husband's bedroom – that haunted, shadowy forest room, hung with green tapestries that always seemed to stir in some unheard wind, to rustle with whispers, echoes from the past. She never went in there. Even passing the door she would start to tremble and hurry on, eyes averted.

Who was in there? It couldn't be that girl. She was in the hospital. The latest news bulletin had said she was fighting for her life – maybe the knife had penetrated her lung. Pity it hadn't entered her heart. If she had one. Women like that never had hearts.

Another creak in the room below. Vittoria sat up in bed, her greying hair awry, shivering a little even though she wore a warm Victorian-style red flannel nightie. Tense and still, she strained to be certain she wasn't imagining it, as she often had before, listening in the night for his footsteps, his breathing, the sound of his laughter, his groans of passionate satisfaction in that bed.

But this was no ghost. Someone was walking restlessly backwards and forwards from wall to wall like a caged animal.

She caught sight of her reflection in the dressing-table mirror; an old woman with a pale face out of which glittered obsidian black eyes. The police had searched the room earlier, and locked it when they left, taking the key with them.

It had to be Sebastian in there.

They had said on television that he was being held at the police station. Helping police with their enquiries was the phrase they always used but she hoped he was under arrest, was going to be charged with murdering the girl. She would have got rid of both of them, then. That would have been a neat finish, a beautiful, symmetrical knot, tying off the whole pattern.

Finally, it would all have ended. She would have won. Her teeth ground against each other. She had to win. She would not be beaten. One way or another she was going to be rid of every shred of evidence of what they had done to her, wipe it all out.

Climbing out of bed she rolled back the carpet – rolled back time with it as she lay down, remembering the misery, jealousy and rage.

For a second she could not be sure who she was watching. Domenico? Her heart beat so fast it hurt; sweat trickled down her body. How many nights had she lain here and watched him?

No. Of course not. How could it be? He was dead.

It was their son, walking restlessly to and fro in that room which, for her, was always haunted by his father.

Chapter Twelve

Looking back over her life, Victoria Serrati saw it as a river whose twists and turns were always dictated by death. Sometimes she wondered if she had been cursed at birth. Why else did those she loved keep dying? Her half-brothers, Alfredo, Filippo, Niccolo . . . She had had so many brothers once, now they were gone, and so were her parents. In bed at night she woke up in terror from a nightmare thinking, Who will be next? Nothing seemed real to her any more. The world was a place of shadows and ghosts . . .

Milan, 1948

Carlo and his wife were too preoccupied with their own lives to notice the sadness and fear buried in Vittoria's eyes. Rachele was obsessed with having a child, but although she became pregnant several times she never managed to carry the baby the full nine months, and each miscarriage had a devastating effect on both her and Carlo. Ravaged with weeping, her sultry face blotchy, her dark eyes red-rimmed, Rachele stayed upstairs in her bedroom all day.

Carlo was either explosive, snarling, shouting, barking orders at the servants, or he sat silent, staring sullenly into space, his brows heavy, his mouth turned down at the corners. Vittoria avoided him whenever he was in the house, which was rare. Rachele stayed out of sight, and Carlo took refuge at the factory. The house was empty and bleak, and Vittoria's life revolved around school and her friends.

Nineteen forty-seven was a bad year for Italy: food was scarce and riots broke out. The government couldn't solve the problems fast enough, but America, afraid of Communist power taking over, came to the rescue, with food supplies and money. In 1948 a new alliance came into being between America and the Western nations, which everyone soon called NATO, and life began slowly to return to normal.

During the spring of 1948, the Serrati family moved into their new house. Rachele was over the moon at having two bathrooms and an ultra-modern kitchen with electricity. She threw parties to show off to her friends, became more cheerful.

One morning at breakfast the post was brought in by Antonio, who was now wearing a livery: black trousers and a striped green waistcoat, which fitted tightly around his slim waist. He looked good in it, thought Vittoria. She was almost sixteen now, her body developing from a child's into that of a woman: breasts rounding and ripening, hips taking on a female curve, her mind prickling with awareness of the opposite sex.

He caught her eye and smiled, his black eyes warm. He was her only real friend in this house. When her mother died she had knelt by the bed, sobbing, until Carlo told her gruffly to go to her room and rest. He wasn't unkind, but he had never loved her mother: he had begun by resenting her and had ended indifferent to her. He didn't share Vittoria's grief. She had stumbled out, almost blind with crying, and collided with Antonio, who held her, wordlessly comforting, stroking her hair, while she wept on his thin chest.

'She's dead, Mamma is dead. And the baby, the poor little baby, it looks so small and white, like a wax doll. Mamma . . .' In a wail, she cried, 'Nobody here wants me. I'm all alone.'

They had both heard Carlo opening the bedroom door and

had sprung apart. Vittoria had run along the winding corridors to her room. Carlo would have been shocked if he had seen a servant putting his arms around her. Ever since, she and Antonio had had an unspoken bond.

She smiled back at him now, knowing that Carlo was looking at the letters and would not notice. If he did, he wouldn't approve. She had to be careful when he was around.

'Who do you know in Switzerland?' Carlo asked, holding out a letter with a Swiss stamp.

'Nobody.' She stared blankly, her mind still on Antonio, who had left the room.

'You must know somebody – this is addressed to you.' He tossed her the expensive cream envelope.

She had only to glance at the black, scrawling handwriting to know who it was from. 'Olivia!' she said, her eyes brightening. 'I wonder what she's doing in Switzerland?'

'Open it and find out!' Carlo teased – he was in a very good mood. Was Rachele pregnant again? Vittoria wondered, slitting open the envelope. Please, God, don't let her lose this one. The atmosphere in this house would change dramatically if Rachele had a child. Even Vittoria could see that the woman was born to be a mother: her face showed the ache of emptiness, of need. Put a baby in her arms and Rachele would be transformed with joy.

'Olivia ... She's the aristocratic one, isn't she? Lives in a palazzo? One of the families whose names are written in the Golden Book of Venice?' Carlo's tone was faintly derisive: he had often been snubbed by members of the aristocracy and looked down on as a tradesman.

Defensively, Vittoria said, 'That's what Olivia told me, but I don't even know if the Golden Book still exists. I don't think it matters any more anyway.'

'Oh, it matters – to the upper classes,' Carlo said, mouth twisting. 'They never stop thinking about their long history. Just because their families were around in the Middle Ages, and their names were written in this book Venice kept to make sure that only the right families got into government, these aristocrats look down on people like us, Vittoria. We're vulgar manufacturers, we aren't blue-blooded, we don't live off the money our ancestors made. We get our hands dirty working to create wealth for this country, for our employees.' He looked down at the letter in her hand. 'Well, is your friend on holiday in Switzerland?'

He took a crisp hot roll from the basket in the centre of the table, spread it with black cherry jam and bit into it aggressively, with his big, white, teeth.

'No, she's at school there – well, she calls it a finishing school, very grand, she says, and she's having a wonderful time. It's not like being at school at all. She's got a beautiful view of a lake from her window. The school's at Lausanne – where's that?'

He snorted. 'Do they teach you geography at that school of yours? Lausanne's on Lake Geneva, just inside the Swiss border with France.'

His mind wandered, as it always did, back to his obsession with work. 'The Swiss drug companies have a big slice of the international market and it will be years before we catch up – but we will, I shall make sure of that. There's a long road ahead of us. We need forward planning, and friends in high places, to take advantage of our position in Italy. Then we can expand into the rest of Europe.' He drank some more of the fragrant black coffee, then said, 'How long does your friend say she's staying in Switzerland?'

Vittoria consulted the letter again. 'Two years. Until she's eighteen. She's the same age as me – she was in my class at the convent school in Venice.'

Carlo tapped the fingertips of one hand on the table, frowning down at the roll on his plate. 'How would you like to join her in Switzerland?'

Vittoria was so taken aback that for a minute or two she

wasn't sure what to say. She had never thought of going away again – she liked her present school and would miss her friends – but it would be a relief to escape the dark moods in this house, Rachele's weeping and Carlo's thunderous tempers. And she would be with Olivia – the only peaceful years of her life had been spent in Venice, with Olivia and Gina.

'Won't it be terribly expensive?' she asked, uncertainly.

Carlo gave an assured shrug. 'Don't worry about that, we can afford it. The factory is doing better every year and I've almost finished paying for the new buildings. We make more money now than we ever did before the war. Look, I'll ring the school and ask them to send us a prospectus.'

'I think I would like to go. I wonder if I'll learn to ski.'

'I expect you'll have to – they get a lot of snow. You'll enjoy yourself, and you can be useful to me, too.'

'Useful?'

'One of our chief rivals has a factory in Lausanne. You might be able to pick up whispers of new ideas.'

She was astonished. 'Spy, you mean? But ... I wouldn't know where to start.'

'Just keep your ears open. Anything you notice or hear could be useful, any gossip about new drugs they're developing. The local people will work in the factory. When you go into town to a café or a cinema, you might overhear something interesting. But be careful! Don't let anyone guess what you're up to, even your friend from Venice. Not a word to a soul, Vittoria.'

'No, of course not.' It might be rather exciting to play at spying, to listen in on conversations, ask carefully phrased, innocent-sounding questions. She smiled to herself. She certainly wouldn't tell a soul. She liked having secrets.

Two weeks later she left for Switzerland, taking with her a large trunk of clothes, sports equipment and books. She was met at the railway station and driven to the school, an eighteenth-century building in the classic style, creamy stucco and elegant proportions, with two wings of more modern design hidden behind it, and beyond that gardens going down to the lake.

The weather was hot, languorous, even though a cool breeze blew softly off the lake. As the taxi came up the drive to the portico-shaded front door, Vittoria saw other girls: playing tennis on grass courts, sitting reading in a rose garden, talking in groups on benches with a young woman who was clearly a teacher. A few girls looked curiously out of the long windows on the first floor. Was Olivia one of them?

Vittoria had written to say she was coming and had received a delighted reply. 'You'll love it here, we'll have such fun! I'll try to get Michie to let you share my room, then we can talk about home in bed at night. Although I love it here, I am homesick, now and then. Nowhere is as beautiful as Venice, is it? We're supposed to be asleep by nine, which is hard when it's still light outside!'

Madame Michelet – Michie to the girls – the headmistress, Swiss by nationality but French-speaking and of French descent, was a slender, chic woman in her late thirties, in clothes Vittoria recognised at once as the highest fashion, with cropped black hair and dark eyes and a face like a razor, smooth-skinned, with a golden tan, but all sharp angles and dangerous lines, warning that she was tough and difficult to manipulate.

She had Carlo's letter spread open in front of her, on her green-leather-topped desk, and glanced at it after welcoming Vittoria politely.

'So. You are here to learn English, French and German, firstly, and various other subjects your brother has requested – Cordon Bleu cooking, typing, fashion, how to drive a car. But I gather that, above all, he wants you to acquire social graces – how to walk, sit, dress, talk to people.'

'Yes, Madame.'

Madame Michelet surveyed her appraisingly. 'I understand you know Olivia d'Angeli?'

'Yes, we met in Venice, when I lived there during the war.'

'So I am told. She requested that you share her bedroom – you're happy with that?'

Vittoria nodded, smiling.

'Very well.' Madame rang a small brass bell on her desk and the door opened immediately, to reveal the maid, in black and a white lace cap, who had admitted Vittoria at the front door of the school and led her to the headmistress's study.

'Jeanne, please show Mademoiselle Serrati to Mademoiselle d'Angeli's room. Has her luggage been taken there?'

'Yes, Madame.'

Vittoria got up. The headmistress said, 'If you have any problems you are always welcome to come and talk to me.'

Vittoria couldn't imagine herself doing so: Madame was not an approachable woman. Getting up, she gave the little curtsy she had been taught by the nuns, and Madame Michelet smiled approvingly.

'I hope you will be happy here, Vittoria.'

'*Merci,* Madame.'

The door closed on the comfortable study, the upright figure at the desk, and Vittoria sighed with relief, then followed the maid up the highly polished oak stairs, the walls lined with prints of famous French and Italian paintings.

She recognised Botticelli's *Primavera,* Leonardo's *Virgin of the Rocks,* a painting of Madame de Pompadour by François Boucher, a Fragonard, some early Impressionist paintings of landscapes.

Olivia's room was on the first floor, right at the end of a corridor. To Vittoria's disappointment, nobody was there. Jeanne•helped her to unpack, hung clothes in a small white-painted wardrobe, filled a chest of drawers with underwear and nightdresses, told her which of the two beds would be hers, then left her alone. She sat on the window-seat and gazed out over the gleaming blue lake. The view was as good as Olivia had promised.

A few minutes later bells began to ring, followed by a stampede of feet on the creaking stairs. The door was flung open and Olivia rushed in, beaming. 'I saw your taxi arrive – I knew you were here.' She was in tennis whites and must have been one of the girls playing on the courts as Vittoria drove past.

They hugged, a little self-consciously because it was three years since they had met and letters hadn't prepared them for the changes in each other.

Olivia was now sixteen, a willowy girl of five foot seven or so, tiny of waist, but with surprisingly large breasts and long legs. She had always been striking; Vittoria could see that she was turning into a beauty, with her family's dark colouring and golden-olive skin.

Vittoria knew that she herself would never be a beauty: her own face was neat but plain, her body faintly dumpy, her hips too wide, her legs short.

'Well, do you like the look of the place?' asked Olivia, complacently, knowing what the answer must be.

'I love it! Isn't this room elegant? And I can't stop staring at the view – the lake is much bigger than I expected. What are the other girls like?'

'Most of them are okay. One or two can be vile, but there are a couple of American girls who are great fun. They think up some pretty wild things to do.'

'What sort of things?'

Olivia giggled. 'There's a boys' school, St Xavier's, along the lake – Trudie and Angie met some of the older ones in town and we're forbidden to talk to boys! It's one of the seven deadly sins here, so they have to be careful or they'll be expelled. They're writing to them – they leave letters in a dead tree and they're planning to climb out one night and have a midnight swim and a picnic.'

'How romantic!' Vittoria's eyes glowed at the idea of swimming in that beautiful lake at night, under the moon.

Olivia sighed. 'Isn't it? Why don't we go, too? Trudie said their boys had two other friends who were really good-looking.'

If they were caught and expelled Carlo would be furious. Heaven knew what he would do to her! Vittoria bit her lip, tempted but scared of the consequences. 'I can't. I'd love to but Carlo, my brother, would never forgive me if we got caught and I was sent home.'

'Oh, Toria, go on! They treat us like little kids here, but we're old enough to get married. Anyone would think the war was still on. Come on! At least write a note to Hal.'

'Hal? What sort of name is that?'

'He's English.'

Vittoria's face set like concrete. 'No, I'm not writing to him. I don't want to go. I hate the English.'

'The war's over and we're all friends again. The English are coming to Venice in droves. We can't afford to go on quarrelling with them and, anyway, the Germans treated us far worse than the English ever did.'

Vittoria didn't want to argue, so she changed the subject. 'What's the food like here?'

'You're being very stupid,' muttered Olivia, then said, 'Well, how good the food is depends on who cooked it. The staff do the breakfasts and dinners, and they're pretty good, but we have to make lunch ourselves – which is fine, so long as you get something from one of the good cooks. Jo-Anne, for instance, can make great pasta, but some of the girls can't cook to save their lives. Just wait till you try Trudie's food – it's disgusting.' She paused. 'Look, Toria, about the boys, you won't tell, will you?'

'Of course not! I'll forget you ever mentioned it. How's Gina? Is she still in Venice?'

'Oh, yes, at our old school. I haven't seen her for months. Her mother still runs the grocer's shop. I expect Gina will work there when she leaves school.'

'I can't see her behind a counter, somehow. Her mother was always so ambitious for her. Do you know what you want to do after leaving school, Olivia?'

'I'm going to art college – I want to paint.'

'Will your family let you?' Vittoria asked doubtfully, remembering that magnificent palazzo on the Grand Canal, the maid in her ribboned white cap, the gossip at their school about the d'Angeli family, their long history and wealth.

'Let them try and stop me! Domenico went to art college so why shouldn't I? The old ideas are dead, we're living in a new world.'

Remembering Olivia's brother Vittoria felt oddly breathless. He had been the most beautiful man she had ever seen, with that golden skin and black hair, like an angel she had seen many times in the Treasury Room at St Mark's – a Byzantine icon of the Archangel Michael, shimmering with gold, great wings spread and one hand raised in a blessing, his face gentle and serious.

'What's he doing now?'

'He's at home. Painting. He leaves college this year and then he says he'll teach.'

'Art?'

'What else, you idiot?'

'And your family don't object? I mean, he'll inherit the palazzo, won't he?'

'He already owns it. Our father's dead and there's nobody to stop Domenico doing whatever he wants, especially now he's twenty-one. Anyway, there isn't much money left, you see – my school fees are being paid by my godmother, who's very rich, but our family estates were lost during the war, and all we have left is the palazzo. Domenico will need to earn a living somehow.'

'Does he have a girlfriend?'

'What do you think? He's had girlfriends since he was about fourteen! But he doesn't take girls seriously, Nico just wants to have fun!'

The bells began again and Olivia got up from her bed, groaning. 'Prep! You can stay here until dinner time, you won't have any prep to do yet. See you later. I'll come back to show you the way to the dining room.'

The patter of feet had begun on the stairs again; doors slammed and laughter and chatter sounded on all the floors.

Standing by the window staring at the luminous lake under the setting sun Vittoria thought of Domenico and sighed. He would never look at her, she knew that – she was too plain. She shouldn't even think about him! Her own common sense told her that she would be wasting her time. That didn't stop her dreaming about him that night and many nights afterwards. If she really worked at her art she could at least be able to talk to him in a way that aroused his interest.

So many people she loved had died she was afraid to love again – yet she yearned for it, for the joy of loving and being loved. Love was like a fire towards which she was drawn, longing to be warmed by it, to be comforted, to belong.

Maybe Domenico would come here soon, to visit his sister. She was aching to see him again.

But as the end of that long, sunny summer term arrived Olivia heard from her brother that he was off to America where he had taken a job as an art lecturer in Calfornia and wouldn't be at home in Venice when she got back.

'How long is he staying there?' asked Vittoria, sick with disappointment.

'He says a year, maybe two. If he isn't back by the time I leave school maybe he'll let me go to America to join him – I'd love to, I'm dying to see America, and if Domenico is there I can live with him.'

Looking back on her two years at Lausanne, Vittoria could remember very little that happened. Too many days were filled with learning social graces which bored her; walking with books on her head to improve deportment, sitting down and standing up as gracefully as possible, learning how to choose clothes and accessories, what colours suited you, what didn't, making small talk about the latest news, a play she had been taken to see, the weather.

The weather was something she did remember, she was left with a lasting impression of deep, white winters, heavy snowfalls, which meant hours skiing at weekends, freezing temperatures in the bedrooms which made you leap into bed as soon as you could get your nightie on; and long, hot summers of blue skies and flower-filled meadows up in the mountains above the limpid waters of the lake.

They played lazy games of tennis in their crisp whites, swam in the open-air school pool, laughed and splashed in the cool blue water, lay on the lawns reading and studying, revising for their exams or simply sunbathing with closed eyes with a striped umbrella fluttering over their heads, chattered in the dining hall.

They walked into town to eat ice-cream, flirted with local boys and giggled. Some of them met boys secretly – one girl got pregnant and a wave of shock went through them all. She was sent back home in disgrace and for a while the others gave up meeting boys and talking about love, but Vittoria went on day-dreaming about Domenico. She stole a photo of him from the family album Olivia had brought with her. Vittoria kept the picture in her missal, tucked into the leather binding; whenever she was alone she slipped it out and gazed passionately at Domenico, tanned and lithe, in brief black swimming-trunks on the beach at the Lido in Venice. One day she would meet him again she kept promising herself. One day.

Domenico was still in America, where Olivia was to join him after leaving school. Lying on the grass beside the tennis courts Vittoria listened to her enviously.

'Over there I shall soon persuade him to let me go to art school. America is very modern, women go to university there as a matter of course. Look at American films! They're full of women going to college. Domenico won't be able to say no.'

Vittoria wished she was going to America when the vacation

ended a week later, but she would go back to Milan where Carlo would probably let her work in the laboratories of the family factory although he would expect her to marry one day soon. Her heart sank at the thought of an arranged marriage with some man Carlo picked out for her.

Somehow she must find the courage to fight Carlo, refuse to marry anyone. There was only one man for her, not that she would dare tell her brother that. He would laugh at her. Marry Domenico d'Angeli? As if he would ever look at her!

Back home she spent the hot summer of 1949 much as she had in Switzerland; swimming, playing tennis at the homes of neighbours, going to parties, choosing new clothes in Milan's designer show rooms. The pre-war life had all come back now. Vittoria, like her mother before her, spent hours in the ornate arcade of the Galleria Vittorio Emanuele II.

None of the rich young men she met showed any interest in her. Expensive clothes could not make her any less dumpy or plump. She began to be bored and pleaded with Carlo for permission to start working in the research laboratory.

At first he refused, but she was persistent and eventually he agreed. She suspected he had been trying to arrange a marriage for her but had failed.

Working in the laboratory was absorbing and exciting. Although at first patronising, not to say scornful, the scientist who ran it began to change his manner to her.

'She has a good mind for this work,' he told Carlo in her hearing. 'She's methodical, patient, very calm and above all she learns quickly. She would be a good research chemist. You could send her to university.'

'University? Women don't go to university,' Carlo growled.

'Of course they do. More and more women are studying for degrees,' the head of the laboratory told him with a touch of condescension that made Carlo redden.

'Not my sister!' he muttered.

Olivia sent her postcards from the States giving vivid

glimpses of her life in California where young women could do anything they wanted.

Towards the spring of 1950, Olivia wrote, 'We're coming home in June. Why not come and stay for a few weeks?'

Vittoria wasn't sure Carlo would let her go. He was finally thinking of allowing her to go to university. 'The doctors say Rachele will never have a child now. So the company will come to you one day, Vittoria. It will be a tough job for a woman to run a big firm. We're expanding all the time, and research is expensive. They say you have a talent for it. I want you to know as much as possible about what we do in the factory. When you finish your chemistry degree you must take an accountancy course, you'll need it if you're to run the business efficiently. You must focus on the future. Work hard. Running a big company is a duty, not a pleasure. Remember, hundreds of workers' jobs depend on you. If the company fails, their lives will be ruined.'

She had listened and nodded, so excited she felt sick, then filling with sympathy for her brother. His own life was such a desert; his marriage, which should have brought him joy, had been tragic and lonely. Was that all she had to look forward to?

She broached the subject of visiting Venice, expecting a short, sharp refusal, but Carlo immediately showed approval and enthusiasm.

'Yes, of course. I will take you there myself. I would enjoy a trip to Venice. I don't know the city and I feel I ought to. I'll book a room at one of the best hotels and stay a couple of days.'

Vittoria was uneasy. What if Olivia felt he was trying to wangle an invitation to Ca'd'Angeli for himself? It would be so embarrassing. Why did he want to go, anyway? He had never bothered to escort her anywhere before.

'You don't need to take me – I went to Switzerland alone, I can get to Venice without help.'

Carlo said firmly, 'We don't want the d'Angeli family to

think you aren't well-brought up. Families like that still expect young ladies to be protected. If your mother was alive she would chaperone you – she's not here to do it, so I must.'

Italy was still a country rooted in the past; many older women wore black, most had lost husbands, brothers, fathers during the war, they guarded the innocence of their daughters with fierce determination. Men wanted their brides to be virgins; where their sisters and daughters were concerned they did not trust other men any more than the mothers did.

They set off on a very hot summer day. The trip to Venice took hours; the train was overcrowded, slow and dirty.

'At least the trains ran on time and were clean when Il Duce was running the country,' muttered Carlo.

Several men in the compartment glanced furtively at him. One of them said, 'Before he got mixed up with the Germans! The 'thirties, those were the good years.'

Carlo had managed to get a corner seat for Vittoria. She ignored the men, her straw hat firmly on her dark hair, her white-gloved hands demurely in the lap of her pale pink linen suit. Mostly she stared out at the landscape running past: the Lombardy plain, fringed by mountains on their left hand, low-lying fields parched with summer heat, dry, bleached grass whispering in river beds where no water ran, tall, flame-shaped cypress burning in black silhouette against the sun haze, and everywhere the stubby silvery-leaved olive trees.

Her stomach cramped with excitement as they came closer to Venice, through the Po Valley, caught glimpses of the distant blue sea. Carlo craned to see the city for the first time; the grey domes and spires of Venice.

'*Bellissima*,' he murmured.

The train drew into the station and Carlo descended on his crutches, in his ungainly way, then signalled to a porter to help with the luggage. While the man got out the cases and loaded them on his trolley, Vittoria shot a look past the hurrying crowds of passengers.

Her heart turned over at the sight of Olivia waving outside the barrier, and, beside her, Domenico, sunlight gilding his sleek black hair and that golden skin.

'Is that your friend? Who's that with her?' Carlo asked, heading for the barrier with Vittoria walking fast beside him to keep up.

'Her brother.'

'The Count?'

'Yes.'

He looked wonderful, Vittoria thought. Everyone who walked past stared at him, especially the women, who fluttered excitedly if he smiled at them.

'He looks like a model,' Carlo seethed, then stopped dead, staring at another man who had just joined Olivia and Domenico.

'I don't believe it,' Carlo muttered. 'I'm not seeing things, am I, Vittoria? That *is* Canfield, isn't it? What the hell is he doing here?'

Chapter Thirteen

Canfield was beginning to show his age: his floppy fair hair had thinned and receded a little from his high forehead, giving him a noble profile. It had also begun to turn grey and shone like silver filigree in the Italian sunlight. Even from a distance, it was clear that he was still as slender as ever, and those vivid blue eyes were even brighter against the tan of his face. He was no longer poor, Vittoria observed, as they came closer, no old flannel trousers for him now, or patched elbows in his jacket. The perfectly tailored summer suit he wore must have cost the earth. She had seen so many wealthy Englishmen in Lausanne wearing suits like that; linen, expensive, in that casual English style, which was somehow formal too. But the pale blue shirt and striped dark blue silk tie had probably been bought here, they were in the new Italian fashion.

The nineteen fifties were Italy's time, a new Renaissance in life-style. Gone were the grey, bleak, poverty-stricken days of the post-war period. The young had money in their pockets. Some had gone to art college, and a new style of clothing, furniture, décor had exploded on to the scene.

The new music was sensual, sexy, light-hearted, downright dangerous, because it persuaded a girl to forget her religion, her upbringing, everything her father had warned her about, and enjoy herself. The sound of Italian popular music was coming out of radios everywhere in Europe during those years.

Their clothes were cheap but classy; pastel-coloured blouses for the girls, laid-back lapels giving glimpses of their breasts, full skirts with tight waists, and underneath frothy, bouncy petticoats that rustled as they walked, sounding sexy and intriguing to the boys in their lightweight, pale trousers and pastel sweaters over open-necked shirts.

After the war Dior's New Look had been popular with the rich, and was already going out of fashion as the decade changed; this new Italian look was for anyone. The young of other countries couldn't wait to get to Italy on holiday. Thousands of foreign tourists from colder countries – Sweden, Britain, Holland – came to experience the delights of dancing at night under the summer stars, sitting at street cafés where lovers ate pasta with tomato sauce and drank cheap, rough red wine.

It was a life-style the young craved, and crowds of them, chattering in English, Finnish, German, Spanish, had climbed out of the train from Milan on which Vittoria and Carlo had arrived, and were rushing off to discover Venice. Vittoria felt a pang. Would the city have changed much since she last saw it? Oh, not physically – the Venetians wouldn't allow anyone to alter so much as a church spire – but now there would be tourists everywhere. Would Venice still be a city of empty, sunny streets and squares, full of the soft sound of water? Of dark alleys, whose small shops smelt of garlic, wine, oranges?

'Are you coming, then?' Carlo demanded impatiently, leaning on his crutches and swinging between them with those over-developed arms.

'Sorry, yes,' she said, flushed and nervous.

Before Vittoria and Carlo could reach the barrier, Olivia ran forward to hug her. 'Oh, I'm so glad to see you! Is it a whole year since we left school? I feel old, don't you? So much has happened.'

Hugging her back, Vittoria laughed shyly. 'Hallo, Livia.'

Olivia stood back to look at her clothes, making a rueful face. 'Oh, what a good little girl you still are! You look just the way you did at school! Where *did* you get that hat? Never mind, while you're here I'll take you shopping for new clothes. My friends will laugh if they see you dressed like that!'

Vittoria reddened, all too aware of the three men listening.

'She looks charming, that colour suits her. I wish you would stop wearing pants, Olivia, not to mention all that makeup!' Domenico said quickly, taking Vittoria's hand and kissing the back of it. 'I remember meeting you, at my house one day during the war – but, like my wicked sister, you've grown up since then. I don't think I would have recognised you if I hadn't known who you were.'

'Thank you for inviting me to Ca' d'Angeli,' she managed to say, her throat dry with excitement. He was even better-looking close to. The last time they had met he had been a boy – now he was a man, so much taller than she was. She loved his clothes, the way he smiled, that wonderful golden skin. 'How does it feel to be back in Italy?'

'*Stupendo!* It's great.'

'Did you like America?'

'America?' he repeated. '*Molto simpàtico!* I loved it! It has such energy, such terrific music – and the art! Amazing! You must go there too. You'll love it, everyone does.'

'Not quite everyone,' a cool, smooth voice murmured, and she reluctantly moved her eyes to Canfield.

'*Ciao,* Toria,' he said, taking one of the hands she was deliberately holding down at her sides.

He lifted it to his mouth and she felt the brush of his flesh with distaste.

She was not pleased to see *him* again, but she couldn't say so in front of the others so she didn't answer, just forced a polite smile and inclined her head. His shrewd, cynical eyes read her expression but he went on smiling, unsurprised, faintly amused, as if he had expected that reaction from her. She had never hidden her dislike and resentment.

'You've become a young woman,' he said. 'And there's a faint look of your mother . . . the eyes, perhaps? The cheekbones?'

'My mother always said I took after my father,' she told him coldly. 'Maybe, if it had lived, the baby she died giving birth to might have looked like her.'

She saw him flinch. Ah! So he wasn't as impervious as he wanted to seem. 'It was buried with her,' she added, watching him remorselessly, hoping to see more evidence of her blows landing, but Carlo, his eyes bulging, interrupted.

'I didn't expect to see you here, Canfield! What are you doing in Venice?'

Vittoria could see the relief with which the Englishman turned to face him. 'Writing a book on Venetian art. Hallo, Carlo. You're looking fit and well, I'm happy to see.' He held out his hand, and Carlo took it, the habit of good manners too engrained for him to refuse.

'Is that how you earn your living, Canfield? I remember you wrote before the war. Do you earn enough to live on or do you still teach?'

'I no longer need to teach. My books on Italy are doing very well and I can live on the money they bring in. How's the factory doing? I've seen your products everywhere so I know you're still in business.'

As Carlo answered, his manner warming a little because Canfield had touched on the subject closest to his heart, Olivia slipped an arm round Vittoria's waist.

'Come on, let's walk down to the landing-stage – our boat is waiting. The porter has taken your luggage down there already. We're going to have such fun, Toria. There's a beach party over at the Lido tonight, and tomorrow an American friend of ours is having a dance for his birthday. His family are meat-packers from Chicago.'

'Are what?' Vittoria queried, bemused by the phrase.

Olivia giggled. 'That's what he calls it. They put beef in cans and sell it all over America. They're rolling in money, Toria, and Greg is gorgeous, blond and blue-eyed. Wait till you see him! He's spoilt but, then, he's an only son and he'll inherit the business. He gets everything he wants – his sister is always complaining about it, and I don't blame her, but he's such a charmer. His parents adore him. They just gave him his own motor-boat for his birthday and he zips up and down the canal, waving to me. The Murphys live in a palazzo round the bend from us, in the Grand Canal. They rent it, of course. It belongs to the Lazaro family, but they can't afford to live in it.'

'Who runs the business in America while the Murphys are over here?'

'Oh, they put in a manager and Mr Murphy goes home every so often to check on things, but Mrs Murphy and Greg and Bernadette stay here.'

'Bernadette is the sister?'

Olivia nodded. 'They're Catholics, of course – Irish descent.'

'Catholics? That's nice.' Vittoria had been wondering how the d'Angeli family would react to Olivia marrying outside the Church.

Olivia grinned knowingly. 'Isn't it? No need to worry about that!'

They both chuckled. Domenico caught up with them. 'What are you two whispering about?'

'You,' his sister told him.

'What else?' His dark eyes wandered over the crowded steps where students in jeans and T-shirts, tourists in shorts, sat nursing their rucksacks and consulting creased maps of Venice. 'Venice is full of Americans again,' he told Vittoria, keeping step with her, riveting the eyes of some of the students with his long-legged, lithe body. He had a physical grace that was mesmerising, especially combined with the unintended arrogance of his self-assurance, the birthright of centuries of d'Angeli ancestors who had been lords and rulers in this city.

'How long have you known Signor Canfield?' asked Vittoria, aware of the man behind her, talking to Carlo. The sound of his voice made her head beat with rage. He had killed her mother. She wanted to scream it at him. Murderer.

'I met him in the States while I was over there. He was lecturing at the same university. When he said he was writing a book on Venetian art I invited him to stay with us.' Domenico smiled down at her.

Vittoria's heart turned over sickeningly. He was so beautiful.

'Charming, isn't he?' Domenico murmured. 'He told me he had known your family well. Wasn't he your brothers' tutor before the war?'

Vittoria swallowed, her throat clenched. He would be sleeping under the same roof. 'Yes.'

'He said there were about half a dozen boys.'

'He exaggerates, as usual. There were four. Carlo is the only one who survived the war.'

He was watching her intently, and saw that she was trembling. Putting his arm round her shoulders to steady her, Domenico said gently, 'I'm sorry, three brothers gone . . . That's hard to bear, you must miss them badly.'

She let herself lean on him, feeling his warmth seep into her. He smelt of lemons and musk and cigarette smoke; she loved the fragrance of his skin. He was kind . . . or maybe he really liked her? It felt as if he did. She loved the way he smiled at her, those dark eyes full of light and warmth. She was so happy she was quite light-headed.

This was going to be a wonderful holiday.

Except for having Canfield under the same roof.

Domenico insisted that Carlo must stay, too, for the two days he meant to be in Venice, and they seemed to become instant friends. Domenico took him around the city, showed him the

Accademia, San Marco, Santa Maria della Salute. They did a boat trip around the canals, went out to the lagoon islands, to Murano to buy dark red glass, to Torcello to see the Byzantine cathedral. Carlo bought lace and linen to take back to Rachele before they went on to San Michele, the cypress-enclosed cemetery island with the white walls.

When they visited Aunt Maria for afternoon tea Domenico came with them. The old woman was pink with pleasure. She had never before entertained one of Venice's aristocrats in her own home. As they left two hours later she whispered to Vittoria, 'Come again, alone, I can't wait to hear all about the palazzo.'

Every evening the men went out – to Harry's Bar, or one or the other of Domenico's favourite drinking spots where he introduced Carlo to his friends, smooth Italians, bluff Englishmen, rich Americans who spent their days moving from the first aperitif of the morning to the last brandy of the night, with many stops in between. There were women, too; tough American journalists, elegant English girls, sultry Italians with red, red mouths and hot eyes.

After his two days were up Carlo stayed on. Vittoria had no idea what he did all day but if she saw him come back he often smelt of strong perfume and was almost always drunk.

She was having a wonderful time, too. Olivia had insisted on taking her shopping, talked her into buying clothes Vittoria would never quite have dared buy without Olivia's persuasion.

Tight-waisted dresses, in pastel colours, poplin shirts in lavender or green, pretty high-heeled shoes or flat black-leather ones. Olivia chose carefully for her to give her more height, make her look slimmer.

Rachele kept ringing up asking when Carlo was coming home. At last one morning she wired that she was coming to Venice to get him.

Carlo grimaced. 'Well, that's the end of my holiday. It was too good to last, but never mind, I've had the best time of my life. I'll go up and pack and catch the next train to Milan.'

Just before he left for the station he said, 'Enjoy the rest of your time here. Domenico's a great fellow, I like him. We've had some long chats, talked it all out, I approve.' He patted her shoulder clumsily. 'I've told him I'd be delighted.'

'Delighted about what?' Shy, excited, uncertain, half hoping yet afraid to let herself believe it, she looked up into his face and Carlo grinned at her.

'Oh, you know! I'm pleased, Toria. It's just what I want for you.'

Questions rushed to her tongue but he didn't wait for her to ask them. Looking at his watch he groaned.

'I must go. If I miss that train, Rachele will be waiting for me with a rolling pin!' He kissed her cheek and was gone, swinging along between his crutches at his usual fast pace. She ran out to the landing-stage in time to see the d'Angeli boat chugging away. Carlo waved to her, then he was gone.

Vittoria stayed on another month. In summer Venice was a place of heady pleasures; glorious open-air parties, dances, picnics on the Lido beaches.

As the heat of August passed into the first, cooler days of September, Domenico took Vittoria out into the familiar, elegant gardens of Ca'd'Angeli and, standing in the shade of a great, ancient yew tree, said, 'Vittoria, I have spoken to your brother and he has given me permission to ask you to marry me. Will you be my wife?'

She was so overcome she couldn't answer for a moment. Domenico had kissed her a few times, gently, once when they walked home together after a dance, once here in the garden after dinner, but he had not spoken of love.

He looked down into her face searchingly, then smiled. 'I promise, I will always take care of you, Toria, you can trust me, I won't ever let you down.'

He took her face between his palms and bent to kiss her, slowly, softly, with a new intimacy, parting her lips, turning her bones to jelly and making her so happy she was almost faint.

He did love her. He must love her. He hadn't actually said he did. But why else had he asked her to marry him?

'Will you marry me, Toria?'

This time she managed to whisper, 'Yes.'

When they went back into Ca' d'Angeli Olivia was waiting, eyes wide and excited. When she saw their faces she gave a whoop.

'She said yes?' Flinging her arms around Vittoria she hugged her like a boa constrictor. 'I'm so happy. Now you'll be my sister. When is the wedding? I *must* be a bridesmaid! Will you have it soon?'

'I'm afraid we can't,' Domenico said quietly. 'Carlo wants us to wait until you are in your last year at university, Toria. He feels you should finish your degree course and then train as an accountant. One day you will inherit your family company and it is important that you are prepared for that.'

'Oh, but I don't want to wait so long, I want to get married right away.'

'Of course she does! It's not natural, getting engaged and then waiting a whole year!'

'Carlo won't hear of you giving up your degree course,' Dominico told Vittoria.

'But I can go back to college after we're married.'

'The university faculty frowns on married women taking degrees, and if we were married it would be very hard for you to concentrate on your studies – and hard for me, too, to let you go away for months at a time.'

He smiled at her, his mysterious dark eyes glowing. 'No, we must wait, Toria. It will be hard, for both of us, but we have our whole lives in front of us. There is plenty of time.'

She returned to Milan a week later to get ready for her first term at university. Carlo was delighted with her engagement.

'Do we have to wait, Carlo? If we got married at once I could go to America with Domenico and start university in California.'

Her brother looked surprised. 'I suggested that to Domenico, but he felt it would be too much of a distraction for you both. If you got pregnant you would never finish your degree. I told him you must get some qualifications. If you're going to run the firm you have to know what you're doing. You could get a manager, but how could you be sure you could trust him? It was a relief to me that Domenico agreed with me and was ready to wait.'

She ached with frustration, poured all her passion out on paper every day. Domenico wrote less frequently. His were not long letters: like Olivia he was a poor correspondent, but he filled his pages with tiny pen and ink drawings of things he had seen during the day, some funny, some fascinating, some sad. He had an eye for the strange, the weird, the pathetic and Vittoria read and re-read those letters every day. They made her feel close to him, although he was back in the States where he was joined by his sister.

Suddenly Olivia wrote to announce that she was getting married. Vittoria was sick with envy but at least the news meant that Domenico was coming back to Italy for a few weeks. In the spring of 1952 Olivia married her American, Greg, with a long and magnificent nuptial mass. Vittoria was her bridesmaid. The wedding breakfast was held at Ca'd'Angeli and many of their schoolfriends were invited. The only one who did not come was Gina, who was working abroad.

Curious, Vittoria asked, 'What job is she doing?'

'She's on a year's scholarship, at an art school in the States.'

'Really? I thought she would go into her family business. Did Domenico help her get the scholarship?'

'He wrote her a reference, I think. Oh, I'm going to miss you. But I'll come back to be your matron-of-honour. And you must write to me! You know me, I hate writing letters, but I'll drop you a postcard every week, I promise.'

She and her husband were going to live in Chicago. The Murphy family had given up the palazzo they had been renting and had returned home. Greg was working in the family firm, learning the business he would one day inherit.

Domenico was sailing back to the States on the same boat as his sister and her husband so Vittoria saw little of him during that spring holiday and when she did he seemed distant and cold. She tried to talk to him about how she felt, to say what was burning inside her, that she loved him and needed him now, not in a year, that she wanted him to make love to her, but he always changed the subject before she got the words out, as if he guessed what she was going to say and was determined she shouldn't.

Then he was gone and she was back in Milan, working hard but intensely depressed. Did he regret having proposed? Didn't he want to marry her? Did he love her?

In her next letter she asked him to name the day. Shouldn't they be planning the wedding? Rachele kept reminding her that there were masses of things to do: they had to book the church, plan the wedding breakfast, make lists of guests, send out invitations. But first they needed to know the date. It would take months to set everything up here in Milan.

'I'll let you know soon,' he wrote back. 'I promise. I can't be certain yet when I shall get back from here.' He filled up the rest of the page with drawings of a beach – girls in bikinis, men with huge chests, children digging in sand. Funny, lively, charming.

Vittoria didn't know whether to laugh or cry.

That winter Carlo and Rachele were driving home from the opera when their car skidded on ice and crashed. Rachele was killed outright. Carlo had head injuries and a broken shoulder.

Domenico flew home the day before Rachele's funeral and held Vittoria while she sobbed into his shirt. She was relieved he had come, inexpressibly glad to see him, yet she had, too, a strong sense of foreboding. Her instincts kept telling her that something was wrong, but she didn't know what it was.

'How's Carlo?' he asked, lightly kissing her hair.

'They won't tell me. They keep saying it's too soon to know if he'll ever be the same. He just lies there, his head all bandaged, so white and still. He's out of the coma but he doesn't react when you speak to him. He just lies there, hour after hour, not moving.'

'I'll come to the hospital tomorrow, see for myself. It sounds like shock to me. You'd expect it, wouldn't you? He knows Rachele is dead, does he?'

'I told him. He just lay there as if he was deaf, staring at the wall.'

'I expect he already knew. Didn't you say she was killed in the crash? He must have realised she was dead.'

'Do you think he blames himself? But it wasn't his fault. The crash was an accident. There was ice on the road. Rachele couldn't control the car when it went into a skid.'

'Poor Carlo. He's had very little luck.'

When they went to the hospital, after the funeral, Carlo was limp, white, silent, but there were glistening tracks down his face where he had cried.

As Domenico drove her home he said, 'He knew. That the funeral was today. He may not react but he's conscious of what is going on around him. The specialist told me he's not too confident about the prognosis. Carlo doesn't have any real future, long term.'

'You mean he's going to die?' She knew her voice sounded raw, as if torn out of her. Domenico glanced at her sideways and sighed. 'I'm sorry to be the one to tell you, darling, but somebody had to. The doctors weren't sure for a while, but now they are. Carlo isn't going to live beyond a year. We must get a specialist nurse for him. But, more than that, he'll need you, Toria. His physical needs are easy. It's the emotional side we have to deal with. We must put off our marriage. I can't ask you to marry me and walk away from your dying brother. That would be too cruel.'

Vittoria was rigid with despair. Time stretched ahead, bleak and grey and empty. But she didn't argue. There was no point. Domenico had made up his mind. In some ways he was as obstinate and immovable as her father, and she was afraid of losing him. Her instincts told her he was looking for a way out of their marriage; she mustn't give him the chance. She had to hang on, by this tiny thread that still bound them together. She wasn't letting go of him. She never would.

Her life became a ceaseless round of work and anxiety. She couldn't have managed without Antonio. They employed a nurse for a while but Carlo disliked her; he couldn't speak but he made his feelings clear enough, growling in his throat like a dog whenever he set eyes on her, and glaring at her. After a month she gave notice, and when she had gone Antonio did most of the physical work involved in caring for Carlo. He lifted him in and out of bed, washed him, dressed him, fed him, unless Vittoria was at home when she took over, and kept him in touch with whatever was happening at the factory, in the offices. God alone knew if he understood it all, but she felt he listened keenly. He blinked replies. One blink for yes. Two for no. Three meant, I don't understand, explain. It took an age to communicate in blinks and long pauses but she often needed Carlo's advice before she made a decision concerning the firm.

She was working long hours every day, continuing with her university course, sandwiching her studies between working at the company in Carlo's role. Normally, she did a morning at the college, had a quick lunch then spent the rest of the day at the firm. Exhausted, pale, at the end of her tether, she would return to the house each evening. Antonio would meet her at the front door and make her sit down. Then he knelt, took off her shoes and massaged her hot, throbbing feet. He gave her a glass of wine, then left her relaxing while he got her meal – melon and Parma ham, soup or bruschetta, heaped with roast peppers or tomatoes, then pasta or risotto or some fresh grilled fish.

While she ate he told her how her brother was, and asked how her day had gone. 'Another glass of red wine, for your blood. You need it, you're so pale,' he would insist.

'I shall get fat.' She sighed, but drank the wine, although she wouldn't have any dessert or coffee.

'You're too thin.'

'They say a woman can never be too thin.'

'Whoever said that wasn't an Italian.'

'It was that American woman, the Duchess of Windsor.'

He made a face. 'Oh, her. She isn't a woman at all. More like a man, with that hard, ugly face.'

They no longer talked like employer and servant, they were friends. He knew her better, was closer to her, than any other friend she had ever had, including Olivia.

After she swayed one evening and fell downstairs out of utter exhaustion, Antonio got into the habit of coming upstairs with her, his arm around her to support her. They would go into Carlo's bedroom and if he was awake, as he often was, drifting in and out of consciousness, day and night, she would talk to her brother for a little while, then she would go to her own room. Once she was so tired that she collapsed on her bed fully dressed and slept there all night. After that Antonio insisted on helping her change into her nightdress. He would lift her between the sheets before turning out the light and leaving her to sleep. At first she had protested, been embarrassed, but when you were almost dead with weariness such intimacies no longer seemed to matter.

It was like a marriage, she often thought. Without the sex, of course. Antonio never once touched her that way. She would never have let him. Antonio was necessary to her, though. He became her other half, who stayed at home while she left to work at a dozen different things, driving herself until she was almost crazy.

In the summer of 1954 she took her exams and passed although not as well as she and her tutors had hoped. She hadn't given her work the necessary concentration. At least leaving university meant she had less to do each day. She decided to put off the accountancy course for a year, to spend more time with Carlo, but he died in the early hours of a frosty Christmas morning. Outside, Milan was still and calm until first light, when the bells of the churches and the cathedral began calling people to Mass. Vittoria and Antonio knelt beside the priest, praying silently, while he gave Carlo Extreme Unction, murmuring the ritual in a sleepy voice. Carlo hadn't spoken since the car crash. He lay with eyes shut, breathing faint – it was impossible to say whether he was listening or understood.

Vittoria had not slept for thirty-six hours. She was past responding to anything, couldn't even shed a tear when Carlo stopped breathing. Antonio made her go to bed while the body was prepared, and the undertaker came to take it away.

She slept right through Christmas Day, and woke in the evening to hear the bells ringing again for Benediction, the last service of the day in the cathedral. Remembering at once that Carlo had died, she thought, It's over. It's finished. I'm free. She couldn't even be sad for him. It had been a release for him, too. He had scarcely been living, more waiting to die.

Her body was light and cool, as if she was floating. Domenico. The name sang in her head, in her heart. At last they could be married.

When she came downstairs Antonio told her Domenico had rung from the States to wish her a happy Christmas. 'I told him your brother had just died and I didn't want to wake you, you were so tired.'

Disappointed, she cried, 'You should have put the call through to my bedroom! How dare you!'

Antonio paled, his mouth tight. 'I'm sorry. I did it because I was worried about you. You don't know what you looked like, white as a ghost. You've been through a terrible ordeal. You needed that sleep.'

'I know you meant well but I would have wanted to talk to

him. I shouldn't have shouted at you, Antonio, after all you've done for me. I'm sorry.'

He bowed his head in acknowledgement of the apology. 'The Count said he would fly back at once.'

Her eyes lit up. 'Did he? When is he leaving?'

A shrug. 'He said at once. Who knows if that meant today or tomorrow? You could try ringing him now while I get your dinner. I have a special meal for you – I had planned it for Christmas. Will you eat now?'

'I'm starving! Yes, please. What is it?'

He smiled indulgently at her. She loved food like a little girl. 'A lentil and chestnut soup, with bay and marjoram and basil, I'll bring bruschetta with it, and then *lepre in salmi*.'

'Jugged hare? Where did you get the hare?'

'A friend of mine shot it up in the hills. I had it marinating for a couple of days in red wine and spices. It's very rich, and so tender it's falling off the bone, you'll love it. You need—'

'The wine for my blood!' she finished, laughing on the edge of hysteria. 'I know. What are you serving it with?'

'Polenta.'

'Sounds wonderful.'

It was. Most of the staff were off for Christmas evening, for family parties, and as she didn't want to eat alone in the big, cold dining room, she ate in the kitchen, which the staff had decked with coloured paper chains.

'And you must eat with me! I don't want to eat alone tonight, of all nights.'

They turned off the electric lights and had candles on the big deal table. Antonio brought across the iron pot of soup, and placed beside it an earthenware platter of hot bruschetta smelling of garlic. Before they began to eat Antonio poured her red wine.

'Your happiness,' he toasted, lifting his own glass towards her.

She smiled at him. 'And yours.'

His black eyes had a wet shine, as if he was almost crying. She understood how he felt, she felt that way, too. She would miss him when she went to Venice, even though she couldn't wait to go, to be married. It was a pity she had to say goodbye to Antonio, though. They had been through so much together.

Then it hit her. Why shouldn't he come with her to Venice? A good servant was hard to find in any city.

Vittoria was married in the spring of 1955 in Milan cathedral, with Olivia as her matron-of-honour. A very large Olivia, who was expecting her first child any day and looked, in her pale lime dress, like a green barrage balloon.

'*Cara,* don't have a baby right away. Take my tip, it ruins all your fun and you look hideous – well, just look at me!'

'You look wonderful, Olivia. And I am dying to have a baby.'

'*Stupido!*' But Olivia hugged her. 'We're sisters now. You must be my baby's godmother. Promise?'

'I'd love to.'

The reception was enormous: hundreds of guests crowded into the hotel, the press outside snapped the famous faces of industry and high society who came. It was the wedding of the year in Milan, the talk of Venice. Vittoria had drawn up the guest list for Milan, while the one for Venice came from Domenico. Before she sent both to the printer Vittoria slid an eye down the Venetian list and stopped dead at one name.

'Canfield? I don't want him at my wedding!'

'He's my friend. *I* want him,' Domenico said, quietly.

'But, Nico . . .' Her head was exploding with images of her mother, lying white and still on her death-bed with Canfield's dead baby on her breast. She met Domenico's hard, dark eyes, and gulped. She had never told him about Canfield and her mother, had no idea if he knew, what he knew, and hated the thought of talking about it, even with him.

'He is my friend. You will be seeing a lot of him. You must learn to like him,' he said.

She could – should, perhaps – have told him the whole story then, but she didn't. It was all too painful to talk about. Oh, well, she told herself, she wouldn't even notice Canfield among so many other people, and she would be too busy on the day to care about him being there.

All the society columnists featured the wedding at great length, with pictures of Vittoria in her wonderful dress, the bridesmaids, people arriving at the cathedral. Vittoria enjoyed it all, the white and gold solemnity of the nuptial mass, emerging to the peal of bells, her long veil blowing behind her, crowds outside applauding, smiling, throwing rice, the reception afterwards, eating the wedding breakfast, listening to the toasts and speeches, and afterwards dancing and talking to people she only half recognised. She even managed to smile at Canfield and hide her hatred, because she was counting the moments until they were alone, she and Domenico. She was half dazed with happiness: she had been so afraid they would never be married that she hardly dared believe she was finally his wife.

They spent their honeymoon in the Caribbean – Domenico's choice, of course, just as he had decided they should marry in Milan cathedral, with a full nuptial mass, and a heavenly choir of boys in lace-decked white cassocks singing the Latin liturgy; he had chosen the five-star hotel, in the centre of Milan, for the wedding breakfast and spent some time discussing with the manager what food would be served and with which wines.

Oh, he made much play of discussing everything with her, but it was always Domenico who made the decisions. She told herself it was natural to him, he was used to authority, both in his home and at the university, with his students. Vittoria still felt afraid to argue with him in case the wedding was called off, so she always said yes to everything he suggested.

'The West Indies are wonderful,' he assured her. 'I've been there a couple of times. I love the hot colours, the light is so brilliant and the local people are fun. The place has natural drama – everything is explosive, exciting. You'll love it, too.'

Looking down from the plane as they landed she did love it. It was so green, the sea so blue, the sands white as spilt sugar. The hotel was luxurious, with a pool set in tropical gardens full of astonishingly bright flowers and feathery, blowing palms, and smiling waiters in white coats served delicious drinks and food. Outwardly that honeymoon was blissful. It should have been the happiest time of Vittoria's life. It wasn't.

Domenico slept with her each night, but much though she wanted to believe he enjoyed it, she couldn't persuade herself of that. His lovemaking was brief, reluctant, she almost felt he had to force himself to touch her. Was he shy? She thought at first, incredulously. Or was it just that he did not enjoy sex?

Vittoria did. She had always known that she would. Her body had ached for it, and now she discovered how sensual, how passionate, her body naturally was. 'I love you,' she groaned that first night, holding him between her open thighs, her naked body hot and eager. She felt the shudder that went through him but misunderstood, believing he was as desperate for satisfaction as she was, and moaned, 'Darling, darling . . .' as she arched up towards him, her hands touching, stroking the lean, smooth body on top of her, able at last, at long, long last to do what she had been dying to do for years.

She explored his body hungrily, fingered along the deep indentation of his spine, down under his buttocks, caressed the curly black hair from which his cock sprang, pressed her face into his chest, kissed with open mouth the faintly sweaty skin, sucking at his nipples, holding his back while he rode up and down on her, and went into orgasm long before he did, crying out, hoarsely, almost in agony, her body jerking wildly, as if in a death throe.

Domenico came as she finished, and she lay there with exhausted contentment, holding his body tightly as his seed leapt up inside her.

'I want to have a baby right away,' she whispered, kissing his hair.

He rolled off her. 'I'd like that.' Yawning, he lay on his side, face turned away. 'You must be very tired. Goodnight, Toria.'

Next day, after a breakfast of fresh fruit, rolls and coffee in their elegant bungalow, he went off to paint down on the beach below the hotel grounds.

She lazed by the pool, in the sun, swam, put on brief shorts and a skimpy top bought in the hotel shop, then walked down to see Domenico's painting and tell him to come back for lunch.

Wearing black swimming trunks, his tall figure gleaming golden, oiled, in the sun, he barely glanced at her, too intent on the brilliant seascape he was painting: blues so bright they hurt the eye, girls half naked on the yellow sand, umbrellas fluttering in the breeze. Life burst out of the canvas and Vittoria was breathless with admiration for his talent.

'Lunch?' he muttered. 'No, I don't eat much in the middle of the day. I brought some fruit down here with me. You go back and eat lunch. I'll see you later.'

She stood there, staring at his profile, a chill stealing up her skin in spite of the hot sun.

'But . . . we're on our honeymoon. Please, Nico, don't leave me alone on our first day here. After all, there will be plenty of time for you to paint, later.'

He didn't even look at her and his voice was curt, indifferent. 'I have to finish this, I have to work fast, before the light changes. Off you go, have fun, enjoy yourself.'

She couldn't make a scene in public. People were watching, listening. 'See you later, then,' she said flatly, and walked back up the sands to the hotel garden.

That first night, first day, set the pattern for their weeks there. She had suspected that Domenico didn't love her the way she loved him; now she knew it, and learnt, too, that when you love someone who doesn't love you life is agony. Pain became her constant companion, walked with her in the tropical gardens, beat in her head, in her blood, slept beside her every night.

At dinner on their last night in the Caribbean, Domenico said, 'Have you decided what you want to do about your firm? Are you going to continue running it, put in a manager or sell it?'

They had discussed all three options before they got married but she hadn't, then, been able to make up her mind. Now she had.

'I'm going to sell the firm and the house. Now that we're married I can't be in both places at once, and you can never trust other people to run a company for you if you don't keep an eye on them. I won't rush into it, I'll go on as I have over the past year, waiting for offers, and make sure I get the best price I can. I'll spend the weekends with you at Ca' d'Angeli, and four days during the week in Milan at the factory.' She smiled at him, her dark eyes passionate. 'It will be hard – I hate the thought of being away from you so much – but with any luck it won't take too long to find the right buyer.'

'And if you find you're pregnant?'

'Then I'll think again.'

Next day they flew home. Vittoria was sick with excitement and nerves at the thought of reaching Ca' d'Angeli. She found it hard to believe that she would walk into the palazzo as its mistress; the schoolgirl who had not been thought good enough to go into the house all those years ago, who had been permitted into the gardens only on sufferance, and given haughty looks by the maidservant who had brought them a tray of food and drink. Did that girl still work there?

If she does, I won't get rid of her, thought Vittoria. No, that isn't the way to get your own back. I want her there every day, waiting on me, jumping when I give her orders. I'll rub her nose in it.

They were met at the airport by one of the servants in the family's motor-boat and arrived in style at the landing-stage in darkness. As they docked, somebody inside switched on the electric lights over the front door.

Domenico helped Vittoria out of the boat and she turned to face Ca' d'Angeli. The front door was open and, framed in the yellow light, Vittoria saw a woman so beautiful she almost thought she was imagining her. Hair of Titian red, swept up on top of her head, wearing a sleek black dress that clung to every curve of her slender body, large, glistening pearls around her pale throat.

For a moment Vittoria thought she was a stranger. Then it hit her.

'Gina?' she whispered.

She had not seen her since their schooldays, but the more she stared the more certain she was that it was Gina, a woman not a girl now, the promise of bud-like beauty she had shown at thirteen now in full, ripe perfection.

Offhandedly, Domenico said, 'Yes. Didn't I tell you? I must have forgotten in all the flurry over the wedding. After she left art school she needed a job where she could work at her paintings part-time, so I asked her to be my housekeeper. She runs Ca' d'Angeli for me.'

She stared at him and then at Gina, and knew, understood, at last. They were lovers, Gina and Domenico. She watched the glance flash between them, the intimacy and passion, secret, hidden, yet burning like wildfire on the Venetian night air.

Everything was clear to her now: her marriage was a farce, a mockery, a lie. Domenico wanted her money but he did not want her. She hadn't imagined the reluctance in their bed. He had forced himself to make love to her because he wanted to get her pregnant, to make sure that his child would be the heir to everything she had inherited from Carlo, but he had hated every second of it. He hated her.

His eyes slid away from hers. There was a stain of dark red along his cheekbones. 'You must be tired. I'll show you to your room, send up a light supper on a tray.'

Did they think they could fool her? Now that she had seen them together. Were they hoping to go on lying, cheating, deceiving?

She walked towards the open front door without replying. In the Caribbean the people talked of zombies, the dead who walk again, brought back by voodoo, yet who feel nothing, their bodies empty of everything but the power of the snake god. Vittoria moved in that lifeless, dead fashion, a blank, fixed, empty smile on her face.

'Welcome home,' Gina murmured to her, in a throaty voice, but she was looking at Domenico, her slanting green eyes shining in the lamplight.

Antonio came out of the house and took her luggage. He had moved to Ca' d'Angeli a week ago. As their eyes met Vittoria saw he already knew the truth about her marriage. His face was angry, protective, full of pity for her, and that woke her out of her dead spell.

His pity hurt. She had thought she was making a brilliant marriage, envied by everyone she knew. Now she saw what she could expect: humiliation, secret mockery, furtive whispers everywhere she went in this beautiful, sly, stealthy city, where what you saw was only the sunlit surface dancing over dark, secret waters where death, decay and corruption hid.

'I'll show you the way, Contessa,' Antonio said, and she followed him into the house and up the wide, marble stairs, listening to the echo of her own footsteps, the echo of all that had perplexed her these last years but which was now so crystal clear.

Domenico had put off marrying her as long as he could. How long had Gina been his lover? All this time, in America?

Far below the front door closed with a heavy clang. Were they in each other's arms, kissing? They had been apart all this time, while Domenico was with her in Milan before the wedding and afterwards in the West Indies. She had felt the desire between them as they stood there, waiting to touch each other again, hunger written on their faces.

Agony tore at her. Domenico. She had thought he was hers at last, but he wasn't, would never be. Gina possessed him.

She followed Antonio up to the second floor and into a large room hung with dark red velvet curtains at the windows and around the four-poster bed. A fire burned in the great hearth, logs from which bluish flames leapt, crackling, but it couldn't warm the room, which was chilly yet at the same time stuffy from centuries of dust and cobwebs.

Antonio put down her luggage and looked searchingly at her.

She met his glance without showing her pain, jealousy and rage.

'Tell me everything you've found out,' she said.

Chapter Fourteen

Venice, 1998

After four days in hospital Laura was allowed to leave. 'You're lucky. You have healthy young flesh and you're healing quickly,' the surgeon told her, his black Italian eyes caressing her face, the curve of her breast, her body under the cotton robe, not offensively, merely with admiration. 'But you must rest that shoulder. Don't start work yet, and lie down as much as possible. I'm afraid we need the room or I would have you here longer.'

'That's okay, I feel fine.' She smiled at him. It was partly true: she was feeling much better, although it still hurt at times as she shifted in bed, and she was taking pain-killers three times a day. She hated being in pain: it made it hard to relax or think clearly. You were always on edge for the next hot stab in your flesh.

She could bear that, though, now that she knew Sebastian had not attacked her.

And, of course, he hadn't sent those letters. She was convinced, and could see that the police agreed with her, that the letter-writer and the would-be killer were one and the same person. So who had sent the letters?

When Sebastian was allowed to see her, on her second day there, she had smiled at him, eyes feverishly happy, and held out a hand that shook. He had knelt by the bed and kissed it with an intensity that made her light-headed. 'It wasn't me who attacked you. You thought it was, didn't you? I saw that look you gave me, just before they put you in the ambulance. But it wasn't me, Laura. I love you – how could you think I'd do that? I wouldn't hurt a hair on your head.'

Tears welled up, one splashed down her cheek. 'I know. Sebastian, I know it wasn't you.'

He leant over her and brushed his mouth over her wet eyelids, slowly, gently. '*Cara, carissima,* it hurt like hell to know you were scared of me.'

'I'm sorry, darling,' she half sobbed. 'I was so scared, in so much pain, just after it happened. I didn't know what I was doing.'

'If I get my hands on the guy—'

'I think it was a woman.'

'A woman?' He did a double-take. 'A *woman*? What makes you think that?'

'It came to me gradually. I remembered little details in flashes. It was her hands mostly . . . I must have noticed them subconsciously. Very small thin hands, with red nail varnish.'

'Doesn't necessarily follow. I know guys with tiny delicate hands who wear nail varnish.'

'And I smelt perfume. I knew it. Givenchy.'

'Guys wear Givenchy, too, honey.' He was deliberately trying to lighten the atmosphere. She was so pale, desperately vulnerable, without makeup and her hair like spilt amber against the white pillow. The beauty was still there, glowing and untouchable, but the assurance had been wiped out: she looked very young.

'I know it was a woman, I'm certain it was, there was something . . . Oh, I can't put my finger on it, I just know, instinctively.'

'Female intuition?' He saw her frown and kissed her palm softly, in apology for teasing her. 'Okay, I believe you. If your intuition tells you it was a woman, it probably was. You've told Bertelli?'

'Yes, although I'm not sure he believed me. The police forensic team have gone over that cape they found floating in the canal and it seems they got some DNA evidence from that. Hairs, flakes of skin – he said we leave that sort of debris on everything we wear. Horrible idea, isn't it?'

'If it can prove who did it, it's terrific. They'll be testing the whole crew for a match, then. Damn it. That will take a day or two out of my shooting schedule, and we're running late enough as it is.'

'You think it's one of the crew?'

'Don't you? And the police suspect it is. They're bound to test them first. Who else do you know in Venice?'

Two days later, as she waited for him to come and collect her to take her back to Ca' d'Angeli, she remembered what he had said. Yes, of course, it had to be someone working on the film. Then a name came into her head. Of a woman she knew, who had reason to hate her.

She shivered. Had it occurred to Sebastian?

Sebastian was in a ferocious rage because they were having problems filming a vital scene inside Ca' d'Angeli. The great arc-lights kept burning out and they were running low on power packs; a bitter winter wind was blowing through Venice, making the electricity surge and howling through the high-ceilinged rooms, interfering with the sound recording.

The sound man threw up his hands in despair. 'It's worse than aircraft noises – at least they fade into the distance after a while, but this stops and starts again without warning.'

Count Niccolo, in a heavy black leather coat, appeared at the top of the stairs and picked his way through the cables and equipment towards Sebastian, who gave him a heavy nod.

'Looking for me?'

'A water-taxi just arrived for you.'

Sebastian groaned, ran a hand through his hair. 'Damn it to hell! I'd forgotten I ordered it.'

'If you cancel now he'll still want paying,' Niccolo told him drily, and went through a door into the private wing of the palazzo.

'Shall I go down and give him some money?' asked Valerie, as always at Sebastian's side, notepad in hand, her audio recorder and a mike clipped to her leather belt.

'No, hang on, let me think. I promised Laura I'd pick her up, but I must finish shooting this scene. We can't afford to get any further behind schedule.'

'Shall I go and get her?' Valerie offered.

Sidney and Carmen glanced sideways at each other.

Unaware of them, Sebastian sighed. 'Well, maybe that would be best. Thanks, Valerie. Explain, won't you? Tell her I'm sorry, I tried, but I just couldn't make it. She's a pro, she'll understand. Oh, and pile a few cushions and blankets into the taxi to make sure she has a comfortable ride. We don't want her wound opening again.'

Sidney shaped words silently in Carmen's direction and she walked over to Sebastian. 'You'll be needing Valerie. Why don't I go? I'd love to.'

'You're needed here. Just do your job, will you? I'll go,' Valerie told her sharply, then walked off fast, a thin, energetic figure in a warm sweater and dark grey wool pants tucked into calf-high black boots.

Carmen went back to Sidney. 'I couldn't very well insist,' she whispered. 'Should we talk to Sebastian?'

Sidney chewed his lower lip. 'We can't do that with everyone listening. What if we're wrong and it isn't her at all? She could sue us for slander.'

'What if we're right and Sebastian just sent the murderer to get Laura?'

He grimaced. 'Don't! Look, she wouldn't dare do anything

between picking Laura up and bringing her here – it would be too obvious, she'd be the only suspect.'

Carmen crossed her fingers at him.

'Yeah, well,' Sidney said, crossing his fingers back.

Sebastian, turning towards them from an impatient dialogue with the soundman, caught the gesture and snapped, 'What are you two playing at? Get back to your camera, Sidney, I want to check this shot again before we go for take fifteen. And give it your best! We're running out of time.'

'It isn't my fault we've got problems!'

'Don't be so damn touchy. Did I say it was? Just make it good, okay?'

On seeing Valerie walking into her room Laura felt a grinding shock and couldn't hide her dismay. 'Where's Sebastian?'

'He couldn't make it – he was too busy filming. Are you ready? I've got a taxi waiting. I'm afraid the water's a bit choppy, there's a lot of wind, but I've told the man to take it nice and slow so don't worry. The ride won't be too uncomfortable.'

The nurse, listening, wouldn't have heard the undertone: the words sounded calm and normal and Valerie was smiling coolly, even if her eyes were full of hatred.

'I'll see you out,' the nurse said, and walked with them to the landing-stage. Earlier she had helped Laura dress in a green cotton shirt, over which she wore a thick, green wool cardigan, with chocolate brown trousers and comfortable boots. After helping her down into the cabin the nurse eyed, with some anxiety, the rough grey water, the sky, which was the same gun-metal colour, full of dark, looming clouds. 'I hope it isn't going to snow again,' she said.

'So do I,' Laura agreed, as Valerie joined them.

The nurse gave Laura a light kiss on each cheek, said goodbye, then left. The boatman cast off and the water-taxi moved away, bouncing and dancing across the waves. Pale,

Laura clutched at the side of the seat. She was wrapped in warm blankets, with pillows behind her injured shoulder.

Valerie sat opposite, watching her from hostile eyes. She took a mobile phone out of her pocket and dialled, spoke into it. 'Carmen? Tell Sebastian we're on our way, we should be back in twenty minutes. I told the boatman to take it slowly to make sure she doesn't get thrown about.'

She switched off the phone without waiting for Carmen to answer, and pushed it back into her pocket. Laura sat rigidly, watching Valerie's small, thin fingers, the nails painted bright red.

Neither woman spoke. Laura's eyes slowly moved up and met Valerie's cold stare.

Don't say anything, she told herself, but to her own horror the words came out. 'It was you, wasn't it?'

'What?' Valerie's face became mask-like.

'You're wearing the same perfume today. Givenchy, isn't it? Clea used to wear it, didn't she? She was always drenched in it and so are you. I recognised it that day although I only realised later.'

'What are you talking about?' Valerie's eyes were brilliant, dangerous, like those of a cornered animal, her lips curled back over her small, white teeth as if she might spring and bite.

What if she had the knife on her? Laura's mouth dried and she wished she hadn't been such a fool: she had known she shouldn't say anything. But she couldn't stop. Had to answer.

'And your nail varnish – I noticed that, too. You wore a mask on your face but you didn't think of covering your hands. They're just as much a giveaway.' Like claws, like talons, those bony, darting little hands with their bright red nails.

Valerie pushed them into the pockets of her anorak. 'You're crazy.'

Tension beat in Laura's ears, so fiercely that she jumped when the boatman peered in from the door, unaware of the atmosphere.

'There soon, okay? I can see Ca' d'Angeli now.'

Laura acted as she had never acted before, smiling, nodding. 'Good, thank you. I like your boat, it's very comfortable.'

The compliment brought forth a wide grin. '*Grazie*, Signorina. I like your films, *bene, benissimo*.' She was glad of his presence: Valerie wouldn't dare do anything to her while he was with them.

The boat coughed and leapt in the water. 'Ahhh . . .' he muttered, and was gone.

Valerie was staring at her. Laura didn't look back, yet watched her out of the corner of her eye.

The boat slowed: they were approaching Ca' d'Angeli. Laura looked out through the spray-misted windows and saw the creamy, fretted stone, the flying cherubs, the rows of carved, protective archangels with their outstretched hands. Even in her state of nerves she felt sudden pleasure. It was so beautiful. Yet there was something about it: a presence, a threat, as if the building were alive and full of secret malice.

'If you say anything to Sebastian he'll laugh at you,' Valerie burst out.

Laura risked looking at her then. They were here now, she was safe. 'Will he? I don't think so. The police found traces of you on the cape, even though it had been in the water. Did you know that anything you touch or wear carries the evidence long afterwards? They're going to test for DNA. They'll be able to prove it was you.'

A quiver, like a wave on those grey waters, ran over Valerie's face. 'That's ridiculous! I was nowhere near the place. I was in a shop, buying cheese! The woman remembered me.'

'You may have gone in earlier, but it was you who stabbed me and they'll prove it. You love Sebastian, too, don't you?' With a leap of intuition Laura accused, 'Did you kill Clea? She didn't kill herself, I never believed she was the type. She was a survivor. And I don't believe Sebastian pushed her out, either. That only leaves you. It was you, wasn't it? You thought he'd turn to you once she was gone, but he probably never even noticed you!'

The boatman was tying up. The taxi rocked, steadied. Valerie jumped up, her hands curling as if she wanted to tear at Laura's face. 'We were lovers, you stupid bitch! He loved me before he ever set eyes on you. He was sick of her, disgusted by her drinking, her men, her foul mouth, couldn't bear to look at her in the end. That day she sat on the window ledge saying she was going to jump, over and over again. Go on, then, do it! he told her. He was desperate to get rid of her.'

'So you pushed her!' Laura had made the accusation on impulse but the reality of it was sinking in. Clea had been murdered. Valerie had killed her. Not Sebastian. A terrible fascination filled her; this neat, orderly, competent woman was a killer. Who would ever guess? She looked so quiet and normal.

Or she had. Staring at her Laura saw through the mask to the madness within. Valerie's mind seethed with maggots; a terrible life hidden behind the eyes, inside that skull.

'He wanted her dead but he didn't have the guts to kill her. I had to do it. He would have married me once she was gone – if you hadn't come along just at the wrong time.' Valerie lunged at her, those small hands grabbing her throat. 'I hate you, you bitch. You won't get away this time.'

Laura wasn't taken by surprise. It had dawned on her that Valerie would make another attempt. Jack-knifing, her booted feet kicked upwards hard between the other woman's legs. Valerie let go of her throat with a scream of pain and staggered back. The boat rocked wildly.

From above them Sebastian's voice yelled. 'Laura? What's going on?'

The boat seesawed back and forth as the women fought. Valerie grabbed Laura's injured shoulder. Laura screamed in pain, but fear made her violent. She hit out with her other hand, punched Valerie's eye; felt the hard bony socket. The jar of impact travelled up her arm.

Sebastian jumped down into the cabin. He pulled Valerie away and threw her sideways. She fell on the steps, sprawled there, sobbing, then scrambled up without a word and vanished.

'Are you okay? Did she hurt you?' Sebastian took Laura's flushed face between his hands. 'What was all that about?'

The words tumbled out hoarsely. 'It was her! She stabbed me! And she's just tried to strangle me.' For some reason that sounded funny and Laura began laughing, couldn't stop. 'If at first you don't succeed, try, try again!'

He frowned down at her. 'You're hysterical. Calm down, Laura. You sound crazy.'

'It's her who's crazy, not me. She killed Clea – you must have known that! You were there, you must have seen her push Clea out of the window.'

His face was totally bloodless. 'What on earth makes you think she did that?'

'She just admitted it!'

'She can't have! My God, if I'd even suspected it don't you think I'd have told the police? I had my back to the window. Clea kept saying she was going to jump and I didn't believe her. I was sick to the teeth of her threatening suicide. It was a battle of wills all the time, she used every weapon she could think of. There was never any peace. I was so fed up I said, "Jump, go on, do it." I didn't believe she would. But she did.'

'No, Valerie pushed her! She admitted it.'

He shut his eyes. 'Christ. Once or twice I did wonder . . . but I couldn't believe it. Clea screamed "No!" all the way down. I've dreamt about it a hundred times. Always felt guilty, wondering if it was all my fault, if I'd somehow made her jump.' He swallowed convulsively. 'Valerie really admitted she pushed her?'

'She said you had been lovers.' She wanted him to deny it, to say it was a lie, but his expression told her that it was true.

'Laura, I was miserable and she was there. But I never loved her, and I never told her I did. I ended it, almost as soon as it started. And I hadn't met you then.

'She killed Clea because she thought you would marry her if you were free.'

He went white. 'Yes. So it *was* my fault. And you. You might have died the other day. She obviously meant to kill you.'

Laura's teeth had begun to chatter. 'I'm so cold. So cold.'

'Shock,' she heard him say from a long way off. He picked her up as if she were a baby and wrapped her round in one of the blankets. She shut her eyes as the boat swung round and round. Or was she imagining that?

The boatman helped him climb out on to the landing stage. There was no sign of Valerie. She must have rushed into the palazzo.

Laura's red hair split over Sebastian's shoulder. He tenderly brushed it back so that he could see her face.

A shiver ran down his spine. Déjà vu. He had been here before, stood like this before on this spot. A ghost was walking over his grave. Instinctively he looked up, as he had that day thirty years ago.

He wasn't surprised to see the Contessa's face framed in the window, white and fixed, staring as if she, too, was looking at a ghost, as she had looked at him from that very same window thirty years ago.

He had been a child then watching his mother get into the waiting boat. Now he was a man coming out of a waiting boat, carrying a woman with wind-blown red hair, hair the identical shade and texture his mother's had been; and behind them rolled the grey waters of the canal, veiled in snow which was just beginning to float down from the cloudy sky.

Why did life always make patterns? Echoes of past and future clanged in his ears, came between what his eyes saw, and what haunted his mind.

Another window was flung open with a crash that made him jump.

'Sebastian!' a voice screamed. 'I'm going to jump, watch me!'

He seemed to see Clea looking down at him, climbing on to the sill.

'No! Don't!' he yelled.

'I love you!' she called and jumped.

Laura was screaming in his arms, fighting to get down.

Valerie didn't make another sound. She fell in silence like the soft white snow. Slow motion, he thought, although he knew it wasn't. His camera eyes followed her, watched the tumble and twist of the body, his mouth open. He didn't hear the sounds he made, didn't hear the whine of the wind, the slap of water on the landing-stage.

She hit the stones with a sound he would never be able to forget. Her head split open as if it had been a watermelon. Blood spurted, the white seeds of brain spreading everywhere. Her eyes were open as if they still saw; had started out of the mess that had been her face, like the eyes of Laura's doll.

She must have done that, too, have somehow stolen it from Laura's bedroom at The Excelsior, smashed it and sent it to her. She must have written those notes, have tried to kill Laura the other day.

Sebastian had never suspected so much violence had been hidden behind her calm, neat face.

The film crew crowded out of the palazzo's open door. Too shocked to make a sound as they stared in horror at the blood and brains on the stones.

The weight in his arms made Sebastian realise that Laura had fainted. He began to walk towards Ca'd'Angeli, skirting the broken body, not even aware that he was staggering as he walked until Sidney met him and tried to take Laura from him.

It brought him out of his shock. Arms tightening around her Sebastian muttered, 'No. I'll look after her. You deal with that.' Without looking, he gestured with his head. 'Don't touch anything. Don't let anyone go near it. Just call the police. I'll put Laura to bed.' He started to move again then stopped. 'Sidney. She should see a doctor, would you ring for one?'

Chapter Fifteen

For two days after Valerie's death Laura was sedated. She slept heavily, haunted by dreams from which she woke with horror, sometimes to find Sebastian sitting beside her, watching her with brooding eyes, or Niccolo in the chair by the bed, a pad on his knee, drawing her in charcoal, with quick, light strokes.

She stared drowsily at him. 'What are you doing?'

'Drawing you. Do you mind? You know, you're just as lovely asleep, you have such great cheekbones. See?' He held up the sketch. 'But to bring you alive needs colour, that miracle of red in your hair, your peachy skin, your green eyes. Black and white doesn't do you justice.'

Laura yawned, bored by talk of her looks, wishing she dared tell him her dreams: talking about them might drive them away, but her eyelids were too heavy and she fell back into sleep.

When she got up on the third day the doctor ordered her to stay in her room, sitting by a huge fire, in a Victorian wing armchair, overstuffed with horsehair, piled with cushions, the back of it towards the windows to keep away the draughts. The police came to interview her again, but kept it brief – they had plenty of evidence about Valerie's suicide. All they wanted to hear from Laura was the truth about what had happened on the boat.

Captain Bertelli looked horrified when she said she had

accused Valerie to her face. 'You told her you believed it was her who attacked you?'

'Yes. And she—'

He interrupted, 'That was a dangerous thing to do, Signorina. She might have tried again.'

'She did. She tried to strangle me, but I kicked her as hard as I could.'

The policeman stared incredulously at Laura's delicate face, the frailness of her body, covered by a velvet dressing gown, sunk in the chair, which half swallowed her. His brows climbed almost to his hair.

'You did?'

'We fought,' Laura admitted, amused by his disbelief. 'I scratched her face and punched her.' Bertelli's expression made her laugh aloud. 'I did! I looked at her and thought, She tried to kill me! She really tried to kill me! It made me very angry. She wasn't getting away with it twice. I hit her, and it made me feel good, let me tell you. But then she deliberately went for my shoulder. It was agonising. I screamed. Sebastian was on the landing-stage, he heard me and jumped down into the cabin and pulled her off.'

Now Bertelli was as alert as a cat at a mousehole. 'Then what did he do?'

'He picked me up and carried me out of the boat.'

'What about Signorina Hyde? What did he do to her? Say to her?'

She frowned. 'I don't remember him saying anything to her. I told you, he pulled her off me and pushed her away. She fell over on the steps of the boat, then she . . . well, she just vanished. I guess she went into the palazzo.'

He looked disappointed, thought for a minute, then asked, 'What do you remember about her jumping out of the window?'

Sickness welled up in her stomach. She put a hand to her mouth. 'Do I have to? It was horrible. I don't like remembering.'

He insisted, 'I'm sorry, but we have to get the facts straight.'

Laura sighed, and gave him a sketchy description of what had happened, not dwelling on what she had seen when Valerie landed.

'After that I don't remember much until I came to in this room.' She stared into the leaping flames. 'She must have been mad, poor woman. I didn't like her, but I can't help feeling sorry for her.'

Bertelli stood up. 'Thank you for seeing me. We would be grateful if you would come to the station to make a formal statement, as soon as you are fit enough. Please do not leave Venice until after the inquest on Signorina Hyde.' A human smile came into his eyes. 'I am glad you are recovering. Being attacked again must have been a terrible shock to you, on top of everything else that has happened.'

'Yes.' That was the understatement of the year, but it was not what Valerie had done to her that made her feel ill. It was what Valerie had done to herself.

When he had gone, she stared into the fire, chilly in spite of its heat. Valerie had loved Sebastian. Clea had loved him. Loving Sebastian was dangerous. She shut her eyes. Stop thinking. Let your mind go blank, she told herself, and slowly fell into a light sleep, exhausted by the interview with Bertelli. She didn't want to dream, but dreams came.

Her mind buzzed like a wasp's nest, images stinging her, until she woke up with a gasp and found Niccolo there.

She was glad to see him sitting on the rug in front of the fire, his long legs bent up, balancing a sketch-pad on his knees, a pencil in his hand now. It moved so quickly, soundless, flowing, as if it grew from the end of his fingers.

He must have heard the alteration in her breathing because he looked up and smiled into her open eyes. 'Hi, how are you now?'

'You're always here,' she said, not complaining, just commenting.

'I wish I was.' His lashes drooped, and he looked through them wickedly at her.

'You're a flirt,' she told him, and he grinned.

'You look so sad all the time. I'm trying to cheer you up. Should you be sitting so near the fire? Would you like me to move your chair back a little?'

'It's fine. If it's too far back I catch the draught from the window or the door. Sebastian and I experimented to find the perfect spot.'

He dropped his pad and pencil and lay back on the rug, his hands laced at the nape of his neck, gazing up at her. 'Ah, yes, Sebastian. Always Sebastian.'

'He is my director.'

'And your lover.'

She didn't answer.

'Every time I see you, you're more beautiful,' Niccolo said softly.

She frowned. 'Don't. Please.'

'You don't like compliments?'

'Not much. After all, I'm not responsible for the way I look. I just grew like this. When I was in my teens everyone told me I was ugly, clumsy, awkward, my arms and legs too long, my body too thin. Then suddenly men started telling me I was beautiful – but I hadn't changed. I looked in the mirror and saw the same girl. I got very confused. And one day I'll be old and men won't rush up to tell me how beautiful I am, they'll look away, thinking, What an ugly old hag, and how will I feel then?'

'No. Never. When you're ninety you'll still be lovely. It's your cheekbones and the way your eyes are set in your head. Your bone structure is ravishing. I may draw your skeleton, leave out all the flesh.'

She burst out laughing. 'How gruesome! You have the strangest mind.'

'And you have the most beautiful body.' He sat up, knelt to take her hand, stretched out the fingers on his palm. 'Even your hands are a work of art.'

'Thank you, but I was not the artist.'

'No, that was God, the greatest artist of us all.'

'You believe in God?'

He looked up at her, dark eyes clear. 'Of course. Don't you?'

'I used to, but I'm no longer sure.' She remembered Valerie, broken on the stone terrace in front of Ca' d'Angeli with the golden archangels staring solemnly down at her.

Niccolo kissed her fingers one by one. 'Don't cry.'

She only realised she was crying when he said it. Pulling her hands away she found a paper handkerchief and dried her eyes, blew her nose.

He watched her, concerned. 'I'm sorry, the last thing I meant to do was upset you. The police talked to me about the woman who killed herself the other day. Is it true that it was her who stabbed you?'

She nodded.

'So she was not your friend.'

Laura laughed feverishly. 'That's a charming way of putting it. She hated me.'

'She was crazy, obviously.'

'She was very sick.'

'Then you must not be sad. She couldn't have been happy. Maybe now she's dead she's happier.'

She gave him a dry glance. 'Somehow I don't find that very comforting.'

They were both silent, then he said, 'When the inquest is over, you will go home to England?'

'Yes, as soon as I've finished filming a couple of scenes for Sebastian. I haven't done any work since I got here and it's essential that I shoot the scenes I was scheduled for.'

'Please, come back to Ca' d'Angeli in the summer. I wouldn't want you to have only bad memories of my house, and I'd like to show you more of Venice.'

'That's very kind, but—'

'Also I still want you to pose for me as the female David. I've made a number of sketches from the photos I took and I'm eager to start work – but I need you, I can't work exclusively from photos. I need to touch, you see, to feel the dimensions of what I'm working on.' He flexed his hands, the strong, tanned fingers eloquent, knelt up and framed her face, holding and touching, caressing all at once.

The hair on the back of Laura's neck bristled. Someone was watching. She felt it, as she had felt it once before. She looked up instantly, and saw the glassy, gleaming eye in the ceiling staring back at her.

A scream broke out of her and a second later the human eye was gone, replaced by the flat, painted one.

'*Dio!*' Niccolo was so startled he lapsed into Italian, talking fast, looking anxiously at her.

She didn't understand a word. 'What are you saying?'

'Why did you scream like that? I wouldn't hurt you – I'd never hurt you.'

The door was flung open. Laura looked across the room as Sebastian rushed in. She was both relieved and alarmed to see him.

'What's going on in here?' It wasn't a question so much as a threat. 'What did he do to you?' He moved fast towards them and Niccolo stood up, squaring his shoulders as if ready for a fight.

'I didn't do anything to her!'

'He didn't,' Laura said. 'I saw it again – the eye.' She pointed. 'Up there.'

Sebastian's hard mouth indented; his eyes spat jealousy. 'I wonder what you were feeling guilty about this time.'

'I wasn't feeling guilty about anything! I tell you, I saw it.'

'Oh, come off it! You didn't see anything up there. You just imagined it!'

Niccolo was looking up at the painted ceiling. 'No,' he said slowly, seriously. 'No, I don't think she did. Laura, was it Juno's eye?'

Sebastian and Laura stared at him.

'Yes,' she whispered.

'And you saw a living eye watching you?'

'Yes.' Laura drew a sharp breath. 'I didn't imagine it, did I?'

Niccolo turned on his heel, and walked out of the room without answering. Sebastian followed him. Laura hesitated for a minute, but she wasn't staying there alone. She went after them, shivering a little as she turned into the marble-walled hall. The two men were on the stairs going up to the second floor and vanished round a bend in the staircase.

The film crew, still busy in the hallway, had stopped to watch curiously: an electrician with black cable wound round his hand, Sidney polishing a lens of one of his cameras, looking older since Valerie's death as if the shock had aged him, Carmen sitting cross-legged on a rug with a pile of shooting scripts in front of her, going through them and scribbling timings in the margins.

Laura wished she was just one of them, lost in the daily minutiae of their lives, doing her job, worrying about nothing except getting her work right.

She waved to them and Sidney called, 'How are you?'

'Okay,' she said, but his eyes told her she didn't look it. She walked slowly to the stairs and followed the men up to the second floor, leaning heavily on the banisters.

By the time she reached the top they were out of sight but she heard voices and followed the sound along a corridor into a large bedchamber, hung with red velvet at the window and on the four-poster bed. The walls were painted dark red, too. The black shadows from the flames in the hearth licked up to the ceiling and made the atmosphere heavy with brooding. The Contessa, wearing her usual black dress, sat at an embroidery frame, sewing with the calm, measured movements of custom.

She put down her needle and the skein of silk she was pulling through the cream fabric. 'What are you doing, Niccolo?' she asked sharply.

He had flapped back the carpet on the floor and was kneeling down. Taking no notice of his mother, he told Sebastian, who stood beside him, 'This is the mechanism. It's very old, probably from the Renaissance – who knows who ordered it to be installed? It was the sort of thing that fascinated them in the sixteenth century. I found this one years ago, when I was about four and crawling about in here while the maid cleaned the silver brushes on my mother's dressing table.'

'She had no business bringing you in here! You shouldn't have been left with a maid at all.'

'Well, I was, that day. She didn't notice what I was doing. I played with it for a while then pushed the rug back over it. It was some time before I realised exactly what I'd found. At the time it never occurred to me that my mother might know it was there. This house is full of secrets. There's a staircase that leads up from the boat-house to the bedroom Laura is using. That was how my father's visitors got up to his room without being seen.'

The Contessa rose to her full height, her face cold and forbidding. 'Please leave my room, all of you. Niccolo, you forget your manners. You know I dislike my privacy being invaded.'

'Why were you prying into Laura's privacy, then?' demanded Sebastian.

She didn't look at him. 'I was doing nothing of the kind.'

'Oh, yes, Mamma,' Niccolo said. 'You were up here, peering down through this spyhole. Don't bother to deny it.'

'Why were you spying?' insisted Sebastian.

'I was not. I heard raised voices – it sounded like fighting. I was worried about my son, that's all.'

Sebastian's mouth twisted cynically. 'Is that why you were watching Laura and me making love the afternoon she first arrived here?'

A spot of dark red flared up in her cheeks. 'How dare you!'

Niccolo asked, 'Did you watch my father through that spyhole?'

She shot him a furious look. 'I am not discussing your father in front of them!'

'But he wasn't just *my* father, was he, Mamma? He was Sebastian's father, too.'

Laura had suspected this, but it was still as big a shock as a volcano erupting. Sebastian was white-faced, rigid, like Lot's wife frozen into a block of salt.

Laura put a hand to her mouth to stop herself from crying out and betraying her presence.

'Gina and my father were lovers, weren't they? And Sebastian is their child.' Niccolo turned to look at Sebastian, his face grave. 'I guessed long ago but I was sure when he came back and I saw him face to face. He and I are so alike. It was like looking into a mirror.'

'No! You're nothing like him! Nothing!'

Her son gazed at her with an expression of mixed pity, impatience and regret. 'I'm sorry, Mamma, but it's time to stop pretending, stop lying. You aren't going to convince me. I have a mind of my own, I can do my own thinking. It's all so long ago. What does it matter, anyway?'

'The past always matters! The present springs from it,' Sebastian said, and Niccolo looked at him quickly, his face mirroring his half-brother's, thoughtful, interested. Watching them, Laura saw again how alike they were, not merely in body but in the creative mind of the artist, inventive, curious, speculative, capable of red-hot passion and cold theory.

'Yes, of course.' Looking back at his mother he said, 'Gina had her baby just before you had me, didn't she?'

Her face worked violently. 'Yes, you know she did. I had such a bad time when you were born that I was ill afterwards, I had no milk, but she had milk enough for two. Those great breasts of hers were fountains of it. They took you away from me. I woke up and you were gone, and however much I cried and begged they wouldn't give you back. They only let me see you once a day! I was your mother, but they kept you from me.'

'That scene in Canfield's book, where the wife's baby is taken from her and given to her husband's mistress? Is that where he got the idea for that? But how did he know? Who told him about it? He knew my father. Those descriptions of tapestries, rooms, paintings always seemed very familiar to me. Was the palazzo in the book based on Ca' d'Angeli?'

'Of course,' Sebastian said, slowly. 'And the love affair, the betrayal of the wife, the plot against her. That was you, wasn't it, Contessa?'

She didn't answer, her eyes black holes in space, empty and desolate.

'So that's why you hated the book so much!' Niccolo was looking at her as if he had never seen his mother before. 'Was it all true, the way Canfield wrote it? Did Papa and Gina conspire to get you married to Papa? All he had were the house and the works of art. He didn't want to sell any of them – but although he loved them passionately he loved Gina, too, and she had no money, either.'

'How on earth *did* Canfield know all that?' asked Sebastian.

'They were at school together, Gina and my mother and my aunt Olivia,' said Niccolo. 'She's dead now, years ago, but the three of them were close friends when they were children. After the war my mother went to the same finishing school as my aunt, in Switzerland – the family photograph album is full of photos of them skiing together. That's how my father and Gina knew you were going to inherit the Serrati fortune,

Mamma. That's what happened, isn't it? They got Aunt Olivia to invite you to Ca' d'Angeli, and Papa and your brother Carlo made some sort of deal.'

She laughed bitterly. 'You make it sound so sensible, Niccolo. You left out Canfield. Oh, yes, he was in the conspiracy. He was obsessed with Machiavelli, you know. He wrote a book about him just after the war. Canfield enjoyed plotting, making things happen, playing with people's lives as if they were puppets. I only saw later what a part he played in my own life. It wasn't just spite or a love of conspiracy – he adored Gina, he was in love with her too. Maybe they'd been lovers.'

Sebastian shouted, 'That's a lie!'

'How would you know?' the Contessa threw at him. 'She was my husband's whore. She could have slept with half Venice for all you know! Throughout those years Canfield haunted this house. He had dinner here several nights a week.'

'None of the books about him mention Ca' d'Angeli.'

She shrugged. 'How could they? I didn't talk to any of the reporters and academics who tried to get in touch with me, so they left us out. I think one or two said he had briefly been a tutor to an Italian family but, again, by the time they wrote about that none of my family were alive, except me. There was nobody to tell them anything.'

'Why didn't you ever tell me?' Niccolo demanded. 'You knew how much I admired his work. I'd have been fascinated to discover he used to come here.'

'I didn't want to talk about him. I loathed the man. All my life I hated him, from when I was very small. And later, after I married your father, I hated him even more. They would all sit talking and drinking in the salon, after dinner . . .'

'Talking about what?' asked Niccolo. 'Can you remember?'

'Art, books, God knows, I never listened. I was usually told to go to bed, as if I was a child. Domenico would tell me I looked tired, didn't Canfield agree? And Canfield would say I needed my beauty sleep – one of his little jokes, a double meaning he seemed to think I wouldn't pick up, as if I couldn't read the mockery in his face, the way he looked me up and down. He thought I was ugly, even as a child. I didn't argue, my pride wouldn't let me – but Antonio used to wait on them, and afterwards he would tell me everything they said.'

Niccolo's face turned ashen as he listened, watching his mother with pity. 'They all betrayed you, even your own brother.'

'Carlo didn't know about Gina. He thought it was an old-fashioned arranged marriage and he didn't see what was wrong with that. He was an old-fashioned man and, anyway, he knew I loved your father, and if he suspected that Domenico didn't love me, well, Carlo didn't think that mattered, so long as I became a lady, one of the aristocracy, the mistress of a house like this. Don't forget, our family was in trade – the upper class in Milan looked down on us even when they invited us to their parties because we were so rich. But once I was the Contessa d'Angeli I was in another bracket. It was our father's dream come true.'

'You brought money to the marriage and Papa brought class,' Niccolo muttered. 'A typical tradesman's bargain.'

'But your father wasn't prepared to marry me until he was sure I had the factory and the money. Only when Carlo was dead did he set a date for our wedding, and all that time he was living with Gina in America.'

Her son and Sebastian both stared fixedly at her.

She nodded, her mouth a thin line. 'I only found out after my honeymoon when I got back here and found her in the house. Domenico said she was his housekeeper, but Antonio told me the truth. He owed his loyalty to me, not to your father. I brought him here from Milan. He and I had been through so much together – it was Antonio who helped me take care of my brother during his last, terrible illness. I needed Antonio then, I needed him even more, later, after my marriage. Without Antonio's support I couldn't have gone on living under this roof, knowing that my husband loved his mistress, not me.'

'God, Mamma, why didn't you throw her out the minute you knew?'

'Domenico wouldn't let me.'

'Don't be ridiculous, Mamma! You were his wife. You had every right to dismiss a servant.'

She laughed harshly. 'In theory, yes, but with my husband on her side, what could I do? Oh, I threatened to sack her, but he said if I told her to go they would both leave. I would be shamed in front of all Venice. A laughing-stock. The new bride deserted for the daughter of a grocer! The whole of Venice already knew, of course. They were waiting, watching, to see how I would deal with it – and all I could think of doing was to pretend I had no idea, play deaf at parties, ignore the whispers, the secret mockery, the smiles and gleeful eyes. How do you think I felt?'

'I don't know how you could bear it, Mamma,' Niccolo said.

'It was like wearing a hair vest. At first it chafed and was agonising, but in the end it became almost an obsession. When I discovered the mechanism in the floor that let me watch them, I couldn't stop myself doing so every night. In the summer, they slept naked without a cover, and I could see . . . everything . . . everything they did. I don't think Domenico knew about the eye in the ceiling, or else he had forgotten it. He came up here only rarely. He hated sharing my bed. He only did it in the hope of getting a child. They never seemed to sense they were being watched. I could listen to what they were saying, find out their plans, hear just what they thought of me, watch them caressing, kissing, doing it . . .'

'Stop it, Mamma! That's enough! I don't want to hear!'

She ignored him. 'I prayed I would become pregnant, because I hoped that if I had his child Domenico might turn to me at last, but then she was pregnant. I was bewildered when she suddenly married the gardener. I couldn't guess at first why she did it. After all, it was Gina who really ran this house. Gina was the hostess at dinner parties, garden parties, lunch. She wore fabulous, expensive clothes he bought for her. With my money! Not to mention the jewels! I was left in the background, and Venice pretended politely that I didn't exist. When she married, Domenico gave them an apartment in the palazzo, but she went on sleeping with him, not her husband, and that was when I knew she was pregnant. She was about four months gone and I saw her walking about naked in the bedroom down there. Her swelling belly was obvious. I nearly went out of my mind with jealousy and rage. I broke some valuable glass in here – it was all over the floor, great jagged splinters of it. I felt they had gone into my head, into my heart.'

Niccolo put an arm round her plump shoulders, said awkwardly, 'Mamma, poor Mamma, it must have been so terrible.'

She leant on him and sighed. 'You can't imagine! And then a month after I found out she was pregnant, I discovered I was going to have a child, too. I hoped I'd get Domenico back, but it was too late. Her son was born first and it was him Domenico loved, never you.'

'That isn't true!' Niccolo's arm dropped and he moved away from her. 'Papa loved me! I know he did!'

'Not the way he loved her son!' She shot a bitter look in Sebastian's direction.

He had listened in silence, his face grim.

The Contessa spat out, 'He hated knowing that his first-born was known as another man's child, was thought of as a gardener's son, a peasant. He brooded on it all the time. Then one day he told me he was going to adopt Sebastian, change his will, leave everything equally divided between the two of you.'

Sebastian drew a harsh breath.

'I couldn't let that happen,' the Contessa ground out. 'He wasn't taking *my* money to give to Gina's child! He told me if I tried to stop him he would turn me out of Ca' d'Angeli, said he would get a papal annulment. He had a dozen highly placed relatives in the Church who would help him get one, on some trumped-up reason. Then he would marry her and make their son legitimate.' She looked pleadingly at her own son. 'I couldn't let him do that to you. You see that, don't you?'

'So you killed them,' Sebastian said.

Niccolo's head swung towards him. *'What?'*

'My mother and our father – don't you see? She killed them. I don't know how she did it, but I've suspected for a long time that their deaths weren't an accident. My assistant went through the newspaper files, talked to the police and was certain their deaths were never seriously investigated. And I met an old man in Venice one day, last August, who recognised me from when I was a child. He told me he had worked at Ca' d'Angeli at the time my father died, and all the servants believed it wasn't an accident. They were all sure it was murder.'

'Servants' gossip,' said the Contessa. 'You can't take notice of what they say.'

'You just said that Antonio always knew what was going on!'

She changed tack. 'I was here all the time – you know that, you saw me yourself. You were outside, you looked up at me, at the window.'

'You may not have done it yourself, but you planned their deaths. You paid someone to kill them.'

She laughed hoarsely, her face ugly now. 'Prove it! Go on, find some proof. You try. It's too many years ago. There were no witnesses then, there are no witnesses now. You can't prove anything.'

For the last few minutes Niccolo had been silent, his eyes fixed on his mother's face. Now he said, very quietly, 'Did you kill my father, Mamma?'

Her dark eyes flicked to him warily. 'Don't take any notice of *him*. He hates me, hates us both. He'd say anything to hurt us. Ignore him. We should never have had him in this house, I told you that, but you would invite him, and see what has happened! He's a jinx. His wife jumped out of a window, then that woman he called his secretary but who was his mistress once, she jumped out of the window upstairs. Don't you think that's a strange coincidence? Two women dying in the same way? He's the murderer, not me!'

Niccolo leant on the back of a red-velvet-covered armchair. 'You were here that day, Mamma, but Antonio wasn't. He was out doing the marketing. In the old launch. You see, I remember that whole day very clearly.'

'Niccolo, don't let him come between us! He's his mother's child! She was the same – she came between me and your father and—'

He interrupted her. 'I loved my father, his death was the worst thing that ever happened to me. I found the old launch, years ago, in the boat-house. The side was stove in, dented and scratched, as if it had hit something very hard. It hadn't been used for years, but I remembered Antonio setting out in it that day to go to market. I had watched him leave and then, half an hour later, I watched Papa and Gina go.'

'No, Niccolo, Antonio had had an accident a week before. The boat was waiting to be mended when your father was killed. He wasn't using it that week. He did the marketing on foot. It's all in the police records – check them!'

'I don't believe you. You had my father murdered.' Niccolo's face had turned bone white.

'No!' She clung to his arm, desperation in her eyes. 'Niccolo, think what they did to me – what they were going to do to you! They both deserved to die.'

He pushed down her hands and stepped away, face cold. 'No. If you had left him, forced an annulment on *him,* I could understand that. He deserved it. But murder? That's something else. I don't want you under my roof any more, Mamma. Or Antonio. You can both leave tomorrow. You can find yourself a nice villa by the sea, but stay away from Venice in future. I never want to see you again.'

The Contessa staggered as if she might fall, tried to grab hold of her son but he took another step away.

'Niccolo . . .' She held out a hand. 'You can't do this to me! You can't turn me out of my home after all these years!'

'You're a murderer. What I should do is call the police, but I won't, because I don't want all the trouble it would cause. But I can't go on sharing a house with my father's killer. I'd never feel safe again.'

Her voice rose almost to a shriek. 'I won't go! You can't make me!'

'I can, and I will.'

They stared at each other, oddly alike in that long moment: obstinacy and tenacity in both faces.

Sebastian turned and began to walk to the door. The Contessa screamed after him, 'You're to blame for all this – you and that bitch you brought under my roof, that whore, your whore, with her red hair and those sly eyes. I know what you see in her – she's the image of your mother, that slut Gina. Do you know she's been at it with my son? I've seen them, watched them, seen Niccolo touching her, naked, his hands all over her—'

Sebastian left the room and shut the door. Laura was leaning on the wall outside, her face wet with tears. He picked her up and carried her down to her room, under the curious eyes of the film crew. There, he put her into the bed and sat down beside her, still holding her.

'Poor woman,' she whispered, her arms round his neck. 'Oh, Sebastian, that poor woman.'

'The Contessa?' His face was flinty, closed to all pity. 'Laura, she's a murderess! She killed my mother and father. Don't waste your sympathy on her. You heard what she just said about you, all that sick stuff about you and Niccolo! Or was it true? Was it, Laura?'

'Don't!' She shuddered. 'You don't really believe I've slept with him?'

'I believe he'd like you to! I've seen the way he looks at you, and I believe he has touched you, at least, even if he's never got you into bed. Don't try to tell me he doesn't fancy you.'

'Maybe he does – but I've never slept with him, or come anywhere near it! And as for his mother, it must be terrible to be so unhappy. Can you even imagine what it must have been like for her? To be in love with her husband and find out he was only pretending to love her too? To have to watch him with another woman?' Laura grimaced. 'My skin crept when she was talking about that. And she loves her son very much. It's obvious she's devoted her life to him. He won't really throw her out of her home, will he?'

Sebastian's face was sombre. 'Can he ever trust her again? What if he married and brought home a wife to take his mother's place in Ca' d'Angeli? How long before she had a fatal accident, Laura?'

'I hadn't thought of that. She wouldn't dare risk it, though, now he knows the truth. Would she?'

'Would you bet on that?'

She didn't answer. No, she wouldn't like to risk a bet on it.

Sebastian stroked her hair, her closed eyes, her cheek. 'You're very pale. You ought to sleep for a while. Don't talk any more, don't even try to think. Where are your pills? The sedatives the doctor gave you?'

He found them for her and gave her two with a glass of water, lay next to her, caressing her until she fell into a doze. Then he slipped away quietly and went down to talk to Sidney, to look at the pink sheets of the schedule for the next day. He kept an eye on the stairs, watching for the Contessa, and another eye on the door into the part of the palazzo where Laura slept. Just before sunset he went back to check on her and found her staring drowsily at nothing, between sleeping and waking.

'How do you feel now, my love?' He bent to kiss her face and at that second they both heard a sound, a sharp crack, from outside the window. Gulls flew up, screeching, their white wings crimson in the setting sun.

'What was that?' Laura sat up.

'Sounded like a shot!' Sebastian ran to the window and looked out.

Laura got out of bed and joined him. What now? she thought desperately. 'Maybe it was a motor-boat backfiring?' she said.

A black gondola with gold stripes along the side was moving away from the landing-stage outside Ca' d'Angeli. It was being poled by Antonio in his black suit.

There was no sign of anything else nearby. Laura sighed with relief. 'Where's he going to, I wonder?' she asked Sebastian who didn't answer.

A moment later, Niccolo ran out of the house and shouted after the gondola. 'What was that noise? Where are you going at this hour, Antonio?'

The Contessa sat under the hood of the gondola, her body slumped sideways, head leaning against the side, a few strands of hair blowing in the wintry wind.

'She's sitting in an odd way,' Sebastian said, opening the window to see better.

'Antonio, come back here!' shouted Niccolo. 'Mamma! What are you up to?'

There was no answer from her nor did Antonio look round or register that he had heard Niccolo. He stood in the gondola, poling strongly out into the Grand Canal. There were almost no other vessels in sight, just a *vaporetto* chugging in the distance, heading towards St Mark's Square.

Sebastian drew a sudden, audible breath. 'She looks as if . . . Do you think she's asleep? Why is she slumped against the side of the hood like that?'

The gondola tossed on the choppy waves, half-turned, so

that, in a shaft of dying sunlight Laura could see the Contessa's face. The eyes were closed, the skin pale. The body was slack, collapsed. Laura shivered.

'She looks ill.'

Sebastian gripped the iron latch of the window, his knuckles white. 'No. She looks as if she's dead.'

Antonio stopped rowing near the centre of the canal. He bent, for a few minutes. then tossed a large metal can overboard.

'Oh, my God!'

'What was it, Sebastian?'

'A petrol can.'

Antonio sat down beside the Contessa, and put one arm around her waist, drew her head down on to his shoulder, stroked her spilling hair. With his other hand he threw something along the gondola.

Instantly there was a rush, a loud explosion.

'Jesus Christ!' Sebastian muttered.

The night sky was lit with a brilliance that dazzled. Sparks flew in all directions, like fireworks. The gondola and its passengers were consumed by crimson and orange flames that climbed up into the darkening sky while the archangels and cherubim watched from the golden walls of Ca' d'Angeli.